Mercedes Leyshon was born in Madrid of Spanish and Anglo-Irish parents. Brought up in Casablanca, she later moved to Britain and qualified as a nurse and midwife, before obtaining a BA (Hons) in Modern Languages at Leeds University, and then training in Esoteric Studies at The Lucis Trust's Arcane School in London. She and her husband divide their time between Andalucia and the Highlands of Scotland. *The Aleppo* is her first novel.

MERCEDES LEYSHON

The Aleppo

A Novel

Matador
9 De Montfort Mews
Leicester LE1 7FW, UK
Tel: (+44) 116 255 9311 / 9312
Email: books@troubador.co.uk
Web: www.troubador.co.uk/matador

ISBN 1 90523750 2

Some incidents in this novel are inspired by real events and people

Cover illustration from an original painting by Ardyn Griffin.
*Ardyn trained at the Ruskin School, the Froebel Institute Roehampton and at
Goldsmiths College. She has exhibited at the Royal Academy and at various
exhibitions in Wales, Cornwall and Gloucestershire. She lives in Tewkesbury.*

Typeset in 11pt Plantin Light by Troubador Publishing Ltd, Leicester, UK
Printed on woodfree bookwove paper by The Cromwell Press Ltd, Trowbridge, Wilts, UK

Matador is an imprint of Troubador Publishing Ltd

Gareth, my secretary, critic, closest friend,
long-time husband and love, this book is for you.

CONTENTS

ACKNOWLEDGEMENTS

Noëlle, for being my most exacting and patient critic and for steering me back on track when I went off on a tangent and for your wisdom.

Ben, your humour, quirky comments, enthusiasm and sunniness lifted my spirits.

To both of you for being the children I ever wanted and for feeding my heart.

My grandsons, Jack, Isaac, Bryn and Jof, you made my writing days and every day brighter.

Maman and Papa, you started it all.

Titiné, Eddy, Jo and Pedrito, for your inspiration and for being with me all along.

Rachel, for the tears you said you shed at the end of the book.

Odile you brought me dreams and sanity in the desert of my adolescence.

Father Benjamin, you opened the window to my soul.

Gloria, you were constant in your interest and support during the writing of this book and it gave me strength.

Sister Petra Clare your prayers throughout this journey lit my path.

Graham and May, your application when reading the draft and your constructive suggestions touched me.

Ardyn for being you and for the beauty of the book cover.

Jeremy Thompson of Matador for all your help, professionalism and reassurance.

Marsha Rowe for believing in me.

Mamá Grande for everything I am and because you were the first to love me.

To each of you, thank you.

PART ONE

And we are put on earth a little space
that we might learn to bear the beams of love.

William Blake

ONE

The Birth

Paloma could not make that final exit nor her first entrance into the world. The ambulance wailed its way towards the Galdós clinic in the Puerta del Sol, in the heart of Madrid. It was dawn, Saturday July the 18th 1936 and the first day of Spain's bloody war.

The young expectant mother who called for help after six and a half lone hours of premature labour, felt scared and forsaken. Her mother Pepa was due the next day from their home in Barcelona, and her husband Elias was returning that morning from a congress at the Chambre de Commerce in Paris.

Rosario's contractions intensified in sympathy with nearby gunfire. Her mother's crucifix held tight against her chest heaved with every breath she took. The indolent auxiliary who escorted her in the ambulance sat on the bench chewing and spitting her nails as Rosario's membranes broke with an outpouring of amniotic fluid and green staining. She looked down onto the saturated crumpled sheet beneath her and yelled that something was amiss, that never before had there been green in her waters. Inside Rosario's womb the unborn heart pounded in distress.

The ambulance came to an abrupt halt. A hulking midwife emerged from the clinic's side door lifting and carrying Rosario from the stretcher, down to the muggy basement, a temporary shelter from the perils above and laid her down on a lumpy mattress on the floor. A sunbeam from a small domed window high on the wall streamed onto Rosario's lap like a spotlight. Two other women moaned as they lay heaped in the dark.

"I'm Encarna", snapped the midwife, bending Rosario's knees up and parting her quivering thighs in one go. "And you?" and without waiting for her to reply, she ordered her to push and pant like a dog between her contractions. "Rosario" Rosario replied dimly, before shouting for her mother and water to drink. "Is everything alright?" she then gasped. "I wasn't due for another fortnight. My husband is away on business"

On seeing the infant's matted hair the midwife eased two of her fingers down the birth canal. The foetal cord had wound itself twice around the infant's neck and all at once, every second counted and her requests became commands. "Come on! Push or else!" An elemental fear revived Rosario's strength. "That's my girl!" the midwife coaxed, stroking Rosario's tense and veiny abdomen. Rosario pushed again then sank into the mattress and with a mouth that felt like sandpaper said that she could not go on.

"Try mooing" encouraged the midwife. "A long moo from the crotch and it'll be all over!" Rosario mooed a long pathetic moo until Encarna shouted that she could stop. The head was out. She loosened the cord from the infant's throat and hooked her index finger under the tiny slippery armpit so that first one shoulder slid out and then the other. Released from the waters of her mother's womb, the infant's body landed motionless on the glowing disk of transmitted light. She was lifted, held upside down and slapped on her back. "Wake up!" Encarna bawled. The baby's wrinkled body shook like a rag doll, choking on frothy saliva before becoming conscious of her own breath. She bleated then screamed and pink shaded her cheeks bringing a burst of hysterical laughter from Rosario and Encarna like jubilant accomplices at the end of a perilous mission. To crystallise the moment further the bombing subsided, only to return minutes later with a convulsive explosion close by signalling that this child was born with the dying of Spain.

Elias arrived as the afterbirth was being discarded into a bucket like unwanted offal in an abattoir. Scarcely aware of

Rosario's ordeal or of the new arrival his eyes searched around the room expecting to see Don Javier de Montesino, the obstetrician in charge.

"Don Javier not here?" he asked concerned. "He must have been caught in last night's cross-fire" replied Encarna. "Or... who can tell these days!" she added, raising her arms and eyes to the heavens.

Elias bent over Rosario at last, held her hands, smoothed her clammy forehead and kissed it . "Listen carefully querida." He whispered this, looking sideways and over his shoulder. "A taxi is waiting and Fermin is in the Suiza with Carlota and your mother. They caught the overnight train from Barcelona when they heard that trouble was imminent." He paused to kiss her hands. "The news on the radio is not good. It's all about the uprising in Morocco and revolts have already begun on the mainland. It isn't safe here querida. We are fleeing to France." He looked into Rosario's imploring eyes and waved at the midwife to assist with Rosario's hasty departure.

It was Fermin, Elias' loyal chauffeur, who had first overheard from fellow drivers that his master's name, amongst many others, had been black-listed by Nationalist and Republican leaders, and swift action was crucial to avert his arrest. Elias had many contacts and knew how to set them in motion, but on this occasion he had had to settle for what could only be an unhappy compromise. When Rosario heard that only four of the six requested safe conduits out of Spain had been granted, she cried for her mother.

Pepa entered the basement, her eyes settling on the baby still lying unwashed and forsaken at the bottom of the bed. She only had to glance at the midwife to know that she might well be skillful at bringing flesh forth into the world but that she was certainly inept at captivating the unique sacredness of birth. "Deo Gracias" she whispered when she picked up the infant, and called for a towel and warm water which she drizzled over her bruised head and body until the new skin began to gleam. She patted her dry, dressed her in the crisp white poplin gown that she had brought with her and had once belonged to her sister Carlota and cradled the snuggled up bundle on Rosario's bosom. "Your daughter" she whispered with a pride she didn't try to conceal. Oblivious, Rosario whined over her mother's shoulder muttering that Elias had only managed four passes and crying that she couldn't do without her. "You know, don't you" Pepa sighed, "that I must stay here, in Spain and care for Carlota." Amidst the tortuous silence that they shared, Rosario estimated that her one year old daughter Carlota would be less burdensome than her new-born, and though she more than anything wanted her mother by her side, Elias only, she knew, could rescue her from the horrors that she guessed, lay ahead. The die was cast. Pepa would team up with the infant and journey back home to Barcelona to be met by Salvador, Pepa's son-in-law. Elias who had quietly observed the evolving scene and anticipated the outcome now pressed for speedy action. Her new grand daughter, Pepa requested, had to be baptised before the family dispersed. In the absence of a priest Elias assumed a reverential stance, cupped his hands together, dipped them in the nearby midwife's china bowl and sprinkled the tepid water on his daughter's head. "In the absence of a man of God" he said in an artificially solemn voice "I, Elias, your temporal father, baptise you, Paloma, Misericordia. May the spirit of light, love and peace enter you and stay with you always..."

He impressed the infant's forehead with his thumb, and concluded "In the name of the Father, the Son, and the Holy Spirit, Amen."

Pepa held Paloma in her arms awhile. "My treasured little one," she uttered in the most tender of whispers, in that moment infusing the infant's entire being with the fullness of her own overflowing love.

Fermin had driven the Suiza to the clinic's back door. He was not wearing his chauffeur's uniform. It was a gamble, but he deemed that looking proletarian in Madrid that day could be life-saving.

Alongside, the taxi waited to drive Pepa and Paloma to the railway station. After a while, the family group emerged from the clinic's back door, looking furtive and hindered by Rosario's condition.

"Don't forget to pray," Pepa tried to say, but her voice crackled and Rosario did not hear her. They embraced, avoiding each others eyes before Pepa scurried to the taxi with Paloma in her arms, lost amidst layers of fluffy shawl. Rosario glanced back at her bent fleeing mother and at the tiny stranger in her arms, unable to speak, cry, or move until Elias hustled her into the back of the car. She had no anguish, nor fear, nor any other emotion, just a numb compulsion to follow Elias' instructions.

TWO

Halts and Barricades

Elias had not expected unrest until the early autumn. The plan was to return home to Barcelona before Rosario's confinement, but the premature birth and the uprising (which everyone mistakenly believed would be contained within Spanish Morocco) had dramatically altered the order of events. He now found himself and his divided family fleeing North through the streets of Madrid. He could not guess what Pepa and Paloma would make out of their journey. He feared for their safety and strangled his thoughts.

Sounds of gunfire and explosions resounded near their route, but Fermin's motoring skills took them unharmed past the Puerta del Sol through a seemingly endless swirling of alleys to the outskirts of the Capital.

Elias wound down his window. He turned back to check on Rosario. Eyes closed, she lay slumped on the seat. "Are you alright Cariño?" he called. "Tell me at once if you are in pain or in need of anything."

In a daze, she replied that she'd had an injection and would be fine.

All at once, he was struck by the horror of his wife's ordeal and a wave of nausea unsettled him.

"Mother of God!" Fermin hushed. The horizon was hazy, with dim brown shapes against it. "Slow down compadre" Elias whispered. "Wind down your window, smile, wave, and prepare to accelerate the second after you've stopped."

It was impossible to identify which side of the conflict the shapes were on until they were within arms length. The men held rusty guns but were not uniformed and must have been a gang of bandits on the prowl. Fermin followed his master's orders. The car slowed down to a halt. The men lowered their guns, only to be left behind, in a cloud of blinding dust, shouting abuse and firing their guns after them.

Rosario and Carlota had been out for the count throughout the incident and Elias hoped that the sedative to calm Rosario down would last a few more hours.

The morning freshness gave way to the still, heavy heat of noon and the road became reassuringly familiar. They had used it often during their business stays in Madrid in previous summers when escaping the furnace of the capital for the cooler climes of the sierras. It was with relief that Elias saw that Rosario was still oblivious when the signpost for Miraflores appeared, as the place held bitter sweet memories of festive family reunions and of Rosario's beloved first child Angelina who was buried there.

The now barren and arid landscape awoke memories of his native Morocco where he had not been since his mother's funeral just before his engagement to Rosario, and a longing for his people and land assailed him until the winding and climbing roads of the Sierra de Guaderrama brought him back to the present moment. This was Spain. Spectacular, beautiful, strong yet vulnerable, and he reflected on how much Rosario and her land had in common.

Freshly felled tree trunks piled in the middle of the road forced an emergency stop, this time waking Rosario and Carlota up with a jerk. "Stay calm," Elias hissed from the corner of his mouth.

Men with guns and hybrid uniforms approached and very slowly circled the car. "¡Alto!" shouted one of them. "Out!" another ordered.

Carlota wriggled her gawky frame into Fermin's arms whilst Rosario, stumbled by Elias' side. One thick-mustachioed man with dark inscrutable sunglasses pointed his gun at Fermin's temple. He came for a closer sniff when he smelt the terror on the chauffeur's breath, "What are you, gentleman or servant?" he asked evaluating the quality of his shirt's cloth. Rosario rushed towards him and claimed him as her brother. On seeing the fresh blood stain spreading on the rear of her dress, the man ripped off her gold necklace with one tug, but the rings on her swollen fingers had to stay on. "¡Adelante!" he shouted. "We don't want a bleeding woman on our hands do we, compadres?"

Their extreme predicament of the last twenty-four hours was hard for Elias to take in. There he was, turned into a fugitive overnight, evading factions of both right and left for fear of calamitous reprisals. But reprisals for what? He was not ashamed to admit that he had always been apolitical and that his own personal credo, if he had one at all, was business. Business had been his life since he left school and now, as always, he saw himself as a businessman merely supplying to a demand from both factions. He was not so innocent as to assume that as such, he would be immune to partisanship and regarded as neutral, but he was baffled at the rapid condemnation that had ensued. Travelling to and from his native land of Morocco to Spain on business since the early 1930s, he had settled reluctantly in Barcelona after his marriage to Rosario and though Spain had become his home for the last five years, he had not formed an emotional bond nor any political alliance with his adopted country. His neutral stance he thought, was wholly acceptable, though others, and his brother-in-law José Luis in particular, had urged him to openly support the Republican cause. Elias had shrugged off his appeal like someone declining the membership of a Bridge Club. If anything, he was a centralist, José Luis had admonished him, someone straddling the middle, afraid to commit, not so much through cowardice but ignorance and the unwillingness to inform himself of the complex issues involved. Inevitably the two extremes would meet in the end as they always did, Elias said, and José Luis feared that Elias could be right.

Elias had known for a while that Spain's political mood was ready to explode. The strife between peasants and the middle and upper classes had simmered for years. The climate was ready for socialism, but Russian communists and Trotskyites meddled and the POUM—the Partido Obréro de Unificación Maxista -was formed. Inevitably anarchy was rife everywhere, affecting Right and Left and causing a pernicious and mutual distrust. As a moderate, or at best a bourgeois republican, a balancing act at the centre, he thought, was the only way to prevent a horrendous blood-bath and he was not ashamed of that compromise.

He sighed as the setting sun mellowed his mood. "Where do you fit into all this, Fermin? " he asked, "I mean, are you a political man?"

Fermin said nothing. Elias was a kind, generous and considerate employer who hired him five years previously at the Port of Algeciras to drive him across Spain to Barcelona, and he had happily been in his service ever since. Elias had never asked him about politics before, and his question disconcerted him. "I am a worker and an Andalucian, Don Elias" he said finally. "I am a Republican. I hate shadowy Generals, but I also hate the communists and their Russian pals. Spain needs an Angel between these two devils Don Elias. I have prayed to La Macarena Herself but we've gone too far already. I am a fatalist Don Elias."

"See that tiny light in the distance? Drive through the field will you Fermin!" interrupted Elias. "And go easy on that track, we don't want to harm the señora ".

It was a small-holding and a pack of barking dogs welcomed them. The commotion startled Rosario and Carlota.

"Señores, buenas!" exclaimed a large figure emerging from under a reed covered terrace and into the dark. "Can I help you?" the man asked.

"We are travelling north and accommodation is scarce round these parts" said Elias trying to sound casual "We would be grateful for a night's stop."

"Nuestra casa es vuestra casa" said the man. "You are welcome here. We have bread and wine... and goat's milk for the wee girl" he offered, waving at Carlota.

Two giggly children aged about seven and five appeared half-way down the stairs in long grey linen gowns to peer between the banister rails.

"Come on down! We've got travellers!" the man called to his wife, but she was already in the kitchen breaking eggs into a clay bowl.

"Buenas!" said the woman with a singing voice to the sudden invasion of her kitchen. "Sit yourselves down, have a glass of wine" she said, placing an earthen pitcher and tumblers on the wooden slatted table. They sat, struggling to explore the dark corners of the room where the lamp's glow did not reach. Quietly, Carlota found refuge on Fermin's lap, and Rosario found hers by Elias' side. No one dared strike up a conversation for fear of saying the wrong thing. The smell of garlic, recently harvested, olive oil and thyme sizzling in the pan brought a cosiness and familiarity which prompted Rosario to break the silence. "Do you get many travellers stopping on their way north?

"No" said the man, "but we leave a light on for welcome and our door is open to anyone who spots us here in the wilderness."

Were they affected at all by what was happening out there she asked again.

"No, not yet. But we will, like everybody else. In the meantime, we live day by day, and when the time comes, we'll face the music!" exclaimed the man.

"And then?" pursued Rosario.

"We'll go north, like you, I guess" he replied. "I'd stay to fight if it wasn't for the wife and children" the man added with a tone of regret.

Satisfied that treachery had not reached these peoples' hearts, Elias let himself sink into the hard-backed chair. Seldom did he think of the age gap that separated him from Rosario, but at that moment and when he glimpsed the shadow of his wife's child-like features dance against the white-washed wall opposite, he felt old, and sad that he was.

"I'm bleeding..." she bent over to whisper.

"Has the Señora recently had a miscarriage?" enquired the woman instantly lifting Rosario's legs to rest on a chair. Her

12

shrewdness and speed of action amazed Elias. "My wife delivered a baby at dawn" he explained, "but it was premature and too weak to travel with us."

"What your good lady needs is a potion of wheat mould" the woman said. She wanted to know where the baby was and who was caring for it. She reached for a brown jar on the top shelf of the cupboard, explaining, when Elias raised his eyebrows, that country women used it for heavy monthlies, miscarriages and the stubborn dregs of after-births.

Later, Elias carried Rosario up the narrow wooden stairs into a bare room with a damp smelling straw mattress on the floor in the corner of the room, and watched over her until she screamed twice and passed fleshy fragments of placental tissue and congealed blood into the piece of flannel that the woman had given Rosario so she could verify that the potion had worked.

They rose in the early morning to the splashing sound of Fermin washing himself and Carlota in the yard. They all drank a bowl of hot milk before Elias thanked them for their hospitality. "No, señor" the farmer said when Elias reached for his wallet. "Help one another is our motto here."

"¡Adalante!" cried Elias to Fermin.

Like a mirage, and still a long way ahead of them, a faint, disorderly convoy, floated against the hazy horizon. Cattle, chickens, dogs and families carrying meagre provisions amongst an eclectic array of basic belongings undulated forwards, like someone's atavistic nightmare. Some scattered to the sides of the road as the car came closer and women and children fell flat to the ground expecting a round of gun fire.

"Don't be afraid. We are brothers!" shouted Elias out of the car's open window and called to an old white bearded man if he had the latest news.

"Troops are marching towards the Basque provinces Señor" he replied, "but it will be days!" Another said Burgos was the place to fear. "The Iron ore and the industries there" he commented, visibly pleased to contribute, "are sure to attract the Nationalists!"

13

"And where are you heading?" asked Elias.

"The young ones are off to Burgos and Valladolid to fight Señor. Fight to the death." He covered his face to conceal the horror. "The rest of us" he added, "are going as far north as we can, and hope it's safe there, but who knows where the lion's den is hidden in this bloody war!" he exclaimed with uncharacteristic peasant resignation. "Are you a foreigner?" he whispered, bending forwards towards the car window. "Yes. We've been caught here whilst on business, and we're on our way to France."

"Safe journey!" shouted the man as the convoy made way for the car.

Guessing what lay ahead or who had supremacy in any particular town or village was out of the question, but it stood to reason that the wealthier the area the more appealing it would be to the Nationalists. Either way, depending on who you or they were, no place was safe.

Fermin headed for Tolosa. It was midday. The engine was heating up and needed cooling, but ahead, another road block made them pull up. A group of soldiers holding rifles headed towards the car. Elias knotted his tie, ran his fingers through his hair and waited.

One soldier poked Elias' shoulder with his gun. "Out! Fatso!" he ordered, "and you, the thin one, bring your papers!" One after the other they were pushed into a make-shift shed of an office off the road where a uniformed officer awaited them. "Who are you?" he roared, pushing Fermin aside and making him stumble.

"I am the lady's brother" he replied, composed.

"What lady?"

"My wife and child are in the car" said Elias, in his most suave voice.

"Go back to your sister" the officer ordered after pondering. "You, stay!"

Fermin, would have blundered sooner or later and a sigh of relief relaxed Elias' features.

"And your destination?" the officer growled

"We have relatives in France and we are on our way there."

"Your occupation?" Elias froze. His answer could save or damn him and his family. "I am in business" he replied, trying to sound neutral.

"What kind of business?" he asked, his nose and Elias' almost touching.

"I export hides to Ireland."

"Anything else?" he asked, groaning as he sat down on a hard stool.

"I import bananas from the Canaries, and gouda cheese from Holland and" he added as an afterthought, "eggs to the garrison in Morocco."

"Eggs! To Morocco? Bananas to the Canaries…!" A thin smile stretched the officers' lips until they were bloodless. "So… you must be one of us!" he said, standing up and with his arm around Elias' shoulder. "I'll walk you back to your car and meet your dear spouse."

Were there were more garrisons ahead Elias enquired. They should have a clear run the officer assured him with a wink, adding that the capture of Irun and San Sebastian by General Mola would seal the frontier with France.

"Water and gasoline for our friends!" he ordered his soldiers when he saw the steaming engine, and he waved them off with the new pronunciamento of '¡Arriba España! ¡Arriba Franco!"

*

They followed a track down the valley to a small grey village where they spent the night in the church's sacristy. The caretaker had beckoned them in after she saw them aimlessly circling the square.

The Angelus rang at six as they awoke. Rosario thought it was a good omen and her spirits soared. Despite the terrors around them, their lives had been spared because thus far, she felt, they had been guided by a posse of angels. The faint images of Pepa and Paloma burgeoned in her mind but refusing to give

15

them further life, she made herself look at the mountain tops and she felt aroused by the romance and the jittery disquiet of this frontier land into which her father Camilo was born.

"Slow down! Your passes!" shouted a grumpy voice from an invisible cabin in the dark.

"This way. To your left!"

They had arrived. "To the belle France!" cried Elias "and two days rest in Saint Jean..." he whispered, watching Rosario's face grow rounder with a rare smile.

The break brought them a new cheer and rhythm. France was new to Rosario. She had only travelled within the Peninsula and once to Italy on her honeymoon and now flutters of excitement filled her chest. She saw France as being better and having more than any other country in the world and she yearned for undiluted self-indulgence and cultural and personal self advancement.

Elias' mind travelled a different path; his was that of survival. Soon he would have to earn to feed and care for his family, as the money reserve he had in Paris was almost exhausted. But his immediate thoughts converged to a more pressing matter: Rosario's state of health which had been seriously neglected after the confinement.

Fermin's musings shifted with the landscape. His guilt for having forsaken his native Andalucia when it needed all its men made him ache the agony of the exile and the shame of the deserter and he welcomed the interruption of Elias' request to call at the nearest hospital for Rosario's check up.

THREE

Agnus Dei

The Puerta del Sol seethed with crowds not long after Pepa and Paloma had left the Clinic for the railway station in the North of the City. Giant banners hung from balconies clamouring for 'More Arms For The People.' It was then that Pepa realised how much more explosive the situation was than she had anticipated. The station would be teeming with northern and Catalan workers attempting to flee from the predicted reprisals of Nationalists and her fear for her grand-daughter's safety grew. She instructed the driver to avoid all main roads as far as possible and to stop at a pharmacy for a tin of powdered milk. But businesses kept capricious hours at this unsettled time and they arrived at the station without it. She pressed a few pesetas into the driver's hand and thanked him after he had pushed and shoved her onto an empty single seat on the train. He refused her offering saying that today they were equal at heart. She smiled and said "Every day comrade."

Pepa wrapped Paloma in her own shawl to further protect the infant against the noxious fumes and human assault. People screamed and stampeded their way onto the train. Like a last call for salvation, the piercing sound of hooting bored into the airless atmosphere and the frenzy redoubled. Obscenely laden, the slug-like train slithered slowly away from the platform. Only the roof remained free of human occupation. Every seat was taken, and every other lap. In the aisle, the late-comers stood glued together in a homogeneous mass. At first, no one could move without causing a minor landslide until the swaying mass developed a sympathetic rhythm of its own. Near the window a man began to agitate and demand urgent

17

access through the aisle. His way blocked, he was met with protest and derision. Undeterred, he loosened his belt, removed his cloth cap, then bent down to defecate into it to shouts of disgust and disbelief. The stench, in the midday heat brought waves of nausea. A pregnant woman threw up and children, reminded of their own needs, screamed for the lavatory.

In time, the drone of the train and the muffled sounds of discordant snoring induced an hypnotic trance. Lingering dreams of loved ones left behind, vomit and excrement mingled without distinction and fed the thick air that was nervously shared. A sudden thud and stop shook them into another reality, then silence. Fear exuded from every pore; a mob of soldiers standing at the platform had invaded the compartment and without a word spoken, a central passage was cleared for them. Stuck together like limpets at the edge of a rock, a cluster of men in the corner stood still, their blatant solidarity and a red neckerchief falling to the ground proclaiming their identity as a bunch of Republicans. Kicked in their bellies and their faces spat on, they were led off the train at gun-point. The soldiers shouted "Arriba España! Arriba Franco!" and the men in chorus shouted back "Arriba la República!" and a volley of shots ended their clamouring.

The sound of the train in motion became louder amidst the bleakness of silence. There was a stir from within the shawl. Pepa parted it. Paloma's flushed face and parched lips alarmed her. She loosened Paloma's gown and fanned her body with her hand. "Please!" she pleaded, looking randomly around, "Please help this child! She needs water!" She renewed her plea before a botijo passed from hand to hand reached her seat. "Thank you, whoever you are!" she called, stretching her gaze as far as she could to the end of the compartment, and dabbed the precious liquid on Paloma's forehead, on her sunken fontanelles, and behind her ear lobes. "That's my girl!" she spoke softly when Paloma began to quiver. All eyes focused on the scene and magically and for a moment a wave of tenderness reconditioned the air. Peering over the bundle the woman next to Pepa asked the child's name. It was the first time someone had wanted to know. "Paloma, her name's Paloma" Pepa replied, full of emotion.

"Paloma de la Paz" the woman said wistfully. "That's what we need right now...A Dove of Peace." And she began to whimper, all curled up, looking vacant at the window.

Irregular stops, some scheduled, others not, punctuated the journey. A nod, barely noticeable, was reciprocated as travellers came and went. No one gave out anything and shifty looks with unfinished smiles were the average measure of exchange. A woman screamed. Amidst the travellers standing in the aisle and like worms at the centre of a rotten apple, wriggled two portly men in hybrid uniforms. Sandwiched between them stood a frail looking young girl following their orders to slide her underpants down to her ankles and hold her skirt above her waist. Heavy belts thudded to the floor and an agonising shriek tore through the compartment as the men's bodies shook in arrhythmic convulsions. Their grunts grew louder and baser in accord with their separate crescendos. Then nothing, until the jangling of their belts indicated completion. The girl stood pale and trembling. "I am dead" she moaned. "I am dead" she repeated. "Dead. Dead."

"Shut up, you stupid nun! You thought we didn't know?... With a face that hasn't seen the light of day for months! We don't need your bloody habit to tell us what you are!" shouted one of the two rapists lighting a cigar. A collective gasp rippled throughout the length of the compartment and he shouted what was the matter. No one spoke. "Aquí no pasó nada! Nothing happened here! Nothing!" But a group of men with menace on their faces came towards him. He pulled a pistol. "What happened you cowards?" he asked louder than before. "What happened?" he demanded.

Retreating, and in unison the men mumbled "Nothing."

"Someone, open a window!" a woman shouted.

"We give the orders here!" growled back the other rapist. "The window stays shut. What's the matter, don't you like that smell ?" he asked, thrusting his pelvis into the woman's face.

Pepa had had enough. Entrusting Paloma to the woman

19

who had asked her name, she pulled a diaper from her bag and elbowed her way to the victim. The man with the pistol made a move to stop her and snarled.

"Look, you!" she threatened with her index finger under his nose, "you've done your bit and no one dared stop you, don't you dare stop me now!"

"¡Cojones! The old crone's got balls!" he sniggered holding his testicles. "Go on then, do your bit, old woman! Hope you are as good as we were!" he laughed.

Pepa wiped the young girl's groins before pulling up her underwear.

"There, child" she murmured, cradling her until the young woman stopped trembling. "I am Pepa. What's your name?" and she lowered her eyes to meet hers. "Esperanza. I was Esperanza but I've been Sister Luz since last April. I never thought anyone would guess without my robes" she said. I am dead Señora ..."

"Listen to me Esperancita" whispered Pepa. "We all suffer many deaths, this for you was one amongst many. It was a martyr's death, and in God you will live and be Luz again. Let us pray for those who raped your body but not your soul and for the healing of our ailing land." The young nun inhaled a long, deep breath. "Agnus Dei qui tollis peccata mundi, miserere nobis..." she exhaled, and repeated her invocation thrice in all, and louder each time.

The last stop heralded a change of territory, mood, political hue and language. Castilla was left behind. TÚ replaced the formal USTED, and SALÚD the usual ADIÓS, signalling the repudiation of anything godly and religious.

So many inconsistencies divided her country and people. A devout Catholic with republican sympathies, Pepa did not feel she could condone the Nationalists, even if they protected the Church, but neither could she adopt the new atheism that had already aimed so much cruelty towards the clergy throughout Republican Catalunya. Yet, and foremost, she felt fused to her people by their language, their industriousness, collectivism, democratic vision, and passion.

Repairs to the engine forced a halt and for the first time Pepa gazed outside the window. The sudden brightness offended her eyes, she blinked and sought the caress of a passing cloud.

"Next stop Lérida!" a woman cried, unable to contain her excitement. "And after that, Barcelona and we are home!"

A silent echo of expectation reverberated through the compartment; whispers, like puffs of smoke, whirled from the aisle and a gradual, tacit exchange began to form. Trust, that forfeited commodity returned with the smell of home and before long travellers confided in each other and predicted who would be there to collect them.

A cacophony of voices exploded as the train came to an uneven halt.

The young nun broke free from the bunched passengers to embrace Pepa and place a small object inside her hand which she then closed tightly with hers. "To my sister in Christ" she murmured, and vanished in a hasty zig-zag into the crowd. Travellers collected their belongings but Pepa remained seated. She could not risk crushing the infant in the outpouring hysteria and prayed that her son-in-law Salvador who was meeting them would stay calm and stand by. She opened her hand as she waited. A silver medal lay sparkling in the centre of her palm. "The All Redeeming Heart of Jesus..." she mused. And she was still smiling when Salvador's voice cried "Pepa! Bebé! Thank God you're safe!" and urged them to hurry. "Things are hotting up here!" he said pushing them along the crowded platform. "How's this for starters" he said, "tomorrow's bullfight has been cancelled. Spain, without its bullfighting on Sunday..! You know what that means, don't you?"

"The bloody corrida is all over Spain, Salvador! So what's the latest crisis?" asked Pepa surprised at the speed of events.

"Keep walking!" he pleaded when Pepa slowed down. "Things were fine till yesterday after you left, then today crowds are everywhere, from the Ramblas to the Plaza de Catalunya and all the way to the Plaza de la Paz by the harbour, shouting for a revolution. The Republican Headquarters are in Colomb. Your fine clothes, the baby's silk shawl, for all they know we could be bloody Nationalists! And here we are, minutes away from it! Let's move!" he shouted, looking over his shoulder. "This way" he commanded, swerving to the right and then sharply left. "I know my alleys" he added with a touch of pride. "And give me the child, this rushing can't be good for you" he said relieving Pepa of Paloma. "We'll stop at the grocer's, just around the corner for you to catch your breath before we make a move for home."

Home was some distance away, near the Monjuic's entrance at the Plaza de España. Josep the grocer wore a red neckerchief which he refused to remove even for bed; he welcomed them into the congested storeroom where the radio blared the latest news. "There's already been bloodshed in the Plaza Catalunya" he mumbled, spitting an olive stone. "Will Lluis Companys save us or crucify us? Who's to know… Meanwhile horses and men are all over the place, nobody knows what the hell's going on, what's for sure is that the trouble is spreading like wild fire and that you must get home within the hour. Paco will push the old lady and the bebé in the vegetable cart. Safer to keep him with you till daybreak tomorrow" he said, signalling his son into action.

Winding their way through the narrow streets, they stopped to hide in doorways when they heard gunfire until they arrived at the Plaza de España, not far from home. From the geranium filled balcony, where they were keeping watch, Lalia and Mingo caught sight of their father and waved frenetically, reappearing downstairs with their mother to meet them in the street.

Barely eighteen years separated Pepa from her eldest daughter Carmela and the closeness of their relationship relied on a blend of motherly and filial love, sisterly affection and intimate friendship. In silence, they hugged and cried as if it had been months since their last encounter. "And Rosario?" sobbed Carmela, at last disengaging from her mother's embrace.

"She's with Elias, that's what she decided." But you knew

that already "said Pepa struggling to hold back her tears and then she shrugged her shoulders.

"Will Carlota be alright?"

"There's no guessing about that child" she replied wistfully. "One thing is certain, she'll get no comfort from her mother. There's too many strange undercurrents between those two, so who can tell?"

"And Elias?"

Pepa hesitated. "He knows Rosario needs me and that Carlota is a trying child. He will send for us as soon as he gets the passes. I know he will."

FOUR

From the Darkened Sea into a Hall of Mirrors

The poky two bedroomed apartment in the Calle Diputación of Rosario's childhood which she had once loved and where her sister's family, Pepa and Paloma now lived, was no more than a fleeting grey image in her mind she had no wish to rekindle.

Her first acquaintance with the villa on the corniche was the most exciting moment of her life. Villa Écume had its own golden sandy beach. Purple bougainvillaea and yellow tufted mimosa trees lined the drive that sheltered the gravelled path to the sea. She breezed from room to room, up and down the marble staircase and doted on the pink italianate tower she claimed for herself. Elias shouted her name as he peeled off the loose white coverings to reveal an antique collection of furniture in the vernacular provençal style, then summoned the four staff to inform them that Madame would be giving instructions as to the running of the household in a day or two.

The nanny was to take full charge of Carlota as of that moment, and Amélie and Carlota's mutual glances left no doubt as to their instantaneous and reciprocal antipathy.

It had been a month, passed in calm and safety before Elias began to fret. He was an energetic and successful man, an 'Export—Importeur de Primeurs' as he described himself, respected by the trading fraternity, who, by a twist of fate had lost his business contacts, and now for his safety, circumstances dictated that he remain incognito. He sat on the chaise-longue on the vine-covered terrace drinking huge gulps of iced grenadine between inhaling long puffs of his Havana cigar. The sea he gazed at through a gap in the clump of pine trees made him long for his own patch of the Atlantic Ocean back home in Morocco. He saw himself as if now with his three brothers galloping bare-back along a sand-duned beach and then slowly undulating their way through the cobbled streets of Mazagan and into the arched courtyard of the Casa Porta do Mar to groom and stable the steaming horses. A passing yacht, the like unseen in Atlantic waters, swept his image away reconnecting him to place and time. He called for Popol the new chauffeur to take him for a drive.

Banished from her mother's sight Carlota languished with Amélie in the small pavillon next to the gate; Rosario left her bedroom only to climb to her pink tower and dream dreams she shared with no one. It was to Josette, the maid, to see to madame's every whim and Elias himself became over-attentive as if to atone for his young wife's trauma over Paloma's birth and its aftermath.

Rosario first came into Elias' life in an office in Las Ramblas, one of Barcelona's fashionable quarters which he shared with his elder brother Joaquín. She was only seventeen. Falling in love with Rosario when interviewing her for a secretarial position was the easiest thing Elias had ever done. Her French and stenographic skills impressed him, but it was her captivating dark looks, her eyes, direct and provocative and the all-pervading duende emanating from her essence that ensured her the post. She found him intriguing from the moment she heard his indeterminate accent and succumbed to his impeccable classical dress sense and winning awkwardness, so different from the smutty youths who courted her. Elias was not attractive, she acknowledged that from the start. He was portly, rather short—no taller than a metre fifty five—with a thinning crown, but his asset was the enigma that surrounded him.

A year passed before he made his feelings formally known and it was her father's response that became Rosario's main concern. Don Camilo was a captain in the Guardia Civil who came from an old but impecunious military family with the word HONOUR tattooed on its soul from birth. Rosario was his youngest daughter and she knew Camilo would embark on a fastidious investigation into the background of this unknown thirty-something man before he would grant his seal of approval.

From a prestigious and well-respected European family on the Atlantic coast of North Africa in the remote fortified town of Mazagan, Elias' pedigree could not fail to impress Don Camilo. Elias' great-great grand father had been an Anglo-Irish landowner from the Irish town of Kilkenny who bequeathed his land and castle to his eldest son, while the nearly penniless younger brothers were driven out of Ireland to seek their fortunes elsewhere. In 1823, Eion, the most adventurous landed in Tangier, married the youngest and most vivacious daughter of a retired sea captain from Cadiz, became a Spanish national and a successful grain merchant. Their only child was Joseph. At only twenty five, Joseph's inherent Irish pioneering spirit, his curiosity and passion for the Arab world, earned him the post of Spanish Vice Consul to the medieval Portuguese town of Mazagan. There, Joseph lived in a smart, balconied Portuguese-style dwelling in the Rua da Carreira within the city walls where Europeans—mainly Portuguese, Spanish, Italian and a few French nationals had settled. Jews congregated in the Mellah, a ghetto, also protected, at one end of town, whilst the indigenous population lived in impoverished clusters outside and around the fortified walls. Venturing beyond those walls after dark was seen as foolhardy by the town dwellers and the tall, heavy, cast-iron gates at the city's entrance closed at sunset. Joseph acquired a sturdy horse and rode outside the walls visiting Arab settlements across the countryside to survey their land and examine their grain and cattle. It was not long before they bestowed on him their gift of respect and affection and Joseph saw no reason to live within the city walls. He became the first European to dare settle outside them and after months had passed and no harm had befallen him, the gates remained open all night. I was this single gesture of trust that marked the beginning of harmonious relations between all peoples in the city.

One day Joseph returned from his travels holding a dark, curly-haired baby boy in his arms, all wrapped in a fringed purple shawl. He had adopted him, he told his housekeeper. His name was Zachariah, Zac to his new family, and she was to care for him as if he was her own. Zac would be initiated into the Catholic and Moslem religions alike and instructed in Spanish, Arabic, Portuguese and French. Joseph's belief was simple—the more pluralistic the man—the less likely he would be to quarrel.

Twenty three years passed before Zac returned from a business trip to Gibraltar having fallen for the charms of Frigiliana Carey, the only daughter of an Anglican pastor. He had asked the Reverend for Frigiliana's hand in marriage, and Joseph finally felt compelled to tell Zac that he was truly his father, and Miriam, a Jewish woman whose amorous alliance with Joseph had been forbidden by her strict Sephardic parents was his mother. It was rumoured in the ghetto that she had died of a broken heart after Zac, only a few days old was taken away from her to be raised in a Catholic convent during his first year of life until Joseph claimed him back and brought him home. Fearing that the shame and the stigma of having a Jewish mother would impede his marriage to Frigiliana, Zac dissolved his engagement, but a year later, he and Frigiliana Carey were wed, yielding eleven children of whom only six survived: Joaquín, Elias, Samuel, Lourdes, Trini and Geraldo.

Though not straightforward, the family background would have satisfied any demanding father, but Don Camilo's cautiousness was unrelenting, for he considered Elias' personal history to be a little dubious. Still unmarried at the age of thirty nine, he reasoned that Elias was just as fallible as any man. Camilo's son, a recently qualified doctor, was to give Elias a thorough medical examination and the Wassermann test for syphilis, the accursed disease of the well-travelled man.

Never had Elias imagined that he would be subjected to so demeaning a scrutiny to marry the daughter of a guardia, but his ardour for Rosario was so irresistible that he willingly submitted to it.

Weeks before his parents could meet Rosario and give their blessing for the union, Zac died of Cholera and heart-broken, Frigiliana followed him to the grave, a month to the day. After a minimal period of mourning for his parents, Elias and Rosario were wed.

Popol and Elias returned from their long drive. Even his hefty body could not prevent him from running up two steps at a time to Rosario's pink tower, where she took her afternoon tea. "We are going to be alright" he panted. "We shall live like kings!"

"Don't we already?" she asked holding an imaginary tiara.

"I didn't want to worry you, querida. The thing is, our money has run out."

That evening, Elias dressed in his tuxedo. Rosario saw him vanish with Popol into the night and for the first time since their marriage she could not fathom Elias' behaviour, nor the purpose of his nocturnal escapade and all night, she sat in bed reading Lamartine's poems to placate her nerves. As dawn broke, she heard a rattling noise arising from the kitchen. Elias had grabbed two glasses and a bottle of Heidseik from the refrigerator and was now standing, beaming and silent at the bedroom doorway, the stud of his starched collar undone. She sat upright, tongue-tied, then begged him to say something. "First, a glass of bubbly for my chiquita..." he breathed clinking the two glasses together and then producing the champagne bottle from behind the door like a stage magician.

"Well?.. she demanded. "Tell me!" she pleaded, her cheeks and eyes aflame. He tried but unsuccessfully, to sit cross-legged in the centre of the bed. "I-have-made-a-killing!" he intoned.

"A killing?" she repeated. "Yes, a killing!" he shouted, relishing her state of puzzlement, and when she could no longer restrain herself, he told her to listen. "I have just won a fortune." He said it very slowly, and savouring every word, "and this," he added, floating ten thousand francs above her head, "will keep us going... and going ...in the luxury you deserve."

"Elias!" she cried, gathering the crisp notes in her lap. "How?"

"The Casino querida! I played Roulette. Where do you think I've been all night?" He arranged two pillows behind his back and continued. "Popol drove me to Monte Carlo this afternoon because the sun glaring on the sea made me homesick and I had to cheer myself up and that was it. I had to test my luck there and then, and I won a few francs—not much—but when I returned to the casino tonight, I just knew it would be our lucky night."

"The Casino! You're back from the casino!" screamed Rosario falling backwards on the bed as light as a candy floss ball. She then looked at Elias through the edge of her gossamer nightdress.

That night and all the following day they spent in bed, laughing and love-making as they had not done for months.

Newspaper headlines about the civil war in Spain became increasingly confused and Elias' concern reflected everyone's. What was clear to him above all else, was that Spain, within the complexity of its long-standing divisions, was split into two camps—the Republicans and Nationalists—and that the war had irrevocably acquired international significance, with the Fascists in Italy, and the Nazis in Germany pandering to Franco and the Nationalist right, against the Russians, not surprisingly eager to become involved with the communists and the Republican left, while the Americans, the British and the French played safe by choosing a policy of non-intervention. Always with a smile, he remembered the Red Brigade, left-wing intellectuals of mixed nationalities, who came, he thought, not so much to fight a war, but an ideal. The war, a localised conflict at the start, was fast becoming the symbol of the polarisation that already existed in much of the Western world, and Elias sensed with dread that the Spanish Civil war was no less than a dress rehearsal for a sinister war in Europe.

A recent radio bulletin reported that Catalunya was engulfed in total turmoil. This was his most pressing concern, and it comforted him that Rosario had missed the report whilst away having a uterine prolapse repair operation.

"Tell your Elias what you would like to do most when you feel stronger?" he asked Rosario the day she came home from the clinic. It perplexed her that nothing outrageous came to mind and said, not meaning it, that she liked surprises best. "I think the theatre" he declared, knowing the idea would excite her. "Then dinner in the vieille ville. And after that you can be my lucky mascot at the Casino." She squealed like a sixteen year old and complained that she couldn't go without a fur coat just like Gloria Swanson's and Greta Garbo's and all the stars. He frowned and told her it was vulgar.

At the theatre, she watched the Pastourelle and her romantic imagination soared. At the candle-lit table, she sipped her champagne as if each were the first and last sip she would ever have, and closed her eyes in ecstasy to listen to the Beluga pearls explode in exquisite juices between the tip of her tongue and the back of her teeth. But later it was the women at the casino in their sparkling second-skin haute couture gowns, the magical language of the croupiers around the gaming tables and the men, palpable re-incarnations of her own cinema idols, that captivated her and made her head spin more than champagne ever could, and more wildly than the roulette wheel. Elias called her to shout a number, any number, and relentless, the wheel turned to shouts of les jeux sont faits, rien ne va plus, until it stopped dead, game after game, at Rosario's given number.

That night she wanted to, but could not respond to Elias' persistent amorous overtures, nor could she sleep. "This child," a voice said in her head, "was born with a golden spoon in her mouth." It was her eldest sister Carmela's voice ringing in her head like an automated musical box until lulled, she granted herself the luxury to drift into her own life dream.

She had been spoiled from day one. Everyone knew it and she could see that. Eighteen when Rosario was born, Carmela looked on her baby sister almost as if she had been her own child. Pilar, her middle sister had conceded to Rosario's every whim rather than compete and her only brother José Luis, who was seven when she was born had idolised her from the start. Even the nuns of Our Lady of Mercy convent school adored her, and as a late arrival in Camilo's life she had become her father's best loved child, and later, he delighted parading her on his arm in the Ramblas of the Plaza de Catalunya during the evening Paseo.

"You're restless cariñito. Are you unwell?" asked Elias dazily.

"I haven't slept a wink!" she moaned, tossing right and left.

"Must be the champagne, I must make sure you get used to it" he said, turning round to face her. "Do you want to make love?"

"Only if it will send me to sleep" she answered unexcitedly. She fell asleep after he had obliged and did not wake until it was time for their customary cup of iced tea on the lawn the following afternoon.

Elias got up early to gather the house staff in the fore-court. Madame would be holding a 'Thé Dansant' early next week he told them, followed by a late swim. There would be some fifty guests and she would give her instructions later. It was early August and the announcement was intended as a pleasant surprise, but the idea threw Rosario into a tantrum. She had not been to a Thé Dansant in her life nor heard of one, let alone given instructions for a party of fifty. Thés Dansant, Elias reassured her were informal garden occasions ideal for beginners in social skills and that Josette knew all about them. "Who can we invite?" she lamented. "We only know our staff, the croupiers at the casino, my coiffeur, couturier and gynaecologist!" That was precisely the point, Elias emphasised, and that was why it was time to invite the société Niçoise. She moaned that her French wasn't good enough to mix in society and he promised her that it was delectable.

"Who'll be coming then?"

"We'll send invitations to all our corniche neighbours and I'll ask Monsieur Gérard to make an announcement at the casino on Friday night when the British are there in force and we'll take it from there."

"Do you think they'll come without formal invitations? You know how stuck-up the English are!"

"They'll think us a little boorish, but they'll come out of curiosity. They're so voyeuristic…" he smiled benignly.

Instructed to play a medley of American, English and French music, the musicians came early to set the mood. Dressed in white from head to toe, Elias was just how Rosario imagined him in his native Morocco and she thrilled each time he lifted his Panama to welcome a new guest. She too wore white. She had picked a boleroed outfit from La Sérénade boutique in the Promenade des Anglais after hours of agonising indecision. Elias had to restrain her from adding to it a pair of large gold bangled earrings he had bought her to wear only in the private realm of their bedroom.

Just as Elias predicted, Casino clients appeared in dribbles of ones and twos. Others introduced themselves as neighbours and spontaneous conversations burst into multilingual animation. Some visitors arrived without formal announcement. Madame la Contesse Isodora Pushkova who had never missed a Thé Dansant showed up with a tiara and full ceremonial regalia, unnoticed by most habitués, whilst Imelda O'Brien, once a speck in the American cinematic firmament, now married to a millionaire Monégasque, already lay flat on the lawn, slowly drowning in Irish Malt and buried aspirations. Immersed in this strange bohemian refinement Rosario vowed, with all her heart, to stay a part of it for the rest of her life. Elias observed her from behind the leafy pergola fearing that the glamour Rosario so much ached for could forever erase the ingenuousness he so relished in her, and he wished that she would forever remain just as she was.

Moving from table to table, Rigolo, the vocalist, intoned requests—'when I close my eyes, I get butterflies;' 'Dada je suis;' and 'Dis-moi Oui, Dis-moi Non' followed by a riotous 'Oomp-pah-pah'! There was laughter and gossip until the band struck a romantic chord and couples gathered on the lawn. Sweet peas, mint, jasmine and mimosa trees exuded their heady mélange of scents. The mood mellowed. Woozy ladies flung their shoes aside and cheek-to-cheek couples danced, looking at the stars and their reflections in their partners' eyes. Then, the magic broke.

Sounding a spoon against an empty glass, a young male with thigh-hugging stripey trousers and a boater stood on a table . "Attention all!" he shouted, and then repeated it until he got it. "Who's for a swim?" he bellowed. The young rushed to the house to change and Elias joined Rosario already sitting on her favourite step by the rocky beach. "Are you happy?" he asked distracted. "I was" she murmured, "but now it's all changed" she snivelled. He told her that she was the perfect hostess and when she didn't respond to the compliment, he suggested a day out soon, a real family day, with Carlota too, who had not been taken out anywhere since they had been there. She replied blandly, why not, adding in the same monotone that she could do with some new outfits from the Coupe Anglaise which she loved, but Elias was only half listening. He had been watching Paco and Mirabel, the honeymoon couple at the party, diving from the rocks into the sea like two puppy seals, and clapping, child-like, at each other's nautical antics. At regular intervals the flashing light from the lighthouse at the end of the pier lit the water's edge in one clean sweep and Elias saw Paco dive from the highest rock to a loud admiring bravo from Mirabel below. But when Mirabel climbed down from the rock screaming for help, Elias kicked his shoes in the air and dived in. Rosario shouted to raise the alarm. Guests rushed to the scene, some jumped into the sea, others gloated whilst the hysterical young bride screamed and hugged Rosario as if she had always known her. Deep into the darkened sea Elias dived, waiting for the flash of the lighthouse to illuminate the waters. The music in the garden had stopped and the musicians and staff ran down the steps with lit torches, folded blankets under their arms, and Cognac. Elias struggled as a sudden shower of torch lights transfixed him. "He can't see, you fools!" shouted Popol as Elias tried to reach the water's edge, dragging Paco's body by his side. "Help me!" he gasped, "and keep Mirabel away. Someone ring for an ambulance, the police, the priest and the family. Hurry!"

"What he needs is a bottle of Cognac inside him!" laughed the boater-hatted guest. "Paco's cracked his skull" Elias said with death in his voice. Paco's dead."

Everyone scurried back to the house, dressed and left in a hurry so as to forget that the tragedy ever happened.

Wrapped in his bathrobe, Elias sat alone in the kitchen gulping whisky from the bottle. He inhaled deeply before he walked up to the bedroom. "Querida" he said as he came in, "let me lie next to you. Let me feel you close." His words came out hoarse, trembling and imploring. "Talk to me cariño!" he insisted wearily, when Rosario remained silent.

"I just knew something was up when that oaf called for a swim" she mumbled.

"You did?" he asked, belching uncontrollably.

"And besides, now no-one will want to set foot in the villa, ever again!" Elias sat upright to belch out the salt water again and apologised for his vulgarity. "You are tired and upset" he said, worn out. "Both of us are" he added. "We need a good night's sleep and we'll see things differently in the morning." He let his body slump on the mattress pulling the white sheet over Rosario's nakedness as he did, and fell asleep. Rosario lay awake, with her eyes unduly wide open, as if afraid to close them. Her nostrils flared as she sniffed the air. She could smell death floating in the bedroom. It touched and tapped her on the shoulder as lightly as a fluttering moth. It was Paco's body, lying flat on his back on the tiled floor, as vivid as when she saw Elias drag it out of the sea. The image drifted in and out of her consciousness for what seemed an age, becoming blurred then distorted, even grotesque, and narrowing and expanding as in a hall of mirrors and steadily assuming someone else's likeness. She tried to shift her tensing body to one side for comfort but she kept very still instead, holding her breath, waiting and watching the lingering shape emerge then grow into a luminous bubble, like an apparition in the centre of the room. She sat up and smiled. It was her first child Angelina and the only corpse she had seen before Paco's.

One unbearably hot Summer, Angelina, aged two, died of an incurable congenital heart condition. Her little angel had gone forever and Carlota, then a few months old, was hated for being alive and was removed from her mother's side, until back from a spell at a private clinic where Rosario's equilibrium had been restored.

In the darkened room, she whispered Angelina's name, willing her child to materialise, before the night drew to a close. By dawn, she forged a living entity, coloured, fed, and wholly energised by her persistence and imaginative force. Over the days and weeks that followed Angelina was there, miraculously re-incarnated, and as Rosario went about her life, she could at any time she chose, behold the velvet of her infant's brown eyes and her gentle closing fist on her own finger, and each time, she felt drawn and dissolved into an inexplicable pool of tenderness far beyond anything she knew this world could offer. A phase of unrelenting piety overtook her and no one at the Villa Écume understood what was happening to Madame. Every day, for weeks, Popol drove her to the local church for early mass. There were no frivolous garments in Rosario's wardrobe. Instead, a few dowdy black outfits she had bought at the Galerie Lafayette hung creased on the rails. Elias' incapacity to deal with emotional traumas paralysed him. He knew that Paco's drowning the night of the Thé Dansant had somehow triggered his wife's metamorphosis, but he could not comprehend how or why and he began to long for Pepa's soothing presence. Pepa had lived with them since returning from their honeymoon and had been a great leveller and comfort throughout Angelina's terminal illness. Now Elias found himself looking at ways to speed up her and Paloma's exits from Barcelona.

"Querida," he whispered, as if afraid to disturb a volcano when he saw Rosario kneeling in the grass one afternoon "What has happened to you?" She moved sideways saying she didn't know what he meant. He touched the sleeve of her black blouse. "Why are you in mourning" he asked.

"I don't need to explain, and you wouldn't understand if I did!"

"Please help me to help you!" he begged, joining his hands together.

"I can't!"

"Tell me why you are kneeling on the grass like that, then!"

"Because!"

"Because?"

"Because, because! Because I need to speak to God. There!"

"I understand that, but why all the black these days? Why don't you wear something bright and summery? After all, isn't summer symbolic of the fullness of life?"

"A poet now are you? And what about Paco and Angelina then!" she screamed. "They died in the summer didn't they? Life? I call that death! Finito! Caput!" He held her in his arms until the inordinate pounding of her heart against his resumed its normal beat. That was what it was. Paco's death had brought back Angelina's and reopened the old wound of loss.

"Angelina has been gone three years now querida..."he whispered.

"But she's back!" Rosario snapped back, unable to temper the wildness in her eyes.

"Back?"

"I see her Elias. She's here. I can even smell the talcum powder on her skin and the stale milk on her bib; she came to me Elias, my little angel is here. She IS here."

Imagination was never Elias' forte and Rosario's esoteric experience totally eluded him, but then he relied on his basic instinct to guide him. "Angelina is in Miraflores, remember?" he said, hoping to shift her back into the here and now. "We buried her there with mountains of beautiful white lilies."

"No she isn't" insisted Rosario, "she's here!" she gestured towards the empty space by her side. "Well I can't see her..." he contended, "because she's dead, Rosario. Dead." He repeated it slowly, making sure the word sounded like a stone hitting the water at the bottom of a well.

"Dead?" Rosario shook her head. "Dead?" she repeated.

"Yes." He paused. "But she's happy where she is and she wants you to say goodbye until it's time to meet again. Please come back to us querida!"

"Have I been away?" she asked as if awakening from a dream.

"Querida, watching you has been like watching a small bird trapped in a cage. Rosario I'm opening the door for you to fly away.. Do it!

*

Elias was taking Rosario to Cannes for a celebration lunch the next day. She had flown the cage, the fog in her head had lifted, and now she threw herself into an orgy of feeding, grooming and pampering every inch of her neglected body before dressing in a salmon-coloured outfit she had purchased that morning. She had turned a new leaf and was grateful to Elias for lifting her out of her long and terrible 'spleen,' as she called it.

Carlota never saw Elias and Rosario. The family outing planned just before the drowning never happened and the distance between Carlota and her parents grew abysmal. Amélie became disgruntled by her charge's wicked ways and without warning, gave her notice and quit. A replacement nanny was needed at once, but the summer was over and the so-called nanny season in Nice was gone. Rosario learned of an agency in Liguria on the Italian border who could send three nannies to be interviewed in a month's time. For Rosario, they were four weeks of torment. It was her secret—she had even kept it from Pepa—that since Carlota's birth she had not been able to see her daughter other than as an intruder, an interloper whom she should never have carried or borne. More than that, she thought Carlota evil, and those feelings of loathing for one of her own flesh and blood tortured her beyond endurance. She tried confession many times for contrition and peace of mind, but nothing ever diminished her guilt and every time she looked into her child's uncanny gaze, an overwhelming desire to harm Carlota overtook her.

The three nannies from the Ligura agency impressed Rosario beyond expectations. Carlota's unruly hair was set in paper curlers to create tumbling Shirley Temple ringlets the night before the interviews and on the day, dressed in layer upon layer of organza, and seemingly floating in a cloud of frothy innocence, she appeared before them, having accumulated a mouthful of saliva, which she spat over them. Wiping their faces the nannies ran out, shouting diabolo. Did madame want her to change Carlota's clothes, Josette asked. Rosario raged, saying she could rot in hell . From her pushchair parked on the landing, Carlota leered at her mother. Like a fury, Rosario charged towards her impelling the push-chair the length of the corridor and towards the open French window, just off the low walled balcony.

"May God forgive you Madame!" cried Josette lifting the screaming Carlota from the wheelchair into her arms.

"Who asked you to interfere?"

"Madame," said Josette, "It's not the child's fault!"

"Whose is it then?"

"Yours madame" she replied. "She's a very unhappy child madame. Very unhappy."

"YOU look after her then, see how you like it!"

"It's you she wants madame."

Down the garden steps she ran to seek refuge on the same rocky beach on which Paco had drowned. She called to the open sea, "if you're there God" she shouted, "help me! At least," she softened, "I beg you to send my mother back to me!" She held her head to stop it from shaking and when it settled, her thoughts, at first confused, followed their own volition, like small emanations to where her own sense of good and evil lay. The 'state of sin', she had been told during countless hours of religious instruction as a child and adolescent, was inherent to humankind. There were of course saints. They, she was told, had manoeuvred that evil out of their being through acts of goodness or martyrdom. But what of ordinary mortals? Was evil then, here to stay? And what was it anyway? And why did she come to think Carlota evil when she could not define its essence? Nothing that she had been taught helped her in her ruminations. But she remembered reading somewhere that the path to all understanding lay not in the known but in the unknown. She did not know what that meant, only that she was drawn to the notion, as part of her longing for a deeper inquiry into the complexities of existence. At the same time, she acknowledged that she also craved for the preservation of the pampered stability she knew and now, as on so many previous occasions, she chose to remain within the known framework of her religious conditioning rather than pursue her questioning on the nature of evil.

As soon as Elias had put down his briefcase, Josette informed him that Madame had had a difficult day.

He always knew where to find Rosario after an upset. For a while, he sat beside her on the rocky beach before venturing to speak. "I have good news Rosario" he whispered.

"You've found a nanny!" she blurted, turning sharply to look at him.

"A nanny? I thought you were dealing with this today."

"She ruined everything Elias. Everything!"

"Who?"

"Who? Who d'you think? Carlota, the devil incarnate, that's who!"

"Easy Rosario, tell me what happened."

"Oh! It would take too long to explain. She just ruined the interviews, that's all!"

Almost ignoring her reply, "Read this!" he said.

"From Spain? It's from Spain!" Rosario shouted waving the envelope in the air.

"Open it" said Elias pulling down the hem of her skirt.

"You open it, Elias" she said, sitting on her rock, "my hands are trembling."

"There..." he said "read it while I walk down the path."

Barcelona April 21st^s 1937.

My dear Rosario,
I have received only two letters from Elias and I am so
happy to read your life is safe and easy and I pray to

God that it will continue. I hope that my other three letters have reached you. I fear that I cannot write openly as so many letters are intercepted and confiscated these days, but I'm afraid I will upset you with news from our José Luis. He has been reported a prisoner of war in some jail down South. We have heard nothing concrete about it and I beg you to pray for your brother's release. Here, I will say that life is difficult but dear Carmela and Salvador are looking after us as best they can. Paloma is a joy. She smiles a lot and brightens everyone up in the bread queue. She is not putting on as much weight as she should but she is a very small baby and needs little food. Her birth was finally registered on the 11th August, and she is now officially a member of the human race. May Our Lady of Mercy protect her and keep her safe under her All Merciful Cloak. I miss you all, my darling daughter, Elias and sweet little Carlota and I long to be reunited with you soon, in our beloved Catalunya.

I hope this letter will reach you. Take care of yourselves, and pray God for your poor country.

With all my deepest and affectionate love.

Your mother,
Pepa

Rosario closed her eyes. "Mamá!" she wailed, "Mamaíta!" and pressed her fingertips hard against her eyeballs to help conjure a sharper outline of her mother. She saw Pepa's thin, lined face, her sparkless eyes and slight frame that were the raw testimonies of a year of want and deprivation. She tried to see Paloma in the bread queue, smiling, but she saw an open red wound instead, amidst screams, cries of women and children, visions of flames, chaos and destruction. She yelled, uncovering her eyes to stop the agony. "No! Please, God, have mercy!"

"Dear God querida, what's happened?" cried Elias hurrying to her side. "Is everyone safe?" he asked, snatching the letter from her lap.

"I can't bear the horror Elias! I saw it, heard it all! I didn't know! I didn't want to know! Mother a shadow, Paloma a bloody wound that won't heal and José Luis in prison! For what, in God's name, for what?"

"Shush..! Calm down querida" he said stroking her arm.

"They must come here at once Elias !"

"I'll do my best. I promise querida, I promise."

FIVE

The Crimson Dove

Treacherous generals:
see my dead house
look at broken Spain
from every house burning metal flows
Instead of flowers..

Come and see the blood in the streets.
Come and see the blood in the streets.
Come and see the blood in the streets!

Pablo Neruda

For Paloma and Pepa life in the streets of Barcelona was like playing Russian roulette. Each morning Pepa dressed Paloma in her cousin Lalia's old baby clothes and wrapped herself and the infant in a pink angora shawl Rosario had crocheted for Angelina. Symbiotically, and in the coldest winter ever recorded in the Peninsula, they made their way to the bread queue, but not before a five kilometre trek through the city to collect Paloma's milk coupons. At the bread queue Pepa picked up the precious tin of powdered milk that would have to last a week, and their ration of bread for all at Diputación. They always arrived late and joined a queue already a few hours long.

Out of months of silent, daily queuing, grew a strange camaraderie. Places were guarded jealously, but now and then a mother and baby were nodded to the front and a ripple of warmth ran through the length of the human chain.

42

Conspicuously absent from food queues were older children. The drudgery of boredom had driven many of them into habitual petty crime and parents considered it safer to keep them locked indoors and out of mischief.

It was late afternoon when Pepa finished queuing and the mostly trouble-free mornings often gave way to edginess as the day wore on. Before starting on her daily trudge back home, laden with milk, bread and sleepy infant, Pepa wolfishly pricked up her ears and scrutinised the horizon for signs of ferment and impending riots. Her instinct seldom failed her and she and Paloma arrived at the Calle Diputación unharmed and at the expected time for supper.

It was the 24th of September, 'Our Lady of Mercy's' day and the Patron Saint of Barcelona. Pepa followed her usual routine and nothing suggested danger until she saw, a few metres ahead, a man in ecclesiastical robes striding towards her, his hands joined in pious recollection. She knew, as did everyone else, that most priests in Republican Catalunya had been shot or were in hiding and that those who had been spared had the sense to wear civilian clothes. Her impulse told her to keep moving but within seconds of her decision a loud explosion shook the square and covered the sky in orange light. Then followed a burst of riotous screams. Pepa could not see, but she could hear the uproar. For a moment she forgot her bearings and was transported back to the June fireworks celebrations of the feast of San Juan. But this was September 1937 and there were anti-fascist posters everywhere urging Catalans to fight for independence, peace and solidarity amongst comrades and street merriment was now a thing of the past. Too late when Pepa tried to run away, she was caught in a dark tide of men dressed as priests that spilled into the square where she and Paloma were standing. The men, as in a black Sabbath ritual, laughed and danced around a towering bonfire of sacred objects and holy books. Passers by, like Pepa and Paloma, caught in the impromptu madness joined in to survive. Cheers of "Viva la República!" and "down with filthy priests!" echoed in the nearby streets. In the middle of the crowd, she saw one slim man thrown like a puppet into the air, then caught by a few men holding a blanket, to laughter and shouts of "Ecce Homo!" until deliberately, the men missed and let him land on the ground with a sickening thud. "Priest," mocked the gang leader chewing on the stub of his cigar "what do you want, your life and your freedom or death for your precious Christ?" "Death for my Christ" moaned the young priest, broken on the ground. "Good choice! The Passion in September!" jeered the leader. "Two Passions in one year! He will be pleased your bloody Christ!"

Standing next to Pepa a woman confided that young Padre Ignacio had been hiding in a friend and his wife's basement since the onset of the revolution after rescuing books, statues, religious garments and what little else he could save from his blazing church. Pepa had arrived just after he had been apprehended and dragged out of the basement into the square, along with his rescued treasures. Both his saviours had been shot on the spot. Pepa felt queasy and alarmed, she looked inside the shawl and tightened it around her waist to ensure protection. She dare not think of what lay ahead when she saw the priest stripped naked to lewd cries of "Wee Willie Wally!" and "No wonder he's a priest with a tiddler like this." One by one the men whipped him with their leather belts until he fell to his knees in a pool of blood. A woman crossed herself when she saw the outline of the map of Spain forming in the blood stain beneath his body.

"Come on priest! Get up! We've even got you a cross!" snarled the leader, kicking the priest's testicles with the metal toe-cap of one of his boots, then a round of gunfire scattered the crowds to clear a space.

"Before you die, oh Christ" taunted the leader, "We, I, the people of the Republic, in our Immense Sincerity, forgive you for your sins and your sins to the Nation!" he pronounced before he laughed, coughed and choked on his own sputum.

"It is I, Christ's humble servant who forgive you in His Name" muttered the priest in his thready voice.

"Well, what do you know….A brave priest!" he sneered "Then

crucify him!" he bellowed, enraged by the priest's meekness.

A loud succession of shots were fired from somewhere in the square and the Padre fell dead, halfway through his final blessing, into the peninsular stain of his own blood. More shots dispersed the hysterical crowd.

"Find him! Find the bastard who shot the priest! He was mine!" roared the leader, scouring the scuffle. His men scattered amid the bedlam and he followed them.

The injured were dragged into side streets by unharmed friends and relatives. The dead remained unclaimed. Pepa and Paloma sheltered unhurt behind a pillar when furtively, a young man emerged from a doorway. "Camarada!" Pepa called, when she spotted him. "What can we do with the dead?"

"I need another man to shift them and pile them in the square, for the relatives to find them in the morning" he said throatilly. "And the priest is mine" he added, lowering his tone.

"Did you know the Padre?" Pepa whispered back.

The man came closer and spoke in her ear. "He was my brother. I had to shoot him before they crucified him!" He burst in stifled sobs. "My own kid brother! May God forgive them Señora, he was a Republican too!"

Pepa smothered him in her bosom against Paloma and the provisions. "Believing in God does not make us Nationalist monsters" she whispered. He nodded. "From his basement my brother fought the Republican cause. He was one of them Señora !"

"May his soul rest in peace" she breathed. "And now my friend, I am your man!"

"And the child?"

"Wherever I go, she goes too" replied Pepa, rearranging Paloma and goods tight in the shawl behind her back to free her arms. "Let's go!" she exclaimed, rolling up her sleeves, "your dear brother to your house first. And we must be fast." Then they lifted and carried the dead and lay them side by side by the fountain in the centre of the square before they hid behind a pillar to sound the act of contrition on their behalf and for their executioners.

"I am Pepa, I don't know your name, amigo."

"Christóbal, Christóbal Aranjuez."

"Christóbal" she repeated, "Christóbal, my brother, let us pray for Padre Ignacio's peace in heaven and for the healing of this lost and sick world of ours."

Soiled, hungry and damaged by the day's savagery, Paloma fretted in her shawl all the way back to the Calle Diputación where the family, even the children, had kept watch for hours. Late that night, when Carmela and Salvador saw Pepa and bundle swaying and bent in blood-stained clothes, reaching her goal like a marathon runner on her last lap, they knew she had cried tears of despair and that she could not speak of the day's horrors. By the flickering oil lamp in the living room, they bathed her and Paloma in warm water and wrapped them each in blankets of tenderness.

Chores and responsibilities at the Calle Diputación were shared equally. From the start of the revolution Salvador had been wrenched away from his small but successful tailor's workshop by the Republican Militia and ordered to work in a factory outside Barcelona making uniforms for their men. Every night on his way home he stopped in unlit doorways to exchange remnants of heavy cloth, reels of black cotton and faulty buttons that he had smuggled out of the factory, for portions of lard, beans, black pudding, paraffin oil and if lucky, the odd candle or two.

After their breakfast of adulterated bread, made moist with a smearing of lard and thinly sliced onions, it was Mingo and Lalia's task to ensure the family's daily water rations. Armed with tin buckets, bottles, saucepans and leather gourds hanging from their shoulders, they joined the children's queue in the street below where stood the communal black, cast-iron water pump, standing totem-like in the middle of the pavement. The street janitor saw to law and order with an old broomstick, but anarchy often broke out in that once-a-day make-shift playground, and a shrill whistle, kept from his refereeing days, sent the children scurrying back to their homes, spilling much of the precious water into the streets, landings and staircases,

46

while from their balconies, mothers screamed at their children's senseless squandering.

Carmela's chronic asthma since childhood had entitled her to more rest and leisure than anyone else in the household. A bowl of malt coffee was brought to her in bed every morning by little Lalia. It was only after she drank it and coughed up the night's accumulated secretions that Carmela got up to see to the pile of mending and sewing of uniforms that Salvador brought for her from the militia, and to Mingo's and Lalia's rudimentary education in the afternoons, if she gave up her siesta. Paloma's contribution Pepa decided was her innate joy which kept the family cheerful. Prepared by Pepa, suppers brought the family together around the mock mahogany table in the three-by-three metre dingy dining room glimmering in candlelight. Bread portions, measured to the closest centimetre and sliced, were passed around and soaked in the cabbage and potato broth, or on Sundays, lentils and chick pea stew. No one ever talked. Only the muffled sounds of food, supped and relished gave the family a sense of oneness.

Salvador later amused the children with his own shadow theatre repertoire where old Catalan folk stories came alive on the bare flickering white wall opposite the dining table until asleep, he carried them to bed one by one. He, Pepa and Carmela then gathered quietly around the single candle flame, listening, like animals in a dark forest, to their mutual thoughts, only interrupted by an air raid on the Tibidabo mountain at the other end of town.

Confined to barracks in early June 1936, one month before the outbreak of the civil war, Camilo smuggled home prized food and other commodities from his barracks to share with the family, when granted a twenty four hour pass. A Republican, through and through, he had nevertheless been stripped of his rank and uniform simply for being a Guardia Civil, and no amount of passes and privileges conceded to him for remaining loyal to the Republic could make up for having been divested of his dignity and his freedom. He too, like most of his colleagues could have chosen to support the Nationalists or joined the Rebel Guardia Civil who, having abandoned their garrisons, now hid in the mountains, living as highwaymen, robbing and terrorising villagers of any political persuasion. But as a guardian of citizens' civil liberties above all else, Camilo viewed their life of vandalism, oppression and fascism as an abominable crime.

It was his sense of honour, that had impressed Pepa, even before falling for his patrician bearing and fine aquiline features. Posted as a newly promoted sergeant to a small village in the Gérona province where she first met him, the young Pepa Claris, only daughter of a local farmer had a poise and confidence seldom seen in a village girl. At fifteen she had already won the first ever scholarship to the school of pedagogy in Gérona.

The attraction between Camilo and Pepa was instant, mutual, and so compelling, that anyone watching them could not help but blush with embarrassment. Within days Camilo had asked Pepa's father for her hand in marriage. Camilo did not know it then, but in the eyes of the law and the Catholic Church Pepa was still a child, until the onset of menstruation .

It did not deter Camilo who pledged to wait until Pepa was ready. Chaperoned by Pepa's vigilant aunt, they conducted their nearly silent but all-consuming courtship in the farmhouse kitchen from each end of the long scrubbed wooden table, until one night and just before her seventeenth birthday Pepa woke the household with screams of jubilation and the trophy of a blood stained nightgown to authenticate her new-found status.

A period of official wooing came when the couple could meet alone, before Pepa and Camilo's nuptials were celebrated in Santa Crúz, the small village church. Their forty-eight hour honeymoon in a one bed roomed auberge in Pau consummated their now unbridled passion, a passion which lasted unabated for the entire eight years of his posting in the exalted Pyrenean wilderness, until Camilo's promotion to Barcelona brought it to an abrupt close. Far from her cherished mountain vistas and plain living, Pepa withered, whilst Camilo gorged himself on the glamour and sophistication of city life.

Their children, Carmela, Pilar, and José Luis were the glue that bound them together with the memories of their idyllic past, but their growing differences and conflicting aspirations insulated them from each other until year by year, if only briefly interrupted by the birth of their fourth child Rosario, they adjusted to a life of separate togetherness. It was on Elias' request that Pepa came to live with them during Angelina's terminal illness that ended their tenuous relationship.

*

A stranger by the name of Ramón arrived at the door with news of Camilo's son José Luis during one of Camilo's visits from barracks to the Calle Diputación. Pepa and Camilo had last heard from him after he had qualified from the Faculty of Medicine in Barcelona and when he was conscripted for military service to Melilla in Spanish Morocco. It was his misfortune to join his battalion weeks before the first shots of the insurrection were heard, only a short distance away from his garrison. News of his imprisonment came later, but without any explanation of why or for how long.

Ramón told Camilo of his son's indefinite imprisonment. José Luis, he told Camilo, had been charged with treason and collaboration with the enemy. He described the tortures that he and José Luis had been made to witness over the past four and a half months, fearing every day, that their turn would be next. Not a day passed he said, without agonizing screams reverberating around the prison's courtyard where the pulling of finger nails, twisting of testicles, and the staging of mock executions took place. José Luis had himself experienced such 'executions' and Ramón, now released from prison, expressed concern for his friend's health and even life, unless an early rescue was urgently contrived.

Camilo was aggrieved but comforted that Pepa was not present at Ramón's detailed description of her son's torment. José Luis' crime was tending to the wounded, regardless of their political sympathies and Camilo considered his stance as laudable. His son's action could cost him his life and to free him became Camilo's crusade, even if, in the last resort, he had to beg his old Commanding Officer, now in charge of one of Burgos' Nationalist garrisons, to intervene in his release.

Soon after her pledge to walk up the stony path of Mount Hilary, a holy shrine in her small village of Arbucias, in exchange for her son's freedom, Pepa dreamed of a letter and when it arrived on cue, she sent for Camilo.

She read,

CÁDIZ 5th, July 1937.

My very dear mother and father,

I doubt that you would have received my other letters sent from Melilla, Granada and Cádiz since I later found out that they fell into the hands of prison guards. I have entrusted this one to Arturo, one of my patients here in Cádiz where I was fortunate to care for the wounded for four hours every day at the hospital whilst serving my prison sentence. He was recently discharged and promised to post it to you, as soon as he reached home near Montserrat. He too, like me, was caught at the start of his national service.

I hope you are safe and well. My thoughts and prayers are with you all constantly, especially for my dear little sister who was due to give birth close to the start of this inferno.

You will be relieved dear parents, to hear that I am due for a transfer to Pamplona, where I will be resuming my full medical duties. To this day, I do not know what powers were invoked for my miraculous release, but I will be forever indebted to those who made it possible.

We all need to talk of our own personal involvement in this common bloodshed but it is difficult to do so impartially with a war which is still raging. I imagine that as in all wars, only retrospection will tell today's story equitably. But even so, history is never tidy, not even retrospectively and if anything, it is only accurate to those who were present at the time and who later, no one believes anyway, because their emotions are still raw. What is being recalled is often tainted by personal experience, which is only a minute portion of a complex and gigantic canvas, and some of it is already so distorted as to verge on the fictional; but what is undeniable is that utter chaos and confusion reigns everywhere. No one knows what the other is doing, saying, feeling or plotting and that uncertainty is at times more terrifying than the firing of guns.

This war has become nothing less than a monstrous game played only by a few, and whose pawns, our people, us, are caught in a web of violence, deceit and injustice. It is against this insane background that multiple crimes are committed at this very moment, brother against brother. And this applies to both sides in the conflict. It is rumoured for instance, that conversations between officials, some high ranking, are listened to by hidden microphones in their offices, resulting in murders carried out at night and bodies being dumped in unmarked graves or in our morgues, for swift incineration before daybreak and identification. I see bodies torn open and left lying in the streets in pools of blood, to terrorise the population. You could not believe such inhumanity unless you witnessed it. As if this wasn't enough, the best of our intellectual heritage, our artists, visionaries, essayists and poets are fleeing the country in droves for fear of their lives and to seek refuge in France and even England. Most, no doubt, will fall into obscurity, ail, or die of sorrow. Those who stay, are dying now of grief and, disillusionment, like our revered Don Miguel de Unamuno who is reported as saying to his captors, "you will win but you will not convince." Others are quietly disposed of when their voice dissents or hints at the truth, as with the recent mysterious death of our Federico García Lorca shot dead last August. And whilst the roar of madness rages all around us, from afar, we hear on the radio, the clear, inspiring and dynamic voices of our friends, Neruda, Gide, Hemmingway, C.Day Lewis, Orwell, Huxley, Beckett, and others, singing our songs, in love, reverence and hope and flying our flag in sympathy; and some, the Brigaders, are even prepared to die for us.

We have always known that we are a great nation and that Spaniards are heroic, noble, courageous and resilient but at the same time we have to ask ourselves when will we learn to temper our innate cruelty, primitive brutality, indiscipline and fanaticism with compassion and intellectual poise? I so crave for justice, equilibrium, truth, transparency and light to shine on our poor broken country.

My dear parents, all is not despair and for your sakes and mine I feel I must finish with a note of optimism. Deep down in my heart and paradoxically perhaps, I am certain that this harrowing turmoil is not in vain. We have held an isolationist position here in Spain, for long enough, but we have made a link with the world out there and as a result of this bloody war, our new friends, through their interest, compassion and goodwill, we have become part of the Family of Nations. This, surely must give us the seed of opportunity to explore new ways of living together, here at home and also in groups of nations; but that, as they say, is another story!

My dearest father and mother, I have rambled on and raged for far too long and I am grateful for your patient listening. My loving thoughts are with you day and night and I ache to hear your news. To hear of Rosario's confinement, the new baby, Elias, Carlota, Carmela, Salvador, Lalia and Mingo. Give them all my love and tell them I miss them so.

Please do not worry on my account. I know that many have switched alliance in order to survive, but be reassured, regardless of where I am and to whom I administer, that my heart remains forever Republican. And do not fret about my safety either, for I believe that I am now out of danger.

I must leave you in hope until we embrace.

Your ever loving son,
José Luis

"Praise be to God!" chanted Pepa, lifting Paloma off the ground and high up into the air. Paloma giggled and kicked her legs against her grandmother's arms for more, but Pepa put her down, poured herself a glass of water which she drank without catching her breath, sighed, and sat down to read the letter once more. She wiped her tears. All that suffering and she didn't even know. Knowing is sharing and she felt robbed.

"You know," she said at last to Paloma on the floor, "I understand what your uncle means about the Family of Nations and about compassion and goodwill. Isn't it what families are about? So why not nations?" She scrunched the letter against her bosom to feel her son even closer. "I know!" she exclaimed loudly, making Paloma jump, "we'll celebrate like kings when your grandfather comes for Sunday lunch. Let's see..." she said surveying the pantry shelves "I've saved a tin of Portuguese sardines...in tomato sauce...That'll do for starters... we'll have our usual broth, but with a chunk of lard, if la Carrobet can spare us a piece... And for desert, guess what? Natillas. Home made custard was always your uncle's favourite! I'll make it in his honour, even if he isn't here, with Salvador's milk ration—that he should,but never drinks. I'll scrounge the sugar from la Sentis on the third floor—she owes me one—And!.." she said, dancing backwards, and swaying her bony hips from side to side, "that bottle of champagne your grandfather hid under the sink after your mother's wedding!"

Days after the family celebration for his release, and without warning, José Luis' showed up at the Calle Diputación. Dressed in shabby civilian clothes, he stood, bent and transfixed in the dingy and narrow doorway.

"Mother!" he whispered holding her tight. For a long time Pepa sobbed against the hollow of his chest, feeling his fleshless shoulders, crying that he was so thin. "Look at you!" she wept, pushing him into the light to see him better. His hair was parted to one side, sparse and limp, and his ashen skin, tight against his cheekbones gave him a gaunt and distant look. "What have they done to you?" she whimpered. "May God forgive me for hating those who abuse the sons of this wretched country!"

"I am all here, mother, give or take a hair, or a tooth!" consoled José Luis, stroking the wrinkled skin of her hands. She hugged him again, this time fully and without the shock of surprise.

"You are really here, you REALLY are!" she cried and taking her time, led him into the living room. "There's someone I'd like you to meet" she murmured.

"My new niece? he hushed back, afraid he would make her cry. "When was she born?"

"Have a guess!"

Not on the eighteenth of July!" He said, his voice becoming loud with shock.

"The very day!"

"A child of the Revolution! And her name?"

"Paloma"

"A crimson dove..." he whispered, after a long pause. "May

54

I hold her?"

"She is your god-daughter!"

"My god-daughter eh.." he said, his voice drowned with emotion. "Her eyes" he added in a while, "green, like yours, and mine! And this?" he asked pointing at Paloma's red spot between her eyebrows.

"It's Rosario's craving for strawberries when she was carrying" Pepa said.

"More like a little heart," he smiled, stroking it with his finger. He returned her to the ground and looked at her, this time with a clinical eye. "Calcium and vitamin deficiency" he stated bluntly with a tone that was different. "This bloody war has got her too." He paused to muster his emotions. "Paloma needs attention mother, wholesome food and she needs to be out in the sun, or this flat could become her tomb."

"I did all I could!" cried Pepa, picking Paloma up. "She's only managed powdered milk three times a week- that was the ration—and there's no fresh milk or vegetables. We've no fish or meat!"

"It's not you, mother" he said, hugging them both. "It's this war. Paloma is only one of many victims. At least she is alive and contented, and she has you. There is hope for her, of arresting the damage, but only if she gets what she needs and gets it soon. Where's Rosario?" he asked, looking around half expecting her to appear in the room.

"In Nice with Elias and Carlota," Pepa replied, abashed.

"Nice? Did you say Nice? What on earth!" He cried pacing the room. "And what kind of arrangement is that, I ask you!"

"It was only possible to have a pass for one child."

"What's all this about?" he frowned.

"Elias was on two critical black lists, son."

"And what's that got to do with it?"

"There was panic, a lot of panic."

"I'm very sorry for Elias, but Paloma should have gone with her mother and Carlota stayed behind. At least she had a year's head-start in life for Christ's sake! Better still, Elias should have gone alone!"

"Son, it was Rosario's choice" Pepa replied, ignoring his last remark.

"And couldn't you have changed her mind?"

"I tried. I wanted to keep Carlota."

"When did they go?" he asked.

"They started their journey on the eighteenth of July,"

"The day of the..?" he gasped. "And you were left holding the baby, to travel back on your own to Barcelona, a raging city!" he yelled. "I don't believe it!" he mumbled shaking his head. "Elias fled for his life at the expense of Paloma's, who was then separated from her mother on day one..." he said, as if to himself. "Does Rosario know what that means? And what was she thinking about leaving you to manage on your own?"

"She is very young, son, and she was very frightened" said Pepa trying to appease.

"Mother, no. Don't let her off the hook. There are no excuses. Duty and responsibility have been rammed down our throats by you and father for as long as I can remember. Rosario knew what she was doing alright. And even if it breaks my heart to say so, she has been selfish and cowardly. Christ almighty!" His eyes burned and he wished he could find a way of atonement but he could not.

"No doubt Elias has been trying to arrange safe conduits for you and Paloma to join them?" he asked, mellowing.

"Yes" replied Pepa relieved at the change.

"When?"

"Any day now."

"These passes should have arrived by now. I'll contact Elias myself and get him to speed up your exits" he said resolutely. "Besides" he added, "the sooner you go the better; Catalunya is on the move. It's like a huge tidal wave out there. Many have already made it over the border to France, others are queuing up and it can only get worse. If we leave it to the winter, it'll be chaos. We must get you safely over the border by the end of the month."

The happy news of his pending marriage to Maruja that José Luis had come to announce faded with the pressing needs of this unexpected reality. "I'll get in touch as soon as I hear from Elias. In the meantime" he said, "gather what you need for travelling. Watch your chest mother and take warm clothes, it'll be chilly when travelling through the Pyrenees." He paused to look at his mother and sighed. "Mother, sweet mother, you are a brave, wonderful and very special woman and I can hold you at last!"

"Son..." she whispered, "I have just found you...Will I see you before we leave?"

"I don't know mother, but this is OUR moment. Yours, Paloma's and mine. How can we ever forget it?"

Turmoil marred Pepa's life in the days that followed. She wanted to bask in the joy of her son's freedom, but emotions never previously experienced in her life robbed her of those feelings she longed to indulge in.

She was about to take a giant leap into the unknown and she was scared. A flicker of her simple mountain village ignited her memory as she tried at the same time to conjure an image of a place she did not know. She craved to stay. Only the thought of Paloma's well-being and to be reunited with the family she had lost at the onset of the Revolution stabilised her once again.

Announcing her impending departure met with a disgruntled Carmela who blamed and resented Rosario for always being on the winning side of life. She had lost her mother to Rosario once before and she was about to see her go once again.

Pepa's and Paloma's exits arrived in a registered letter from Elias. He had responded to his brother-in-law's urgent message and there was no time to lose. Warnings of unscheduled delays caused by refugees fleeing daily reaffirmed José Luis' predictions of chaos and Pepa began to gather the bare essentials for the journey. Salvador donated the leather tailor's bag given to him by his father to accommodate Paloma's belongings and Carmela lined it with a cheerful floral cretonne fabric and fitted it with inside pockets. Mingo and Lalia gave their precious cloth patchwork ball their mother had sewn for their last Christmas present and a rattle Salvador made of old wooden curtain rings for Paloma to play with during the journey.

"Mamá! Yaya! Come and see! Quick! It's uncle José Luis with a pretty lady!" shouted Lalia from the balcony. "It's true!" confirmed Mingo excitedly.

"A lady? With your uncle?" exclaimed Pepa and Carmela with synchronised amazement as the door opened.

"I've missed you all so much!" cried José Luis, on seeing his family for the first time since his imprisonment and they hugged all at once. Conscious that this was about to be a momentous occasion Pepa waited in the back room. "Mother..." he said softly as he entered it, "this is Maruja, my fiancée, we are planning to marry at Christmas, and we have come to have your blessing."

Feelings of loss and gain overwhelmed Pepa when she said "My blessings and my love to you both." She hugged them in one single embrace. "You deserve all the happiness there is! May God be with you."

"I have heard so much good about you Doña Pepa. José Luis tells me that you are his favourite heroine!" said Maruja, in a crystalline Catalan voice which won Pepa's heart.

"Mother," José Luis said, taking her aside "I've come to say you are leaving next week and I shall organise the Red Cross car to escort you to the railway station. Be happy mother, all will be well. Those exit passes are Paloma's salvation"

"That's it then" said Pepa with a hollow voice. "Everything is happening so fast. Me leaving you just after meeting Maruja..."

"It's a new beginning for you too mother"

"Who knows if it is son, but thank you for being strong for me, and for taking care of Paloma. My vow..." she then cried woefully.

"What vow, mother?" he asked, cradling her face in his hands.

"I vowed to climb Mont Hilary bare-foot for your release."

"I'll go for you, Doña Pepa!" offered Maruja.

"Pray instead that I may return soon to keep my vow."

58

"I promise I'll pray" Maruja replied solemnly.

"And your wedding, son, your special day, without your mother!"

"My mother dwells here in my heart, how can she not be with me, always?"

"I am becoming a foolish old woman with all this..." wept Pepa.

SIX

Antonio and the Tic Tac of Time

Silence enshrined the flat at the Calle Diputación, until last minute preparations turned the hush into hysterical activity. Carmela blew out the candle, lit for farewell prayers for Paloma's and Pepa's safe journey when Mingo shouted from the street that the Red Cross car had arrived. After wordless embraces, tears and clasping hands reluctant to let go, Pepa and child were gone. They waved from the balcony. Pepa looked up. A cramp crushed her chest like a vice, which she recognised as the same pang as the day she left her beloved mountain village to settle in Barcelona. The red and white flag hoisted above the car bonnet flapped its single red and white wing in the gentle autumnal breeze. Paloma fretted. Pepa cradled her in her arms and sang lullabies both for her benefit and Paloma's until the car stopped at the station. "Are we there?" she quivered, surveying her surroundings.

"I might as well use the flag to drive you as close to the gate as possible" the driver replied, starting the engine again. "Don José Luis has booked you in the VIP wagon. I'll take you right up to your seat."

"I didn't know they still..."

"There'll always be VIPs" he interrupted, trying to sound impartial.

They had the luxury of a window seat with luggage space underfoot for Salvador's old tailor's bag, a small travel blanket, a billowing pillow case Pepa had filled with clothes and a brown paper bag bulging with food to last them for the journey. The compartment was full but orderly. Passengers had arrived hours early to ensure seats, and all eyes converged on

Pepa and Paloma until a new arrival, anyone, redirected their attention elsewhere. The frenetic crowd of men, women and children pushing for entry onto the train reminded Pepa of their 18th of July exit the previous year, but this time, hope had left the travellers eyes, hunger had stunted their children and despair had turned them into sneaking fugitives seeking refuge in a foreign land.

"The train is now full. Please leave the platform" announced the loudspeaker to those till jostling for last minute space. In their eagerness to board some were separated from their less agile loved ones. Others, sometimes entire families, were turned back, often without explanation. A lump of shame lodged in Pepa's throat for the privileges she had been without for a year and was now receiving.

"Five minutes stop at Gérona and Figueras. Then, the frontier. All out at Le Boulou" the conductor's bland voice detailed like a recitation.

Sitting opposite Pepa was a young man, his pale face pressed against the window, gawping at every passing tree, bird and inch of blue sky with the intensity of a dying man. He was without luggage and alone. On his knee rested his clenched fist closely guarding its contents. "My soil. It's a handful of my soil" he said, carefully opening his hand to show Pepa, who had been staring at it.

"Forgive me, I didn't mean to intrude..." she said, embarrassed that she had invaded another's privacy.

"No, please señora, no harm done" he interrupted. "I saw you looking. We have nothing to hide from one another; we are all part of one family in this country of blood and tears." He offered her his free hand. "My name is Antonio, Antonio Machado, I am a poet" he smiled. "My voice has been stifled here" he said, "and I must empty my bleeding soul before it's too late. Before the tictac of time expires." He looked out of the window again. "Maybe I will, across the border, one day inspire my broken country anew with the meditation of my verses. This dry clump of earth you see" he said, opening his fist again, "is from my pueblo, for my grave, should I die in exile. And how many more, like me, carry their little piece of Spain with them for their grave across the frontier!"

Pepa stayed silent, then with a small bowing gesture she thanked him for sharing his thoughts with her.

"I feel deeply honoured, and I pray that you will one day fulfil your poetic mission for the new generation to come" she said, offering her unfolded white handkerchief for the clump of earth. Antonio let the red dust thread through his funnelled fist into the centre of the cloth, then tied the four corners together into a tight knot. "To the Nueva Generación!" he exclaimed, turning a few heads. "And the child?" he asked., feeling embarrassed at having drawn attention to himself. "Is she your grand-daughter?" Pepa nodded. "Paloma. Her name is Paloma... she was born on the 18th of July last year..." she offered to say, sensing this was a landmark for him too. "Paloma...Paloma..." he whispered, diverting his gaze onto the landscape again as if it was his only source of inspiration. "Paloma de la Misericordia..."Yes, that will be my next poem. My first, dedicated to Paloma and peace."

Antonio's passion and longing for a better humanity brought José Luis' thwarted idealism back to Pepa's mind and for what seemed a long while, she found herself pondering about the evil committed throughout history, so often in the name of God.

"La Junquera!" shouted an official, startling her. Some passengers desperate to reach the frontier had risked travelling without papers and when found out, were ordered off the train to some unknown fate, like lost souls in the netherworld. The fortunate stayed on the slow-moving train until it stopped at Le Boulou only a few kilometres away where Antonio helped Pepa and Paloma off the train and on to the frontier's gate.

"To Peace... And to dreams..." he whispered, making those few words sound like poetry. He lifted Paloma in his arms, looked at Pepa, his eyes made tender by their new-found comradeship and embraced them both as if part of his family; then he began his weary walk alone, some fifteen kilometres ahead to his new, and perhaps final destination in Collioure.

Long queues of travellers with fear on their faces waited to have their passes checked and restamped before they were finally allowed to cross over to France. Cold and weary refugees from earlier trains still had to be waved through the border, and make-shift clearing centres were organised to deal with the increasing bedlam. The fortunate ones, the families that had safely crossed the frontier, were now separated on their last lap of the journey and left torn with agony, their hopes of freedom and togetherness dashed, as they watched their loved ones wrenched away from them, transported in trucks and randomly allocated to different camps, known to be no more than make-shift huts with little or no sanitation and surrounded by barbed wire, until fate, if kind, reunited them one day.

Lost and all alone with Paloma inside Angelina's pink shawl, Pepa searched for the platform for the next train to Nice. They had missed it. A kindly porter directed them to the waiting room where they dozed, huddled together on a bench until dawn.

Few boarded the early train and Pepa and Paloma enjoyed the luxury of an entire compartment, all the way to Beziers where the train stopped, filled up and carried on to Marseille. Pepa smiled and greeted each new traveller, but none returned her greetings, and trouble-free though the journey was, it felt uneasy and endless. She recalled Antonio the poet saying pro-Franco newspapers circulating in the French border regions, dscribed the Republicans fleeing to France as filthy criminals, lower than beasts and infected with unimaginable infectious diseases and she surmised the reason for their hostility.

Nice was minutes away. Pepa washed Paloma's face, combed her own hair back into a tight bun at the nape of her neck, and dabbed herself with the precious eau de Cologne La Sentis had given her as a leaving gift.

The train pulled into the Gare du Sud well after midnight. The deserted platform made her anxious until Elias tapped her on the shoulder from behind. He called their names as if to concretise their presence and embraced them in that awkward way Pepa had forgotten. "You are six hours late, you must be exhausted" he said escorting them to the car, adding that tired of waiting, Rosario had returned to the villa, but that she was waiting up. He embraced them both again, this time with ease. "I can't tell you how difficult it's been" he sighed "and how much we've missed you."

"It's been hard on all sides Elias, my friend" replied Pepa, "but we are the lucky ones, the ones who have been spared. Is it far?"

"No, not long now."

"Where's Fermin?" she asked.

"Ah! dear Fermin had to return to Andalucia or he would have died of heartache" replied Elias. "I heard he took up arms with his fellow peasants. I still miss him. He saved our lives. He was a friend."

The car turned left into the mimosa-lined drive and slowed down. Outside, lights flooded the garden and down the paths to the sea. "Is this it?" asked Pepa raising her eyebrows.

"Yes Yaya, it's your home."

"Home" murmured Pepa with trepidation. "Home" she repeated mournfully.

Rosario spotted the headlights sweeping the drive from her pink tower and Pepa could see her running downstairs in her long pink satin nightgown, her bare feet hardly skimming the stairs. The beam on her face was that of a child as she flung the front door open and ran faster still to meet her mother. "Mamá! Mamaíta!" she cried throwing herself as a well aimed shot into her open arms. Pepa stumbled.

"Thank God you're here." Rosario sobbed, "I've needed you so much!" Pepa stiffened.

"Your daughter" she said softening and lifting Paloma off the ground for Rosario to hold, just as she had done after Paloma's birth almost a year and a half earlier. "She isn't mine!" Rosario blurted, stepping back. "She's yours. You keep her."

To protect Paloma from her mother's denial Pepa held her tight against her heart and asked to be shown to her bedroom. "Yours is next to Carlota's and the new one goes with her."

"Paloma stays with me, Rosario" she stated. "At least until she settles in her new surroundings."

Pepa was tearful on that first night in Nice, and numb and empty. Strange as it seemed to her, the animation she felt during the past year was fast draining away from her being. It was as if the love, comradeship and mutual caring which had so profoundly sustained her and bounded her to her compatriots against the bloody and battered landscapes of her country had all been in vain. She struggled to rekindle the vibrancy she felt then but the air she now breathed, clear as it was, had lost its substance and the airy space she occupied in the large bedroom she was given, seemed obscenely opulent and wasteful. Her youngest daughter struck her as being even more spoiled than she remembered and though gentle and kind, Elias' compliance to his young wife was excessive to a fault. In twenty-four hours her life was overturned from the dynamic and basic to the dull and extravagant and from the profound to the fickle. Nothing she could think of could change those circumstances in the short term and all that was left for her, was to adjust to a different beat, certainly for her own sake, and for Paloma's mostly, lest Rosario's steely arrow of rejection on arrival, fester in the child's heart.

Next morning Pepa took Paloma to meet her sister for the first time. Carlota sat up in bed, silent, wary and sombre, until a faint and distant recollection of her grandmother's face began to lighten her own.

"I'm your Yaya sweetheart, remember me? I've come to get to know you again and to be with you" said Pepa reaching for her hand. "Carlotita" she said, taking it, "this is Palomita, your little sister"

"Mita!" Carlota exclaimed after a long mesmerised glance at her sister. "Mita, eh!" smiled Pepa. "Paloma, meet Carlotita, your big sis."

"Tita..." uttered Paloma, touching her sister's face.

"Tita! Did you hear that Carlota? Your sister has just baptised you 'Tita'! Well, 'Tita' and 'Mita' it is!"

Carlota took to her sister with the same curiosity and

adoration she would have reserved for a new pet. Following her everywhere, she cooed, smiled and stroked her and when once, captivated by Paloma's speckled green eyes, she poked them, expecting a magical response, Pepa explained that it made little Mita cry, and a vague stirring of remorseful concern struck within her, sowing the first seed of tenderness in the core of her derelict heart.

From day one of her arrival, all maternal responsibilities were delegated to Pepa, and Rosario, once again became a child, trying every subterfuge to obliterate her own daughters from her mother's attention and so regain her position as 'favourite child'. She talked for days dramatising the account of her last confinement as the worst event in her life and expounded on the terrors of her exit journey from Madrid to Nice and how she was robbed of her expensive necklace. Pepa listened, unable to respond to her ramblings and it was only days later that Rosario asked her mother, in passing, about her brother's ordeal.

SEVEN

The Captivity of Freedom

Casablanca, where his brothers and sisters had settled became a more and more compelling idea to Elias as their next destination. There, the roar of battle would sound more like the echo of distant guns, loud enough to be kept connected but not that close to be imperilled.

Spain was in the throes of war; he knew it would be years before he could feel safe there again and the solution for a better life seemed increasingly dependent upon moving to his own country of birth.

Soon, he would have to impart his intentions to Rosario and Pepa and booking a table for a family lunch at the Rivoli seemed a conducive move towards a positive outcome.

Pepa's response was not as Elias had envisaged. The only thing on her mind she told him, was her son's wedding in December and her absence from it. Elias was quick to reply that he had already arranged for crates of champagne to be delivered to Maruja's home in time for the big day.

"Shall I ask you after the wedding?" he whispered, trying to sound less pressing, and Pepa conceded, reluctantly, that since the subject had been raised, they might as well talk about it. What she wanted to know was for how long would they be gone.

"Until the end of the troubles in Spain, allowing some time after that for an economic recovery" Elias replied.

He asked her to trust him, saying it was for everyone's safety and went as far as to suggest the New Year as a possible departure date. Pepa reminding him that the move to Nice was initially meant to be until the end of hostilities and now he was talking of settling further afield with little time allowed for readjustment and for an indefinite period.

"You couldn't possibly think of leaving me and the girls could you?" intercepted Rosario sensing Pepa's quandary. "And anyway, I am your youngest and I need you the most!"

"You have Elias," Pepa said, "his large family and all the servants you'll need. You'll lack nothing. Isn't that right Elias?" Elias nodded.

"And Paloma? Would you leave her?"

Rosario had delivered the one blow Pepa could not deflect. A life without her grand-daughter was unthinkable. Paloma was Pepa's lifeline and Pepa was Paloma's salvation. They had not been apart once since Paloma had been handed over to her within an hour of her birth. So close to her had she become, that Pepa had, for a moment, considered returning with her to Spain. But she could not forget her son's plea to take her away from the chaos into which she was born. "Well?" asked Rosario defiant.

For a long while and with consummate tenderness Pepa contemplated Paloma and then Carlota. "I'll come!" she cried, banging her fist on the dining table. It was a decisive gesture she needed to effect, so she could not be tempted to change her mind.

"To our new life in Morocco then!" toasted Elias, incredulous at his good fortune. "You'll all love it there!" he enthused. "I promise! And now, let me tell you about my family" he said, bringing his chair nearer the table "You've already met Joaquín, my elder brother. Joaquín has been the patriarch of the family since my parents died. And there's Samuel. Well, he's tremendous fun and everyone adores him, and you'll love Colette, his French wife, Rosario. She's a grande artiste, trained at the Conservatoire de Paris. Plays the piano like an angel. Then there's Lourdes, now living in Paris, married to a painter after her first husband's assassination in Chile, where he was the Spanish Ambassador. It's quite a story, I'll tell you about it another time; and then there's the baby of the family, Trini. Trini's husband Carlo is a tennis champion and an unstoppable playboy. And there's a couple of nephews... Well...you'd better wait until you meet them. It's quite a tribe!" he exclaimed between alternate sips of champagne and Grand Marnier.

"What about Geraldo, your youngest brother?" Rosario asked.

"Oh him!..." said Elias dismissively.

"What about him?" she insisted.

"He's a good lad, very gentle, a keen horseman, but we don't talk about him in the family" whispered Elias with his index finger on his lips.

"But why?"

"Because he's the black sheep... that's why..!"

"Why is he the black sheep?" she demanded. "I might as well know. I'll soon find out anyway..."

"Our father disowned and disinherited him."

"How fantastical! What did he do?" she begged, consumed with curiosity.

"He ran away at eighteen with an Amazon" said Elias wriggling in his seat with embarrassment.

"An Amazon! From Amazonia?" asked Rosario nonplussed.

"No, no, no. Marina was a horse woman in the circus. That's what they're called, you know, when they ride side-saddle with a long split skirt thing and a funny trilby type hat. And she's Italian, from Naples."

"Was she beautiful?" asked Rosario entranced.

"Very" replied Elias. "I mean supremely! She was a beauty."

"And what happened in the end?"

"They got married..."

"They got married? This is so romantic Elias. I want to meet them!"

"You can't. None of us has seen them since he was cast out of the family home. Geraldo has made a new life for himself with the Pavarotti's, Marina's Italian circus family."

"I think that's stupid and cruel!" lamented Rosario.

She would have stacks of interesting relatives and friends to meet he reassured her without the need to know Geraldo and Marina, and he made her promise to forget the whole thing.

Pepa had kept silent. Her life, Elias vowed, would be made as comfortable and happy as possible in their future home and he said he would continue to help the family back in Spain with regular food parcels from Morocco until the end of the war.

"And I will do my best to help in whatever way I can" said Pepa, sounding like someone bound by a solemn vow.

"Will the new year be too soon for you?" he ventured to ask.

"Elias, once I've made up my mind, I'm ready for action." She spoke firmly to reinforce her resolve.

"And the wedding?"

"José Luis said himself that I lived in his heart—as he does in mine" she struggled to say. "I am now facing up to the inevitable."

"So when do we begin the preparations?" erupted Rosario, unconcerned about her mother, wrestling with her emotions.

"I must liquidate my assets and transfer them to my bank back home" Elias detailed, and get Joaquin to order a car and find us a villa to rent in Casablanca, and I must apply for exit permits at once. I'll book our passage today and God willing we should be sailing from Marseille by the end of December."

Pepa's priorities were different to Elias'. Every night she stayed up late, agonising on how best to write farewell letters to each of her children and to Camilo, explaining her motives for following Rosario. Busy keeping the girls happy whilst preparing their clothes and other paraphernalia for the journey, she also found demanding.

The few weeks leading up to Christmas proved frantic. The busiest seemed to be Rosario, packing the many possessions she had accumulated during her time at the Villa Écume. She filled trunk after trunk with her haute couture collection, matching shoes, accessories, hats in neat hat boxes, and a leather-bound collection of the complete works of Victor Hugo she had begun to read. All the silver and the multi-coloured Murano glass chandeliers, she packed in crates, with FRAGILE painted in red on each side, ready for registration and shipping.

Obtaining visas to Morocco for himself and family was easy, and the date for sailing to Casablanca was set for New Year's Eve. The voyage would last two days, with an evening docking at Palma de Mallorca and a few hours in Tangier. Rosario exploded like a child opening a birthday present when Elias announced that there would be a masked ball on board to welcome in the New Year. She thought of the magic of the characters in the 'Commedia dell Arte she had seen performed in Venice during their honeymoon and she knew she had to be Arlecchino, the multicoloured male character madly in love with the beautiful but invisible Columbine.

A letter from Joaquín arrived a week before departure, advising Elias that a villa had been rented for them in the smart residential district of Anfa and that two maids, a gardener and a chauffeur were already cleaning the house, tidying the garden and polishing the new black Buick Elias had ordered. He would be at the quay to meet them.

Don Marcial del Olivar was amongst the travellers. Now Spanish Consul to Baghdad, he had helped Elias formalise documents in the past for his import and export business. Don Marcial, strolling on deck while his wife wrestled with a Marie Antoinette crinoline inside the narrow cabin in preparation for the masked ball, confided that he too was eager to leave his country behind and his own depiction of wild anarchy and haphazard acts of revenge throughout the peninsula during the past year, convinced Elias that not only had his move to Nice been correct, but that the timing of their migration to Casablanca was also astutely judged.

Passengers came out on deck late that afternoon as Palma was glimpsed in the distance against the open fan of a tricolor sunset of gold, pink and aquamarine. They watched it without a word spoken until the colours faded. Some of the Spaniards on board realising at that moment that whatever the consequences, they would be unable to live as exiles, disembarked to return home, while still in Spanish waters.

The Bishop of Palma, a small ancient figure buried in folds of gold and red brocade, came aboard with his solemn entourage to bless the last civilian ship to dock at the island before it served as a naval port, and to give benediction to its passengers bound for what he described a heathen land.

The city of Palma was invisible but for the lights from the awesome cathedral on the hill. Looking ominous in the darkened harbour, several Italian naval patrol boats sheltered eerily in a safe zone.

Elias and Rosario stood on deck gazing at the stars and reminiscing about their first romantic holiday together, still unmarried, at the Formentor hotel on the north tip of the island. Pepa had accompanied them as Rosario's chaperone. It had been a week so idyllic that they had wished their wedding had not been postponed by the enforced period of mourning for Elias' parents. Elias caressed Rosario's hair. "Mucho... mucho... mucho... Yo te quiero mucho..." he crooned. Do you feel sentimental cariño?" he whispered, nibbling the lobe of her ear.

"About Formentor you mean?" she asked evading him.

"Wasn't it just wonderful..." he said recapturing her.

"And we didn't...well... you know..." she said coyly.

"But we're married now... we are afloat on a ship off the most romantic island on earth and la Yaya's with the girls..."he whispered it, while his searching lips caressed her smooth cheeks.

"I must get ready for tonight..." she objected softly. "Columbine awaits..."

"It's two hours to the ball... Come on...let's go and lie down, and celebrate the old year our way..." he said luring her to their cabin, with music filtering like a descending mist through the entire ship.

*

In half a day they would dock in Tangier. The sky looked clearer than it had for weeks. "It must be a good omen" commented Elias, asking Pepa if she felt a new beginning was about to dawn. The world was making sure of that she replied and she hoped that when the dawn finally arrived, it would bring better times, and mostly peace. She wanted to believe that as travellers in a newly consecrated ship, bound for a sun-blessed land and at the advent of a new year, their lives would, at least, be bestowed with grace; but there were others she could not forget and remorse for the uncertain fate of her loved ones and for her people gripped her.

A noon arrival at Tangier was announced, but the notoriously rough Straits of Gibraltar still had to be traversed and passengers were instructed to return to their cabins. Only Elias who had prophylactically swallowed a dozen oysters washed down with several glasses of neat vodka escaped the ravages of sea-sickness. The ship docked for a two hour break, but with everyone jaded and weak, the lunch Elias had promised at the El Minzah Palace was cancelled. Instead they hired a taxi to see the sights. First, the Medina, then they headed down the Rue de la Marine into the kasbah, past the Kasbah Mosque and its octagonal minarets to the enchanted Sultan's gardens. It was when they reached one of the hilltops overlooking the sea below and the small white pebble-like houses of Andalucian villages gleaming beyond it, that Pepa felt her heart heave. She had touched alien soil and there was no going back.

"I must come back here Elias!" exalted Rosario. "The geography! The mystery of the place. D'you think we'll ever return?" He reminded her that Tangier was part of his roots, that his great grandfather Eion had come there from Ireland, and that they would be back one day. But Pepa declared the place unholy and as if fearing contamination she scurried with the girls back to the taxi, and back on board.

Casablanca, their final destination was three hours away and capturing that first glimpse of the coastline, together, as a family had long been Elias' dearest wish.

"They say that it's the journey that matters" uttered Rosario wistfully, "but for me, it's as much the arrival. I feel so different! So alive already!" she cried enfolding Elias' waist.

Square, white, piled on top of each other box-like houses floated eerily against the heat haze between sky and sea, and that magical moment Elias had dreamed of since leaving home had almost come. "Home! Can you see?" he asked, pointing as far as his arm would stretch. "We're here" he shouted, lifting Rosario off the ground.

"It's good to see you so happy, Elias," said Pepa moved by his exuberance.

"We shall all be very happy here Yaya, you'll see."

Rosario pulled a small mirror from her handbag, bit and licked her lips several times to make them glossy, pinched her cheeks, smoothed her eyebrows with her saliva and checked her shoulder length hair before putting on her Barbara Stanwyck hat bought especially for that moment. "Are we ready to disembark?" she asked looking mysterious from under the brim.

"Wait here with your mother and the girls" Elias instructed, "I'll hunt for Joaquín." he added, scanning the quay for his brother and his servant Abdul.

"Elias! Hombre! Welcome back!" shouted Joaquín who picked out Elias from the swarm of travellers. "Joaquín! Bandido! Where did you spring from? It's good to see you. God, it's good to be here!" he cried, punching his brother's chest. "Where's Rosario got to? Let's find la Yaya and the girls."

"La Yaya?"

"It's Catalan for granny, Rosario's mother, the girls' grandmother."

"I approve. Yaya! it's a good name!" he exclaimed.

"Porteur! Porteur! Par ici, les valises et les malles! Attention c'est fragile!" Elias shouted at the sudden throng of porters.

"Have you forgotten your Arabic Elias?" laughed Joaquín, "You've been away too long!"

"Habit." replied Elias. "And where are we going to put all this?"

"There's room in the Chevrolet" said Joaquín, "and Abdul has come with the horse and cart for the big trunks;

everything's under control! Rosario... there you are!" he exclaimed, recognising her in the crowd. "I thought Elias had decided to leave you behind!" He chuckled as he embraced her lightly. Rosario recoiled at Joaquín's physical contact, sarcasm and the gaze of his penetrating ice-blue eyes, but she was surprised to find his bearing distinguished and even handsome in an uncomfortable, ascetic kind of way. "You look terrific in your colonial outfit, Joaquín" she said, adding "just like a film star!" and disliking herself for the cheap flattery.

"The novelty my dear, that's all it is! And where's your dear Mamá?" he asked, genuinely interested.

"Mamá, this is Joaquín, Elias' older brother, do you remember? He was also in Barcelona when I first met Elias."

"Of course, Joaquín, I am delighted to meet the elder of the Butler family at last!" she said, squeezing his hand in the French fashion.

Carlota here, is our eldest, and that's Paloma, and of course my mother, Pepa Claris de Iriondo."

"It is a pleasure to meet you Doña Pepa, I hope this will be a wonderful place for you all," and he bent down to pinch hard the girls' cheeks. "Your little cousin Binot will have company at last..." he told them in a strangely conspiratorial whisper and a prolonged wink that not even Pepa could interpret. "We're ready!" cried Elias. "Let's go! Fissa! Fissa! Baleck! Baleck! Hurry, out of the way!" he shouted to the porters, as the family jostled with their baggage towards the car.

PART TWO

You cannot step twice into the same river;
for fresh waters are ever flowing in upon you.

Heraclitus

EIGHT

The Orchard

"Clever of you to arrive in January! Best time of the year— not a soul on the beaches and the ocean, delicioso..." said Joaquín licking his lips as if he had just tasted the salt. "You swim in January?" asked Rosario.

"All the year round my dear. Doesn't Elias?" he chuckled, looking at his brother's overweight frame. "Why don't you join me for a swim tomorrow?" he challenged.

"After the spring, brother" replied Elias.

"You're not a great aficionado of the water, are you?"

"I prefer horses."

"Let's go riding then!"

"After the spring, when we've settled in."

Joaquín drove as if alone on a race-track, prompting Rosario to ask how much further to the villa. "Hey! Take it easy sister! Enjoy! Make the most of what you see! You wont be coming back this way often. Bad things happen around here... Not a place for nice ladies like you..." She squirmed at being called sister by this man she found objectionable.

"Doña Pepa comfortable at the back? It won't be long before we hit the boulevard" he said looking back at her. Pepa made the sign of the cross each time she saw the familiar baroque façade of a Catholic Church, and she was comforted that there were so many. The car swung into the wider road and Joaquín let go of the wheel. "Anytime now we'll pass the El Hank lighthouse, one of Elias' special spots. Wonderful at low tide, and the sunsets! What happy times here..!" he sighed, turning towards his brother.

"Ah..." inspired Elias, winding down the window, a whiff of that air is worth all the gold in Mejico! And listen to those breakers.. God Almighty.." he whispered, with quasi religious fervour.

Carlota's demand for a wee prompted Pepa to ask Joaquín to get a move on. He revved up the engine to a screeching pitch and set off again. "Isn't our corniche every bit as glorious as the Riviera?" he tittered. "And wait for it... are you ready... here's... your villa!" he cried, reversing into its drive in a wild, single manoeuvre.

"Pink! like the Villa Écume and it's called 'La Vie en Rose'. Isn't it dreamy!" exclaimed Rosario.

"Well!" said Joaquín, "traditional houses in this area are white, but this is an arty-farty rendition of the neo-Provençal style" he added with a hint of disapproval.

The villa, thought Elias, was on the small side, but Joaquín stated that it was ample until they found what they were really looking for. He clapped his hands and seconds later two men and three women appeared from their quarters in the basement, bowing like mechanical toys. "Salam Alaikum" greeted Elias, touching his chest and then his forehead. They approached in automated unison with greetings of Sidi Lebesses and more bowing. "Madame Wahed—Madame number one" said Elias, introducing Rosario, "and Madame Jooj—Madame number two, both your mistresses. And Mamselles Carlota and Paloma."

"M'sier...M'sier..." they chorused with stifled giggles and still bowing.

"How can the women work in these clothes?" whispered Pepa, dazzled by their apparel and jewellery.

"These are their best ceremonials to greet us!" laughed Elias.

"This is Ahmed your chauffeur," called Joaquín, "Bouchaib the gardener, Zorah your chambermaid, Fatima the nanny, and here" he said taking Aisha, aside, "is the best cook south of Tetuan" explaining that Aisha's grandmother was cook to the Butler family in Mazagan years ago. "Let's have a quick look

80

inside shall we, I'm due at the Lido for tennis with Carlo in an hour."

Smaller than the villa in Nice, the house had no view to the sea and the garden, albeit large, gazeboed and tropical, did not lead to a private beach. "We'll make do here for a while" said Elias keen to lift Rosario's visibly deflated spirits. "I thought..." hinted Rosario "well, perhaps we shouldn't bother to unpack. It's such a pain, if we have to pack all over gain!"

"As you like querida. I'm sure there's everything we need here for the time being."

"Does Joaquín live in Anfa?"

"Joaquín...how shall I put it, is obsessed with work and lives closer to his Real Estate office."

"In town?"

"Nobody here lives in town!" he laughed. "No, he lives between the racecourse and the Lycee de Jeunes Filles, in the Quartier des Palmiers, a Bohemian sort of place."

"Bohemian..." repeated Rosario, inwardly savouring every image the word conjured up—painters in flamboyant neckerchiefs, poets with translucent faces in floating cloaks, and women, dying of doomed love or consumption, or both. "Can we look for a house there Elias?"

He thought Anfa was her kind of place, but agreed to see Joaquín about properties elsewhere.

"And he should give you a good deal" remarked Rosario.

"Cariño," he said, "I wouldn't bet on it..."

Life in La Vie en Rose was characterised by all the tediousness of a transitional stay. Restless and eager to resume her previous life of indulgence, Rosario fretted with every day that passed without a thrill. Now hardly ever in the house, Elias' concern was to resume his business contacts and find a suitable warehouse near the port to store his merchandise before he could begin his import and export business in earnest.

"That was Samuel on the phone!" he shouted. "He's back from Paris where Colette just gave a recital. I've asked them to dinner tonight to meet you all!"

"Samuel! Colette! Dinner! From Paris!" Rosario flapped.

"Calm down Rosario. They won't bite you!"

"I'm trembling Elias. D'you think they'll like me?"

"Like you? They'll fall in love with you querida! And you with them. I guarantee that."

"Tell me again, what are they like?"

"He's enormous fun. He's got the loudest, most infectious laugh you've ever heard and Colette...well, she's your typical femme française—a little too clever for me—but you'll love her."

"Mamá!" she called in a dither. "Did you hear? Samuel and his wife are coming to dinner and I really want to impress them!"

"Ask Aisha, the best cook south of Tetuan" Pepa replied in a long drawn monotone voice.

"Yaya," intervened Elias, picking up on her feeling downcast after Joaquín's flattering introduction of the cook which had evidently made her feel excluded, "I would be very honoured if you prepared one of your fabulous paellas for tonight. What d'you say? A Spanish night, but with champagne!" he added flamboyantly.

"Where's the market, and I need plenty of assistance!" she cried, rolling up her sleeves.

"Just give the orders!" Elias replied.

Pepa's mood lifted. The market at the Spanish quarter of the Maârif was an Aladdin's cave of gastronomic treasures, of colours, aromas and sounds. It was a whiff of home—as it was before the revolution—it was Pepa's kind of heaven on earth.

"The crockery is so artisanal" Rosario scorned.

"I bet Colette will take to it!" retorted Elias. "The peasant look is in......" he added mockingly.

"Anyway, what matters is what's on the plate" yelled Pepa who had overheard Rosario's concern from the kitchen.

"Wise old Yaya!" shouted back Elias.

"What d'you think, sailor suits for the girls, and will my white piqué two-piece do?"

"They're family querida.... you don't have to change, just stay as you are..."

*

"Élie, mon cher Élie!" Diminutive, theatrical and lost in a boa of feathers, Colette mimicked a kiss on each of Elias' cheeks. Transfixed, Rosario peered at the scene through a chink in the kitchen door.

"Rosario? Mais ne vous cachez donc pas mon petit!" Colette beckoned. "Charmante...your wife is delightful Élie! Cucu! Come and meet Rosario! So Goyesque!"

"Did she say Cucu?" Rosario whispered in Elias's ear.

"Yes...It's what she calls Samuel..." he whispered back. "She's French, and an artist to boot. Anything goes! Ah! Samuel!" he cried.

"Elias mon vieux, lebbes? And Rosario, I presume!" said Samuel, embracing them in one generous gesture. "You've got yourself a real cracker!" he chortled in Elias' ear, then he lifted the girls off the ground one by one to hug them. The contrast with Joaquín was startling and thrilled Rosario. She could really like Samuel, but it was to the eccentric and waif-like Colette that she felt irresistibly drawn. She knew at once that what captivated her was something far more intangible than her unconventional demeanour, the fluttering feathers caressing the feline angle of Colette's jaw, or the overly painted crimson cherry of her lips. It was not just the pool-like vastness of her purple eyes either, or even the delicious way to which she couldn't roll the R's of her name when she had first called her Rosario. It was beyond all that, and she felt off balance, as if she was about to enter a forbidden garden full of unknown, intoxicating and dangerous scents.

"You're in for a treat my friends!" called Elias. "La Yaya is cooking one of her Paellas Royale in your honour!"

"Yaya? Rosario, chérie" asked Colette, "you didn't bring your own Spanish cook with you, did you?"

"She... I..." blushed Rosario until Elias rescued her. "Isn't Yaya such an evocative word for grandmother!" he exclaimed.

"Your mother? You brought your mother to live with you? What an absolute hoot! I want to meet her. Yaya! Yaya!" she called, small stepping her way to the kitchen and bringing Pepa out to meet Samuel.

"Cucu, mon chéri, meet Yaya, Rosario's charming mother."

"Bienvenida, Doña Pepa! Elias has told me you are a jewel!"

"Yaya will do" she said "and please don't get up. It's a real pleasure to meet you Samuel."

"She's a sweetie Rosario, and a cook! My dear, you'll be the envy of every hostess in Casablanca!" said Colette, inhaling on a 'blonde'. "Do you smoke, chérie?" she asked, offering her a cigarette from a silver and mother-of-pearl case which seemed to click open by her just glancing at it.

*

In the days that followed, Rosario plagued Elias with umpteen questions about Samuel and Colette. She wanted to know every single detail of their lives. They were an odd couple, he told her. Colette was about forty, some ten years older than Samuel, and they had been married for seven years. Samuel's limp was caused by a fall from a horse, which left him with a chronic leg wound that needed daily dressing, frequent visits to Arcachon for the water cure, and to Switzerland for yearly check-ups. Rosario's appetite was whetted and she made up her mind to invite Colette for afternoon tea, soon.

"La Vida en Rosa indeed!" grouched Pepa.

"You must learn French, mother! LA-VIE-EN-ROSE!" Rosario chided.

"Whatever. Look Rosario, life's not that rosy in the villa. We've been living out of our suit-cases for I don't know how long. Ages anyway. It's not a home!"

"So?"

"So, get a move on!"

"Me?"

"Elias has enough on his plate; why don't you talk to Joaquín yourself about finding a house?"

"Or Samuel."

"Property is Joaquín's business."

Rosario learned that a large house was available in the bohemian quarter of Les Palmiers at the corner of the Rue Blondel, a major road used by caravanserai on their way to the souk every Friday. The thought of camels, passing the house weekly, laden with multicoloured silks, rugs, intricate gold and silver filigree jewellery, exotic spices and dyes of crimson and indigo packed in cellophane bags in huge weighty baskets, hanging from the flanks of camels, made her feel like a thousand Christmases, and she persuaded Elias to view the house with her that evening.

Two jacaranda trees guarded either side of the iron gate. Squarish, the house had a flat roof and an overhanging border which protected the windows below from the worst of the sun. It had three spacious floors, a vast crescent-shaped dining-cum-living room and two terraces, one on the first floor, and the other opening off the master-bedroom. As was customary, the basement was the servants' quarters. Pepa and the girls would love the garden, and though small, by comparison with the villa in Nice, it came already with ducks in the yard, a full chicken coop, two Alsatian dogs, a one-horse stable, a small orchard with orange, plum and peach trees, and Rosario's favourite, a titan of a fig tree for sitting under on lazy summer afternoons. At five minutes from Joaquín's villa and fifteen from La Cigalle, Samuel's and Colette's apartment near the Sacré Coeur cathedral, it couldn't be better positioned. She told Elias she wanted it because it had a fig tree which looked old and wise. The house was near family, and was big enough for entertaining, even though Rosario would miss the grandeur of the Villa Écume. But to compensate, nearby were the shady palm tree parks, replicas of the Le Notre parterres in Versailles, and the artist's ghetto that Elias talked about, minutes away and still to be investigated.

A brass plaque with a fig tree motif on it went up and "The Orchard" was home. Pepa was relieved. The house was what she wanted, a family home with a garden that would be alive in no time with carnations, geraniums, roses and Rosario's favourite, gladioli, as well as scented herbs, vegetables and fruits in the small orchard. What Pepa could not have anticipated was Rosario's slavish reliance on Colette's advice on every aspect of the task ahead. For hours, every day and for weeks, Ahmed drove Colette and Rosario to the centre of town in search of the definitive furniture at the exclusive Tout Pour La Maison and La Kasbah Éxotique.

"Don't you think the house is difficult to please? I mean, it hasn't a definite style of its own, has it?" Rosario ventured to ask Colette.

"Au contraire, chérie. It falls fair and square in le style moderne which was all the rage after the Paris exhibition of Les Arts Décoratifs, which was probably the time when the villa was built. The shapes are angular and geometrical—poached from the Cubists, of course. And with lots of ceramics, mirrors, glass, and Lalique, you could have heaps of fun with your house chérie! Even if you are the very first to dare, here, in Casa!"

"You're amazing Colette! Your knowledge...I've never known anyone like you!"

"You're young. You'll catch up!"

"Isn't Déco very risqué, and how do I know if I'll like it?"

"Let's go back to my place" Colette suggested, "and peruse through my Déco books!"

Kiki La Doucette, the cat, met Rosario at the door, then disappeared into the depths of her prodigiously large black satin cushion with its appliquéd purple sphinx and the initials KLD embroidered on it in gold silk threads. "Come and look chérie" Colette beckoned as she opened the French doors to the terrace. "Sublime isn't it?" she added dreamily. "With The Sacré Coeur to the right and the quartier des diplomates only five minutes away. Come inside" she said, closing the door with a shiver. Rosario sounded a doh as she passed the grand piano. "Do you give recitals here Colette?"

"Less and less, though Sami chose the flat for the size of this room."

An aspidistra, the size of a small tree in a cache-pot, by the side of a dazzling array of satin cushions with shimmery fringed shawls, caught Rosario's eye; she had never seen the like of it before, except in the domestic section of Le Foyer magazine. "This is out of this world!" mused Rosario. She hesitated, "What style is it?"

"Chinoiserie, Orientalisme. Delacroix invented it when he visited Morocco and its freedom and restlessness bowled me over... D'you like it Rosario?"

"It makes me feel wild! And sinful! It makes me want to wander, to forget my roots..!"

"That's promising..!"

"Who's painting is that over there, catching all the light...It looks familiar."

"Ingres. Alas, a reproduction. It's the portrait of Mademoiselle Rivière. Sami bought it for himself before we lived together because he missed me... Such a cucu my Sami... "

"To remind him of you... Of course..!" exclaimed Rosario still gazing at it. "You two are like twins! How uncanny..."

Sprawled like courtesans on the soft mountain of cushions, they leafed through the book Rosario had come to study. Their shoulders touched. Rosario trembled at their intimacy. Never before had she felt so perturbed by a woman and so desiring to be closer. "There, look!" Colette said kissing the lobe of her ear, "this is very stylish and uncluttered. It gives you room to think, to be who you want to be... You could almost meditate in it. Do you think Élie would like it?"

"I've got carte blanche" Rosario said hoarsely after recovering from the exquisite tingling of Colette's kiss, "but I know that he's basically conservative. Would you believe, he's still got some furniture from Ireland that Papi Joseph took to Mazagan from his parents in Tangier. Can't imagine where it could go!"

"A bit of anarchy adds spice..." whispered Colette, making the word spice hiss and sound wickedly exotic.

"Anarchy! Good?" Rosario asked, afraid of the answer.

"What do you think?"

"I was brought up with Loyola's 'Examen de Conciencia' —

and oh boy, does he like discipline!" Rosario replied.

"He was more of a bloody soldier than a Jesuit chérie. What's the army got to do with the soul? I'm afraid you've been had, my sweet!"

"You frighten me, Colette..."

"Good!" Colette stared at Rosario. "Well?"

"Tell me, how is anarchy good?" Rosario trembled, resisting the longing, new to her, to feel her body pulsing against Colette's.

"Simple" Colette responded. "Anarchy is chaos, and chaos brings harmony. It leads to freedom chérie—self-governing freedom. But it doesn't happen just like that. There's destruction first. Annihilation even. And then a new dawn...D'you see?" she said, sounding different and peering into Rosario's eyes. "Vaguely" said Rosario. "So, I mean, are you an anarchist?"

"Sometimes. But I'm not strong enough to sustain the struggle. I still need the familiar. I wish I didn't, but I do!"

"And can it be dangerous, I mean to yourself?"

"If you want to move on chérie, you have to take risks. The trick is to know how far you can go without causing damage to yourself and others. But even if you go too far, there's value."

"How far is too far?"

"Look at Rimbaud!" exclaimed Colette, her face now lit by a kind of fervour. "He's up there with the best of them. A genius who sacrificed his entire life to the principle of anarchy, breaking all conventions so that WE can sit back and experience, second hand, his journey to hell. And all the time you can hear him saying, that's what's ahead of you, if you want to follow this map!"

"You've lost me Colette!" Rosario breathed.

"Forgive me chérie, I got carried away. Now then, you haven't said what is it to be, du Moderne, ou quoi?"

"Sorry?"

"The furniture! Modern? Art Décoratif? Moroccan? or what?"

"I'll talk to Elias" mumbled Rosario in a daze.

Elias wanted whatever Rosario wished and within a month an entire houseful of Déco furniture and accessories arrived at The Orchard

"Take it easy with that sister-in-law of yours Rosario" warned Pepa.

"Meaning?"

"She's extravagant and free to please herself—you have a family to consider."

"Can't you see she's educating me?"

"Be careful Rosario, that's all" Pepa said.

"You're jealous!"

"You misunderstand me Rosario. Let Colette expand your mind, but find balance in your life with everyday happenings. Just now you're either with Colette, talk about Colette, or read what you've borrowed from her. There's Elias too, and the girls. And what about sharing my domestic burdens? You are not the first person to seek, Rosario. We all do, but we must keep a focus, get on with life and relate to it at all levels..."

"How would you know?"

"I've had my moments of torment," confided Pepa, "like everyone else. It wasn't easy for me to leave Spain at the start of the year, and if you must know, I have cried inside ever since. And when I left your father to live with you and help you look after Angelina, it was agony. I needed help, strength and direction. I was lost. I was desperate."

"You?"

"Yes me! I have my weaknesses too, Rosario!"

"And how did you get out of it?"

"Not by reading and debating all day. But I understand that each to his own. My way was to pour as much love as I could onto you all, until I forgot my troubles. And then, yes, there was a book which I read over and over again."

"Avila's Camino?"

"It helped me."

"And now, have you stopped searching?"

"You never, ever stop. But now it's different. I'm on a plain and it's fine for a while"

"Anyway," Rosario broke in, "Samuel's asked me and the girls for a ride in his buggy. Will that do for a start?"

"Yes, diversify Rosario. Spread yourself a little. Your head can only take so much."

The girls, announced Rosario were off to Le Nid Nursery School in October. Her out of nowhere and categorical statement dismayed Samuel when he came to collect them for his promised ride. "They're only tots" he objected, asking how old Mita was. She was older than she looked, Rosario replied. Pepa interjected that this was an absurd reply. Paloma was barely two and that besides, she needed stability after what she had been through.

"What has she been through?" asked Samuel.

"Nothing" snapped Rosario. "As usual mother's being overprotective. The fact is, the girls need to meet other children. Shall we go?"

"Whoa... Whoa... ma jolie... Tout doux... tout doux..." shouted Samuel. "Easy… Easy…" Dame, his new mare, steadied herself for the ride. "And where to, madame?"

"Le Nid!" she blustered, and no, she added, neither Elias nor her mother knew about the visit.

Le Nid was a large ugly tomb of a house enclosed by Cypresses at the edge of Anfa. In the office, with the blind pulled half way down, sat puny bespectacled Monsieur Fourrière beside formidable Madame Fourrière.

Were Rosario and Samuel the parents, Madame Fourrière wanted to know, and were the girls bilingual, and more importantly she asked, were they fully potty trained. They collected and delivered, Mme Fourrière said (as if the girls were parcels in a postman's cart.) The discipline was strict and the learning process began the minute the children entered the school gate and in some cases, she continued, glancing tellingly at the girls, that was not a minute too soon.

It was far too soon for the girls to start full time at the nursery, Samuel protested after their visit. She was at home all day, so was Pepa and Fatima the nanny. He was astonished when she burst into a tirade, saying that she had no choice, that the girls were always there, like ticking clocks, reminding her of things she would rather forget and that she needed time and space for herself, time just to be.

She had to take it easy, he said, his voice softening, and to call in at the flat to talk it over with Colette, who would be enchanted to see her and the girls.

Despite Pepa's fierce opposition, came October, the girls began full time schooling at Le Nid. Rosario had easily persuaded Elias that their lives would be so much more enjoyable without them, and touched by what he perceived as her need for togetherness, he arranged a week-à-deux in Gran Canaria just before Christmas.

That week, Pepa kept the girls away from school and invited Joaquín to bring his son, the elusive cousin Binot to meet them at last.

Circumstances, Joaquín warned Pepa, had been far from propitious for young Binot and as a consequence he was somewhat retarded, but that would improve when his mother returned from Paris. He said nothing about why she was away from her only son. In the meantime Binot lived à la ferme, out in the country, which Joaquín had acquired for growing wholesome foods, keeping chickens and goats, and a couple of mules and as a retreat from the hurly-burly of his business. A childless Moroccan couple cared for the estate, all the animals and Binot. Binot hardly ever left the place and an outing to meet his cousins was something of a major event.

"There you are!" shouted Joaquín pulling his son out from behind a rose bush. "Say hello to your cousins. The tall thin one is Tita and the plump tiddler is Mita."

"Woof! Woof! Woof!" barked Binot, without a smile.

Paloma woofed back and then Carlota and they all barked woofs together and laughed a lot.

"The thing, you see Yaya," Joaquín said, telling the children to be quiet "is that Binot hasn't learned to talk. He barks well instead. He can also do cockerels, chickens, and you should hear his neighing..!"

"Can't talk?" exclaimed the girls in incredulous unison.

"That's enough!" cried Pepa. "Under the fig tree everyone. You too, Joaquín" she ordered, conscious of the fact that no one ever ordered Joaquín. But Binot had disappeared again, then found inside one of the kennels with Lobo the puppy from where he was coaxed out and emerged on all fours. "Up you get" said Pepa lifting him up by the scruff of his neck and dumping him onto a chair. "Eat!" she commanded. He woofed again before leaping to the ground with his plate full.

"See what I mean, Yaya, I can't take him anywhere!"

"If you ask me, he needs to get away from that farm pronto and be with other children" Pepa said. "Why not leave him here with us for a week until Elias and Rosario return? Wouldn't that be great girls?"

They shouted Yeh! Yeh! And a congruous humour bound Binot, Tita and Mita together. They were inseparable and by the end of the week, Binot conversed with his cousins in an animated hotchpotch of basic Spanish, French and Canine.

"We taught Binot how to speak!" Paloma spouted proudly as soon as her parents returned from their escapade at Las Palmas, begging that he stay with them forever and be their brother.

"God almighty! I go away to rest and clear my head, and I come back to this!" hissed Rosario. "What were you thinking of, mother?" she hissed again, feigning to be calm.

"Did you know the poor mite hasn't seen his mother since birth?" Pepa asked.

"Of course I know" screamed Rosario. "Why the hell d'you think I've kept out of it? He's trouble, big trouble. Just look at the pathetic creature!" she muttered looking at Binot sucking his big toe. "Little animal!" she added in disgust. Joaquín was there to collect Binot that evening and at Binot's request, he joined Carlota's and Paloma's class at Le Nid the following week.

"Let's hope that one isn't retarded too!" spat Rosario when Paloma's first school report arrived.

"She's as bright as a button, is our Paloma" Pepa protested. "She has fetching ways, everyone says so, she never falls or breaks things like other children of her age often do, and she speaks two languages and without a trace of an accent!"

"That, dear mother, only makes her a good parrot."

Their time in the Canaries had brought a new intimacy to Elias and Rosario. In some way, Elias was Rosario's best friend. Not that she would confide in him her innermost and darkest thoughts—she would surely lose him if she did—but it was what she perceived as his unconditional love (despite her erratic moods and frequent sexual withdrawals) that placed him, among other men, in a category all of his own. He never reprimanded her, always offered solace and she was grateful for his sweet nature against her often acrid and virulent temper. She didn't know if she loved him, and if she did, she wondered how or why. But she knew that she felt deeply for him. Onlookers puzzled at how compatible they looked despite their age, aesthetic and temperamental differences. Their relationship, no one who knew them would deny, was the scaffolding, the bricks and mortar, on which Rosario constructed her life, even if Samuel and Colette were now providing the gilding.

Something different began to happen. The more Rosario visited Colette, the more she beheld Samuel in a new light—less and less as Elias' younger brother and more as Colette's husband. Beneath Samuel's debonair good looks and seductive boyishness, Colette always insisted, lurked un homme sérieux, and it was by chance that Rosario discovered that Samuel could only reveal his depth of feelings through disclosing his love for Colette. He wasn't usually given to introspection, but caught off his guard, he once confided that he met Colette in the Spring of 1930 at the Clinique Pasteur in Paris, which he attended for treatment to his leg. She was Mademoiselle de Granville, the virtuoso pianist, who returned every year for a rest cure after her gruelling tours. "See you next year" she had said as she breezed out past him, on that first meeting. He smiled now at the thought.

He was there the following year to keep their rendez-vous, only to discover that Colette had been transferred to Switzerland for treatment.

It was days before he found her sitting in a chaise-longue in a lake-side sanatorium, struck with tuberculosis. Her cheeks were two bright purple plums in her tiny face and he felt the flash in her eyes when she smiled at him, almost unbearable.

Samuel's face altered as he remembered the silence that fused him to Colette like a live electric wire and that when Colette finally spoke, her voice was much deeper than he remembered it. She told him that her next tour would be in the colonies, for the clemency of the climate, adding that her agent was negotiating a contract in Casablanca. They laughed at life's coincidences and agreed their meeting was fate, and that their destinies had long been decided. Samuel smiled again. There was no woman in Morocco remotely like Colette he said, adding how turbulent and restless her life had been from the moment she became a student at the Conservatoire de Paris. He explained that with all her might Colette believed that the French aesthetic theory of the Esprit Nouveau of the Twenties was the most exciting period since the beginning of history and she was proud to have been allowed into Aragon and others' inner sanctum and to be received as one of their lesser Enfants Terribles.

But it was Rimbaud, or le Papa de tous, as Colette called him, with his knowledge of the occult, of Plato, the Cabala and Buddhist scriptures who was her model, and it was from him that she drew her own codification of life. Samuel conceded that though he was not a cultured man, Colette had made sure he knew all about that. He smiled at Rosario. "She told me to read 'Un Saison en Enfer', you know…" he uttered distantly as if still lost in a rêverie. "But I never did" he gasped, his voice drooping with remorse.

"You still can!" cried Rosario ardently.

"It's too late. Le moment juste was then, and I missed it."

"But you rescued her all the same!"

"Rescued her?" he laughed. "I was purposeless before she materialised into my life, a rolling stone. Only she, has given me balance and peace."

"Peace? From Colette?"

"Is that so strange?"

"She's so restless Sami…"

"But through it came a kind of wisdom."

"Are you still in love?" Rosario asked, after she had puzzled and reflected on his words.

"More than in love. We met on the crest of a wave and I have ridden that wave ever since. Except recently."

"What happened?"

"She isn't well. Sometimes" he murmured, afraid to hear his own words. "I don't recognise her." There was silence. Sami's utterance terrified Rosario. "Can I help?" she gulped.

He tousled her hair. "See her more often." he suggested. "Be vibrant. Give her the gift of your youth when you visit. And now," he whispered touching her lips, "not a word of all this to anyone—you are the only one who knows."

They had forgotten about the girls playing in the wooded park near the Sacré Coeur. "You like children, don't you Samuel?"

"I love the creatures."

"Do you miss not having any?"

"I did at first, but I only have time for Colette nowadays, except when she throws me out of the house to see you!" he laughed. Rosario saw Colette and Samuel as heroic and tragic figures hiding behind a glittering façade, and her obsession with them grew deeper.

*

Pepa opened the envelope. José Luis' letters were scarce, and she trembled as she began to read.

Barcelona, 19th March, 1938.

My dear mother, Elias, Rosario, Carlota and Paloma.

On the 23rd of December the Nationalists assaulted Catalunya, and Barcelona was captured by Franco's men on the 26th of January. As a Catalan, this was one of the most tragic days of my life, but we must try to rejoice that our war is over, despite the Generalísimo's victory. At least, it has put an end to the blood-shed and terror and God willing, in time, it will open a way to a new era, even though it is not easy to foresee what a dictatorship can offer a country, except more cruelty, injustice, repression and the loss of freedom. Many of our compatriots are so demoralised and worn out that they will settle for the promise of stability—any stability, and that is a measure of their desperation. The rebuilding will take a very long time, and the countless and horrendous hardships suffered by millions, won't go away by magic. I remember your theory, Elias, that our troubles were just a prelude for a larger scale onslaught that would engulf Europe; and now it's happened. Herman Goering himself admitted that his massacre of Guernica was but a trial run to see what his air force could achieve, and the rumoured invasion of Eastern Europe by Hitler's troops seems inevitable and imminent. I would say to you all, stay where you are until this other terror is over. Elias my brother, I thank you for your kindness and generosity. Your food parcels are a life saver to us and those at the Calle Diputación and there is even enough to treat our friends and neighbours!

Salvador, I am sorry to report, is receiving treatment at the sanatorium after I diagnosed tuberculosis. He is dying. Father too, has suffered. He lost his sight quite suddenly one morning when he got up and now lives with us on the ground floor. Carmela and the children are frail but surviving. Do not grieve dear mother. For your consolation, let me say that father's blindness has blessed him with an inner peace that he never enjoyed before, and you would be so proud of him. As for me, I have started a free weekly clinic for the destitute in my district and I will complete my training as a cardiologist at the end of this year. But my best news, and I want to leave you with this in your hearts, is that Maruja is expecting our first child. Can you believe this mother, your son, to become a father? We've already decided— if a girl—she will be called Pepa and Camilo if a boy.

How is my glorious god-daughter? I often think of the little red heart between her brows and I smile. I miss you all. Sometimes it aches, but I would rather see you safe than here.

Father sends his love, especially to you dear mother, and so does Maruja who prays daily for you all.

I embrace you one by one, with my deepest tenderness. Happy Saint Joseph's Day to us both mother, I'll miss your natillas!

Your always loving son
    José Luis

Pepa fell to her knees. The tears rolled down her cheeks. Her Camilo was blind, Salvador was dying and a new life was forming all at once. Agony, joy, offered in a single cup to swallow. She shook her head. "Dios..." she murmured.

"There you are! I've been calling you for ages. Have you been asleep?" shouted Rosario.

"Look, a letter from your brother..." Pepa said picking it up from the floor. Rosario began to read. "So it's all over then!"

"What?"

"The war! He says the war is over."

"Yes... And..?"

"You mean about father and Salvador?"

Pepa looked down. She could conceal her crying better that way. "Yes, that..." She quivered.

"I can't imagine father blind. He so loved beauty!"

97

"He can still see it."

"We must think of new life mother, be happy about the baby!"

"I am, more than I can say... Renewal. Hope..." she struggled to say, "and..."

"I came to tell you I want an early lunch" interrupted Rosario. "Is it ready?"

"You'll have to make your own. I have something to do here first" Pepa said, striking a match to light a candle.

*

Binot turned out to be a great companion for Carlota and Paloma. The enfant sauvage was now a normal, boisterous boy. Schooling, for him and Carlota was a kind of game and in the same perverse way, school dinners were fun and something of a novelty. But for Paloma, the thought of letters and numbers were the stuff of nightmares, and institutional meals an ordeal she could barely endure. But worst of all were the pangs of separation from Pepa that struck her with daily panic as she left home, until the cart turned the corner and she lost sight of her grand-mother.

An increase in pupil intake following the Easter break made it necessary for the school to open the roof terrace during recreation to relieve the overflowing playground. Carlota told Samuel that Filomène, Madame Fourrière's sixteen year old daughter and her twin brother Barnabé were put in charge of the roof terrace. Rosario complained that the girls never confided in her when Samuel asked if she knew about it. "We're going there to check that terrace" he said, "And it'd better be safe... And those twins..!"

They looked like two paragons and after careful scrutiny, the terrace was declared as secure as a jail's games room. "There was no harm in checking," he said, when Rosario mumbled I told you so.

The twins were in great demand. It was rumoured throughout the school that exciting games were played up on

98

the terrace, and that the latest, most thrilling game of all would soon be taught.

It was the Thursday before Corpus Christi.

Clapping her hands like a seasoned schoolmistress, Filomène ordered everyone to form a circle and reminded them that this would be the best game they would ever play and it would only work if it was kept a secret, even, she emphasised, from her mother, Madame Fourrière. The girls were to follow her instructions, and Barnabé would lead the boys. Filomène shouted for attention as she might not have time to show them how to play the game again before the bell. Off came her nipple-high white cotton knickers and out popped Barnabé's modest and limp organ as he fumbled to undo the flies of his shorts.

"Come on, come on. Off with them!" she hurried the girls.

"I don't need the toilet" argued Carlota.

"You'll do as you're told!" barked Filomène.

The circle of girls giggled at first, then as they watched their instructress they became reticent and restless. Filomene sat on the cement floor, with her back resting against the low terrace wall; she parted her thighs and began stroking her genitals until her breathing deepened and her groans became screams of "Ouis!"

Barnabé, still kneeling and trailing behind his sister burst into a syncopated Marseillaise. "Why... he's peed on his hand!" said a boy putting his tongue out in disgust. "It's not pee, you stupid, it's man's stuff and you can't make babies without it" sneered Barnabé, drying his hand on the boy's hair. "Now, you try it!"

No one dared not to. Some girls mimicked Filomène's 'Ouis' and the boys feebly chorused 'le jour de gloire est arrivée'.

"That was shit" bullied Barnabé. "We'll need a lot more practice, every day if we have to, and 'til you get it right. Right?"

"And remember..." Filomène said with a wink and a menacing twist of her mouth, "it's a secret."

After a couple of weeks of assiduous practice on the terrace, Paloma, Carlota, Binot and a few others got the hang of the new game. Carlota and Paloma often felt the need to practice at home outside the circle on the terrace and feared that this was against the rules. The thought then struck them that if it was a secret, something about the game must be amiss and Carlota wondered, since they were all at it, if they had been contaminated by some disease passed on by the twins. "Do you mean like Señor Consul next door? I mean he had diarrhoea and his children caught it" said Paloma knowingly.

"Yayita said he had an amoeba or something" suggested Carlota. "But I don't feel sick, do you?" she asked holding her tummy, "could be something else" she ventured.

"I think it's just a good game. Don't you?" said Paloma trying to sound grown-up.

"Yes. And Binot said he wanted to be the best and he's practising a lot at home too."

"Maybe we should warn him it might be dangerous" worried Paloma. "But I think we should tell Maman first, before him I mean."

"They told us it was a secret" admonished Carlota.

"If we tell Maman, she will be pleased with us" said Paloma nodding hard.

"She could be angry."

"We've done nothing wrong!" Paloma protested, shrugging her shoulders.

Paloma had just divulged their secret. A strange expression crossed Rosario's face which Paloma took as a smile, and Rosario waited before she spoke. "You did very well girls, to come and speak to me about this."

The girls glanced at each other with smug relief. "You haven't told anyone else, have you girls?" she asked, scrutinising their eyes.

"We haven't!" they chorused shaking their heads furiously.

"Is it a good game, d'you think Maman?" Paloma dared to ask.

Rosario paused. "Not really" she said. "It's more something that happens."

"But is it a disease and can I die?" enquired Carlota.

"It won't kill you" Rosario replied, "but it can make you very tired. So tired that you want to sleep all the time."

"Can it be stopped?" ventured Paloma.

"It can. But you have to want to. Some people try to think of something else as soon as they feel the tickling." She didn't know what else to say, and wished she could have been more inspired. Nevertheless she congratulated herself. She had not reprimanded the girls nor made light of the situation or given it excessive importance. All the same, she decided to confide in her mother.

At three and four, the girls were far too young to be exposed to such practices Pepa commented, and wanted to denounce Mme Fourrière and withdraw them from Le Nid at once. It was one thing for the natural response to be awakened at the right time, she said, quite another to prematurely manipulate it in a covert group.

*

Elias bought Rosario a hooded buggy driven by Hamido, an aging local jockey, and drawn by Péricles, the gentlest of palomino horses. It was summer, and Rosario and the children spent the mornings swimming at the Lido beach and the afternoons at the Parc du Sacré Coeur by the cathedral, some hundred yards down the road from Colette's, whom Rosario visited whilst Fatima took the girls to an ice cream parlour. Soon Rosario managed the buggy herself, giving her the freedom to shop, spend hours at the beauty salon and see a great deal more of Colette, without anyone knowing where she was.

She got into the routine aafter a while, of dropping off the girls for their weekly ballet classes at the Petit Conservatoire at the corner of the busy Rue Colbert and afterwards meeting Samuel on his own at the Café Koutoubia by the Marché Central. Colette, he revealed, on their last encounter, required surgery to remove a part of her bowel infected by tuberculosis and he begged Rosario to boost Colette's morale by frequent visiting after their return from Paris in a month's time. Bereft by the horror of Colette's predicament and by the loss of her friends for several weeks, Rosario began piano lessons to ease the pain and tedium that lay ahead.

Old Madame Avril was dressed in black, with a gold lorgnette permanently fixed to her eye socket, like an aristocratic widow at the turn of the century. Once Colette's teacher at the Conservatoire, she too had been seduced by the colonial life. Now long retired from the dizzy whirl of the Conservatoire, she enjoyed sipping a very full glass of medium dry Amontillado sherry every day before lunch, and in the evenings, she lay still in her chaise-longue amidst the pinkness of her bougainvilleas, listening to the world fall asleep and knowing that this was music. Hardly ever touching the keyboard, except to play the first note of the scales with her crooked index finger, she spoke only to greet her pupils on their first lesson, usually to say she was to be addressed as 'Madame' and that she was eighty three years old. The metronome, and the tapping of her tiny feet enclosed in doll-like, lace-trimmed shoes, were her only teaching tools. Rosario saw her every other day, and acquiring her own piano to practise at home became a must.

*

"Children!" called Pepa. "Bring your baskets, the chickens have laid ten eggs, all spotty brown, and if you hurry you'll see the eleventh pop out. Where's Binotte?"

"Binot..O..O!" he corrected. "O!, O!" he shouted.

"That's what I said" asserted Pepa, thinking how confident he had become.

"No. You said Bino-tte" he argued.

"Leave my grandmother alone—she's Spanish, not French" said Paloma rising to her grandmother's defence.

"I didn't know she couldn't.. ...Binot mumbled.

"Now, now. We must learn to communicate peacefully, mustn't we?"

102

"What does 'cominate' mean?" he asked.

"It means to understand one another" replied Paloma faster than Pepa could open her mouth. Still astounded by Paloma's verbal precocity, she told Binot it was the girl's bed time and that Fatima would walk him home, and to come for breakfast the next day. She grabbed him by the shoulder as he was leaving and said "Don't I get a kiss?"

Pepa always had supper with the girls before bathing and putting them to bed. And then came the story, except when Rosario took over the task if she needed to soothe her guilty conscience. Paloma tickled her grand-mother's chin and pleaded to let her come to her bed for the story, and to stay there all night if she fell asleep. "You know how your mother complains when she finds you here in the morning." Paloma implored again and kissed the tip of her grandmother's nose. "We'll see" Pepa conceded. "Jump in. You too, Carlota" she said, without further cajolery. It's got to be a short one tonight girls, because..." she sighed, "I'm tired after the laundry."

"Érase una vez en un lugar lejano... once upon a time in a far away place..."

"Where was it?"

"It was far across the ocean in a land so large no-one has ever seen where it ends and it's called the Americas. And there, beautiful people called Red Indians live..."

"Do they wear red clothes?" interrupted Carlota.

"No, they are red because the sun has made their skin look like the earth after rain. One moonlit night, the wise old chief gathered all his people in a huge circle and said, we are here to play an important game together, so listen to the rules carefully for I will speak only once."

"They taught us this game already at Le Nid" shouted Carlota aroused.

"Not that game, Carlota. This is a game you would do well to learn. And the chief called the game 'The Talking Stick.'

"Sticks can't talk!"

"Carlota, I said listen!"

"Everyone in the circle looked at each other amazed that

there could be such a thing as a talking stick, but they didn't interrupt the chief. His name was Gold Feather. As if by magic, he made the stick appear from the side of his boot, and they all hummed when they saw it. It was the length and thickness of a church candle—like the ones you lit in the church in Nice to pray for the healing of Spain when you were very little—and it had a horse's head carved at one end. A small feather hung from its collar and all the way through the stick were carved the words: HEAVEN, EARTH, WATER, AIR, and FIRE. It was the most beautiful object they'd ever seen. "Now" the chief said, in a deep cavernous voice, "I will pass the talking stick to Little River by my side and she will think of something important to say, and she has to think very carefully, because she only gets one go. In the meantime" he said, "the rest of you will remain silent and listen to what Little River has to say, and after she has spoken, she will pass the stick to Fire Horse next to her and then he will speak, and so on, until each one of you has had a turn."

And so the stick went round the circle very slowly and each person spoke whilst everyone else waited in silence, until Gold Feather held the stick again. 'Any questions?' he asked.

Why is this game important? enquired Big Cloud. 'Because it teaches everyone to think carefully before they speak, and to be very clear when they do, because they only have one chance. It also makes everyone else patient listeners. But most importantly, it links us together with our thoughts, just like Heaven, Earth, Air, Fire and Water are linked together.'

And the Horse and feather? asked Silent Fish.

'That is for the journey of the soul—the horse's head stands for the passage from this world to the next, and the feather stands for truth which is the soul.' And the chief made the people sit in a circle at the time of every full moon when he said there was a golden thread linking men and women of goodwill with the sacred beings in the heavens. At that very moment, he told them, they could unite as a group and invoke spiritual light, spiritual love and spiritual power." Pepa yawned. She blessed her grand-daughters pretending to be asleep, smiled, and tired, she too, slid between them under the covers.

Every evening, as the sun mellowed and the air cooled, Bouchaib watered the orchard, lawns and terraces. It was often then that the children came out to play after sheltering indoors from the worst of the afternoon heat. Always the first out of the house to seek the freshness of the grass underfoot, or the shade of the fig tree, was Paloma. This time, she stood by the duck pond with Carlota and Binot, inhaling the wetness before she bent, scooped a fistful of mud, smelled it, and smeared her face with it. "Look at me!" she cried "I'm one of the Red Indians in yaya's story!"

"Red Indians are red all over, ninny!" shouted back Carlota.

"Dare you to take your clothes off, and roll yourself in it" challenged Binot.

"Maman will be cross with me if I do."

"Maman will be cross with me if I do..oo..oo.." mocked Carlota. "Wimp" she jeered.

"I'll do it after you" assured Binot with a beguiling smile. The seduction worked. Paloma undressed before sinking ankle deep in the mud and falling on her back like a puppy waiting to be tickled. She squelched and smeared the slippery red mud all over her pink body.

"You're not supposed to eat it!" shouted Carlota.

"I want to" Paloma mumbled shoving the mud into her mouth as fast as she was able to. The cackles, screams and convulsive laughter alerted Rosario who came to her bedroom balcony. "What's going on down there?" she called. "Come over here and let me see what you're up to!"

"She started this" hissed Carlota, pushing her sister forward.

"What's the meaning of this and where's that woman?... Fatima!" she called. "Never there when you want her. And you" she ordered Paloma, "come up at once!"

She had just washed the mud off Paloma's body, and a twinge of tenderness welled up inside her. She had never been that physically close to her child and for a moment she felt sad

105

that she had not discovered before now that Paloma was ticklish behind her knees and that she bit her nails.

"Why did you roll in the mud?" she asked, surprised at the softness of her tone.

"I wanted to" Paloma replied. "It was like having a cuddle."

She could not punish Paloma for the mud incident Rosario admitted to Pepa who said there was nothing to punish, because Paloma probably needed to do it. What an odd thing to say, Rosario remarked, but it wasn't, Pepa retorted, seeing that Paloma was an imaginative child and literally in need of earthing to reassure herself that she really existed. "But you know what I'm getting at…" she intimated, adding "but it was good that you bathed her, Rosario. I mean, really good."

Samuel called at The Orchard. He was back from Paris. Colette now had a permanent colostomy and a full-time nurse stayed with her at home until she became familiar with the management of her new predicament.

She wished to see no-one but Rosario.

Sunk deep amongst her heap of bright cushions, Colette looked paler and more fragile than ever. The nauseating stench emanating from her friend's body assaulted Rosario's nostrils and impregnated her skin. She held her breath for as long as she could and felt ashamed that it was revulsion rather than sadness or compassion that overcame her.

"Chérie! called Colette, her voice as thin and lost as a thread come loose from an embroidered canvass. "Come" she said, outstretching a fleshless hand. "I have so much to teach you before…"

"I have just started piano lessons" interrupted Rosario, seeking to avoid a situation she persuaded herself she could not handle.

"With Madame Avril, I hope chérie! Isn't she unbelievably…"

"Unbelievable!" shouted Rosario unduly exuberant.

"We can choose a piano together when I'm better."

"Let's!" she cried, cheered by Colette's faith in her recovery.

"But now..." Colette said patting the leather folder that rested in the cradle of her lap.

"What's in it?" asked Rosario.

"That, chérie, is Surrealism!" She lifted the slim folder high above her head as if it weighed a ton. "Help me keep it vibrant, Rosario!. It's all here chérie" she said, fondling the folder like a photograph album of a favourite child. And so began Colette's own style of tutoring. Throughout her life, Colette had been the artisan of her own spirit, but it was not before she had first sunk to the depths of surrealism, lost herself in the extreme emotions of her passion for Sami and music, that she emerged bolder and wiser. She wanted Rosario to follow in her steps but saw that she was not yet ready for such a fearful confrontation of self. She looked at her protégé in the manner of an over-zealous mother, driven by desire for her child's accelerated advancement, but she would have to proceed at a speed Rosario could accommodate.

"Open the French door, chérie" she pleaded. "It's time for a breather."

"It's so good to see you up!" said Rosario, gasping for fresh air.

"Hold my arm chérie. Isn't that something!" marvelled Colette, as she habitually did whenever she looked at the view. "And that austere building on the left. Is it a monastery?" Rosario asked.

"Gracious me, no!" she laughed. "Here they hide their monasteries in the mountains. That, my dear, is the Institution Sainte Jeanne d'Arc"

"A prison then?"

"Heavens no! It's a convent and THE school for girls in the whole of Morocco! And can you believe it, all the nuns there are aristocrats. And only the crème de la crème send their daughters there."

"That's definitely for my girls then!" cried Rosario.

The right moment was now. Elias sipped his pre-lunch scotch. In a triumphant tone that he could not miss Rosario declared that she had found the perfect school for their daughters and that she had to enrol them at once.

Despite Rosario's enthusiasm Elias objected that Paloma was far too minute for proper school. It was only the rickets Rosario said. She was really taller than she looked.

"You should consult your mother on this one" he advised, then changing the subject he asked about her visits to Colette. "She's educating me Elias!" she said fervently. "It's as if I had my own private college tutor. We're reading Les Fleurs du Mal next, and guess what, she's helping me choose a piano!"

"Will you mind if I join you?"

"Of course not, cariño, I want you to be there."

A Playel Grand Piano in glossy palissandre wood with natural shades of purple arrived at The Orchard.

On it, Rosario could not wait to float a very large embroidered Manila shawl she had been given as a wedding gift. And on top, she placed a tall Chinese vase which, she said, should never be without gladioli or arum lilies.

When Rosario told about the convent for the girls, Pepa lashed out. "You abandon Paloma at birth to save your skin. You reject her outright when you see her a year later. You send her to nursery school at two when I was there to care for her, and finally, you want to send her to convent school when she's barely three!"

"And what's more, the girls will be boarding!" exploded Rosario. "They're starting this October, and you'd better start sewing their name tags on their uniforms!" she screeched and stormed out of the room. Pepa dragged her back. She would have nothing to do with this decision, she wholeheartedly opposed it and Rosario had better remember it for as long as she lived.

It scared Rosario that Pepa did not shout. She never knew how to deal with her mother's scorn and retreated into a sulk every time it happened until in the end she came to see herself as the victim who had to be rescued by her aggressor. This time she knew Pepa would not budge an inch and she sought Samuel for consolation and approval. Girls, he told her, came out of the convent with brains, manners and poise, how could he not approve? "I do so value your opinion Samuel. It's so important to give your children a good start in life, don't you agree ?"

"Even more so nowadays, than when we were youngsters" he commented. "Mind you," he laughed, "our parents, bless them, enjoyed having us around and kept us home till..."

"Paloma isn't very bright" cut in Rosario.

"Not bright?"

"She is hopeless with numbers and letters and Madame Fourrière was very critical about her."

"That old bag! What would she know about children like Paloma? Paloma is different. She needs time, that's all."

"I have an interview with Madame Notre Mère at the convent. D'you think she'll take them?"

"Without a doubt. Two years pre-registration is time enough."

"I want them to start this October."

"Rosario..., they are only babies! Palomita barely looks three!"

"And they'll be boarding" she said casually. "Samuel?" she called when he backed away. "Samuel please say something!"

"I can't. I just can't! "

"Will I see you next Thursday?"

"No, not for a while."

In their crispy white shirts and navy uniforms of double-breasted blazers and plaited skirts, still impregnated with their shop smell and shod in black, knee-length, laced-up boots, the girls looking puzzled and forlorn, waited by the gate, ready to be driven away and dropped off like stray seeds in a gust of wind only two kilometres away from their own soil onto the sterile pitch of their new school playground.

Pepa suffered her worst asthma attack for years, and was unable to see the girls off. The emotional blow of losing her grand-daughters, decreed the doctor, had most certainly precipitated the crisis, and he cautioned Elias and Rosario that Pepa needed care and sensitive handling.

Pepa, Elias told Rosario, was sure to take the girls departure very badly and pleaded with Rosario to consider enrolling them as day pupils instead.

It was too late. Rosario's tone was unyielding. Their ballet classes and piano lessons had already been transferred to the school. In addition, she had booked a deportment class, because God only knew how badly they needed it.

"And what about La Yaya?"

"She'll get better. She always does."

"At least," he said, lets make sure they spend Sundays with us, for Yaya's sake as much as for the girls."

"We can pick them up after High Mass at the Sacré Coeur. And anyway" Rosario said, "I'll visit them every Thursday afternoon."

"On your way to, or from Colette's?" asked Elias, a note of sarcasm blatant in his voice. He had never used it before and though a part of Rosario panicked, she was also defiant. "After" she replied. "Satisfied?"

"Fine querida, fine" he murmured.

Paloma kissed her grandmother's damp forehead and smoothed her long unplaited hair.

"I want to stay with you forever and look after you Yayita."

"Palomita..." Pepa said propping herself up in bed with a groan she could not contain. "Look! I'm already better. You mustn't worry about me sweetheart."

"I will run away from school at night to look after you."

"You'll do no such thing. You'll see, I'll be better when you come back next Sunday and I'll be able to give you cuddles and tell you stories to last you the week" Pepa puffed between every word.

"Why doesn't Maman love us as much as she loves auntie Colette?"

"Your mother is not quite herself sweetheart."

"Is she ill too?"

"She has a kind of illness. It's called Rosario-itis!"

Samuel had stopped his visits to The Orchard after his confrontation with Rosario over the girls' overhasty boarding and her calls to Colette also came to an abrupt end. The piano

110

and Elias were her solace. Elias' business boomed. Invitations to glittering social events came pouring in. Cocktails at embassies, afternoon teas in Consulates and late night cabaret with the Chambre de Commerce members became their way of life, converting 'La Belle Rosario' as she came to be known, into the most sought after socialite in town. Rosario's appeal transcended her beauty as Colette's intensive tuition paid off, when at the "cercle littéraire" she once held the undivided attention of a small but distinguished côterie of visiting illuminati during a visit to the Grande Foire de Commerce et des Beaux Arts.

At The Orchard, the tempo beat to Pepa's reduced rhythm. The servants became her friends, bolstering her up with their simple friendship at a time when the loss of the girls and her protracted convalescence had pushed her to the brink of depression. A sense of worthlessness and desolation became daily enemies that she could not find the will nor strength to fight. Blind to her plight, Elias and Rosario saw nothing of her except for fleeting glances from her bedroom door when on their way to a night out. There were Joaquín's flying visits, always dispensing assorted naturopathic advice she never followed, and Samuel who came before lunch, when he confided that Rosario had not visited the girls at the convent on Thursday afternoons for weeks, and he had filled in for her.

*

During the autumn afternoons that led to her recovery, Pepa sat in the armchair by the side of her bed and began to review her life and pray for direction. She had been broken into pieces and now she longed for wholeness, even while knowing that this notion of wholeness was itself a delusion. She told herself that the key to happiness was to bring the gift of serenity back into her daily life, but she found it a laborious task when she had been so blatantly exploited and used. She had come to this foreign land for a clear purpose—to care for her grand-daughters, and bring a degree of balance to the family in a state of disarray. Now, she saw herself redundant and the real challenge, she knew in her heart, lay in the wise use of the materials at hand: the now childless Orchard, Rosario's egotistical nature, and Elias' feebleness. She closed her eyes and stepped a long way back to her beginnings far away into the clear light of her mountain village. Whenever wisdom failed her, this going back in time served her well, and now and for no reason she knew of, her memory summoned up her school days and Doña Alfonsina's one and only history lesson, 'Rural Spain throughout the Ages.' Life in Spain, Doña Alfonsina had taught her, had been based on family and communal living since the Middle Ages and had remained, until as late as Pepa's own childhood. Those rural communities were autonomous and independent of one another but, Doña Alfonsina had said, with a warning inflection in her voice, that when the web unifying family and group broke down, there was no one from outside to help them out of their quandary, and that was the heavy price they forfeited for their jealously guarded exclusiveness. She added that this idea was irrevocably tied up with a complex web of land reforms, redistribution of wealth and class structures, but she never elaborated on this.

Pepa tried, but could not see the relevance of her teacher's lesson to her present predicament and why it had come to mind in the first place, since she had always viewed the family not as a separate entity but as the jewelled microcosm of the Greater Whole. By serving it with love, deliberate effort and without undue attachment (and this she found hard to achieve) she was confident that she was offering the very best of herself to her small unit, to the Human Family and mostly, she hoped, also to her God. The warning Doña Alfonsina had spoke of, she then recognised, was that for true service she must physically stretch her hand beyond that small unit that was the family.

As her breathing eased, she graduated from her armchair to going for afternoon strolls in the garden. Aisha, no longer the rival cook but housekeeper and friend, poured her sweet mint tea until the pot was empty. Bouchaib reduced his gardening chores to sit by her side and once broke his customary silence to murmur a Sufi saying; 'When the heart weeps for what it has lost, the spirit laughs for what it has found."

Gradually, and as a child traces an existing drawing through a transparent sheet, Pepa saw her own map of directions appear just as clearly before her eyes. It showed that she would once again be of wise counsel and would always be treasured by her grand-children. And through the telling of stories, old and new, she would be the transmitter of wisdom and the facilitator of their spiritual potential. She would go on relishing the newness of each dawn, the rushing of the animals in the yard, the intoxicating smell of the Monday laundry, and the blessedness of the Eucharist on Sunday. A well of clarity spiralled up within the centre of her being. Her mind was made up. She would confront Elias and Rosario, stating her conditions if she was to remain in the household.

For a minimum of two hours during their weekly Sunday visit from the Convent, the girls would be with her. They would never (as Rosario had intimated) be deprived of their family holidays and sent miles away to Summer Camp instead, and she would have equal say as to their physical, emotional, and spiritual welfare. She would, as she had wanted since her arrival, run a weekly soup kitchen at The Orchard for the poor of the Medina and Ahmed would drive her weekly to the Parish of Saint Vincent de Paul to spend the day there as a voluntary worker. Finally, Rosario would join her in the Rosary during the month of May to celebrate and revere the Marian qualities of love, compassion and wisdom which Pepa felt all mothers needed, if they were to fulfil their life's purpose.

She summoned Rosario and Elias to her bedroom which she had adorned with candles and pink carnations and called for a moment's silence as they entered the room and before she made her announcement.

"Oh my, Oh my! The Phoenix has finally risen!" sneered Rosario.

"And you'd better watch it, for I'm still hot from the ashes!" replied Pepa, blowing on her finger tips.

"Yes!" exclaimed Elias. "Yaya, yes!"

"Yes what?" objected Rosario.

"Yes to every one of your mother's requests" he replied firmly.

"That's that, then" grumbled Rosario with a sweeping gesture of her arms.

"Good. I'd better get going." said Pepa, rearranging her bun with a single hair-pin.

With his Master of Ceremony's voice, Elias toasted, "every one, even you girls, please raise your glasses this Sunday lunch to our dear Yaya's return to health, and that she may long stay with us, and be happy!"

"I want to know everything about you and your new school, everything" said Pepa taking the girls upstairs to her room after dessert.

"The nuns like me! Especially Madame Dominique" Carlota rushed to say, waving her gangly arms about.

"Madame? I thought they were all nuns at the school."

"Maman said they are, but she told us that they once were ladies who lived in castles in far away countries." said Carlota.

"Well I never!" Pepa exclaimed "And what about…?"

"Mita hates school and she eats the toothpaste straight from the tube…"

"Let Paloma speak for herself."

"I miss you Yayita!" she said, hiding her face under her grandmother's armpit.

"She cries every night too, and keeps the others awake…" Carlota said, deliberately adding kindling to a spitting fire. Pepa rocked Paloma in her arms as she did when she was a baby. "Is that true sweetheart?" Pepa asked at last.

"It's Madame Valéria…"

"Is she your teacher?"

"She said I was a cretin because I can't do numbers and letters and she sent me to stand outside the classroom, and everyone that passed thought I had done something wrong."

"Have you told your mother?"

"I'm afraid to."

"Is there anything you enjoy doing in school?"

"Polishing my boots. I like to polish my boots before going to bed until they shine and I like to eat toothpaste and I like it when the House Mother, Madame Aglaee, gives me a bath on Saturday night because she is very kind and she cuts my toenails and she sings all the time and she takes off her coiffe and I can see her hair."

She paused to breathe, "and I like it in chapel before breakfast because it's all quiet and nobody can shout at me there. I hate the uniform and hands review after mass because I bite my nails and the inspecting nun hurts my fingers with a ruler and she shouts at me when my boots are wrong and I can't do my laces properly and I...."

"She looks stupid with her boots the wrong way" sneered Carlota. "Everybody points at her and laughs!"

"Enough!"

"But I look after her!"

"She does Yaya" assured Paloma, "she's only naughty at home."

"I can believe that" Pepa said. "Right! Let's get them boots and laces sorted."

Paloma did not know her left from her right side, nor could she do knots. She had developed her own convoluted method for tying up her laces which did not meet with the approval of the school's regimented ways.

Pepa slipped Paloma's hands inside her boots and asked if they were on the correct side. "Hold your boots close together" she told her "and tell me what you see?"

"They're straight!"

"Very good. From now on, slip your hands inside your boots before you wear them and make sure you get the tips straight next to each other, then, one at a time, put the boot from one hand to the foot on the same side, and abracadabra, they'll be straight on your feet too!"

And when Paloma had mastered it, Pepa said "Next Sunday, lace practice!"

*

Paloma stopped eating in school, lost weight, and a spell at home was prescribed by the convent doctor. She slept in Pepa's room, and it was like the old days again.

"Tell me about your dinners at school" Pepa asked after watching Paloma wiping her plate clean with relish with a piece of bread. "Yuk! I always throw them under the table when no one's looking."

"You cunning thing! And does Tita really look after you?"

"Sometimes she does, and is very kind, but sometimes she's ashamed of me and pretends I'm not her sister."

"Are you the smallest, sweetheart?"

"Yes. I'm always the first in the line for everything and everybody calls me 'Quito'"

"Quito?"

"You know... short for mosquito."

"Cheeky devils!"

"I don't mind because I go buzzzz..buzzzzz..and they all laugh, and then, they like me a bit."

"Palomita, you're not a mosquito, nor stupid, nor anything else. You are the loveliest little girl I have ever known!"

"That's because you're my Yayita..."

"Uncle Samuel and Binot think so too.."

"I want Maman to love me and the teachers too."

"Mita, grown-ups are funny. They only like people like themselves and anyone different puts them off, but I'm sure they like you sweetheart, because you're so cheery and polite."

"I think grown-ups are very muddled Yayita. All, except you."

"If you're better, you might as well come down and help me with the decorations!" shouted Rosario from the living room.

"Run along Mita, and show your mother how clever you are with your hands!"

A mountain of tissue paper, glue, tinsel of every hue and the Christmas decoration box she had saved since her own childhood surrounded Rosario.

"I want you to trace those on this pink and yellow tissue

116

paper, I want you to cut them very carefully and gather them with this piece of string. A rosette, look, you see?" she said, sounding unintentionally stern.

"Can I make more pink ones than yellow ones?"

"What's wrong with yellow then?"

"I like pink best because it's the colour that comes to your eyes when you love someone."

"How do you know that?"

"I can see it!"

"You must be dreaming!"

"Not now, but I dream a lot at night."

"What about? Watch it...you're cutting through your dress!"

"About you sometimes."

"Is it nice?"

"No, not really. You always leave me under an old tree, all by myself, and I cry until the branches come down and hug me and I'm alright again."

"I've never left you under a tree, old or new!"

"You have."

"Nonsense!"

"I've finished my stars. Look maman!"

"I said "Rosettes" Paloma, but these stars are very good. Have you learned cutting at school?"

"No. But I like it. I love making things Maman."

"Hands are all very well, but you have to use your brain too, Paloma."

"Where is it?"

"In your head, silly! And the bigger it is, the better you can think!"

"Perhaps my brain is small, because I'm small."

"That's no excuse."

"Can I eat something to make it grow bigger?"

"Lentils. Eat loads and loads of lentils and it'll make you clever."

"They're horrid!"

"I used to hate them too, but then I ate them everyday until

117

it made me a very clever person."

"I should stay at home then."

"Why?"

"Because we never eat lentils at school."

"Who says you're daft eh?"

"Can I go now?"

"Not before you tidy up."

"I always do, Maman. Are you a tidy person too?"

"I have better things to do. That's what the maid is for."

"Or yaya."

"Crafty, and impertinent! I'd better watch you!" muttered Rosario.

*

Carlota was home from school for the Christmas vacation. She had enjoyed her brief respite from Paloma's tribulations in school, but they were always happy to be re-united.

The crib was Pepa's undertaking and every year Bouchaib was sent on his ancient moped, to gouge a few clumps of moss from the river bed of the Oued Nefific for the girls to put at the base of the crib. Pepa had bought nativity clay figures whilst in Nice, where they were known as Santons de Provence which she and the girls positioned on the patchy moss under crunched-up brown paper meant to look like a cave. It sat on a small console table in the hall with an everlasting candle by its side, lit by Pepa to encourage a seasonal thought from visitors.

But Rosario saw to the tree. She ordered it each year, months ahead and it never failed to arrive on Christmas Eve by special freight from the Middle Atlas, above the fertile plains of Sais.

Why was the tree brought indoors, was a question the girls asked Pepa every Christmas to which she invariably replied that it was to remind every one of the cross that joins heaven and earth and of our commitment to live a spiritual life. The girls nodded. They were not sure they understood all that their grandmother said, but the glow they always felt as she spoke made them feel somehow cognisant and content.

It wasn't until Christmas eve that the tree was decorated. Paloma's hand-crafted tissue decorations floated everywhere like falling stars, but the miniature candles attached by minute metal clips to the branches were by far their favourite decoration . Rosario glowed. She did not know why but the spirit of motherhood had a habit of stirring deep inside her belly like a stray butterfly every Christmas and every Christmas Pepa said it was a response to Mary's pregnant womb and the Seed of Love She carried.

With Pepa's recent illness in mind, Ifrane, at over sixteen hundred meters above sea level was the ideal location for the family to spend their customary New Year celebrations. Elias could not have been more discerning in his choice. The pine covered mountains, green soft valleys and fruit orchards took Pepa back to the beauty of her own fertile homeland, but the markets back home did not display dazzling fossils, mellow coloured minerals and bright geometric patterned Berber rugs on sale in tented stands in every village. And at fruit stalls, piled high with oranges, lemons, limes and silky skinned dates, that Pepa could not have bought in her mountain village, nor almonds, still cocooned in their furry shells and small, red, shiny apples no bigger than cherries. Bare-foot children came running to them, sign-talking with the girls and once mime-taught them a game they played with the smooth bleached bones of a sheep's spine which they tossed deftly from their palm to the back of their hand and which spurred the two girls later to entertain themselves in the hotel bedroom with small, polished stones they found on the hotel drive, instead of bones.

The unusually clement weather and the absence of snow in the mountains that winter prompted Elias and Rosario to take leave of Pepa and the girls to drive further towards Taroudant and into Ifrane de l'Anti Atlas, a town Elias had always set his heart on visiting for its Jewish cemetery where a 2000 year old grave inscription indicated that the first Israelites fled there during the reign of Nebuchednezzer. It was a kind of pilgrimage in memory of the sephardi grandmother Elias never

119

knew and whom no one ever mentioned, as if she were some hideous fungus on the family tree, and seeing the sight had been a healing moment, Elias confided. They headed towards the Seyad valley and the first fortified granaries in Morocco. He had only been there once before as a very young man to inspect grain prior to exportation. He had learnt of its existence from his father Zac, who had travelled there, and his grandfather Joseph, before him. Little had changed since then and it was Ahmed who advised them that the path, only accessible by mule would be too hazardous for Madame.

Dusk fell before they began their way back through scattered clusters of decaying villages, some of them with lokba roof tiles engraved with the hand of Fatima and other cryptic symbols to protect their families from the evil eye. Now and then, Elias told Ahmed to stop. He chatted awhile with the women and children walking in long meandering files from village to village, precariously balancing their loads on their heads, and then he told Rosario their stories. As he shared his knowledge of people and places and expounded on the essence of his own roots, Rosario saw him unfold like a rich and colourful paper frieze until she felt herself unwittingly falling a little in love with him.

NINE

Wings, the Rose and the Butterfly

Germany had just invaded Poland and it was France's turn to fall prey to the Nazis whilst the rest of Europe shuddered.

Spain's upheaval during its three years of terror had convinced Franco it was safer to remain neutral and Elias found himself saying that it was the Generalísimo's only wise action. Morocco, he feared, would not escape the Fuehrer's wrath and he began stock-piling provisions for the likely dearth to come.

A letter from José Luis arrived soon after the New Year echoing life's ambiguities. Maruja gave birth to their son Camilo the very day Salvador died. He wrote that to him, these two events symbolised the death of the ailing Spain and the hope of the new. Salvador, and many others, he said, had been sacrificed on the altar of so called historical progress, and he prayed that their deaths would not be in vain. He thanked and begged Elias to continue sending food parcels, as Carmela, now widowed, cared for the children alone.

Pepa began her weekly beggars day on the Feast of Epiphany which commemorated the adoration of the Magi and the transmutation of water into wine at Cana. In the same way, she was convinced that the single loaf of bread, the quarter kilo of sugar, broken in pieces from the sugar cone, and the glass of milk she gave each beggar that queued at the gate, were symbols for a much greater sharing in the world. Thereafter, and every Thursday before the Islamic holy day on Friday, Pepa enlisted Bouchaib's and Aisha's help to distribute the portions until the queue faded. The news that 'Zahah'—giving to the poor—did not come from a Muslim like themselves, but from an old Spanish woman from Les Palmiers district, had reached every ear at the Derb Jalef medina, swelling the queue with newcomers each week until the numbers settled at around twenty or thirty. She knew each beggar, with whom she conversed in Catalan, and was replied to and thanked for in Arabic as if they had spoken the same language. Paloma played with the children in the queue during the Summer vacation and once asked her grandmother why beggars existed at all. They weren't there—At The Beginning—Pepa replied, adding that they were beggars now because of the greed and injustice in the world, and that unfair as it may seem, their presence was not in vain because it reminded us of our own shortcomings. She added that no one must ever assume that they would always be the ones to give.

"I won't mind being poor." Paloma said.

"But would you like to be in this queue, with flies in your eyes, sores on your legs or even have no legs at all, like little Yousef?"

"He's always smiling" said Paloma. "That means he must be happy."

"Some children are blessed, others are oblivious, but if you look at the grown-up beggars eyes, you will see that they had to die inside or they could not survive the suffering".

Rosario made a point of being away on Beggars Day and returning late, when the last whiff of the queue had evaporated. She despised her mother's morbid interest in the afflicted and when Pepa explained that an attempt—no matter how insignificant—at imitating Christ's way could not be too much of a bad thing, she retorted that trying to imitate the Big Man Himself was nothing but sheer arrogance, adding that mendacity was always self-inflicted and best left to those who practiced it.

Pepa blamed her outlook on the seditious literature Colette gave her to read, and feared Rosario could lose herself in labyrinths of irredeemable sinfulness without her realising it. She was convinced that Rosario urgently needed to find a lynch pin, like the down-to-earthness of family life to hold her back from plummeting into the abyss.

She was malingering, Rosario said, when Paloma began to shiver one Sunday afternoon, but after checking her temperature, just before returning her to the convent for the week, Rosario decided to keep Paloma at home from school, at least over-night. She tip-toed into her grandmother's bed when she heard the thud of her parents' bedroom door and knew they were in for the night. "Hold me tight Yayita" she said, "I'm really afraid of her."

Pepa lifted her grand daughter's chin to peer into her eyes. "Madame Valéria?" she asked.

"She's like a statue" said Paloma stiffening herself like a corpse. "I swear her skin is marble. And she has no eyes."

"Is she blind then?"

"No."

"You mean she doesn't notice you?"

"She never looks at me, or smiles or speaks to me and her face never moves" said Paloma looking like a mask.

"And?"

"And" said Paloma struggling to tell, "she sent me to the cellar all day last Friday."

"She did what?"

"And forgot about me until Carlota reported that I wasn't in the dormitory that night."

"Madre de Dios!"

"And I hadn't done anything wrong..."

"Why did she send you to the cellar then?"

"Because I jumped from a high wall in the playground."

"Jumped? Why were you up there?"

"I was only practising my flying. Like I do at night."

"You can fly at night?"

"In the blue sky, with the wind on my face, and I'm very happy and everybody below looks up and they stretch their hands up, but they can't reach me and I can't pull them up and then I stop flying and I come down with them again."

"You mean you fly in your sleep?"

"Yes. I don't know why I don't take off when I practice."

"Palomita, when we sleep we can do things we can't do

123

when we're awake, and flying is one of those things. You have to wait till night to go flying. Day time is for touching the ground and learning to walk. So no more jumping from walls. Promise?"

"But I never hurt myself, or cry if I fall."

"But you shouldn't take chances. Besides, it gives Madame what's-it Malaria, something to punish you for."

"I never want to go to the cellar again Yayita. It's so dark. Nobody heard me when I screamed. I couldn't see anything. I wanted to get out but I couldn't find the door and I couldn't reach the light switch."

"My poor sweet. Has she sent you there before?"

"No, but I've been in another dark room like that before."

Pepa raised her eyebrows.

"Another time..." she whispered into her grandmother's ear.

"When?"

"A long time ago..." she replied, suddenly looking quite old.

Darling" Pepa said, becoming aware that Paloma had unconsciously regressed to her foetal state whilst in the cellar. "That was such a long time ago!" She stroked her face. "If only I could speak French, I'd give that Malaria statue what's what!"

"Don't Yayita, and don't tell Maman either!"

"I think she should know, she is your mother."

"She won't like me if you tell her."

"What if I tell uncle Samuel? He can call in and warn Madame Notre Mère about the Malaria who pesters you."

"But he might tell auntie Colette and she'll tell Maman."

"No, just him, you and me, sweetheart."

She pulled the bed-cover over her grand-daughter. "Go to sleep" she whispered "and flap your wings."

"You are a love" Pepa said. "Thank you Samuel. How was your interview with Madame Notre Mère?"

"She is a riveting woman! She's very queenly and belongs more to a throne than a prie-dieu!"

"Did she know you were a lapsed Catholic?"

"At once! She said I looked too carefree to be a functioning Catholic! About Paloma. The dinner nuns have reported misbehaviour at the dinner table."

"She chucks her food under the table" Pepa interrupted "and why shouldn't she, wouldn't you, if its disgusting?"

"She's the last to leave the chapel every morning and evening."

"She has peace there..."

"She eats her toothpaste."

"She needs some comfort!"

"She doesn't mix with her peer group."

"She's different."

"But older girls adore her."

"Well then?"

"She's very sweet and full of smiles during the day but cries her eyes out at night."

"Tita told me" said Pepa aggrieved and then added that the irony about Paloma's so called misbehaviour, was that Paloma herself found it logical, but that others translated it as wilful, and it would only be a matter of time before she felt inadequate, odd and unworthy.

"She asks to be excused from class too, and then is found climbing up walls."

"She's loftier than most children... And what about the cellar incident?"

"Notre Mère went very silent then."

"Do you know why?"

"Well, as it turns out, La Malaria is a Princess! Comes from Austrian aristocracy, is a graduate of the Sorbonne, had a life before she took the veil and brought a fabulous dowry that keeps the school going!"

"Great! She can get away with abuse then!"

"Notre Mère was very reluctant to take action, but she did promise another teacher for Paloma."

"That's a start."

"She was about to call Rosario for an interview, you know!"

"I hope she doesn't. Paloma wants to be in her mother's good books. It's the old rejection thing…"

"What rejection?"

Pepa recounted Paloma's birth and her first separation from Rosario soon after delivery. "She was born with a thorn in her heart" Pepa said, and Samuel remarked that it had to be plucked out.

*

A very young nun, Madame Justine, and Madame Valéria's replacement, suggested in a letter to Rosario that to ensure Paloma's upgrading for the next scholastic year a practice of daily homework in arithmetic and penmanship throughout the whole summer vacation was crucial. Rosario took it upon herself each morning, at precisely ten o'clock, to sound the bell normally used to summon the servants, whereupon Paloma rushed to the living room to unfold (which was a task in itself), the all-in-one pine desk that her mother had especially bought for the Summer homework. She opened her exercise book at a new page and raised it to her face to inhale its newness. She placed her pen in the groove for pens at the top of the desk, unscrewed the ink pot, positioned a new square piece of blotting paper exactly under the first line of the page and waited, knees close together and arms crossed on the desk top as she would in school.

"Today" Rosario declaimed vaguely acknowledging Paloma, "we'll start with the alphabet. First, the letter 'a'. Good. Now 'b'; Good, she said peering at the page. 'c'… take your time. I want a lovely rounded 'c' with fullness where it's due. Good. Now 'd'; I said 'd!' 'd!' Paloma, not 'b'.

"That's what I'm doing Maman…"

"Start again. Write 'b' first. Good. Now look at it. You agree it's a 'b'? Good. Now write a 'd'. No! I said a 'd'! d! d! Rosario shouted until Paloma screamed back that it was.

"Let's move on. No.., 'm!' Paloma, not 'w'. 'O's a jolly letter isn't it, and you've given it a smile! Whatever will

Madame Justine say when she sees it!"

"She's always doing funny things like that to make me laugh!"

X, Y, and Z! You like those don't you?"

"They're the last letters!" laughed Paloma, putting her pen back in the groove and pulling her tongue as she pressed the blotting paper all over the page with the ball of her fist.

"You look very pleased with yourself Paloma. Would you say you've done well?"

Paloma smiled "Yes, very well!"

"What about those letters you can't get right?"

"Which ones?"

"It's good Rosario to see you giving up so much of your time to spend with Paloma, but go easy on her" Pepa advised.

"What do you think is wrong with the child?" Whatever was wrong, said Pepa, was unimportant.

Rosario told Elias of Paloma's idiosyncrasies. He said children, like horses, needed rewarding sometimes. Rosario replied that Paloma was so eager to please she did not need bonuses of any kind. "Whether you agree or not cariño," Elias retorted, "Paloma has her own God-given gifts and she will find her niche."

"Like what for instance?"

"She has a lovely nature, she's kind, she sings...." he smiled, "is a good little Rat de l'Opéra and she is learning the piano."

"So....?"

"She'd make a wonderful gouvernante to an ambassador or even a king! What more could we wish for her!"

"And she can't read music either!" Rosario cried, aware for the first time that musical notes were like numbers and letters, and she vowed that she wouldn't let her daughter's affliction beat her.

Pepa made sure that afternoons were for play. Binot walked the short distance from his home near the CTM (Cars et Transports Maroccains) down the camel road in the Rue Blondel every day and Zouzou and Dédé from next door climbed the wall into The Orchard, whilst trying not to disturb

their father's beehives, . They built castles in the sand pit, filled
their arms with puppies and fed them milk from baby bottles.
They poached food from the refrigerator for picnics on the
lawn which Paloma always prepared and enjoyed the pleasure
others derived from her concoctions, usually uncooked and
sometimes imaginary.

It was not unusual for Rosario to remark how much Paloma
resembled her grandmother. But animals were Carlota's
domain. She hugged them, talked to them, fed them, wiped
their sticky eyes with her own handkerchief, and de-fleed them.
No one had ever taught her how to remove a tick from a dog's
ear but she knew. They all watched her as she pricked the
parasite with a pin to release the blood on which it had fed,
until, like a vampire pierced with a stake, it would let go of its
prey. She sighed every time she did it and said it made her feel
better, as if she, herself, had been freed from an invisible hold.

Rosario lost weight and looked drawn; tests revealed that
she hosted two very different guests in her belly—a growing
foetus and a tape worm, both of which had to live in harmony,
since any attempt at flushing out the worm could result in a
miscarriage. She was carrying a son, she was certain of that. A
son who adored her already beyond anyone's imaginings and
would continue to do so, long after other men had ceased to
worship her. Never doubting her forecast of a son, Elias was in
heaven and Rosario became a repository of whims he found a
pleasure to indulge.

Carlota, only a year older but an outstanding pupil, now
that Rosario had withdrawn from teaching Paloma, was
assigned the task until a Summer tutor was found.

The girls lay, tummies down on the mosaic floor to keep
cool, and the desk, so crucial for Rosario's tutoring, stayed
unopened in the corner of the room.

"Let's use a pencil instead of a pen and if you make a
mistake" suggested Carlota, "you can rub it out and no one will
know. Shall we draw?" she asked.

"I'm not good at it Tita" said Paloma looking stricken.

"I'll show you. You draw a circle, like that, then smaller

circles around the big one, then a straight line down for the stem, then half circles . And look. A flower!"

"I wish I was as clever as you so that Maman would like me."

"She likes you better than me, though I'm cleverer!"

"She doesn't!"

"She does!"

"She doesn't like either of us very much, but she likes the new baby" announced Paloma dolefully.

"How do you know?"

"I heard her talk to it. I think it's in the bedroom somewhere, because she whispers nice things to it when she's having a nap, like coochicoo and coocoolin" Paloma giggled.

"Yuck!"

"It'll be nice when we can hold it" Paloma said beaming.

"I don't like babies, I prefer puppies" Carlota said, picking her nose and nibbling at the dried mucus. "Shall we draw a puppy?"

"We'd better not" said Paloma turning a new page.

"Letters or numbers first?"

"It's all the same."

"Letters then. Don't press so hard Mita, you'll break the nib. Write a,b,c,d for me. Look, b and d are the same, interrupted Carlota, but they stand opposite, like two friends. So draw two lines and then add a circle at the bottom on either side—remember the flower—it's the same with letters Mita, they're only curves and lines! Easy!" Paloma's page became a happy collection of dancing numbers and letters and in a while she began to see a pattern.

Every single day away from school during the summer vacation was special, but Monday was Paloma's favourite, as it was the start of a new week and she was at home. It was also Pepa's, because it was laundry day. When she was a child, Pepa had helped her own grandmother with the sorting of the clothes into whites and colours, the scrubbing, the rubbing, the bleaching and finally the handing of pegs to hang the clothes on the zig-zagging line across the field, all the way down to the pig-sties. Sometimes Pepa and her grandmother chased each other across the field until out of breath her grandmother caught her and tickled her helpless on the ground. And now Pepa saw herself in Paloma.

Pepa could not think of a more intoxicating smell than the aroma of fresh laundry and nothing else she knew could be more comforting, more grounding, humbling and exalting than to metamorphose a mountain of soiled clothes into clean and fragrant linen. She often thought of washing day as confession day—an opportunity to wash away stubborn stains and be renewed if only until the next confession.

It was evening before she had collected everything from the line when Bouchaib began a relentless watering of the garden. He was still there past midnight. "Sirocco coming Madame Pepa, very much dry for plants" he replied, when Pepa shouted from her bedroom window why was it taking him so long.

A huge swirling of sand reddened the entire sky at noon the following day, sending every creature to search for shelter. Animals were rushed into the basement, doors and windows bolted, toilet paper compacted and stuffed inside keyholes, and the largest bath towels soaked in water, rolled and placed at the door's base. Apocalyptic fear gripped everyone whenever the Sirocco struck. It descended from the heavens with unpredictable irregularity and blew its spiralling Saharan pink sand as if from a titanic funnel, attacking the inanimate and paralysing the animate right where they stood. "It's the fickleness of the monster and the ferocity that confounds me" said Rosario watching her first Sirocco from the bedroom window.

"It is its fickleness and ferocity that the Arabs respect and see as divine attributes" retorted Elias. "They say the wind symbolises their own elusiveness and transience in this world. Most of them" commented Elias "have learnt to sense it before it strikes and seek cover well before it happens, and that in itself is a measure of their own inherent and idiosyncratic wisdom."

"What if they're caught outside?"

"It happens. They use their own Jellabahs as a tent and keep very still inside it. But there are casualties every time. Children are blown away like paper kites and anyone left outside can suffocate in minutes."

"How terrifying! Were you ever caught outside?"

"Once, with Joaquín when we were youngsters."

"What happened?"

"We were riding and the horses became agitated even before the first spin of sand, and we knew. We rode fast towards home, but the horses turned wild and we had to dismount and let them loose. We took the reins and tied ourselves to a tree and covered our faces with our shirts. The sand got inside our trousers. You can imagine the rest..."

"You squirmed for days!" laughed Rosario. "Why do you suppose Arabs are so fatalistic?" she asked, amazed that nothing was ever done to avert disasters.

"Fatalism? That is what the West calls it. Here they call it serenity. And......since we're into local wisdom, querida, there's a saying that the Sirocco is also for bringing people together and catching up with news, because they are forced together in a confined space."

"Have you news then?" Rosario asked expectantly.

"I want you, la Yaya and the girls to spend September in Meknès. The baby inside is tiring you. You need a rest Rosario and I'll join you at week-ends."

"Why not Fez, the holy city?"

"Precisely! There's too much to see and you'll be tempted to visit everywhere."

"Is there anything interesting in Meknès?" she moaned.

"I can take you to the Medersa Bou Inania one Saturday. And before you ask, the Medersa is a fourteenth century Qur'an school. We can get a guide to tell you all about its history and architecture. There's also the Imperial City and we can see the Fantasia festival, and, if you're still up to it, I'll take you to Moulay Idriss for the day."

"Sounds wonderful" Rosario said eagerly, "but the girls are having their tonsils out the last week of August and I don't know if they'll be up to travelling by early September."

"Their tonsils out? What on earth for?"

"It's all the rage for children."

"Some fashion!"

"They say it will stop sore throats and stimulate growth. God knows Paloma needs it, and Joaquín wants Binot to have it done too."

"But he's dead against medical interventions! He even let his daughter die, rather than take her to see a doctor!"

"Well, he said Binot was on the scrawny side."

"What's this obsession with size all of a sudden? Yes, the Butlers are short but they are sturdy, all of them! And removing bits of flesh from the back of the throat isn't going to add centimetres to anyone. Is it?"

"You never know with science, Elias."

*

Pepa complained that Rosario had not consulted her about the girls' operation. "I thought I had a say in their welfare Rosario" Pepa scoffed, when she found out.

"Sorry, I forgot about our deal. Honestly."

"It seems a little drastic and pointless to me when nothing's wrong" argued Pepa.

"Prevention, mother, the medicine of the future. Forecasting trouble before it hits. It makes sense doesn't it?"

"When is it to be?"

"The day after tomorrow. The girls and Binot will be done in the morning and they should be home for lunch."

"What lunch if they can't swallow?"

"They'll be on loads of ice-cream for the first twenty-four hours to stop the bleeding."

"I'll make it myself."

*

The children told everyone they were having their tassels out and were not afraid. But who would be the first to go under the

132

knife became a blustery argument until Binot said that they told him in school, that girls were always first.

Eager to gain extra praise from her mother, Paloma offered to start.

She was lifted into a large, thickly padded operating chair, her head tilted backwards and her mouth forced open with braces. Rosario sat in the far corner of the dazzling operating theatre. One nurse assisted while a gigantic Sudanese woman sang an aria in the middle of the room.

"Bene, no..? It e helps me,.. How do you say.. It..." said the Neapolitan surgeon Dottore Azini.

"No necessary for anaesthesia" he added "because dee operation is e called guillotina, quick, capisca?" he said, clicking his tongue against his palate. "So...it is e one esnip, then due esnips and finito! No une problema for la bambina. Bene, no? Andante with dee Aria por favore.."

Azini incised and Paloma's eyes filled with tears she would not release.

"Bravo! Ecco!...One little estrawberry in dee backet! Favore, dee backet under dee chin for dee blot, many blot...ooh mama mia!"

Rosario craned her neck and shouted if Paloma was alright.

"Tuti fan fruti! Ha! Ha! Fruti. Capisca? Jbel! Sing dee Aleluhiah for dee ragazza. She very brava... no crying....una rara avis! Paloma, avis, funny, no? More louder, more loud, Jbel! Ecco... estrawberry numero due and... ecco!" Azini pulled some flesh from the back of Paloma's throat and clicked his tongue again.

"Is that it?" asked Rosario stunned by the scene that she had witnessed.

"Dee clamps off, rinse dee mouth and now go to la Mama for dee gelatto. Pronto, dee ader bambina!"

Paloma was lifted out of the chair and carried by Jbel to the next room, almost entirely filled with an enormous Mama Azini sitting next to a vast refrigerator.

"Bella!" cried la Mama, taking her into her fat short arms.

Binot squealed like a slaughtered pig during the procedure

and later, Carlota had to be strapped like a lunatic and the singing nurse made to use the drum as well, to supplement her vocal chords and drown the bawling.

"This Azini fellow is a butcher!" Rosario complained to Elias.

"You chose him querida."

"The Umbertos swore by him. A genius, they said!"

"These Italians are as thick as thieves!"

"That's them off my social list!" cried Rosario.

"Let's hope it works after all that carnage" said Elias.

"I want our doctor to check them over and Binot's staying until he's recovered" said Rosario, expecting congratulations for her generosity.

A make-shift bed for Binot was placed between Carlota's and Paloma's and the girls cheered up instantly at having their cousin convalescing with them.

Pepa brought them her home-made lemon ice-cream, and when they became over-excited she told them to sit quietly and listen to her story.

She began. "Érase una vez en un lugar lejano....right at the western tip of the Iberian peninsula—a place called La Coruña, where there lived a wise old woman who knew more about animals than any other living being. She knew about birds and beasts and fishes and even about the smallest, tiniest insects on earth, and she shared her hermit's hut with Ladrón, a spotted brown snake that liked to curl up under a stone by the open fire, and a wolf that lay peacefully like a lamb on the straw bed beside her.

One day, a woman and her child made their way from a far away village down south through the dark woods to seek her advice. The mother told the wise woman that her daughter was seven and could not walk or talk, smile or even cry, and she grieved day and night to see her child enclosed in a tight cocoon. "Cocoon is the very word," said the old woman in a man's voice. "Your child is still in her cocoon, the cocoon she should have shed when she came to life!"

"But what can I do to release her from this place of

darkness?" cried the mother.

"What do you most wish for your child?" asked the old woman.

"I wish...I wish...I wish that she will be successful in every sphere of life. That is what I wish for my beloved child" replied the mother.

"Ah..." sighed the old woman. "Ah..!"

"Ah..? asked the mother.

"Yes. I said Ah! because you, and you alone are the cause of your dear daughter's ailing."

"Surely not, I love her so!" objected the mother.

And the old woman took a deep breath and closed her eyes and kept silent before she spoke again and said that her child was truly a butterfly, the most beautiful insect in God's kingdom, but, she added that she could only evolve outside her cocoon, if she was freed from expectations and constraints. The old woman stopped.

"What must I do? I beg you to tell me, wise old woman" prayed the mother.

"Take your child back and expect nought from her, and she will speak and walk and smile and even cry. And that is what all mothers must do."

Only Paloma stayed awake until the end. She kissed her grandmother goodnight and asked if she, one day, would be a butterfly, and Pepa assured her that she would become a rose.

*

They travelled to Meknès after dusk to avoid the heat and dust. It was a cool ride and all were still asleep when Ahmed drove into the long palm-tree drive of the Hotel Transatlantique. A burst of cricket song awoke them.

"Smooth ride Ahmed" said Elias. "Report to reception. Your room is in the chauffeurs' quarters."

When they opened their shutters in the morning they were convinced they had arrived at the Garden of Eden. Beneath their feet, the whole of Meknès gleamed in the morning sun.

Families of Storks nestled on pise buttresses; ancient olive and fig trees no longer bearing fruit, sprouted on roof top gardens; creamy wild roses, brambles and creeper tumbled down in one single cascade over massive crumbling walls. There were arches everywhere, some new, others decaying and overgrown with scented herbs, and minarets with domed pinnacles shimmering in the morning sun and blue and white flapping flags, to remind the faithful to praise and glorify the name of Allah.

"Will it do querida?" asked Elias.

"It's simply heaven Elias! It's fabulous! It's pure Sheherazade! What more could I possibly want!"

"Good. That was the idea cariño."

TEN

Ludwig von Carosfeld

A communicating door linked the girls' room to Pepa's. Elias insisted that during his absence Rosario was to keep their suite for herself to ensure complete rest.

Mademoiselle Ginette, a young woman from the Montpellier École d'Instruction Physique, collected the girls from reception for their swimming lesson after breakfast each morning. Paloma learnt to float within minutes, convinced it was like flying and could not be coaxed out of the water, but Carlota's limbs wouldn't obey instructions and she had to be taught on the lawn before venturing into the pool.

A walk alone along the formal paths of the hotel gardens after her siesta, became Rosario's routine. She sat on the shaded benches as she went until she met up with Pepa and the girls for afternoon tea at the orangerie.

"Madame... May I?" For a moment Rosario felt displaced and like a heroine in one of her favourite movies. "Please... Do sit down" she replied, in a way that she imagined her heroine would.

"I hope I haven't offended you Madame. If you'd rather..."

"You mean because you're German and an officer?"

"Yes, Madame."

"How can I possibly judge an individual by the actions of one madman!"

"You are indeed a brave lady to insult my Führer to my face, Madame."

"I thought I was being truthful!"

"You have my admiration and my deepest respect!"

"So you won't shoot me?"

"Please Madame. I am not a soldier. I am a restaurateur of Classical art."

"But you are in uniform!"

"Let me introduce myself. I am Count Ludwig Von Carosfeld" he announced, standing up to click his heels." "Von Carosfeld as in the House of..."

"You know of it?"

"Indeed. And that's why you are an officer?"

"Precisely."

"And why are you here in this hotel?"

"Morocco being a French Protectorate, it is French territory, and therefore under German occupation" he replied reluctantly. "You may be aware" he continued "that a couple of years ago overseas possessions passed under the jurisdiction of your Maréchal Pétain of the Vichy Régime Madame, and as a consequence German officers were posted here to Meknès."

"He is most certainly not MY Marechal, Count. Why Meknès?" asked Rosario.

"Did you not know that Meknès is Morocco's strategic city and that we are occupying the French barracks as our prime base in Morocco?"

"But it still doesn't explain why YOU are here, in this hotel and not in barracks?"

"I am here to recover from pneumonia, Madame"

"Forgive me. I shouldn't have pried" she apologised.

"Please Madame."

"You must miss the excitement of garrison life" said Rosario thinking of what her heroine might say next.

"Is war ever exciting Madame?"

"Are there many Germans like you?" she smiled.

"Many of us have been forced into this horrendous war against our principles and wishes. We too are prisoners of the Führer, like the Jews."

"Forgive me for laughing," Rosario scoffed, "but I can't see a single Jew recovering from pneumonia in this luxurious hotel!"

"That was grossly insensitive and unforgivable of me

Madame, and I beg you to overlook my last remark."

"I'll try!... Oh..!" she said as Pepa arrived, "do stay to meet my mother and daughters."

The Count stood up again to salute Pepa.

"Madame, Mesdemoiselles" he said bowing. "I must leave you to your afternoon tea."

"Is he real?" asked Pepa.

"He seems to be. He's a German officer on leave from the garrison, here in Meknès."

"Odd, don't you think?"

"He says he's convalescing from pneumonia. He's a Von Carosfeld. An aristocrat" she added, when Pepa showed no sign of recognition.

"Is he really German?"

"I know... We never think of them as civilised and sensitive, do we?"

"How will people like him ever live with themselves after it's all over!" Pepa remarked.

"If he lives! Elias says that many high ranking officers will be shot by their own side after the war, whether they win or lose."

"We know all about that, don't we!" Pepa sighed, alluding to her own country. "And here we are, in paradise, when all that monstrous fascism is going on out there!" she added. "D'you know, I have, God forgive me, prayed for Hitler's annihilation, instead of asking for grace to descend upon him."

"We're only human mother" Rosario remarked softly.

"And that's why we need prayers to transcend our physical limitations and a belief that our prayers, whatever form they take, do make a difference" Pepa said.

"Well, I don't pray any more."

"I know... It'll come back Rosario, I promise you it will."

Elias arrived early. He could not wait until the weekend to see Rosario. "You seem awfully thin for someone so pregnant querida" he said, feeling her shoulder blades and then the sharp bones of her pelvis.

"You don't expect me to grow in a week, do you?"

"I suppose I do." He caressed her lips with his finger tips and played with her hair.

"I feel fit actually, really fit!"

"I know what's coming..." he said, looking at her sideways.

"What?"

"You want me to take you somewhere in the town, don't you?"

"Well..." she said, touching the rounded chick pea-like tip of his nose. "Yes, I do need to get out. Can we go to the Medersa?"

Opposite the Grande Mosque, the Medersa Bou Inania stood guarded by doors decorated in an intricate pattern of carved Koranic prayers. Immediately above towered an imposing cupola. The guide whom Elias had hired was already standing in the courtyard waiting for Rosario. He wore a cream djelabah and turban, did his solemn salamalecks and stood upright until she came closer then pointed at a symbol on the wall. "It is the 'Barakat Mohammed'" he intoned, "and it means 'the chance for faith'. This, you see," he said in excellent French, "was a place of opportunity, a place to know God. It is a school you understand, for the learning of the sacred Qur'an. And here, by this beautiful conch" he whispered, caressing it, "was the Tolba where the student reciters of the Qur'an gathered."

Rosario noticed how white and deeply lined the palms of his hands were when he opened them wide and side by side to signify the sacred book. "Was the teaching spiritually advanced?" she asked, all at once fired by the same old mystical flame she had kindled as a youth in her convent school.

"Not as much as in other centres of learning. Here, it was mostly recitation of Arabic poetry from the Qur'an" the guide told her.

"Is the recitation a spiritual goal in itself?" she asked, wondering if it was like reciting the Rosary or the Litanies.

"Indeed" the guide replied, "the Misbaha is a rosary with ninety-nine beads. It has been used by us in religious meditations for hundreds of years. The word Misbaha means guidance in glorifying and praising God and all of his ninety-nine Sacred Names. But it is still an exercise. A preparation for something greater. Then there was a silence between them that was both heavy and light. Rosario waited until the guide muttered that the Qaadria, was something else It was a group of disciples of Moulay Abd El Kadar El Gjilani of Baghdad, formed around the twelfth century. It had evolved through reflective prayer—and over a lifetime it taught them to lose their selves and their egos. The Sufi, he said, initiated this practice and it was this form of worship which was the purest of all.

They walked side by side as Rosario became aware of a change in the quality of the light and of her own pulsation. "And who is that man?" she asked, stopping in her tracks. She could see a frail old and white bearded man, as still as a sage in a child's picture book, and with a twinkle in his eye, sitting cross-legged on a square cushion on the azulejo floor at the end of a very long pillared room. "Our Marabou, madame" said the guide, touching his brow and then his heart. "A holy man and a seer. Listen" he said, "he is glorifying Allah, Allah the All Embracing, Allah the All Forgiving, Allah the All Hearing, Allah the All Seeing, Allah the Avenger, Allah the Restorer......"

Rosario closed her eyes, Allah's sacred names reverberating in her head and filling it with brilliance. She had never been so close to anyone as holy and she felt galvanised by his proximity. When she opened her eyes, the Marabout had dematerialised and she thought she must have been dreaming or seen a vision of a saint.

*

Ludwig Von Carosfeld became Rosario's regular escort after her short siesta and walk through the gardens to the bench by the fountain, known as 'The Fountain of Night and Destiny', and she began to look forward to their meetings more than anything else during the day.

"Look at this exquisite volubilis!" he marvelled, holding an electric-blue, bell-shaped flower between his thumb and forefinger. "So unique, and still so much part of the whole. Perfection in itself and yet so diminished without its own foliage and the red earth beneath its stem." He looked at Rosario. "You look surprised Madame..."he said.

"I never thought a German could have so poetic a soul!"

"Do you not know Goethe Madame?"

"As in Faustus?"

"He was also a scientist and his 'Metamorphosis of Plants' and theory of colours are masterpieces of beauty and wisdom Madame." He paused, "but let me hear about your own French literature."

"I am a Spaniard."

"Forgive me, your French is exquisite. Spain!" he exclaimed "such a culture! Cervantes, Calderón de la Barca, Saint John of the Cross, Bequer...."

"You know of Bequer!" she exclaimed amused.

"I am a Romantic Madame... And a classicist."

"You also favour the classical?"

"If you permit me to say it, like the Roman features of your beautiful face Madame..."

"You are too gallant, Count......"she whispered.

They talked about wars through the ages and this terrible war and how it was tied up with the notion of good and evil. Ludwig Von Carosfeld's belief was that where there was good there was also evil and that this was not a new concept. "Take the Chinese" he proposed, "an older culture than our own whose central philosophy is the integration of opposites." He stopped to entwine the fingers of both his hands. "Like that" he said. "Like a man and a woman. But permit me to return to Goethe, and this time to his 'Prologue in Heaven' from Faustus where he shows a clear sympathy between God and Mephistopheles, which he terms the 'Spirit of Negotiation'. Evil and God are not a contradiction, Madame, he said when Rosario looked puzzled. In fact, they become one in their scheme to help the Journeyman on his quest to his unique developmental force, which will, eventually, lead him to a spiritual life. So, you see Madame, evil, or our friend Mephisto, is God's greatest collaborator when it comes to man's long struggle in this world!"

Rosario gave up her siestas for longer encounters with Ludwig Von Carosfeld. Never had she experienced such depth of intellectual intimacy, not even, dare she formulate it, with Colette, her friend and mentor. But as days passed, it became the proximity of his physical presence, his noble bearing and his gaze, blue and caressing, that she hungered for the most. She lay at night, coaxing and fearing the piercing of Eros' arrow, knowing that if Eros came, what she knew truly aroused her about this man, would vanish, and by morning she tried to settle for the exquisiteness of their Platonic stance.

The recent edginess in her daughter Pepa observed, had to do with the Count. A shrewd move Pepa thought, would be to invite him for coffee and liqueurs with the family after lunch.

"Would Mademoiselle like a sun on her plate?" he asked Paloma. She nodded, made dumb through not knowing what language to use. He picked an orange from the fruit bowl, shone the peel on the table cloth and reached for a paring knife. "Now watch my hands carefully and you will see the sun rise from within them" he said, turning the sectioned peel face down on Paloma's plate to reveal a glowing sun. "Voilà!" he cried "Un petit soleil pour un autre!" Paloma clapped.

"Isn't my daughter beautiful" Pepa said, when she saw him seeking Rosario's eyes. "Women can be so radiant in this state don't you think, Count?"

"Forgive me Madame!" he said perturbed. "How very obtuse of me not to have noticed. I should have been so much more attentive had I known!"

"She is rather delicate" Pepa said standing up, "and must rest for longer periods in the afternoons. Shall we meet you for coffee here at the same time tomorrow?"

"Indeed. And you Mademoiselle" he said, turning to Carlota, "shall have your rising sun tomorrow."

"Why on earth did you have to tell him that I was pregnant!"

"Why conceal it?"

"I didn't want him to think of me like that. That's all."

"You mean a pregnant woman is perceived differently by a man?"

"Yes!"

"The temptress and the mother don't mix, do they? You and your fantasies Rosario... You complicate your life so..."

"All I know is that you've killed something special."

"What I have done, is to nip something potentially dangerous in the bud!"

"Rubbish!"

"This man is besotted by you Rosario!"

"Besotted? Rosario whispered. "Besotted.." she repeated, savouring the lushness of the word.

"As if you didn't know..."

"I know..." She trembled. "And what's more, I love the terror of it, the fear of falling."

"Look, in ten days we'll be back home and that'll be the end of it. Don't seek his company alone, promise me that."

As Rosario had suspected, the disclosure of her pregnancy had dispelled the entrancing spell she and Ludwig Von Carosfeld had shared, next to the 'Fountain of Night and Destiny'. She was now the Mother, a demi-goddess, a kind of female pantheon he could no longer pursue and felt compelled to revere, leaving Rosario bereft of the bit of herself she most wanted to hang on to.

The return journey from Meknès was silent. "I can tell you've got news Elias, and something tells me it's not going to be all good" Rosario said to break the unease.

"Could be worse. The thing is, everyone" he said with a goodbye gesture "we've seen the last of our Buick. The Germans have requisitioned it."

"No car!"

"They are giving us a Citroën Traction Avant instead, querida."

"One of them! I've never liked them. So vulgar!" grimaced Rosario.

"The police use them because they're nippy" Elias said, to offset her derision.

"At least I've got my buggy!" Rosario sighed.

"About your buggy....."

"Have they got that too?"

"I've got you another one....." he said scrutinising her face, "with an engine!" he exclaimed dramatically.

"A car! You mean I've got a car!"

"I don't want my chiquita taking any risks with my son, and horses can be so temperamental."

"What is it?" Rosario asked, covering Elias' face with tiny kisses.

"A Topolino. Très à la mode for ladies" he said, prodding her gently. "And you will be driving by Christmas."

"You've booked me lessons at the Auto-École as well?"

*

It was mid afternoon, midweek and mid-term when Pepa's heart sank. She saw Paloma's diminutive figure push open the gate. "I never want to go back!" she cried, as her grandmother came hurrying down the stairs to meet her. "How did you manage to find your way home sweetheart"

"I watch Hamido when he takes us back to school on Sundays and it only takes as long as eating an orange."

"What on earth is going on here?" shouted Rosario from the terrace.

"I'm as much in the dark as you are!" Pepa shouted back. "She's only just got here!"

"Well? asked Rosario now facing Paloma.

"It's...Madame Justine..." .

"Your new teacher, well, what about her?" barked Rosario. "She's..."

"She's what? How come you're mute all of a sudden?"

"She's in shock" interjected Pepa "and she needs a drink

before she can tell us."

"She's gone!" said Paloma with a burst of tears.

"Is she dead?" asked Pepa.

"Madame Justine has disappeared and the big girls say she's eloped."

"Eloped? But she's a nun for God's sake!" exclaimed Rosario.

"What does it mean, "eloped", Maman?"

"Oh never mind that. Who has she eloped with?"

"I don't know about elope, but they say she's gone with a German officer like Monsieur Ludwig."

"And where on earth could SHE have met a German Officer!"

"Some are living in the big houses near uncle Samuel's, at the back of the school."

Rosario's mind drifted back to the bench by the fountain at the hotel in Meknès and she wanted to say good luck to her, but instead she shouted "outrageous! simply outrageous! A fine example for the girls I must say!"

"A little compassion perhaps, Rosario?" said Pepa with a hint of irony.

"She didn't have to become a nun, did she?"

"And you didn't have to be married, but you were......"

"Has she done something very bad then?"

"Of course not Mita" Pepa reassured her, "she's young and has changed her mind about certain things, that's all."

"Anyway," interrupted Rosario "what's all this got to do with you?"

"I liked her a lot Maman, and she liked me and now I have to go back to Madame Valéria! Please, can't you teach me at home Maman?"

"I'm taking you right back. And don't you ever run away from school again."

ELEVEN

A Package from Monségur

A letter arrived from Madame Notre Mère warning Elias and Rosario of possible expulsion following Paloma's truancy, but Paloma was reprieved and chastised instead.

Decided by the community of nuns, her punishment was to polish the silver during playtime for the rest of term.

In the absence of the eloped Madame Justine, a lay, private tutor supplemented her school work as necessary but Madame Valéria remained her form teacher. Dissatisfied with this arrangement, which she knew would harm Paloma, Pepa insisted on keeping her at home until a transfer to another school was arranged.

She was too compliant and anyone would think Paloma was hers, Rosario told her. Not in a conciliatory mood Pepa asked if she had forgotten why she was still in this foreign land. Rosario chose not to reply, but Pepa told her anyway. It was, she reminded her, to atone for her mishandling of the girls and especially of Paloma and she challenged Rosario to get on with motherhood so that she, now nearing her seventies, could take a back seat.

Things were as they were and there was nothing she could do to change them, cried Rosario. Then it was time she let others try and salvage the wreckage said Pepa. Carlota was not a problem vaunted Rosario and then wished she had kept her mouth shut. Carlota, Pepa reminded her, was a survivor and if she was drowning she would take her own mother down with her, or anyone else.

"These two have been the curse of my life from the start" moaned Rosario. "But this baby!"…..she said, stroking her belly. "This one is going to be different. This one is special, you'll see."

"Rosario.....What are you saying!"

"That I'm loving my son inside me."

"Can't you see that you are already manipulating your unborn child and further alienating the girls?"

*

Twice a day, Paloma thrived in her punishment. Wearing a large sack-cloth apron reaching down to her ankles and tied high up around her waist, she stood on a stool and was made to polish a mountain of silver cutlery, ornaments and altar pieces heaped on the large refectory table. After each item shone to her satisfaction she positioned it with delicate precision in its respective velvet case ready for inspection. A new sense of purpose, order, and beauty entered her life.

One dawn, a package arrived from Monségur, a mountainous stronghold of a gnostic sect in France, where beautiful gold chalices were made. It was left outside the tabernacle of the Eucharist, in a wooden crate nailed on all sides, and no one knew who had delivered it. The House Mother opened the box as if she was entering a secret room, before revealing a small gold chalice commissioned long before the outbreak of war by Madame Notre Mère for the school chapel. She placed it reverently on a red velvet cloth and asked Paloma to savour the moment before tackling the task of polishing it as she would never handle it again once it had been consecrated by Monseigneur Delecluze.

Paloma felt a quickening of her heartbeat before she even touched it. She had seen a light, if only for a moment, but so white and burning, that she had to cover her eyes to shade them from its fierceness. A warm flush surged through her body making her wish for a mountain breeze. She held the chalice above her head as a priest would at communion and as it gleamed against the diamond-shaped window on the high wall of the Sacristy, she saw her own glowing heart mirrored in it.

148

"That was a sign to teach you to polish your own heart too" Pepa said, when Paloma told her what she had seen when doing penance in school, "or it will tarnish and be of no use." Paloma wanted to know how could she keep her heart shiny, and Pepa replied that she must always speak the truth, be kind and do no harm. "That Paloma" she said "is what will keep it shiny."

Her private tutor had made no impact on Paloma's progress and as a last resort Paloma was sent to be assessed by Madame Notre Mère. She entered her office, curtsied and climbed onto the chair that was offered so that her legs dangled down high above the ground.

"Is 'Paloma' Spanish?" asked Madame Notre Mère when Paloma had stopped swinging her legs.

"Yes, Madame Notre Mère, it means dove."

"And do you speak Spanish Paloma?"

"Yes Madame Notre Mère. I spoke it before French because my grandmother and mother are Spanish and I was born in Spain" Paloma said, as if reciting a lesson.

"Do you speak other languages?"

"I understand Catalan because it is what my grandmother and mother speak when they don't want us to know something."

"And you understand it?"

"It is like French Madame Notre Mère."

"What about Arabic?"

"Only a bit, but my father speaks it like an Arab."

"Is he Moroccan?"

"No, he is really Irish but he doesn't speak English. His family came here from Ireland a long time ago, I think. "

"Do you enjoy talking?"

"Yes, because words are magic and they can make you sad or happy."

"What else do you like?"

"I like stories, my mother playing the piano and my grandmother's cuddles, and natillas, and I like to make my sister laugh."

"And does she?"

"She thinks I'm a clown and always asks me to pull faces."

"Do you enjoy that?"

"Yes, laughing is happy."

"Now tell me, what do you think is wrong with the school?"

"Madame Valéria, books and dinners, Madame Notre Mère."

"What is wrong with books?"

"They are empty Madame Notre Mère."

"But they are full of those magical words you like!"

"I can't see all the words Madame Notre Mère."

All at once Madame Notre Mère realised the root of Paloma's troubles.

In her report to Madame Valéria she praised Paloma's intelligence and directness, but an urgent visit to the optician was recommended.

However, Paloma's sight was declared flawless and she was pronounced a manipulative liar who had to be disciplined with the most degrading and punitive measure known to the Convent. She would parade in the playground before the whole school, bearing a cardboard hat with donkey's ears and a heavy placard that said, in medieval script, 'I AM A LIAR AND NO BETTER THAN A DONKEY'. But as dressing up was one of Paloma's favourite games and as the placard gave her a penguin-like gait and made everyone laugh, she was happy. She did not mind being a donkey either. She had always thought them beautiful, friendly and cuddly when she saw them passing the house with their heavy loads and was unable to feel degraded.

It was different for Carlota, and though burdened by the humiliation of having Paloma for a sister, she followed her everywhere to ensure that no harm befell her and when one girl kicked and pushed Paloma to the ground, Carlota was there to rescue her.

Paloma kept jolly throughout the Sunday lunch at The Orchard, but sighed, then wept, when alone with Pepa. "It's the Malaria again, isn't it? cried Pepa exasperated. "Keeps coming back like a bad fever!"

"I wish she was dead Yayita but my heart will tarnish because I wished her harm."

"Palomita, if someone hurts us, it is natural not to feel kindly towards that person, but after the anger has gone, you will come to wish that person well and your heart will shine again."

"She did it again Yayita."

"The cellar?"

"Yes, after the donkey parade."

"What parade?"

"I didn't mind that, but the cellar was horrid and like in a cave full of monsters and I was cold and afraid but Madame Aglaée said never mind about the fear if it makes you stronger. But I didn't understand."

"It takes time before you know how strong you are Mita."

"And will I have to go back there to get stronger?"

"Perhaps not there, but there will be other caves sweetheart."

*

"Coupons? You mean we're going to be deprived?"

"Not as much as some, Rosario" Elias replied. "Our warehouse is bulging with supplies."

"What about shoes, and clothes, and face cream and perfume?"

"As la Yaya said, those are non essentials and we'll have to make do."

"Non essentials? And how long will this misery last?"

"Till the end of the war, I guess."

"The beggars" worried Pepa, "can we keep that up?"

"Joaquín has promised us as much milk and potatoes as we want from the farm."

"It will be the worst Christmas ever!" moaned Rosario.

"No, the finest Rosario!" enthused Pepa. "For the first time in The Orchard, everyone will have to bring their own offering, just as Christmas should be!"

"Boy! You must have lapped it up during the Civil War! I'll never understand people who thrive on want!" scorned Rosario.

"I'll tell you Rosario. It makes you appreciate the insignificant, feel alive and part of a community. It makes you self-reliant and creative about every aspect of life and it connects you with each and everyone in the human chain. Are these good enough reasons for you Rosario?" replied Pepa, not succeeding in remaining collected.

Samuel sent for Rosario. She had not visited Colette since her argument with Sami and it was Colette's rapidly failing health that prompted the request. Rosario wished she did not have to see her friend and when she beheld Colette's face, small and taught, looking the palest it had been against her sea of dazzling cushions, she wished she could run away.

"Ma chérie..." Colette breathed. Her fleshless hand reaching for hers. "Here... sit on the pouffe, that's it. Not too close...The baby...must think of the baby..."

"Colette... I'm..."

"It's alright. I know you wanted to come, but Sami, your argument...about the girls boarding...I know. I just wanted to see you, my sweet."

"Where is he?"

"In the study, should I need him."

"I've missed you Colette. I couldn't..."

"Sami......the baby... I know... "

"It's going to be a boy, I know it!"

"I'm sorry I won't be there for his coming..."

"Colette, don't..." begged Rosario.

"Listen, that's why you're here. Remember those times we shared together, the books, the reading, the passionate debating..."

"I shall never forget."

"The point is, chérie, the point is, all-that-was-a-load-of-rubbish!"

"Colette!"

"I've just found out you see..." she gasped, sinking deeper into her cushions. "This box here," she said painfully pointing

152

at her head, "it's all a con, a mirage. The pot of gold we chase, an optical illusion. The reality, my sweet" she breathed, sliding her hand over her heart, "is here."

"Yes..." croaked Rosario with emotion. "I know...I know."

"I mean Love, Rosario. That's all there ever was, is, and ever will be."

"You have loved Colette" choked Rosario.

"Yes. I have known men and as many women, but I have only loved Sami. And you..." She whispered this with a tremor and then let her body slump, as if released from a hefty burden.

"My dearest..." wept Rosario.

"I love you chérie. That's what I wanted to say." Her misty and wide eyes bore deeper into their purple sockets. "Don't go yet" she murmured. "See that bundle under the piano? It's for you, my music. I want you to have it. I want you to feel me by your side when you play it. Now go Rosario. Tutto e finito! Adieu ma chérie until we meet again, and we are free to love. You, me."

Even before Samuel phoned the news the following morning, Rosario who had seen Colette dancing in her dreams that night knew that she had died, gone the lingering way of the heroine's death—a death that consumes the body as it liberates the soul.

For a long time afterwards, Pepa answered the girls' questions on the nature of death. She described it as a gentle entering into a stream, then floating on a river of molten gold and arriving at a place where you had always wanted to be, without past, present or future.

Shortly after Colette's death, Rosario was rushed into the Clinic Moulay Yousef with a threatened miscarriage. A week's sedation and complete rest saw her home ready for her confinement. In her absence, her bedroom had been painted sky-blue, the drapes renewed, and the balcony converted into an exotic aviary and botanical paradise. When in it, she disappeared into a world of maternal fantasy previously unknown to her. She learned new cradle songs, knitted booties in angora wool—dozens of them—then scattered them on her counterpane like newly hatched blue chicks, and decorated the cot with satin ribbons and crisp embroidered linen ordered from La Maison d'Irlande in Tangier. The transformation pleased Pepa until Rosario began reading again. Resting her mind as well as her body Pepa cautioned her, and surrounding herself with God-made beauty and simplicity was what she needed now, but Rosario complained that all she could do was read, and that anyway, she couldn't hear herself think, with Elias' crazy canaries in the aviary, except that she had thought about what she wanted her son to be when he grew up. To imprint her desires on the unborn child Pepa warned her, interfered with a journey which was not hers to travel.

Rosario's waters broke soon after Elias had left The Orchard to oversee a shipment at the Port. Within minutes the midwife was at her bedside and the infant wriggled out of Rosario's womb like a glow-worm out of the dark, blinked, then wide-eyed, inspected his surroundings. Pepa massaged his wrinkly feet and head with oil of pine kernels and bathed him afterwards in a small enamel bowl. On Rosario's orders Elias was not to know that he had a son until she could see his face when he discovered it for himself. Samuel collected the girls from school on special leave to meet their new baby brother. They arrived as Elias, with an eagerness that later embarrassed him, parted the towel in which the baby was wrapped. "A son! Thank you querida" he sobbed. "Did you suffer much?"

"I hardly knew he'd arrived. He was eager to get out that one. Not so, for the wretched worm! It will have to wait until my insides have settled, the midwife said." She took Elias' hand. And said how different she felt this time.

"What shall we call him querida?"

"Something magnificent. I thought Alexandre!"

"Alexandre, Elias, Samuel!" he pronounced, embracing his wife and son. "You've made me the happiest man alive."

"Was he inside a parcel?" asked Paloma, tip-toeing over to the cot.

"In a way" replied Pepa. "You're very quiet Carlota. do you want to hold your baby brother after Paloma?"

"No! Will he suck your teats when he's hungry?"

"Only animals do that" Rosario replied, irritated by Carlota's crudeness. "And primitive people. The baby will be fed with a bottle."

*

Mid-summer night, Rosario decided, would be a momentous time of the year for Alexandre's christening.

Samuel, now reconciled with Rosario after Colette's death, was to be the godfather and replacing Colette as the godmother, was the wife of one of Elias' associates. Every Butler was there, except Geraldo, Elias' banished younger brother and Marina, his circus wife.

Friends and colleagues of Elias were all known to Rosario but not Dionisio Atalaya to whom she took an instantaneous liking. One of Elias' distant cousins, Dionisio was there on business from New York, where he was a Director of the General Motors Company.

The champagne, saved by Elias in his warehouse popped, bubbled and spilled, as if this was a time of boom and not of privation. Trini, Elias' younger sister, performed her usual repertoire of improvisations on the piano, and Madame Kuntz, a large Teutonic beauty with a yapping Pekinese in her arms bellowed Lili Marlene until Samuel stuffed an egg en aspic in her mouth. Outside, between the goat-house and the kennels, the children played the 'I'll show you, if you show me' game.

Bouchaib was never wrong about his divinations and the plague of locusts which he had predicted the day before the christening came to pass, devastating the crops and trapping guests in The Orchard overnight as millions of winged grasshoppers descended from the skies in apocalyptic clouds, crashing with a rhythmic metallic sound against windows or any obstacle they encountered in their erratic flight. Cars and pedestrians came to a blind halt. Only the foolish or the greedy stayed out with their make-shift muslin nets to catch, then roast what they regarded as delicacies. It was said that not far from the Derb Jaleb the previous year, a pregnant woman who ventured out with a net to catch the locusts to feed her family, was eaten alive by swarms of them, until nothing but her hair and her unborn infant's eyes were left. Pepa dare not voice her thoughts on what the symbolic implication of the plague of locusts striking on the day of Alexandre's christening might be.

*

For weeks Elias' chest felt tight on awakening. Docteur Goslin, a young cardiologist newly arrived from France said Elias' health was deteriorating. His life-style had to change or his diet of fatty foods, alcohol and cigarettes would kill him within five years.

"Didn't I tell you?" jeered Joaquín. "Living for the present is all very well Elias, but you're a family man and they need you."

"And what do you propose I do?"

"Stop smoking, no booze, no meat and take daily exercise, just like the good doctor told you!"

"You really expect me to give up my steak tartare, paté de foie gras, my Camels, my whisky, vermouth and table wine all at once? Why don't you give me a monk's habit and shove me in a cell? The trouble with you Joaquín" he went on before his brother could interrupt, "is that you are a zealot. If you'd said to me, 'cut down Elias, piano, piano, I would have listened! Moderation Joaquín! ….Not bloody fanaticism!"

"No one could accuse you of leading a moderate life Elias!"

"That may well be, but all the same, you don't know how to get the best out of me."

"What about Alex. Don't you want to see him grow?"

"Leave it Joaquín…"

"Well don't come crying to me when things get tough Elias!"

"Wait a minute! As I recall, it is you who has done the crying in the past!"

"Crying? Me? Come on… When?"

"When you lost all your money!"

"What are you on about? I've never lost any money in my entire life!"

"No? What a short memory you have. Barcelona, 1932. You were wiped out through your own miscalculations. And who baled you out? Your brother Elias, that's who. You started again from scratch with the capital I gave you, no questions asked and I've never had a repayment!"

"Oh... that?.."

"You owe me Joaquín. And don't you forget it!"

"The best is to look after yourself Elias, then you won't need me!" he chuckled.

"Let's change the subject" Elias said, hating himself for losing control. "How about a swim twice a week then? And let's have lunch at the Lido afterwards with Rosario, the kids and Samuel."

*

Alexandre could tread water at three months and for Rosario, that and everything that Alexandre did, was a momentous sign. He floated and bobbed along, his tiny face barely above the water and for a brief period he was the Lido's undisputed aquatic star, until Hassan, Morocco's young Prince, eclipsed his stardom when he and his sister began to use the pool. Hassan pirouetted from the highest diving board to be met under the water by the two girls and other admirers.

For Elias and his brothers a swimming pool was nothing more than an expanded bath, suitable only for children and their mothers, or the frail and infirm. They never swam there, preferring to cut through the frothy Atlantic waves and swim far out to sea. At lunch, Rosario ventured to ask why Geraldo could not be amongst them and why he was still a persona non grata.

"He's our little black sheep, that's why!" sneered Joaquín, adding that as it happened, he was working for him.

"Can't be?" they all chorused.

"He's asked me to teach him the real estate business!"

"Geraldo? Our little Geraldo?" Elias gasped.

"I had to. He hadn't got over his spot of trouble...you know..."

"No!" said Elias.

"You knew about his horses didn't you?"

"I heard he sometimes supplied the Sultans' stables, that's all" replied Elias.

"Well, an infection wiped out the lot before he could sell them, and he's bankrupt."

"Has he got any horses left?"

"If you knew him Rosario" said Samuel, "you wouldn't ask that question. They are his life! Of course he has. A couple of them at least, for his personal pleasure."

"D'you know, I could have sworn I saw him passing the house in his racing buggy the other day" confided Elias. It annoyed Rosario that he hadn't called her when he saw him and he promised that if she was discreet, he would point him out next time he passed The Orchard. "Anyway," Elias chanced, turning towards Joaquín, "isn't it time for a truce?"

"Not so fast. My seeing Geraldo is business. He knows, only too well, what he did to our father when he left the family for that circus woman and we can't forgive and forget just like that!" he replied snapping his fingers.

"God almighty Joaquín, that's a lifetime ago!"

"Family honour Rosario. You, as a thoroughbred Spaniard should understand that, and I, as the elder of the family must carry that burden."

"We're not talking Calderón de la Barca here, are we? This is the twentieth century for God's sake!"

"Caldo who?"

"Never mind Joaquín" said Rosario downcast, "it was just a facetious literary remark to do with Spanish honour."

"And Irish honour too, don't forget!"

"I didn't know they had any!" Rosario hurled back.

"Rosario!" Elias rebuked.

"Sorry Elias, sorry Joaquín, sorry Samuel and sorry to all your ancestors of Kilkenny!"

"You should drop Binot at the house before Rosario leaves

for the Lido next time!" butted in Elias, hoping to rescue Rosario from her deliberate faux pas, "it would be fun for the girls"

"He's with his mother" Joaquín said in a lacklustre tone.

"Is Olympia with you?" asked Rosario intrigued.

"No, no, no, she's in Paris."

"So Binot's with her?"

"We flew there at the end of term, and she'll bring him back in August. Would you like to meet her?" he asked Rosario.

"I'm very curious about Olympia," Rosario admitted, "tell me about her."

"We bumped into each other at a Theosophical Convention in Aix when my Maria was dying of Tuberculosis. She was wonderful to her and a great comfort to me."

"I didn't know Olympia was a Theosophist."

"Actually she's a Spiritualist, but sometimes the two get mixed up. We're divorcing you know…"

"We didn't!.." Rosario and the others exclaimed.

"I'm not too happy about her influence on young Binot."

"But he's with her now!"

"He is young and I can easily debrief him when he's back with me."

"That bad eh…" Rosario mumbled.

"At least he's not in boarding school. Not until he's older and he has a strong base" he chided.

"The girls love it in boarding school" protested Rosario.

"Correction" interrupted Samuel. "One does."

Rosario was to meet Olympia at a conference in the Arab quarter near the harbour, the day after her return from Paris. The occult nature of the assignment worried Pepa and she begged Rosario to ask Simone, her piano teacher's niece, who had attended several spiritualist seances, to accompany her. Ahmed drove them through the dust, mélée and the cacophony of the medina, with water vendors and shouts of 'harira,' 'kepta,' all touting for custom. He pointed to the spot between his eyebrows when they stopped, and told Rosario and her companion to watch for the evil eye. And to protect Madame from Gnus, he pressed a small medal of Fatima's Hand into Rosario's palm.

They entered a long, dark, stone floored corridor and were met by a woman who introduced herself as Madame Vladimira, and as Olympia's spirit sister. She drifted, bare-footed, in a full length maroon muslin gown, and led the way with an oil lamp which she held at arms' length leaving a suffocating trail of black smoke behind her. Rosario's high-heeled shoes echoed like a hammer on an anvil on the stone floor until Madame Vladimira ordered her to remove them, lest the rhythmic tapping disturbed the spirit world. She rapped three times at the studded door when they arrived. It opened into a cave-like room. The name of Madame Petrova Blavatsky was written in large red letters on a gold banner covering the entire wall facing the audience. Below it, sitting very still and crouched on a child's desk, was a woman with a serene, translucent blue gaze, and a purple scarf wound several times around her throat. "Rosario et compagnie?" she asked in a rich voice.

"Olympia?" checked Rosario with a small voice.

"C'est ça. Asseyez vous au premier rang" she said, like a school marm.

Someone bellowed "Silence!" and announced that Madame Olympia C. Narfios was about to address the brotherhood.

"It's all women here!" muttered Simone stifling a giggle.

"Friends!" Olympia thundered with her arms wide open, "let me now read to you a passage from the Old Commentary of the Secret Doctrine.

"William Butler Yeats—was a Blavasky disciple, did you know?" whispered Simone.

Stimulated by the Irish connection, Rosario lightened up. The lights went off leaving the hall in darkness and Olympia brought the flame of a candle nearer to her script. "Darkness" her cavernous voice orated, "is a place of fruition, a place where the seed in the soil will later grow into a flower, opening its petals for the sun to feed and nourish it." She was supremely precise and enunciated her words like a priestess, her eyes flickering before she continued. "We need the darkness of the

160

deep earth for without it there would be no appreciation of the light"... But Rosario had stopped listening and though much taken by Olympia and her quotation, something about the intangible claustrophobic eeriness of the hall warned her that all was not well. "Let's go" she whispered, dragging Simone by the elbow and feeling overwhelmed by a sense that she was being taken over.

"Not everyone in that hall had pure intentions" Simone explained, when they were outside in the fresh air. "Some were there to misuse their psychic powers for their own ends and that is what you picked up. But be in no doubt" she added, "that those words from The Old Commentary, perfectly interpreted by Madame Olympia are gems of wisdom for all time."

*

Quite frankly" cried Rosario as she slumped on the armchair and kicked off her shoes in the air, "I'm not too surprised Joaquín is weary of Olympia's activities."

"What happened there?" asked Pepa.

"It was heady stuff" she said pretending to wipe her brow. "I'm jolly glad Simone was with me."

"And Olympia?"

"I felt she was out of place. She's strange alright, but I honestly sense that she belongs in a brighter, sweeter, finer sort of place. I can't really explain it."

"But is young Binot safe with her?"

"It's not Olympia who's dangerous, it's what surrounds her I'm sure."

"All the same, children should not be exposed to occult forces. They need to develop their own protection first. Once they have it, it's up to them."

*

The episode at the theosophical hall had given Rosario a craving for open spaces with limitless horizons and she began riding

161

lessons with Martin Fierro, an exiled Argentinian gaucho.

Let's discover new places and see the world, she told Elias after hearing Martin's impassioned talk of the Pampas. She hadn't begun to explore the wonders of this beautiful land, he remonstrated.

"Why don't we, then! We never go anywhere wild and exciting!"

"Now is the time to stay put querida" he said. "You can see that!"

"The war you mean?"

"We're safer here than anywhere else."

"And the invasion?" she asked as if that was the next most exciting thing.

"It will be over before we know it."

"And then what?" she asked, overtaken with boredom.

"The Americans will drive the Germans and Italians out of North Africa and create a safe zone for the Allies to get into Europe."

"They'll be around a while then?"

"Till the end of the war."

"I wonder how it will affect life in Casablanca" she said perking up.

"There'll only be a few based here. Most of them will be in Tripoli and Egypt guarding the Suez canal."

"It's all quite exciting!"

"So why go elsewhere when all the theatre is right here under our very noses?"

"Is it true that the Americans will be lodging with families?"

"So I hear."

"Shall we welcome one in our home?" she said teasingly.

"I don't want any Yanks ogling my beautiful wife when I'm not around."

"You... Othello you..!" She dramatised, as if she was on the stage.

"Who?"

"Othello, you know!......."

"Is he the one with the hump?"

"Never mind " she said with a dismissive gesture, "I wouldn't like it either. Having an American as a lodger, I mean. They're so immature, arrogant and uncouth. Gary Cooper aside."

"By the way" Elias said, "how are the art classes with madame Truffaud?"

"I love it!" she exulted. "I'm painting Mina, madame Truffaud's maid, in oils "

"Talking of which..." Elias said.

"I can feel a treat coming on Elias... What is it?" she cried, "tell me!"

"I've commissioned El Señor Cruz Errera!"

"The famous painter from down the road? To teach me?"

"For your portrait!"

Rosario gulped then hugged Elias too tight for his comfort.

"Can I dress as a Gran Señora for it?" she asked, pointing her nose up in the air.

"You are a Gran Señora, querida!"

Don José Cruz Errera announced himself, lightly kissing Rosario's hand and guiding her by the elbow towards the window. "With the blind pulled half way down to catch this sol y sombra..." he said, talking to himself, and at the same time handing Rosario a sensuous silk mantilla and a sleeveless figure-hugging corsage in midnight blue brocade. Rosario had never worn such a bewitching garment in her life, but she felt herself tremble with a sense of recognition.

"Doña Rosario, the lady, is in there somewhere too....." the maestro mused. "I mean, the 'Lady with the Rosary... The Virgin..." he went on, arranging the milky-white mantilla loosely over her shoulders. "But... this!" he added taking a dramatic step backwards, "is the woman I want to see!"

"Who is she, Don José?" she asked, almost daring not to .

"The demi-mondaine, señora ..." he whispered. And she worried aloud about what others might think. "Only you, Señora, and Don Elias will see through the double-entendre..."

"And the mother in me?" she found herself asking.

"That will be encapsulated in the black pearl pendant nestling in the small hollow of your bosom."

Rosario asked him to explain and he hushed in her ear that the pearl was lunar, dark, mysterious and female, adding that a painting was an exercise of the imagination, a careful deciphering of layers and that the painter and the sitter had to be as one.

"The Maja!" Elias gazed at the finished chiaroscuro portrait. "My Maja, my private Rosario." he whispered .

*

The girls stumbled upon two trenches. They had strayed from Fatima on their way to the Medina to collect the daily milk. They looked down, then ran, but not before they peered into the second trench.

"We must tell Maman" said Carlota breathless. "But if we do, she'll never let us leave the house ever again and our holidays will be horribly boring!"

"Let's tell yaya instead" suggested Paloma and they told her what they saw in the two trenches near the milk farm.

"You kept away from them I hope."

"We only looked inside."

"That's alright then."

"They were playing with their tongues."

"Who were?"

"The man and two women inside the trench."

"Did they see you?"

"The man stood up when he saw us and said 'Viens! Joie garantie' and we didn't know what he meant and he lifted his djellabah and we saw his thing, bigger than Alexi's and Binot's and we ran."

"Bendito sea Dios!"

"But we had to look inside the other one because they were moaning."

"Who were?"

"The two men."

164

"Had they been injured?"

"They were stuck together like doggies."

"Ave Maria Purísima!" cried Pepa, crossing herself.

"Is it that bad?" asked Carlota.

"Men are not dogs, Tita. They were made to look at each other in the eye."

"Will you tell Maman?" she asked.

*

Anywhere near the milk farm was banned for the rest of the Summer vacation. The girls had to stick by Fatima's side at all times whenever they went out. This meant that she took them to her home in the Medina on her day off where they sat cross-legged drinking mint tea around a brass coffee table with her nine sisters and umpteen female friends, before they took off for their weekly Hammam. Altogether and amidst indiscriminate splashing and laughter they scrubbed their legs and arms with huge loofahs until their limbs were left hairless and glistening. They washed each others' long hair under continually running water from a rusty pipe along the wall and giggled and sang like children at a birthday party. The girls pleaded to return every Friday. They could, Fatima said, only if they did not tell their mother.

But when the doctor was called about their incessant scratching and ringworm was diagnosed on the girls' scalp, which he said must have been contracted from someone in the medina, they had to tell.

Despite calls for mercy from Pepa, Fatima was summarily dismissed and Alcaya, a beautiful young Berber widow succeeded her and moved into The Orchard with Abdelouakil, her twelve-year-old son.

*

The Americans began their attack to remove the German presence in Casablanca. Every night, sirens announced an

165

impending air-raid. Samuel suggested the girls became day pupils until the cessation of hostilities as the German Head Command was only minutes away from the Convent. Rosario thought him unnecessarily alarmist and declined. The Convent's own air raid siren reverberated in the dormitories every night and the House Mother, organised the pupils in the basement with prayers and hymns until the end of the raid.

Out of habit from the war days in Spain, Pepa listened to the six o'clock news with her early morning bowl of coffee. That morning, news came of an explosion at the girl's Convent. She ran upstairs to inform Rosario when Samuel phoned to say his flat, a few hundred yards from the school, had shook with the force of the bombing and that he was on his way to find out about the girls.

It occurred at five-thirty in the morning, half an hour before Mass when the pupils would have been crossing the playground on their way to the chapel. Leading the column of nuns for the Angelus before the start of Mass was Madame Valéria. The exploding bomb left a huge crater, separating the school from the chapel. Madame Valéria and four other nuns were killed instantly, their remains were never recovered.

The Americans had targeted the German Headquarters but missed.

Samuel arrived amidst screaming girls still in nightgowns, the spared nuns, flapping like bats, gathering their pupils together as best they could, distraught neighbours and flashing lights from Red Cross ambulances.

Crouched together, Samuel, found Carlota and Paloma under one of the refectory tables and he did not wait for anyone's permission to take them away. Within hours the debris was partially cleared and the whole school evacuated. Those children unclaimed by friends, neighbours or relatives were transferred, bewildered, to the main aisle of the Cathedral of the Sacré Coeur nearby, for parents to collect later.

The two girls huddled together in the buggy on the way home, like chicks in a nest after a storm. No words Samuel spoke to them could dispel the horror of their ordeal. The nightly raids had become a boring routine like so many others the girls endured at the school, and the bomb was a disconnected event which made no sense to them.

Joaquín was at The Orchard as soon as he heard, and Rosario, Elias, Pepa and the servants waited for Samuel. The girls ran to Pepa first, then to their mother, who knelt to embrace them.

"Alabado sea Dios" intoned Pepa. "Thanks be to God" the rest echoed.

In silence, they sat inside the house drinking coffee and warm milk for the girls that Alcaya had made for them.

"It was like that time in the other place Yayita" mumbled Paloma, after downing her milk in one gulp.

"What other place Mita?"

"A long time ago before Carlota. Do you remember?"

"When you were inside the shawl?" asked Pepa.

"And you were always running and I was bouncing in the shawl. And my head hurt."

"I forbid you to make up stories!" said Rosario exasperated. Paloma cried that she didn't. Then Rosario warned the girls that the bombing was no excuse for a holiday. They would have to behave or they would not have Sunday leave when school began again..

Every day, Pepa took the opportunity to teach them the rudiments of cooking. "Maman said the kitchen is no place for ladies" moaned Carlota.

"Ladies or not, food preparation is good for the soul."

"What's the soul Yaya?"

"It's the best bit of you..." answered Paloma, "the bit you cannot see and the bit that cannot die."

"How do you know that?"

"I don't know how I know!" Paloma cried, holding her palms upwards.

"You're freaky! You know that?" Carlota said, unleashing a sudden flood of tears in Paloma, who wept that she had killed Madame Valéria—she had wished her dead, and it had come true, with the bomb.

"You'll be punished for having bad thoughts about her" Carlota snarled, "and you'll meet her in Purgatory and you'll have to spend millions and millions of years with her and she'll send you to the burning basement there, forever."

"I'll ask her to forgive me" Paloma snivelled.

"You can't, she's dead."

"I'll talk to her soul then."

"Only saints can do that."

"Everybody can."

"Enough of that you two. Get on with your vinaigrette, Carlota. And if you stop squabbling, I'll even tell you a story."

*

In November 1942, an ill-planned British-American force floundered ashore between Casablanca and Fédala. The might of the Atlantic in the late Autumn took the navy by surprise and the army waded ashore, sea-sick and exhausted. Although a humiliating fiasco, that landing was nevertheless the first step towards the liberation of Morocco. The German occupation was over and a mood of celebration set in, mostly among the French colonials. But for some, this was far from liberation. Overnight, male residents of Italian descent were rounded up and herded into concentration camps in the barren surrounding countryside.

Carlo, Trini's Italian husband, three generations away from his country of origin, saw Morocco as his only home but he (as hundreds of others) was bundled into an open truck destined to be a prisoner of a war he had never fought, simply because his name was Costello.

"Pourquoi mon Dieu!" Trini wailed when she came to Elias as she did when she needed support. Penniless, with a twelve-year- old daughter, she had never worked (nor did it enter her mind that she should),and a weekly account was settled for the duration of her husband's internment. Her small luxury pavillon at Ain-Diab on the Corniche had to be relinquished for a minuscule basement flat in the less than prestigious district of the Maârif.

Trini swore that her balding, already in an early stage had intensified, since her parting from Carlo. She began to chew her fingernails until her fingers bled, and her one sole asset—to spontaneously reproduce any tune on the piano (and for which she was sought after at social occasions) vanished with the stigma of Carlo's internment. Pretty and dainty in her youth, it was easy to understand how Carlo—playboy extraordinaire— had been smitten by Trini. She was eighteen when they married, and when their daughter Tania was born the following year, Carlo's philandering resumed with a vengeance, plunging Trini into a permanent state of masochistic adoration of her husband.

Powerless to help, except financially, Elias hinted that Rosario might. "I can't" she protested. "She's such a misery. And" she added, when Elias looked at her pleadingly "she's terribly jealous of me!" .

"Why shouldn't she be. You've got everything!"

"She's got what she deserves" Rosario said unreservedly.

"What? For her innocent husband to be sent to a concentration camp, completely out of the blue? Rosario, have a heart!"

"I've never seen her trying to improve her circumstances."

"That's because she lacks confidence!"

"Intelligence you mean!"

"Well, both."

"Why should I spend an afternoon a week with her whining and crying!"

"Crying is her only weapon, Rosario."

"And boy... doesn't she know how to open the flood gates when it suits her!"

"She's a victim, Rosario. I beg you, visit her and take the girls, for Tania's sake."

"That one!"

"Now what?"

"You'd think she was eighteen, not twelve!"

"What do you mean? She's the scrawniest child I've ever seen!"

"Scrawny, yes. But have you looked at her eyes?"

"What about them?"

"Not of her age Elias. Surely as a man you must have noticed! I bet you anything she's no child. I can't think how our girls could amuse her!"

"Heaven forbid that all you say is true, but whatever, pitiable as she is, Trini is my little sister. Families stick together Rosario, for better or worse. Will you do it for me?"

*

She began her weekly mercy missions (as she called them) by handing Trini an envelope with the financial settlement from Elias which sustained her and Tania. Trini thought Rosario beautiful, elegant, witty but too clever by half. Intelligent women, she thought secretly, should at least not look it, for not only was it an unattractive trait but a barrier to getting what a woman wanted. She took the envelope from Rosario's hand and said how fabulously glamorous she looked.

"What matters is how you carry yourself Trini."

"You carry yourself beautifully."

"Everyone can, Trini."

"You are younger than me Rosario."

"By six months!"

"I've aged since they took my Carlo away" Trini said, adjusting the bandeau that held a few strands of her hair together.

"Is everything to your satisfaction in the flat? Elias asked me to check that you had all you needed."

"He's our guardian angel. He's the generous one in the family, always helping the rest of us. Joaquín, Lourdes and now me. He never could say no. Such a sweetie, our Elias!"

"Perhaps it's time sweetie started saying no!"

"Then he wouldn't be our Elias!"

"Is there anything you'd like Trini?"

"I don't know how to ask this...it's..."

"Out with it!" shouted Rosario not concealing her impatience.

170

"It's just that…it might sound…how shall I put it…"

"I'm waiting…"

"Rosario" she said, plucking up courage, "have you any clothes you don't wear any more?"

"Ah!"

"I knew it, I shouldn't have asked!"

"On the contrary, I have a bundle ready for the poor of Saint Vincent de Paul parish."

"Can I have them?"

"Ahmed will deliver the lot."

"You're so kind" she whined.

"Is there anything else?"

"I thought… maybe…"

"What?"

"You'd let me play your piano sometime?"

"It's very finely tuned" Rosario said sharply. And after a silence she added, "you'll treat it with respect, won't you?"

"As if it was my own!"

"That's what I'm afraid of" she mumbled between her teeth, and then she obliged grudgingly. "I'll send Ahmed to pick you up on Wednesdays."

"Could you bring the girls next time Rosario if they're still off school because of the bombing?"

"I'll send them instead of me."

Rosario's eyes surveyed the flat without moving her head.

"Quite small isn't it? Where are the bedrooms?"

"Voilà!" cried Trini, unhinging a double bed from the wall.

"My goodness!" exclaimed Rosario moving sideways.

"They say it's an American invention."

"It would be. And the kitchen?"

"Voilà again!" squeaked Trini opening a cupboard door.

"Gracious me! How amazing" adding how dark the room was.

"We have no windows here and have to run up the basement stairs when we want to see daylight."

"A bit of a rabbit warren then?"

"Beggars can't be choosers, Rosario…" Trini replied with a calculated tremor.

"At least you don't need servants!"

"Thank heaven for small mercies!" said Trini looking heavenwards.

"There you are then. Not all bad, eh?"

"One last thing Rosario..." said Trini pressing herself against Rosario getting ready to leave.

"Yes..." she hissed, stepping backwards as if Trini had halitosis.

"Do you think we can borrow the car and Ahmed for our monthly visits to the camp?"

"Your Elias will say yes of course..." jeered Rosario.

"Will you have a glass of Porto before you leave?" Trini pleaded, attempting to prolong the visit.

"Porto? How quaint! D'you often drink during the day?"

"When I'm lonely."

"I must get going. Plenty to do" Rosario said, gathering her handbag and gloves. "I'll send the girls, the envelope and some fig jam from la Yaya next week."

"You're so very kind Rosario..." she whimpered.

"Please don't cry Trini!"

*

"Checking up on him, are you?" said Rosario.

"Just making sure he behaves himself" Joaquín replied walking into the lounge uninvited. "He says he's cut down on cigarettes" she whispered, following him in, "but I've seen stubs floating in the toilet bowl" she added, biting her tongue afterwards for telling on Elias.

"He never had any will-power" he retorted, "ever since he was a toddler. Five, before he was potty trained."

"Not everyone has your will of iron Joaquín."

Elias came into the room and she whispered not to mention the stubs.

"Ah... Joaquín, pirata!" shouted Elias, "I've just spent a couple of hours with Samuel. Did you know he was a partner with the Dubails?"

"New business between them?" asked Joaquín, raising his eyebrows.

"They've become associates!"

"Do you know this couple? I mean, who are they?"

"The wife seems very canny" continued Elias. "Perhaps we ought to keep an eye on things. Samuel's not been quite himself since Colette. They've even been to Arcachon together" he added.

"That's a bit odd!"

"This place holds too many memories. Maybe he needs a change" Elias said, "and he also told me that social life in Casa had become unpleasant with Americans swarming around!"

*

In a deluge of tears the like of which Rosario had never witnessed before, Trini welcomed her when she dropped Carlota and Paloma off at the flat for the afternoon. She had just come back from her first visit to the concentration camp in Siddi Bennon. She cried that it was a sad and bewildering place, where many of the American guards in the camp were themselves of Italian origin and looked upon their prisoners as brothers. Carlo was reasonably well but she sobbed that he was wafer-thin from worrying himself sick about Tania and longing for his Trini (and she placed her hands on her crotch as she told Rosario this.)

Rosario begged her to stop dramatising and wailing, since the news about Carlo was not good, but neither was it bad. She cut short her visit, and left a bottle of Porto on the trestle table, some provisions in a cardboard box that Pepa had prepared, a discarded riding skirt and the money envelope.

"Your mother's the kindest of all, and isn't she a picture!" cried Trini, loud enough for Rosario to hear as she climbed the stairs to the street.

"Everybody in school say she's like a film star" said Paloma proudly.

"I wish I was her!"

"Maybe that's why you're bald" suggested Carlota.

"She means you shouldn't wish for more than what you have" amplified Paloma, trying to minimise the criticism.

"Carlo adores me just as I am" she said trying hard to look theatrical.

"What shall we do, auntie Trini? And where's Tania?" asked Carlota.

"She's gone for a ride in an American jeep."

"That's lucky!" said Paloma.

"They bombed our school, did you know..." added Carlota in a derogatory tone.

"They didn't mean to, everybody knows that. It was a terrible mistake" replied Trini.

"D'you like Americans, auntie Trini?" inquired Paloma trying to sound grown-up.

"They're good to my Carlo in the camp and bring things here for my Tania and me."

"What things?" asked Carlota.

"Coffee...sugar...nylons...gum...nice soap and..."

"D'you have to pay lots of money for them?" she asked again.

"Tania is nice to them."

"Yaya says that's best" said Paloma. "Be kind to people, I mean."

The girls told Trini the Americans drove around in their Jeeps and followed the nuns and the crocodile of boarders on Thursday afternoons, whistling and enticing them with stockings, cigarettes, and french letters, though they puzzled why the letters were not inside envelopes.

"Have some of their gum girls!" said Trini, throwing each of them a pack.

"Maman wont let us have any. She says it's vulgar."

"Well, she isn't here now" she told Paloma. "And come and sit by me and then we'll have some Liptons and thin toast."

"Papa only drinks Earl Grey" said Carlota.

"I know, but that's what I get from my American friends. Do you like stories?"

"Yeh!" the girls bounced excitedly.

"A real one or one from my head?"

"A real one" they echoed.

"About Papachito?"

"Who's Papachito?" they asked.

"You don't know? He was your great great grandfather, Joseph.

What Papachito loved most girls, was to travel and explore new places."

She paused for breath and to inhale several short and successive puffs on a Camel. "Then, when his son Zac, your father's father, was old enough, Papachito travelled all the time. He even visited the well divers in the desert and desert lakes" she said without any response from the girls.

"But one day he set off alone on his best horse—a racer called Bismillah—with only a few provisions, a cowhide to lie on at night and another as a blanket. He always wore a Djellabah and a turban so he would not be taken for a European and be attacked by highwaymen. Just before dusk, he spotted a huge oak tree and as he was about to settle under it for the night—are you ready for this girls? (and her voice dropped an octave) he saw a group of men galloping towards him. They were wild and shouting, brandishing their guns in the air, and some of them even fired them, and then they disappeared in a cloud of red dust. But Papachito knew they hadn't gone because he couldn't hear their horses galloping away and when the dust settled he saw them right in front of him. They stood still, eying each other for a long, long time. The chief, on his Palomino horse and all dressed in white had his face covered like a Tuareg. Then Papachito broke the silence. He spoke in Arabic. "Chief, your eyes are the eyes of a friend."

And the chief revealed his face and it was Ali Ben Kassem. Trini stopped for dramatic effect. The girls had not moved. "Don't you know who Ali Ben Kassem was?" she asked amazed.

"Was he a good man or a bandit?" asked Carlota, afraid to know.

"Ali Ben Kassem was an important man who once was a farmer and advisor to his village" Trini went on, "he and his family lived for many years outside the walls of Mazagan on the plateau near the lighthouse, where all our ancestors had acres and acres of land. Ali was then the proud owner of goats and asses, many horses and good land near to Papachito's. And then, during a very dry summer, the drought claimed all his animals and later, locusts ravaged his crops. He had nothing left and he and other farmers left in search of another patch of land. But no other land yielded as much as his land by the lighthouse and so, he continued to travel, looking for good land to feed his family. He travelled far, and after two more years of famine he became the most feared highwayman and looted villages and robbed travellers in order not to starve."

"Did he rob Papachito?" asked Carlota.

"He would have, but when Papachito uncovered his own face and Ali Ben Kassem saw who he was, he decided to kidnap him instead, and to keep him in his village until Papachito had taught him and the other villagers how to make their land bountiful, for it was Papachito who had once taught Ali Ben Kassem a system of planting in rotation, like Papachito's ancestors had done in Ireland. And Papachito stayed as their prisoner until the crops were plentiful again. He was happy with them and they loved him and called him 'Pacha' and asked him to become the village chief. But one day the governor of Mazagan sent a halallah to find him and when they found him, they brought him back home and all the family cried with joy."

Trini opened the Porto and took a sip straight out of the bottle.

"He was lucky Ali Ben Kassem remembered him, or he might have been killed!" exclaimed Carlota, trying not to get her words jumbled up in her excitement.

"Did Papachito always come back safe from his adventures?" asked Paloma.

Trini covered her face with her hands and wailed. "The...He...Papa...chito... never returned from his last journey!" she cried, between grotesque sobs, like hiccups from a sick cow.

176

"He didn't?" asked Carlota aroused. "Why?"

"I can't! I'll tell you another time. I'm too upset..."

"Let's have some tea!" suggested Paloma cheerfully.

"Yes. Tea. But first, come and curl up against me girls. I feel like a cuddle coming on." And she held them so tightly against her thin chest that their breathing nearly stopped.

The girls had nothing but praise for their aunt when Rosario asked about her and what they did. "She told us a story" replied Paloma. "A real one."

"At least it kept her from crying!"

"She did cry Maman" said Paloma.

"She cried in the story?"

"It's when she said about Papachito's last journey" whispered Paloma confidentially.

"She told you about Joseph?"

"Why don't you tell us stories about him? complained Carlota.

"I'm not good at it. You should ask your uncle Samuel. At least he'd make you laugh!"

Next from Trini came the story of her young brother Geraldo, of whom they knew nothing, not even that he existed. "We were babies together" she told them. "The others were older than us. We two were like twins, but he left home when he was still a boy, and no one ever forgave him." She gasped a deep sigh caught halfway to its completion, and wiped her tears with a multi-coloured handkerchief she pulled from inside her blouse, inscribed with 'I love you babe'.

"He ran away..." she expired at last, "with Marina, the ringmaster's daughter, when the Pavarotti circus came to town and they fell madly in love and were married within a week. He went to live with them and became a lion-tamer and he was so fantastic they called him El Supremo. My Geraldo was the best" she cried exploding in another flood of unquentionable tears.

"Did a lion eat him then?" asked Carlota certain he had come to a grizzly end.

"Lions adored him too..." she cried, her face drowning in

her own secretions. "I'm so sad girls, so sad...My little brother, Aldo...Gone."

"Do you feel a cuddle coming on?" asked Paloma gone all maternal.

"I do... I do... Come girls, sit down, your heads on Trini's heart. That's nice..." and she hiccupped her sick cow's hiccups again, then became silent and began to rock. Their heads heaved against her chest and Trini mumbled to the girls to suckle her nipples like babies. Her body convulsed. She stopped and stood up all at once, letting the girls fall off her lap. She muttered that she did not know what had come over her, and begged, "you mustn't...you mustn't tell..."

"Are you unwell?" asked Paloma confused.

"That's it...I'm ill. I've just had a fit girls. Yes, tell your father, that's what it was. A fit. And you'd better not come again until I'm better!"

"You mustn't cry, auntie" said Carlota. "We'll be back for more stories, and more cuddles."

Elias called in to see Trini as soon as Carlota told him about the fit. The girls, he told Rosario, should resume their visits as soon as possible to cheer her up. But Rosario found them quiet and withdrawn after their last visit was undecided, and told Elias as much.

"We send the girls there to sweeten her dreary life a little" Elias said. "So... she tells them stories and, cries a lot" he admitted. "She gives them tea and madeleines and even gum! What harm is she doing Rosario?"

"She's unstable Elias."

"Only once more then" begged Elias. "Anyway, don't they start school again next week?"

*

Rosario had led a sedentary life since Alexi's arrival. She marvelled at his least achievement and thought him the most beautiful and accomplished of children. She pampered herself less, and Elias' ardour for Rosario found a new vessel in his son. This unabated idolatry could easily destabilise the child, and Pepa was relieved at Dionisio's arrival from New York. Like the god himself, Dionisio's gift was his prodigious capacity for enjoyment and it was to Volubilis, the ancient Roman city with large mosaics depicting the revelling god Dionysius, that they took him to visit. And to satisfy his prodigious appetite for nightlife, every night, it was candle-lit dinners à trois, cabaret at the Guinguette, billing the young Piaf on tour that week and Sidney Bechet, to whose tender pitches he and Rosario found themselves dancing in the Guinguette's darkest corners, cheek to cheek.

A message that he had left for Paris on urgent business was pinned at the hotel reception board when they called to collect him for another soirée of indulgence, but Rosario knew at once that he had left hastily because she had bewitched him.

Bemoaning the loss of a budding romance she let herself sink into an orgy of self-pampering, and like a love-sick adolescent she lay in bed, listening to 'Que Reste-t-il De Nos Amours?' the closing down song at the Guingette.

"Here's a cup of broth" Pepa shouted, rolling up the shutters. "Playing games again?"

"What games?" said Rosario barely surfacing from under the sheets.

"It didn't take you long, did it?"

"It didn't take me long for what?" growled Rosario.

"Languishing over Dionisio! That's what!"

"D'you think Elias knows?" she asked sitting up and relieved that her secret was out.

"Elias hasn't a suspicious bone in his body" Pepa said dismissively.

"He has!" objected Rosario, sitting up. "In business, and things..."

"Things? What things?"

Rosario hesitated, then blurted out that it happened a long time ago just after they were married, and then half wished she hadn't said anything. When, exactly?" pursued Pepa.

"On our wedding night" Rosario said looking down.

"I see..." said Pepa trying to explore the thoughts behind

179

her eyes. "Do you want to tell me?"

She looked at her mother. "He was gentle and everything. He didn't hurt me..."

"But?"

"It was horrible!" she cried covering her face, before she could continue. "He made me roll out of bed onto the floor, you know... after we... and scrutinised every millimetre of the sheet for a blood stain. He said I couldn't be a virgin and that I'd tricked him and then he wanted to know who the first man was..." she whimpered.

"Cariño..."

"I couldn't believe that he, of all people" she snivelled, "could do a thing like that. He went berserk, mother!"

"Think, Rosario" Pepa said after a long pause. "Sure, Elias is a well-bred European, but remember he was raised in a different continent to us and who knows if checking like that isn't an accepted custom in this part of the world!"

"It's just that he spoiled the romantic thing, you know...between us."

"What happened after that?"

"Well, the following night he pushed further when we... and I had a bleed, and when he saw it he begged me to forgive him, and he cried for what he had done, and said over and over again that he would make it up to me for the rest of his life."

"And did you find it in your heart to forgive him?"

"Sort of... I kind of put it aside. He's always been so kind and generous, it didn't seem to matter any more."

"Why does it now, all of a sudden, Rosario?"

"I don't know..."

"You do!"

"I think you think it's to do with Dionisio don't you, and that I'm using this wedding night thing to justify my feelings about Dionisio..."

"Aren't you?"

"Maybe. But it did happen. Really. And it did spoil the romance from the start, and now that Dionisio......"

"Is a knight in shining armour?"

180

"It's like being sixteen again!"

"But you're not!"

"What harm is there? He's gone God-knows-where on his business trips and for God knows how long!"

"So why nurture something so unreal?"

"Because it makes me feel alive again!"

"You mean a part of you does. But there's so much else going on in your life! Focusing on one thing alone is bound to upset your balance and you know what happens then!"

"What?" she snuffled.

"You suffer, and everyone else with you. Alexi, Elias, the girls, me, your hobbies, and most important of all, you lose your own peace of mind."

"It isn't that I don't love Elias..."

"I know that..." said Pepa holding her in her arms.

"But I really feel special with Dionisio. He's funny, lively, tall, handsome and he knows so many glamorous people! Did you know he played golf in Estoril with Alfonso, and that Maria de las Mercedes just adores him?"

"And who are they?" Pepa asked, letting her go.

"Mother! They are our exiled Royals!"

"Ah them."

"Amazing isn't it?"

"What is?"

"His knowing the Royals."

"It's inconsequential, trivial and valueless to know royalty unless they happen to be very special people, which they may or may not be."

"Inconsequential!" she shouted. "Inconsequential!"

"Forget the glitterati. Do you love this man?"

"Love?"

"Yes, love. Not fascination, infatuation, fancy, but love. As in—for better for worse and till death us do part—growing together through strife, commitment, you know?"

"How can I ever find out if I am not free to develop the relationship? I mean, isn't attraction the first of all love impulses?"

181

"Yes. It is" said Pepa certain of her reply.

"Well then. How can I possibly answer your question?"

"You have a point Rosario. But attraction, when love is to follow, is supplanted by a spark so radiant that it touches your heart in a different way to any other encounter. Have you felt that spark Rosario?"

"I can't say I ever felt one. Oh..!" she murmured as an afterthought, "perhaps a little..."

"With the German Count?"

"Yes. He came close to it" she said clearing the emotion netted in her throat. "Did you feel it with father?" she asked.

"We sparked together Rosario, at exactly the same split second and we both knew it!"

"And now you live apart!"

"That's cruel."

"But true, mother, true!"

"It's also true, that apart, we still love each other fiercely as well as sweetly.

"Love without compatibility!" cried Rosario.

"Yes, tragically so for us both."

"And with me, it's compatibility without love!"

"It's not quite like that Rosario, and you know it."

"I know. I love Elias. Deeply."

"Now, tell me, would you jeopardise this kind of love you have for Elias, for a liaison with Dionisio?"

"I..."

"Do you see yourself visiting his hotel suite every now and then when he visits Casablanca? Well? And come back to Elias wearing a mask of pretence, and then put up with Dionisio's long absences until his next unannounced visit?"

"I..."

"It doesn't appeal, does it?"

"Not if you put it like that! And you've just destroyed our romance!" Rosario cried enraged. "Just as you did with Ludwig!"

"If it takes that little to destroy it, it can't have been that true, can it? What you are really after Rosario, is the thought of

182

a man falling madly in love with you. To have control over his desires. Just as you did with Ludwig!"

"What's the harm if I keep the fantasy to myself!"

"Fantasies are lies Rosario, or at best, they're approximations of the truth and as such they deprive you and others from the beauty of reality"

"What if my fantasies keep my marriage alive and safe?"

"Is that what they do?"

"Maybe!"

"I suppose we all have a different yardstick of integrity. This is yours. It isn't mine."

"You make it sound as if fantasy is a mortal sin!"

"If a fantasy is a lie, then the sin of fantasy is no better or worse than the sin of lying, and no, it isn't a mortal sin."

"My marriage is in danger of withering unless I feed it with fantasies born of another man. Isn't that safer than having a full-blown affair with Dionisio and jeopardising my marriage?"

"Neither is desirable."

"And what if Elias senses or knows what is going on and enjoys it, you know, actually enjoys it, vicariously. What then? Have you thought about that?"

Marriage!" she sighed, "who would be foolish enough to write a book of rules about it!"

*

Carlo was out on leave from the concentration camp for Christmas and thought it proper to spend Christmas quietly with his wife and daughter at home. Samuel had gone to Arcachon with the Dubails, and Binot was skiing with his father in Oukaimeden in the High Atlas.

Only Josh, Binot's older half-brother joined them at The Orchard that year. A lawyer at twenty-two, he was all of five foot in his bare feet. Everyone thought him benign until he began to speak in a falsetto voice which reminded them of the villain in a gangster film. His mother, and Joaquín's first wife, had died in labour of a spontaneous ruptured uterus, caused by the precipitous expulsion of Josh's abnormally large head, making Josh the recipient of his mother's vast fortune and at the same time incurring his father's lifetime loathing for causing the death of his beloved young wife. Motherless, the newly born Josh and his older sister Maria were handed over to their grandmother until Josh was sent off to boarding school in the French Pyrenees. Twenty years later, having qualified as a lawyer, he returned to his father's home having seen him on no more than four short occasions.

"You lot are very animated!" Elias shouted from the living room. "What's it all about?"

"We're reminiscing about the good old days in Barcelona before the revolution, when I spent all my Easter and summer vacations with you, uncle Elias!" Josh shouted back from the kitchen.

"D'you remember little Lalia making fun of your Plus Fours?" laughed Pepa.

"Do I ever!"

"You always had a soft spot for her didn't you?" she added.

"Eyes as big as holy hosts and all that blonde hair! What is she now, fourteen?" he falsettoed.

"Josh!" cried Rosario, "you're not..."

"I like them young. At least I know they're not after my money!"

"What a sad thing to say!" said Pepa holding his hand.

"But true Yaya. How can I trust a woman to like me? Look at me!"

"You don't have to divulge your fortune!" advised Rosario.

"Easy if I live in Europe, but everyone knows of my fortune here in Morocco and every ambitious parent will make their daughter pretend they're in love with me!"

"You'll make someone very happy one day Josh. Think of all the jewels and furs you can spoil a girl with!" exclaimed Rosario.

"Money is to be stored, not poured, auntie" he replied.

"Meaney..!" she mocked, tightening her lips and making her eyes into slits.

"That's me. A mean old dwarf that nobody wants."

"Now Josh, where's that happy-go-lucky sixteen-year-old who sat in the kitchen helping me shell peas?" asked Pepa.

"Those were the days! You were my family. You even introduced me to José Luis when he was still a medical student and he took me and old Sis to cafés and bars."

They were silent as they remembered the vibrant Maria, who dated José Luis before she died of tuberculosis.

"If father had listened to José Luis, I would still have my sister!" he burst. "Your father's a fanatic!" Pepa said.

"...And sent her to some weird naturalist doctor in Germany who plonked her in a vat of ice and fed her only boiled rice! And father wasn't even there when she died, you know!" shouted Josh, pitching his voice to a despairing timbre. "But Olympia was! My step-mother for God's sake!"

"Calm down, Josh" said Pepa. "You can't spend the rest of your life angry, or your blood will turn into vinegar. It's Christmas and you're one of us. Come and get your present!"

"I only ever get presents here. Elsewhere I don't exist!" He brandished the newly unwrapped tennis racquet, threw it in the air and caught it, shouting they had saved him a good few francs.

*

Days later, Elias was taken ill during the New Year's Réveillon at the Spanish Consulate given in remembrance of the 1936 Civil War. Everyone talked, but furtively, of Franco's brutal dictatorship and reprisals. Rosario saw Elias' blood drain from his face, until a paroxysm of coughing stopped his breathing. Someone next to him slapped his back and loosened his tie, another opened the windows wide, but the Consul's wife, who was a Red Cross volunteer at the military hospital, shouted that it was oxygen Elias needed and to rush him straight to the Clinique du Sacré Coeur.

The diagnosis was terrifying. Acute emphysema, a liver twice its normal size, distended lungs that had caused excessive enlargement of Elias' heart and a blood pressure that was up with the gods.

A programme of no smoking, no alcohol, a low fat diet, physiotherapy, and a month at a chest clinic in the Atlas mountains with Rosario by his side, was put in place.

*

"Are we eating in the kitchen?" cried Paloma the minute they had waved their parents goodbye.

"You know we do when your mother and father are away" said Pepa with one of her rare winks.

"Smoked kippers!" screamed Carlota lifting the glistening gold fish from the plate to smell it.

"And pamboli! And grapes, and guess what to drink?"

"Lemonade!" they chorused

"Oh... what a shame, it isn't" Pepa said teasingly.

"What then?" asked Carlota, looking around for clues.

"It's...Co..ca..Cola!" cried Pepa making a large bottle appear from under the table. "From the Americas..." she added whimsically.

"We've had it once at auntie Trini's" cried Paloma, stealing Pepa's thrill.

"Let's have a blessing before we start, shall we?" said Pepa, closing her eyes to gather her thoughts.

"How about we give thanks to the waters, the earth and the sun without which nothing would be, and the Americans, for what they bring us to drink here today."

"Why can't we eat like this every time?"

"Because, Mita, this is peasant food" answered Pepa.

"Is peasant food bad?" enquired Carlota.

"No, it is the best food in the world, but your mother wouldn't approve and she would have kittens if she saw you eating kippers in the kitchen without even a table cloth; you, Paloma, licking your fingers, and you, Carlota, not wiping your mouth before and after drinking! Your mother wants you to be ladies, not a yokel like me!"

"You're not a yokel Yayita, are you?"

" 'Course I am Tita, and proud of it!"

"What's a yokel anyway?" asked Carlota.

"A peasant" answered Paloma.

"What's wrong with peasants?" asked Carlota, with her mouth stuffed.

"They talk with their mouths full and they never curtsey!" said Pepa.

"Everyone does it at school" said Paloma standing up to perform.

"Very pretty sweetheart, but it's not my style."

"We like your ways best yayita, don't we Tita?"

"And you tell us the best stories!" said Carlota.

"And I suppose you want one after lunch" said Pepa, interpreting their complimentary remark.

"Is it going to be scary with monsters and things?" asked Carlota, making claws with her fingers and squinting awfully.

"Well... let's see... I think it might be one of those stories...... So why don't you get closer together, just in case... And this is true girls. My mother told it to me and her mother before told it to her when she was little.

It happened in the very field my father bought from a farmer to cultivate his crops. It was midsummer's day. June the twenty first, the summer solstice, when the earth is like a furnace, and the crickets are going wild, but otherwise everything is very, very, very still. So still, some people think the world has died.

"What's solstice" asked Paloma, making use of Pepa's pause.

"The solstice is that very special time when the sun reaches its maximum distance from the equator, and the equator, before you ask Carlota, is a line circling the centre of the earth, like a hoola hoop. People say it is the time when strange happenings occur, sometimes good, sometimes... well... Anyway, Artura, the farmer's wife went to the field with a basket full of bread, butifarra from their own pig, curdled cheese from Manchego the goat, figs and a botijo of wine for the men's lunch break.

She didn't stay for lunch with them because of el Ninet, her eight-month old baby she had to suckle later. She placed the basket under the shade of an apple tree and called for Jaime, her farmer husband between the hollow of her funnelled hands. (Pepa demonstrated and continued.) Then, Artura slowly began walking her way back to the farm. She felt very hot and her breasts were heavy, because the baby was due to feed. She sat to rest a few moments against the trunk of an old gnarled olive tree. She loosened her girdle and unbuttoned her blouse to feel the coolness of the breeze, and she heard the men in the distance laughing and enjoying their lunch as she fell asleep. Then—gather round girls—she woke up feeling very cold, and when she opened her eyes, she saw a snake as thick as my arm, slithering up her body. She tried to scream, but no sound came out of her throat and without moving her lips she began to pray Our Lady's prayer. Do you want me to stop girls?" she asked, when they covered their faces.

"No! Please don't tease us Yaya!" cried Carlota.

"Artura prayed and hardly breathed not to anger the snake. Slowly it reached the top of her blouse and stopped. Her heart beat so loud she thought she would die. The snake's cold and raspy skin against her arm made her shiver with horror. She kept her eyes tightly shut, feeling every move the snake made. But now it had stopped and she didn't know what to think next. She thought it might have fallen asleep against her warm body. She half opened her eyes and she saw the snake's mouth wide open ready to suckle her breast. At this point Artura's terror was so great, that she passed out as the snake's mouth suckled just as her hungry Ninet would. Artura came back to her senses after the snake slid down her body and hid under a rock to digest. She thought she had been dreaming until she saw deep teeth marks all around her nipple and she fainted again. It was el Ninet's starving screams some time later that alerted Jaime who found his wife asleep.

"Artura! Mujer! Por Dios!" he called, shaking her. "El Ninet is frantic. What's happened to you?" In a half stupor she told him the story and Jaime was certain his wife had become mad with the summer solstice. But the older women in the village knew that Artura had told the truth for it was not the first time that a snake had suckled a nursing mother nor would it be the last and it was said that those who survived would never, ever, be afraid again. But the fright dried up Artura's milk overnight and el Ninet was given a wet nurse. She remained mad until the next solstice when... But.. that's another story!"

"Was it really a true story Yayita?" asked Paloma dazed.

"It was, Mita. For Artura, it certainly was."

"I'm always going to stay indoors in the solstice!" avowed Carlota.

"In or out, the solstice's about!" chanted Pepa. "But come along!" she said, clapping her hands. "We've passed the solstice. Besides, who said only bad things happen then!"

*

The girls were back at school after the bomb incident, leaving Alexi to be cared for by Pepa until Rosario returned with Elias after his 'cure' in the mountains.

"Did you know" Samuel asked, "that La Maison Blanche has been acquisitioned, and the whole of Anfa is to be cordoned off?"

"What for?"

"The Summit, here, in Casablanca, any day now!" he cried. "Imagine Roosevelt, Churchill and Stalin all here, right on our doorstep, to discuss Europe's future!"

"Right here?" she breathed, incredulous. "I wonder why? I mean why here?"

"The right geography I suppose."

"A turning point in our history, whatever the reason for the choice of venue" Pepa said.

"I thought you'd like to pray, Yaya."

"Thank you Samuel. I shall. For goodwill to infuse their hearts and minds..."

"And common sense!" he added. "These people never see further than their own noses and will do anything to ensure their own secret agendas!"

"Will you join me in prayer Samuel?"

"Telling you about it is as far as I can go Yaya!"

*

"Come down from there! I told you to fly only at night!" Pepa scolded Paloma, when she saw her balancing with one leg on the terrace edge, arms outstretched to the heavens, and ten feet high above the ground. Paloma turned, jumped and bending her knees first, hit the ground flawlessly like a gymnast then tip-toed towards Pepa to whisper "El Espíritú" in her grandmother's ear.

"El Espíritú..." repeated Pepa.

"El Espíritú de la Naturaleza..." expanded Paloma.

"What about the Spirit of Nature Mita?"

"It spoke to me" she continued, still whispering.

"Like we're speaking to each other, in whispers?" asked Pepa.

"Yes. There's an oak tree at the bottom of the school playground which didn't die with the bomb."

"And does it talk to you?"

"It keeps on repeating the same thing, over and over again. It says to take time to love one another and to listen to each other."

"Wise old tree! Maybe the tree is saying we talk, and do, and think too much, Mita" proffered Pepa. "Our brains get jammed up with clutter and our poor old souls don't get a look in! Have you told anyone about this?"

"The voice said not to tell anyone until I found the right person."

"And is that me?"

"Yes, because you don't laugh at me and because you understand and because you love me Yayita."

"Whatever you do sweetheart, don't tell the nuns you hear voices!" Pepa said, pondering on the fate of St Joan of Arc, the patron saint of the convent school.

190

Pepa had set aside a letter from the Convent for Rosario to open when she returned from Elias' rest cure. "It's Carlota" Rosario said sombrely after reading it.

"Not Paloma?" asked Pepa, astonished.

"And I haven't a clue what to do about it!"

"Is it a reprimand, or what?"

"It appears our darling Carlota goes walkies at night and is becoming a compulsive liar!"

"Is she sleep-walking then?"

"Well, she's missing from her bed when the night nun does her rounds."

"I bet you she's in the kitchen, scavenging for any scraps of food she can get, we all know how gutsy she is!"

"What do you think I should do?" asked Rosario confounded.

"Since you ask Rosario, this is what I think. Take them out of that hell hole!"

"Hell hole! The Convent? I never thought I'd hear that from you!"

"That's no Convent. It's a luxury rest home for failed women."

"I've got Alexi and Elias to think about. The girls stay."

"I can look after them at home" Pepa said, or if you prefer, the local school is minutes from the house.

"Let me speak to Joaquín first."

"What on earth for?"

"His way of looking at things is different. He might come up with a clever idea."

"Like keeping Binot hidden in a farmyard? Him and his high falluting notions and his half baked ideas! All head stuff. Reads a bit of this and a bit of that and ends up with no heart left and knowing nothing!"

"I'll ask him all the same."

*

Carlota was most certainly possessed, declared Joaquín. A negative entity had entered her, which made her roam in the dead of night and err irresistibly from the truth. The two were linked, part of the same thing. If one was tackled, the other would fade away. He had read of such cases and it seemed there was only one remedy. Rosario listened with the attention of a devotee, but Pepa raised her eyes to the heavens, then her arms in disbelief.

Carlota was to have a warm soapy enema daily to rid all evil particles lurking within her bowel. Once they were flushed away, the possessed Carlota would be purified and returned to normality. Paloma, he added as an afterthought, would also benefit from the treatment, as bowel toxins contributed to stunted growth, and the girls were made to take a week's leave from school.

The tubing, funnelling, canulae, vaseline and his emollient son Binot—on which to demonstrate the technique—were all provided by Joaquín. But Binot disappeared when all had been set up and instead, Joaquín demonstrated on Paloma. She lay curled up on the bed and though she did not enjoy the violation of her intimacy, she yielded to her mother's praise and encouragement.

Carlota failed to retain the soapy churning fluid and irresistibly, she soiled the sheets. Joaquín was not in the least apologetic when a resounding slap landed on her behind, saying that the entity in her bowel had rejected the treatment and that mastery and perseverance were the keys to debilitating this negative force into submission.

On the seventh day the long awaited catharsis arrived when Carlota, weary of the daily abuse, confessed to raiding the Convent fridge at night because she was starving. The binging and the lying was a logical outcome of a disturbed childhood Pepa told Rosario, and Joaquín's methods were unhelpful, brutal and even dangerous.

*

Elias' health improved and a stroke of luck combined with

business acumen made him millions. More jewellery was commissioned at Monsieur Espressati for Rosario's growing collection, an extra share purchased in the ancestral home in Mazagan to turn into rentable flats, and twenty acres of land bought near the lighthouse on the Plateau which Papachito had once owned.

The Orchard had not had a party for months and Alexi's birthday seemed the perfect occasion. Birthday celebrations should last a week Rosario often said when her own birthday was due, and Alexi's did. There were visits to the zoo and the circus, the Red Cross Charity Fair held in the Parc Lyauté and the Petit Poucet ballet at the girl's ballet school. But best of all was a matinée of Laurel and Hardy at the Rialto, and to bring the festivities to a close, there was an afternoon of indulgence at the Trianon salon de Thé, famous for their sugared almonds, piled up high on the counters, fresh strawberry ice-creams stabbed with crispy langues de chat, served by gracious waitresses, dressed as eighteenth century shepherdesses and each night, the girls whispered to each other in bed that their mother was the best, ever, and that she must truly love them.

It was inevitable that after all the feasting and merry-making, Pepa's insistence that that the girls begin their annual spring- cleaning chores, would be unpopular.

TWELVE

Tikkun

Every Spring, households spill their furniture onto terraces and gardens to be cleaned, dusted and polished, and chatty chambermaids beat the dust out of prodigiously large rugs with giant carpet-beaters, free rooms of nesting insects, fumigate and white-wash the walls. Pepa forewarned the girls that they would not always have servants and learning housekeeping skills was essential, hence the assignment of tasks to each girl, though Carlota only tackled those she liked and hid until Paloma had completed those tasks she loathed.

The Scissor-man's harmonica call for custom made Paloma rush to the cutlery drawer to gather knives, scissors, and every other blunt instrument. She loved to hear its rippling sound, as it announced the coming of Spring and because the scissors man always told her how much she had grown and she would not hear that comment from anyone else until his next visit. She watched him sharpen the blade of a knife held lightly between his shuddering thumb and index finger and against a fast-moving silex wheel driven by a foot pedal from his cart. He splashed water on it when it got too hot and she smiled and moved away, covering her eyes as it sparked bouquets of stars.

Ice sellers chugged along the camel trail ringing their large cast-iron bells for housewives and servants to come out with their empty buckets, and every Friday, a troupe of Berber acrobats, mostly children, stopped at every gate to perform rare feats of fundambulism with their ropes until someone came out to throw a coin inside the gaudy crocheted cap held out by their smiling, youngest, non-performing member.

In a black full-length buttoned-down gaberdine robe and as

if stuck to his crown, a skull cap, a long-bearded Jew cried in his veiled voice "Mt'las! Mt'las!" and Pepa scurried to the balcony to respond to his call. This same Jew revamped The Orchard's mattresses, year in year out, ever since they had lived there. Only Jews were proficient at this craft, which they had practised to perfection over centuries. Many of their ancestors it was said, had fled from Andalucia to escape the hardships of the Expulsion. Pepa did not know exactly how long ago this was (she had no head for history), but every Easter, and after the Jew's visit, a kind of unwilled shame set in as she recollected her country's "Limpieza de Sangre"—the dehumanising Cleansing of Blood that forced thousands of them either to flee the persecution or forcibly convert to Catholicism. Every year the same question puzzled and disturbed her as to why it was that the Jews, and no other race, had been banished to a life of perpetual wandering.

She confided her disquiet to Monsieur Clémenceau, a scholar of esoteric history at the École Charles de Foucauld, and a specialist on 'The Jewish Question' as it was known. He began by saying that no one could define the Jews, or whether the problem that surrounded them was one of religion or race or whether our accumulated knowledge derived from actual history, Bible stories, myths or facts. To give a specific answer was no easy matter as there were as many theses on the subject as there were scholars. But his own view, shared by some, was that their greed, long ago, was the worm in the apple that began to rot the fruit. And it was this forsaking of the spiritual law which then created a separation from the spirit and hence their fall from grace and the beginning of their nemesis. The race now having plummeted into matter were no longer in 'spirit' and its status as the 'Chosen Ones' was lost. Their mission now was to climb the evolutionary ladder all over again through the continuous practice of good deeds and humility. Only then could the light that would reveal the Spiritual Mysteries they had been entrusted with by God and lost, be regained.

To Pepa's enquiry as to the nature of their greed, he replied that it was the greed of power—the desire to keep that power they had as the 'Chosen People' to themselves and never to share it nor be inclusive with their neighbours. That sin of power and exclusiveness was the beginning of darkness for the Jewish people and also, because we are all brothers, the rest of the world.

There was an undue long pause after he had spoken those words of condemnation. Pepa thought it unfair, she told Monsieur Clémenceau, to still believe that ethnic and religious hatred towards the Jews had to do with so remote a moment in human history. She was right, he replied, adding that the time for the de-demonising of Jews was long overdue, that what was needed most, was a good old dose of 'TIKKUN,' which, he explained, was the Hebrew word for healing, repairing, and transforming the world.

The mattress Jew never spoke and had always fascinated Carlota. She stood all the while watching him work, as he sat cross-legged on the concrete floor of the large covered terrace at the basement of the house. There he spread the yellowing wool from inside the mattresses and piled it up high into several mounds of equal height, after tugging at the string he had sewn in one continuous stitch the previous year. She sneezed every time the wool was released from its case and when he signalled, with his claw-like index finger, she came to look inside his black leather bag from where he chose a hook, with the same deliberate exactitude as a surgeon at the operating table, to thereafter fluff the wool, one ball at a time, until it expanded to thrice its original size and the mounds had risen to the ceiling like candy floss mountains.

*

When Monsieur Déchaumes offered his orange plantation in Azemour to the family for the summer vacation, Rosario did not complain although it was only eighty kilometres from Casablanca and some twenty from Elias' ancestral home in Mazagan, which she had already visited. Elias longed to steep himself in his nostalgic past and he was grateful that she accepted.

196

The gate keeper saw the advancing Traction Avant through a haze of swirling dust and pulled open the solid iron gate. He bowed repeatedly as he waved them into the property, a large, squat terracotta house with a crested tower rising from the back. It was dusk and everything glowed. The orange trees surrounding the house and beyond were like a sea of creamy frothiness. They had already produced fruit once and now, in late July, the heady scent of the blossom infused the warm evening air for a second time. Four women and three men servants waited to welcome them. They watched the family drowsily roll out of the car one by one and smiled when Elias greeted them in Arabic. Several courtyards and two pinnacled extensions came to evidence only from inside the house. The architecture had been left intact since the fourteenth century when it was built for the local Pasha, as a small palace in the Hispano-Moorish style, with graceful arches and geometric azulejos from floor to ceiling. Only its name had been changed to 'La Maison du Levant.' It was bought from the Caid's son by Monsieur Dechaumes' grandfather, who had developed the extensive land around it into a profitable plantation. Slumped into the cushions, chosen for their bright colours,Elias sighed, and rang for mint tea. He could hear the birds splashing lightly in the pond of the shady garden beyond the filigree patio portal. He closed his eyes to savour the sweetness of their evening song, and for the first time in years he gave thanks for being alive.

The Pasha of Azemour's offer to Elias and his family to share a traditional Moroccan meal at his palace was accepted, and as a token of appreciation Elias was to introduce Rosario to his host in full Moroccan dress.

At the Kisseria, she selected lengths of silks, laminated with thin threads of gold and silver for a sumptuous Kaftan, as worn by high ranking Moroccan women and Sultanas. The housekeeper from the plantation escorted her to the Souk to bargain on her behalf, and to the doorstep of the small white-washed house of Zaiane, the Pasha's wives' own seamstress. Elias instructed Rosario, Carlota and Paloma on the rudiments

197

of Moroccan etiquette, and what to expect from a day at the Pasha's palace.

Sidi Abdul Kassim was a Maghzen, a high ranking government official and also a business man. He sprinkled Elias with rose water on arrival, bowed to Rosario and the girls (whom he called jolies demoiselles) and led them to an anti-room. He complimented Rosario on her authentic attire and the Pasha insisted that she join his wives and the ladies of their entourage in their boudoir.

Sidi Abdul Kassim 's grandfather and Joseph Butler had travelled together in the Middle Atlas in the past to settle tribal disputes, and the bond that he developed with Elias was strong and instant. He whispered into his Chaoui's ear, who left the room returning with a gift wrapped in a coarse woven cloth which the Pacha offered Elias. Elias embraced Sidi Abdul Kassim like a brother, as he knew the offering of bread to another was the most sacred sign of fraternity in Moroccan custom. They walked through the palmeraie and into the Minzah, a garden pavilion within the palace enclosure with a rectangular pool of floating white lilies. Alongside the pool, low, square tables were laid side-by-side for the feast, with cushions positioned on the floor around each table.

Even though his adolescence had been spent in Paris, when at home, Sidi Abdul Kassim chose to eat with his fingers, as dictated by Moroccan protocol. A wooden spoon for Rosario brought her relief and Sidi Abdul Kassim apologised that it was not silver, as Islamic law forbade the use of table utensils made of precious metals. Baskets of limes, shaddocks, quinces and pomegranates, fresh purple figs and almonds—still moist from their shells, sat on each table and an aromatic extravaganza of spiced kefta, succulent and tender mechoui and other exotic delicacies were brought in copper trays and clay pots balanced on the heads of floaty, bare-footed servants. Swept away to the stables for a pony ride through the gardens before their gluttony made them ill, the girls disappeared eating a honeyed gazelle, their favourite sweetmeat. After the feast and without warning, Rosario felt herself air-lifted by two large ululating

Senegalese women in white ballooney sarawells. They carried her into the ladies' chambers, through an arch, which opened into a venetian style chandeliered room draped with purple and gold sensuous hangings, too high on the wall to be caressed. Sitting on geometrically patterned cushions, arranged a la Mauresque, women of all ages in gaudy Kaftans and adorned in finely chiselled red and gold jewels stared at her as if with one eye as she entered their fanciful domain. A woman, slender, and wearing a grey two piece (which Rosario recognised as Patou's) introduced herself as Zaiane (the Pasha's number one wife) and told Rosario to sit on the red satin pouffe in the centre of the room. Zaiane snapped her fingers twice and the women converged on Rosario like a flock of brilliantly coloured, twittering birds. Some came to peck-kiss her hands lightly, others massaged her feet with oils of jasmine and frangipane. Rosario smiled and drank without qualms the cup that Zaiane offered her. Filled with an ambrosian liquid made of fresh almonds—said to be an aphrodisiac—it was Zaiane's last parting gift before Rosario was returned to Elias as a delicacy ready for his delectation.

*

"Joaquín phoned while you were out" announced Pepa. "He's wondering about a picnic in Oualidia and can you ring him back."

"Marvellous!" exclaimed Elias. "Never mind Paris, querida" he told Rosario. "See Oualidia and die…"

"Is Binot coming?" Carlota asked. The girls held hands and whirled in a circle shouting "For -mi -dable!" when Pepa said yes.

"Why is Oualidia so special?" asked Rosario.

He smiled. "Wait and see…ee" he hummed.

Pepa rose early to prepare the picnic. "We'll stop at the Cap Blanc for oysters and arrange to collect a couple of Veuve Cliquots on ice" said Elias, up before anyone to help Pepa.

The coastal road to Oualidia followed a barren plain on one

side. On the other, a natural sea wall opened to an incandescent clear blue lagoon as still as a painting. Further ahead it broke into an eerie meandering of estuaries and shimmering sands where sky and sea converged. Salt was extracted from the salinas, but there was no one to be seen in this eerie landscape, not even a single orange billed oyster-catcher strayed from the reed beds, and Rosario was moved that Elias should love such a place.

The car rolled slowly along on the stony road. Pepa keenly surveyed the sparse cultivation of tomatoes, peppers and aubergines covered with mended brown muslin or broken window panes. An old woman, shrunk and bent with a load of wood on her back walked barefoot behind a man sitting on a donkey and Pepa wanted to shout her indignation, but remembered she was in a land where men had a different regard for their womenfolk.

Rosario was restive. The landscape, open and beautiful as she saw it, made her feel edgy, without her knowing why. It was the same feeling of angst she had experienced in the darkened hall where Olympia gave her recitation, though she was now out in the open. This was a dark spot in a land with uncanny spirits, some were evil, and they persisted in the atmosphere, leaving an indelible imprint said Joaquín. This was Morocco.

*

She was eight years-old and Carlota became inseparable from her little book of catechism as she prepared to receive her First Communion. She grew so withdrawn and pious, that the nuns at the convent hailed her as a budding saint. They did not see that at home she despised and humiliated her younger sister who, because of her learning difficulties would have to delay her own instruction before being allowed to take the Eucharist.

Her sister, Paloma thought, had turned into a crazed wretch and she was relieved at the respite.

When Carlota's special day arrived, dressed in white

organdie, with a mother-of-pearl missal held between her joined hands and gliding towards the altar, Rosario was moved to tears and was convinced that for the first time in her life, Carlota was indeed good and pure.

A week later, stirred by her own childhood memories of devotion, Rosario returned to the Catholic fold, and was certain that it was her new-found faith that a month later blessed her with a pregnancy. It was May, and Pepa said that the timing of conception—the month of Mary—was a felicitous sign for both mother and child.

THIRTEEN

In Secula Seculorum

"What's out there, where that woolly mist is gathering, Elias?" Rosario gazed pensively from the terrace of the
La Mamounia hotel in Marrakech, where they had come to spend their summer vacation.

"It's the Ourika valley querida.

"Ourika...Ourika..." she repeated entranced. "If it's a girl" she said stroking herself, "I'll call her Ourika... It's the most evocative name I've ever heard!"

"Rosario... Cariñito... you're such a romantic!"

"Can we go there instead?" she pleaded. "It's...I don't know... oppressive here and the opulence is getting me down."

"The opulence is..." He shook his head in disbelief.

"I know, I know Elias. It's difficult to explain."

"You don't have to. Ahmed will drive us there tomorrow and then we'll see."

"Amorcito..." she cooed, ruffling his thinning hair, and she ran to tell Pepa.

They left the sumptuousness of the hotel, the crowds of the teeming souks and the unbearably sweltering heat of the medina. For Ahmed the journey through the Oued Ourika was paradise revisited. He had spent his childhood there, left, and never returned. He stopped the car to kiss the reddish earth, known by his Shluh Berber ancestors as hamri. They planted lush vegetable gardens and olive, cherry, plum and even apple trees bloomed there in the spring, he said. Further up the valley at Arhbalou there were prehistoric rock engravings, and the view of the Atlas range beyond and the Haouz Plain was something, he said, only Allah would dare to describe. Allah was good to him, and Monsieur Elias, he murmured with a quiver in his voice, for bringing him back to his sacred roots once more before he died. He saw a man on a donkey and stopped to ask him about accommodation for his master and family but the man did not know of anywhere at which a European family could stay.

Minutes later, around a bend on the deserted dirt track, walked a small boy of indeterminate age, flanked by two grey mules. He held a staff and his feet and head seemed to gleam. He told Elias in flawless French that he knew of a woman and her son who kept a small auberge five kilometres off the track further into the mountains and that they needed to leave the car behind and use his mules to carry them there.

"Is this a vineyard? asked Elias squinting into the sun as they finally approached the Auberge du Perpétuel Retour.

"To make grape juice... yes" said the boy with a smile that shone. "And these are strawberries growing inside the verandah" he added.

"That can't be! Down on the coast, we have to import them from France!" cried Elias. The girls jumped up and down shouting that they wanted to live there, forever. A slight woman emerged from the Jasmine-scented verandah with a basket full to the brim of strawberries she had just picked and which were as big as plums. "Welcome" she said passing the basket around, with an accent that needed no guessing as to her origins.

"I'm Alegria " she said. "My husband Jeannot, may God keep him, was French, from the Ardèche."

"I understand you take guests here" said Rosario in Spanish.

"Castilian! Music to my ears Señora ! Yes we do, but we are full up just now."

"Full? Full!" exclaimed Elias incredulous.

"We have only two bedrooms Monsieur."

"Please" begged Rosario, "you see, we must stay here."

"Of course you must" the woman replied. Her eyes searching Rosario's then Pepa's and again Rosario's. "Come with me, we have a small azib, a summer croft, behind the house." She led them to a white-washed hut, no bigger than a shepherd's shelter, with a thatching of pink and gold bougainvillaea next to the derelict donkey stables and a small bubbling river. "That?" asked Elias.

"Let's stay here!" begged Rosario.

"Yaya?" he asked, hoping for a more sensible decision.

Pepa nodded. "We were guided here Elias."

"Shall I settle now?" he asked, holding his wallet.

"Only guests at the Auberge pay Monsieur. The hut dwellers come and go as they please if it was Brahim who brought them" she said.

"Brahim?" Elias asked, not seeing anyone.

"The boy who brought you here. Our friend from beyond the valley." She turned to Pepa and smiled, for she knew that, unlike Elias, she had not failed to notice that Brahim was no ordinary boy.

Elias returned to the La Mamounia hotel to stay the night and collect their belongings. He could not understand what had made Rosario favour a white-washed mud hut in the remote mountains of the mid Atlas to the luxury of one of the most prestigious hotels in the world and he doubted he could cope with living in a hut, if only at weekends.

"Can you believe this!" gasped Rosario when she saw inside the hut.

"I can" nodded Pepa. Narrow oblong apertures high up on the walls let in the light that glowed like crosses on the wall opposite.

"This place was meant for us, wasn't it mother?" said Rosario.

"Yes." she said firmly "And we must give thanks."

It was dawn when Elias arrived with the boy Brahim whose two mules had appeared at the same spot as the previous day to carry the luggage from the car. Along with Alegria's trio of cockerels, their arrival welcomed the new day and no one for miles around could ignore their cacophonous salute. Rosario came out of the hut to meet Elias, still in her nightwear. "They must be millions of years old" Rosario said observing the mountains that looked like the carved faces of ancient warriors, adding that she felt like a speck of shiny silex that had been dropped into the valley for some unknown purpose.

"It's like a vision of the promised land..." mused Elias, surprising himself by what he had just said.

"D'you really mean it?" asked Rosario, gladdened by his declaration.

"I do, and I don't" he replied, tilting his head from side to side. "You see, it is easy for me to take in the beauty of this place, and it stirs me, but...the spirit of it, or whatever..." he paused awkwardly, unable to complete his sentence. "Well, I would feel lost and fearful here, after a while."

"It might have the opposite effect" suggested Pepa, now by his side.

"It would take millions of years for me to evolve in that way Yaya, just like this landscape!" he laughed.

"You underestimate yourself Elias" said Pepa. "You are a good man, a thoroughly good man."

"Those trees over there" asked Rosario, "what are they?"

"They are holm oaks querida, the oldest and most majestic you'll ever see" said Elias, still pensive after Pepa's words.

"Don't you just want to hug them!" she cried with fervour.

"But don't you ever hug those!" warned Elias as she walked towards a prickly pear, "only goats can get close to eat their fruit unpeeled!" Later that afternoon Alexi bit straight into one, of which its treacherous, almost invisible down-like thorns embedded into his tongue. Pepa used a liberal quantity of olive oil to loosen them off his tongue then plucked them one by one with an old tweezers found in Paloma's Red Cross Kit, and his cries of agony resonating down the valley, were louder than those of the poor lambs sacrificed at the end of Ramadan.

The Auberge was waking up and Pepa could hear Alegria singing a seguidilla as she collected water from the well. They had used up their provisions the previous day and Pepa wondered about breakfast. No sooner had she formulated the thought when she heard someone behind her. "Jerónimo. Yo

Jerónimo." It was a young man carrying two baskets balanced over his shoulders at each end of a broom-stick.

"Buenas, Jerónimo" said Pepa. "Are you going to the fields?"

"Fields." he said, blankly.

"Those baskets, where are you going with those heavy baskets?"

"Baskets!" He laughed, and lowered them to the ground.

"For us?" she asked.

"For us!" he answered, this time laughing out of control.

"Breakfast everybody! Jerónimo's brought us breakfast!" Pepa cried with a distinct modulation of her voice reserved strictly for her most joyous moments. She asked Jerónimo to join them, but he had gone, still muttering "for us" to himself. She rolled two empty wooden barrels standing by the stable, just outside the hut and called to Elias to fetch an old door lying behind the hut to use as a table top. A tin of nestle condensed milk, malt coffee, two round loaves baked at dawn in the Auberge's oven, and a large-bellied earthenware jar of home-made strawberry jam were laid on the make-shift table. Alegria brought crockery of bright cobalt and orange Moroccan patterns and an assortment of rusty folding chairs. "You will find supplies of food, paraffin and a trestle table in the cellar, beneath the Auberge" she said. "It's always open, just help yourselves."

"I thought you'd never wake up!" cried Rosario, when the children peered around the hut's door.

"We're eating outside!" they screeched, looking at one another with glee.

"Come on! Grab a chair and tuck in children, but first give thanks." said Pepa, sweeping the entire landscape before them with one deep gulp of her unimpeded breath.

Every morning, Paloma's first impulse was to rush to the river to make sure it was still there. That water, she told her grandmother, was not just for washing and playing, it had an angel living in it. Pepa said it was the sun, the moon and stars at night that animated the water in the river and made it special.

One morning, Paloma filled a bucket with the river's gurgling water she had longed to make hers from the beginning.

"Is the water in your bucket gurgling now?" Pepa asked, watching her from the doorway of the hut. Paloma looked at the water, dark and lifeless in the bucket, then at her grandmother's face.

"Well?"

"It's dead" replied Paloma, her voice breaking as if caught in a snare.

"Dead is it?" asked Pepa. "Listen to me Mita" she said crouching by her side. " If you want life, you must let go of it— the river is only a river when it flows and it only flows when it is a river."

Paloma clung to her bucket and to her grandmother's riddle, until a flash of insight, like the striking of a match, revealed its conundrum. Ponderously, and to prolong the intense rapture of her brief ownership, she let the water run back into the stream. "The river is only a river when it flows..." She murmured.

*

"I could stay until Tuesday" said Elias, when he arrived at the Auberge for a weekend, "and if you like, we can take a trip into the mountains".

Pepa would not risk too high an altitude and declined. But a touch of adventure after four weeks at the Auberge suited Rosario, and even more so after Elias promised to take her to a Fantasia celebration in one of the remotest Berber villages. Ahmed alerted Elias that he could only take them there as his guests, and even then, only if they posed as Arabs. Elias didn't have to worry, his fluency and mannerisms being convincing without even having to put his mind to it, but the correct attire for Rosario had to be borrowed from one of Ahmed's aunts who lived nearby in the Oued below the Ourika valley.

Off at dawn to avoid the worst of the heat and so that they could return before nightfall, they met no one during their journey along the precipitous dirt track to Tahines, and when they reached the summit, they could see Tahaleh and several valleys beyond. They stopped to breathe the rarefied air on the mountain plateau and as Elias inhaled, his blue complexion turned pink.

Guns were fired into the air. The Fantasia had begun and they could hear the horsemen's wild cries well before they arrived. The riders, covered in white creamy muslin saw the Traction Avant skim into their compound and the galloping horses came to an abrupt halt. The women, clad in shluh berber glittery jubile robes and jewels of red coral and amber, broke into a deafening wail. Away from his roots too long, Ahmed could not decide whether this was a friendly or hostile welcome. Some had never seen a car and ran to hide. Others were transfixed. Ahmed approached the chief horseman and explained that he was the son of Jacoub and Nizam of the Goudafa tribe and that Elias and Rosario were distant relatives from Agadir. As a measure ot their acceptance, Elias and Ahmed were offered horses to join in the festivities and the women who had stopped ululating, welcomed Rosario with lengths of dazzling cloth and dried leaves of henna for her to paint symbols of luck on her hands, feet and forehead.

Their faces, aged before time by the rigours of mountain life, bore no cruelty, greed or despair, and behind her yashmak, Rosario decreed that to think of them as the 'chosen people' was not too much of a romantic notion.

*

Their lives, Pepa thought, needed to be punctuated by a daily rhythm to set against the disconnecting timelessness of the Auberge du Perpétuel Retour. At twelve a clock and not a minute later, Pepa announced lunch by ringing the heavy bell that had once served to call the faithful to prayer at a Qur'an school down the valley. Every day she roasted red peppers and fresh goose eggs on a flat white boulder with the reflected heat of the mid-day sun. Alegria joined them at the table after their dessert of figs or goat's cheese coated in wild herbs, for a miniscule cup of malt coffee and a sugar lump soaked in curaçao. Jerónimo, she said, had not been so happy since before his father died.

She had met her husband Jeannot in her native Seville during the Holy Week celebrations which he had come to photograph. He was a mere boy, in his twenties, and he wanted her for his wife before the Fiesta was over, even though she was forty and greying. Back at his home in the Ardèche, their son Jerónimo was born a year later. "You have a Mongol child" the midwife pronounced at his birth, and they did not know what that meant, since she was Spanish and her husband French and there was no knowledge of any Asian blood in either of their families, until the doctor explained the meaning of the term. Their love for their child grew deeper and their search began for a place to live without having to endure the intrusion of prying eyes. Their pursuit took them to the Pyrenees, the Jura, the Dolomites, the Alpujaras and finally to the Atlas mountains. They found Ourika and followed Brahim to the spot where they built the Auberge du Retour, as their home. There was weightlessness to the silence after Alegria spoke. Joyfulness is the silence that sounds, mused Pepa looking up at the so-still mountains. "How could anyone deserve such undiluted and effortless peace?" she asked Alegria.

Alegria replied that it was not a reward but a blessing.

"The jackals are restless. You'd do well to light a bonfire tonight Pepa. I can smell them" Alegria said inhaling the air. "We've put in a new metal door, because they destroyed the old wooden one so don't open it if you hear scratching, it will be them!"

It was lit and the bonfire became a ritual that they all wanted to renew at each dusk. At first it was hard to keep the children from danger as they danced, laughed and screamed savage cries whenever wood exploded, but they surrendered to its magic after a few nights and sat to watch the smouldering embers slowly turn into a pile of ash. Pepa told Alexi when he asked what fire was, that it was like the spirit of life itself.

Though the true fire, she expounded, was invisible and burnt in the hearts of men, but only when it was kindled, like the bonfire. The bonfire did not keep the jackals away. Every night after they had gone to bed, they circled the hut, howling and scratching at the door, leaving only when they saw the flame of the oil-lamp Pepa placed high inside the communal bedroom, on the narrow aperture in the wall.

Rosario got into the rhythm of waking up early and walking straight to the edge of the clearing. She smoothed her arched back with her hands, and each morning, she invoked the strength of the mountains beyond, to behold her unborn child. If she woke up early, Paloma joined her, her face pressed against her mother's side, waiting to be fondled. Sometimes a slithery movement against Paloma's cheek—like soap in the bath—made her giggle and her mother said how lucky she was because it was the baby kissing her from inside.

The girls sat on Rosario's lap, as if this had been their lifetime practice and in the afternoons, they sat by their mother watching the rabbits she embroidered multiply each day at the edge of a cot sheet for the new baby. Carlota did not baulk at her mother's touch when she bathed her by the river. Nor did Rosario think Carlota evil any more. Here, she was Rosario, pure and simple, and just as God intended. And she was beautiful, Pepa told her.

His family's contentment after their ninth week in a place so deprived of amusement baffled Elias. He saw that Rosario had not looked at any of the books she had brought with her to read, that she tendered to the children effortlessly, helped Pepa with the cooking and joined her for the devotional praying of the rosary every evening by candlelight before the bonfire was lit. Pepa's and the children's affinity with the place he understood, but not his Rosario who so craved the city. He did not know whether he could live with a woman so tame and placid and hoped this to be a passing phase to do with the mountain air and her pregnancy.

Sunday evenings at the Auberge's restaurant, before Elias returned to Casablanca for the week, was a family treat There were black glistening olives served in earthen bowls with chunks of Alegria's home-made bread and a simple, one course supper that Alegria had learned to cook as a girl in her native Andalucia. If encouraged, she burst into a soulful canto hondo which she sang mostly for herself.

The girls loved the restaurant because of the oil lamps flickering everywhere and because there were never any other children and they felt like grown-ups. On one night, an American soldier occupied the other table and with him was a young woman. The girls giggled and christened them 'les amoureux' because they only conversed with their eyes. Paloma declared she wanted a man to look at her just like that when she grew up. Rosario called her precocious and asked her to lower her voice, but Alegria said that Paloma's wish would come to pass. Of that, she had no doubt. Her beau, she said, would be a celtic knight, with eyes as blue as a lagoon at dawn and hair as red as the flames of a bonfire at San Juan."

"A knight? For me?"

"Shut up" spluttered Carlota. "Alegria's only a peasant, she knows nothing. And anyway, you are almost invisible and nobody will ever notice you."

She didn't care about what her sister had just said. She had faith in Alegria because she was special and she dreamed that from somewhere in another land her knight would find her, and that his lagoon-blue eyes would melt into hers.

*

"I do believe I have another special child in here" said Rosario patting her bulge.

"How special?" asked Pepa, feeling the baby.

"Different to Alexi. This one is watery and it sleeps a lot."

"Or meditates?"

"Yes... something like that."

"Your seed, sewn in the month of May and growing in all this beauty and peace is such a blessing for the babe, Rosario, and it will stay with him all his life" smiled Pepa.

211

"You said 'him', mother! I know it's a boy too!"

"Have you thought of a name?"

"It came in a dream the third night we got here" confided Rosario. "Like Paloma's, the very night before the horror started." They were silent and Pepa touched her daughter's hand, "and his name?"

"It's Mickael. After the Archangel."

"Not a very watery name then!" Pepa laughed. "If any angel's got fire in his belly, it's Mickael!" Pepa and Rosario felt close, but did not dwell on it. They saw their closeness as a state of grace and part of the natural order of life that abides in such a clime.

The next week would be their last at Ourika. The wrench from their Eden seemed unbearable.

"Tomorrow" said Pepa, when they were all gathered around the bonfire, "we will plant a tree on the spot where we sit to have our meals. It will be there long after we've gone, so that a part of us will remain here forever, and when we feel troubled and lost we can each think of our tree growing on this patch of earth and also deep in our hearts. "Now, what shall we plant?" she asked, her glance forming a circle.

"We won't ever leave here!" cried Paloma.

"I think you know we must, Paloma" said Pepa making certain she sounded resolute.

"Yayita..."

"Look, sweetheart" she said, opening her arms wide, "this, was a benediction. It's ours forever, but only if it lives in our hearts. So we must let go of it without too much fuss, and in that way alone can it stay with us forever."

They chose the Aleppo Pine, a hardy native tree that flourished on the precipitous slopes of the High Atlas amongst the holm oak and the juniper. It was the smallest of the three, but also the most yielding, and like a reed, it could endure storms as well as droughts. It was a brave tree and a survivor said Pepa.

Brahim travelled on his mule for two days and a night across the parched Zat river at Ait Ouir and up the Tizi n'Ait

Imgver pass, then round the steep serpentine curves that followed, to find and bring the tree that waited for them. His perilous journey, Pepa told Brahim, was the symbol of their own journey through life and that it would not be forgotten.

Alegria and Jerónimo turned up with a spade and manure gathered from Brahim's mules. Pepa dug the dry earth first, then the children, with their hands, to better feel and smell the soil, and when the tree stood proud, they watered it with water from the river. Pepa shook the earth that clung to her pinny and began to invoke the Spirit of the Creator, as she had seen her grandmother do, after her grandfather had planted an apple orchard.

"Ripen into a wise old tree, Oh Aleppo!"

Pepa then started to chant when everyone thought the ceremony over, and were moving away.

"Be a link between high and low,
And with each and every one here
And with all the elements that surround you.
We thank you Aleppo, tree of the Atlas,
For your Presence now, and in our hearts, forever."

The sapling's tender branches swayed as if to acknowledge her chant, and everyone whispered 'In Secula Seculorum.' They danced around the tree singing thank you Aleppo tree of the Atlas until Pepa felt giddy, sat on the ground, and sent the children to look for a goose feather, the wool of sheep caught on brambles, twigs and a pebble from the river bank which they then placed as gifts at the foot of the well-pleased young tree.

Alegria and Jerónimo had shed all their tears by the time they waved their last goodbye from the Auberge's gate. Alegria could not speak except to shout "Don't look back!"

Just as an Ibis, with his long, thin, down-curled bill flew past, Brahim appeared smiling through a diaphanous haze. His mules carried their luggage to the car where Ahmed was waiting at the same spot where Brahim had first met them. "Go with your God, whom ever He may be" he said, and he was gone.

FOURTEEN

The Morning Star

Two Mariquita Perez dolls, the latest craze in girls' playthings awaited Carlota and Paloma on their return from Ourika.

To welcome back Alexi, there was a donkey foal, grazing between the kennel and the chicken coop. An exquisite cloisonné box rested on top of the piano, next to Rosario's prized Chinese vase, with a surprise inside, which Rosario took to her bedroom to savour in private. And for Pepa, in the laundry room, a goat she spontaneously named Bienvenido, fretted to be milked.

Elias had yearned for the return of his family, and their lukewarm response to his carefully chosen gifts, and their measured tempo since coming home from the Atlas, disconcerted him. Ourika, he failed to perceive, had been a chink of light in each of their lives, a magical window that had opened just for them at the right moment, and nothing that followed could be as complete as their stay at the Auberge du Retour. Not that any of them would notice, but over the following weeks, each began to enjoy the minutest of happenings, a fresh sense of purpose and to formulate new resolutions, the most startling of all being Rosario's withdrawal of the girls from the Convent, and her placing them within walking distance of The Orchard, at the École de la Palmeraie. For Paloma, it was love at first sight with her new form-teacher Madame Cavalier, the first to express a belief in her.

Seeing this new order emerging, Pepa, for the first time, seriously contemplated a return to her native land.

*

On no account was Rosario to leave the house. Her blood pressure shot up two weeks before the baby was due and the opportunity to take things easy and to play, incessantly, Debussy's La Mer for which she had developed a fixation, was heaven.

"For God's sake, come quickly!" panicked Elias from the bedroom. "It's her waters!"

"Call the midwife." Pepa shouted "and remind her its number five this time!"

Rosario's waters had erupted on her way to the bathroom, like an opening dam. Pepa laughed. "More water than baby in that barrel of yours!"

"Is it alright, too much water?" Rosario asked.

"It's clear, there's no green stuff... of course it's alright. I see you've lit a candle, Rosario."

"It worked for Alexi."

"And it will work now. You're not anxious, are you, cariño?"

"No. First time I've been so calm. I feel as if all is being taken care of."

"That's the spirit, as long as you do your bit, you'll get help. I would wait downstairs if I were you" she told Elias pacing the room, "unless you want to witness the birth."

"I'll wait for the midwife" he said relieved at the option.

"How about the Rosary between contractions?" asked Rosario.

"Singing would be better" said Pepa, "it will help with the breathing." Rosario exploded into a heartfelt Sole Mio before Pepa could think of a song. "Maravilloso!..." she exclaimed, soon after Rosario's long scream pierced the dawn and the child's head appeared with a mass of black glistening curls as it moulded through the dilated cervix.

Pepa called to Elias from the balcony that a morning star was born. They named him Mikael, Elias, Joseph, as was Rosario's wish. His two sons carried his name as the Butler tradition dictated and Elias felt that with the birth of his second son, he had fully ensured the continuity of his lineage. But without remorse he knew that Alexi was his number one.

"Are you thinking what I'm thinking?" Rosario asked gazing at her new son.

"Angelina?" hesitated Pepa, massaging the infant's pink feet.

"Isn't it extraordinary?"

"She was the same" Pepa said softly. "Black hair. Placid, soft-eyed, and the radiance..." uttered Pepa, moved by her vivid recollection of Angelina.

"D'you...?"

"Don't even think of it Rosario. Leave these half-baked ideas to Joaquín. Angelina is up there, and Mickael is down here. He is a new soul, starting now."

"If he is her reincarnation, think what joy for me!"

"That's beside the point. For the child's sake, see him for who he is!"

Before the procession of relatives and friends were invited to visit mother and child, Alcaya the house maid, came to bestow her own blessing. She had nurtured Rosario through her pregnancy as if she were her own sister, and out of friendship and gratitude, she was sent to be taught reading and writing in preparation for the Brevet d'Études Élémentaires which Rosario knew was her maid's secret ambition. Educating servants in Rosario's social circle was considered as misguided and as 'quelque chose de mauvais goût.' and she was shunned by the Société Casablanquaise.

*

"Guapo!" cried Pepa.

"And what's that twinkle in your eye..." teased Rosario. "Own up Samuel, what's happened?" she pressed.

"First things first" he said, peering inside Miko's diaper. "Another nephew!" he chanted, as if he had discovered a small treasure. "Congratulations you two!"

"We're waiting..." baited Rosario.

"I can't believe you lot haven't noticed anything different

about me!" he said smoothing his hair, ultra sleek with gomina.

"We've told you, you look like a boy!" said Elias, "but we don't know why!" he said, chuckling to himself.

"For Christ's sake, can't you see?" cried Samuel walking up and down the room.

"Your stick! You're not using your stick Samuel!" exclaimed Pepa. "How come?"

"Penicillin!" he exclaimed leaping into a failed double entrechat.

"Penny what?" asked Pepa, catching him before he stumbled.

"A wonder drug, discovered since 1936, but only available now. I've been on it for the last three months whilst in Arcachon and I feel, well, a new man!" he cried, this time perfecting his leap.

"Are you cured?" asked Pepa astounded.

"It's helping beyond my wildest dreams, but the osteomyelitis has been with me for far too long."

"Dearest brother!" wept Elias coming to embrace him.

"Allah is merciful" whispered Samuel in his arms.

"Allah-u-Akban—God is Great- Elias added.

*

Chosen as godparents for the goodness of their hearts (which they attributed, not to themselves but to their respective ancestors), Saint Domingo and Saint Romero, Javier de los Barcos, the Spanish Consul at Fez, and his wife Maria de las Constelaciones, Miko was baptised in the miniscule Spanish hermitage of Maria del Mar, in the Medina near the harbour. This was followed by a picnic under The Orchard's fig tree, just as Maria de las Constelaciones had wished. "Such a humble start for Miko" said Rosario.

"You're comparing it with Alexi's" commented Pepa.

"His went with such a bang!"

"They have different paths..." said Pepa, in an allusive way.

"He's my baby you know..." said Rosario moved by words

217

she had never before uttered.

"Of course he is cariño..."

"I mean... I feel like a REAL mother! Did you hear me mother?" she almost howled, overcome by the flood of her own emotions.

"I heard you cariño" said Pepa, holding her daughter in her arms. "And it's truly wonderful that you do."

"I can't believe I actually said it!" snivelled Rosario.

"I'm very happy for you and little Miko. More than I can say."

"I love Alexi too mother! God knows how I love that boy. He is... he is the jewel in my crown... but this one is my baby, my little sweet baby."

Pepa wanted to ask about the girls and if they had a place under that new-found cloak of motherhood, but she didn't, because she knew the reply would blemish the moment.

*

It was not just the coming Spring that tinted the air with riotous shades of pink and gold, and filled it with heady scents. Rumours circulated that the war was ending and peace was within reach. A kind of expectation, new and fresh—as if people had forgotten what the world was like before— brightened faces in the streets. Some, for whatever reason, were indifferent, others were loud, and there were those who kept silent, lest they disturb the fragile balance that hangs with any contest, until victory is declared.

A letter from José Luis arrived that wrote of an imminent world peace. Spain, he said was slowly regaining a semblance of normality under the Generalísimo's dictatorship, but the pride and purpose of the nation and its readiness for a New World Order, would only come, if and when a true democracy returned. The raging had gone but there was a heartlessness amongst those who had lived the war and at best, a numbness dwelled in peoples' hearts. Even though Spain now seemed safe, Pepa could not envisage Elias leaving his beloved Morocco ever again. This was his home, and he needed the stability of his own roots now that increasingly, his health was failing. Pepa cautioned Rosario, eager to start afresh, not to hustle Elias until peace was officially declared, and when on armistice day, Rosario spoke to Elias about returning home, she saw a glaze cover his eyes and his greyish-blue complexion turn white. She called if he was alright and to say something.

"Give me a second or two will you?" he murmured moments later. "You were saying querida?"

"I said I wanted to go back to Spain, Elias."

"Oh yes... that was it, I remember now."

"Are you sure you're alright?" He wished he did not have to give an answer. "Aren't you happy here cariño?" he asked fearfully.

"Something's missing here Elias."

"You have everything!"

"I need to see my family. It's been nearly ten years Elias, ten years!"

"We could go on a holiday, somewhere you've never been before."

"No. I want my folk, I want my culture, I want to belong."

"Belong?"

"Yes, like you belong here. Surely you must know the feeling. You felt it in Nice, you told me so yourself, the longing for your birth-place, your kind. The smells, colours, sounds, sunsets, everything!"

"Europe" he said "is old and dying. We are new here, we're still pioneers. There's a better future here for the children. It will take years for Europe to reconstruct. It's derelict there cariño! Chaos! There'll be hardships for years to come and I may not be able to work, not like here. Think, cariño, think!"

"When you left Spain" she said tight-lipped, "you promised it would be temporary, until the end of the revolution. It's been over for six years now Elias, and we're still here!"

"I thought you belonged here now. I thought you were happy. I thought you liked this country and my family. I thought you made friends, I thought you had scope for your

219

own needs. You never complained about it before!"

"It's been good here Elias. And yes, I've been very happy here, but there is always a time for change, and the time is now."

Elias confided his terror of reprisals to Pepa, of secret police lists, checks made on those returning, and of murderous revenge still committed in the dead of night. Those blacklisted in 1936, he was convinced, were still being hounded and when found, given unconstitutional trials, found guilty and shot, or disappeared without trace. He had no doubts in his mind that executions would continue until long after Franco's demise. Pepa reassured him, with more than a tinge of disquiet for she was not certain herself that the present regime would have no recriminations against him. "Why don't you talk it over with Javier at the Consulate? He can make direct enquiries on your behalf to the powers that be, let you know, then you can decide. But I should share this with Rosario if I were you."

"I'm ashamed to" he said, turning away from Pepa to hide his embarrassment.

Taken aback by his lingering fears, Rosario agreed to ascertain Elias' safety before embarking on a major move.

It was 1945, the war was over and to Elias a move seemed ludicrous at this time. Harmony, so elusive since their arrival in Morocco, was finally theirs, tangible, throughout the house and garden. Pepa remarked that moreover, it was a reflection of a more peaceful world outside, until days later, on the 6th of August, news came of the bombs dropped on Hiroshima and then Nagasaki. "So much for the perfect natural order of our wonderful Ourika!" Rosario ranted. "And where does this leave us?"

Pepa was fully aware that Rosario's 'us' had nothing to do with the fate of humanity but for her own needs.

Rosario was not the only one to feel confusion and outrage, Pepa told her, but things had to be turned around, beyond helplessness and apathy. Like so many others, despite her optimistic words, Pepa too, sank into an abyss of depression over the horror of Hiroshima and with loathing, watched how

Rosario's outrage about the bombing lighten, the moment news came from the authorities in Madrid that Elias' name had been erased from the dreaded black list. Rosario goaded Elias until he began official proceedings. He said nothing about his distrust for the declaration of his clearance not even to Pepa, still convinced a secret force was at work to lure him into the lion's den once he set foot in Spain. He agonized with an all-consuming fear, but agreed for proceedings to commence on condition that Tangier would be an intermediate stop to finalise his Moroccan business.

The compromise cheered him up and he declared over a glass of champagne one evening, that he would follow Rosario to the Pillars of Hercules. The following week he had assembled a bundle of papers from the Chambre Internationale de Commerce, a licence to practice business in Spain, permits of various kinds and new passports for himself and his family, having taken the calculated precaution of registering the children on Pepa's passport and Rosario on his own, as a guarantee that Rosario could not go anywhere without him. Carlota and Paloma could not imagine a world without Binot and meeting their much older cousins, Mingo and Lalia in Spain, was no consolation. News of their leaving was left until the last moment. Trini's tears soaked several of Elias' handkerchiefs and Samuel, only half surprised, promised to visit in Tangier before their final crossing to Spain. The house, Joaquín pledged, would be kept just as it was, until its contents were ready for shipping to Spain, and as Rosario wished, he would see that her trusted maid Alcaya and her son stayed at The Orchard until then.

FIFTEEN

Tingis

The last week of Ramadan was the most unyielding to endure not only for the Islamic faithful but also for the infidels, and it was no surprise to Elias and his family to see men at the end of their physical limits, quarrelling or dozing everywhere on the streets of Tangier, like disorderly juveniles or lost souls in the nether world.

It was the Spanish Consulate that found them a house.

The Villa Graziella was perched above the bay of Tangier on the Charf hill overlooking the straits of Gibraltar. It had recently been vacated by the Italian Consul Signor Conti, now posted to Beirut. Raziz, the Contis' chauffeur, took over from Ahmed who returned to Casablanca in an uninhibited torrent of tears.

Rasiz was no ordinary driver. His employer made it a priority to only engage literate staff and Rasiz was no exception. He had been a teacher of the Qur'an and a multi-lingual guide at the Dar el Makhzen. He apologised for some of his countrymen's un-Islamic behaviour during Ramadan, and wishing to atone for what he knew most Christians felt about that period of their religious calendar. He told them that it was a very important month of fasting in which the Qur'an was revealed as a guide to all men and as evidence for the true religion. He saw Pepa's disapproving look and added that the truth was indeed in a person's heart.

They were privileged to stay at the Villa Graziella he announced, for they could look daily into the stormy waters of the Straits where currents flow their different courses—a reminder of man's polarities and inner struggles—and he recounted the story of Poseidon and Gaia who mated there and produced the giant Anteus who, in time, married a Moorish nymph called Tingis; to honour his mother, their son Sophyx, named his city Tingis. What Rasiz did not tell, was that the Charf hill, where the villa stood, had become a burial ground for the holy, but they would see that for themselves as they wound their way up the hill dotted with white-domed Marabouts.

"It's the only house on the hill!" Rosario exclaimed dismayed when she caught sight of a shimmering roof at the very top.

"Look behind you Madame" said Rasiz slowing down, "where the road curves to the hillside, clinging right at the edge. Don't you see it? There's another house. It was once a small palace and now it's a retreat for novice monks, but you'll never see them, for they are also hermits."

"So we really are on our own up here!"

"To the left of the road" Raziz continued with his guide's tone, "is a narrow path that takes you to Monsieur Lilius' place. Monsieur Lilius is a writer and a recluse."

"We're most definitely on our own!" confirmed Rosario.

"Here, you are surrounded by beauty and peace Madame, and these are your true neighbours."

"Perfect, if you want to become a nun!" she snided.

"You love solitude! Think of Ourika!" exclaimed Elias, already enamoured with the place.

"That was different. For a start, the town is there" Rosario pointed at the sprawl of buildings down the hill. "You just can't ignore it, and if it's there" she argued, "you might as well enjoy it!" .

"Shall we look for a house in the town then?" Elias asked dispirited.

"Let's at least look inside the house since we're here" suggested Pepa, desperate not to be amidst the hurly burly of souks, nightclubs and shops.

Rasiz pushed the prodigious wooden gate guarding the villa to reveal the full extent of the property. It was built on several levels of adjoining blocks with cantilevered balconies suspended from the cliff side overlooking the sea and the sandy beach below. It was not Pepa's idea of heaven, but to Elias and Rosario it was a grand and fabulous folly. "Changed your mind querida?" asked Elias.

"Absolutamente mi amor!" she exclaimed opening her arms wide, to better breathe the biting sea air.

"This is like nowhere I've ever been!" she cried in one of her yet most melodramatic tones.

"Not so absolutamente safe for the children..." interrupted Pepa pointing at the cliff.

"We like it here Yaya!" cried Alexi, already inebriated by the howling wind "and we can play zoomy games" he added, becoming an airplane dangerously close to the edge.

The biting wind wouldn't do her chest any good, brooded Pepa, trying not to breath in the abrasive sea air. But if Rosario wanted it, the deal would be sealed, and that would be that.

Rasiz remarked that Signor Consul was renowned in Tangier for his extravagant entertaining of gangsters, drug dealers, cinema idols and royalty, and that they would do well not to advertise their presence there, if they wanted a quiet life.

For all its furnishings, chattels and glitter however, the house sounded hollow and it was conspicuously empty of servants. It was customary for owners to keep retainers on while away, even for prolonged absences, but in this case the Contis had kept on only Rasiz and Mohtar, the gardener, who was also a calligraphist. Pepa insisted that if they stayed at the Graziella, all unused rooms remain locked to avoid unnecessary housework. She pleaded that Rosario refrain from rushing into a social life, and that she tutor the children herself since they would not be starting school until they arrived in Barcelona. Rosario planned a programme of dictation, composition, the reading aloud of Don Quijote de la Mancha, Le Livre de Mon Ami, a little Arithmetic and Spanish history, beginning with the story of El Cid, one of her romantic heroes.

Pepa improvised a small altar on the sill of her bedroom window so that she could begin a purifying ritual for the house as she was edgy about what she felt were the years of corruptive resonance drenching its walls.

The last thing she anticipated was that she would make a friend of Rasiz. It came about congenially during his chauffeuring of her to the souks where she shopped every day, for fresh fruit and vegetables, and during the to-and-fro-ing from church on Sundays. She confessed that she was apprehensive about Tangier. Wasn't it a dangerous city, a detrimental place in which to live? Rasiz nodded. Here he was, a polyglot, teacher of the Qur'an and an historian, chauffeur to an absent sybaritic diplomat—lover of the demi-monde. Often, he had asked himself why had he long endured this depraved city and after much reflection he wanted to believe that whatever the answer was, the response would be in favour of his soul's plan.

Not everyone recoiled from the city. Won over by Tangier a second time, Rosario thought it to be the most captivating city in the world. Soon after settling, she subjected herself to Mrs Fogg's class. Affectionately known as Foggy, she was a ruddy woman of a certain age who in her youth had run away from home in Hampshire to Morocco and had fallen in love with tangier (even though, she reminded her students, Mark Twain had called it "That African perdition"). Foggy gave classes in Moroccan history in a quaint mixture of English, French and Spanish, and always started with a theatrical reading of the Merchant of Venice, Act 2, Scenes 1 and 7, when the Prince of Morocco came to woo Portia, and after she finished her recitation, advised that Shakespeare was by far the best way to become proficient about Morocco since there were more than sixty references to it in his works, and all of them, she said, were based on reports from English traders and envoys who had close links with the Saadian rulers. Her students, she insisted, were to become acquainted with Samuel Pepys on the Tangiers Expedition, James Richardson's' works on the abolition of slavery, and with Charles de Foucauld, a missionary in the Sahara desert. Then spoken sotto voce, she told them of Isabelle Eberhardt, a woman who became a

Bedouin man and died young and in a desperate state. Not even Rosario's fanciful mind could have invented the extravagant and chimerical lives of those eccentric, extraordinary travellers and it excited her to know that through Papa Joseph, Alexi and Miko had similar romantic and fantastic origins.

That was in the past. Today, writers, film directors, actors and painters, met at Le Club des Artistes, sometimes feet away from her, and Rosario luxuriated in their nearness and thought of how Colette would have relished its Bohemian spirit.

For Elias, pleasure was watching the small fishing boats preparing to sail at dusk, and to sup a glass of mint tea with Rosario by his side, on the terrace of the Rif Hotel, silent and dreaming of his own patch of the Atlantic back in Mazagan.

He was taken aback when Rosario enquired about their impending move to Spain, muttering that he was in the middle of something big, something that would keep them going when they got to Spain. The deal, he revealed, was importing tea from Gibraltar for the English contingent in Tangier. Was that really big, she asked. The demand would never dry up was his reply, and when she enquired about how long it would take to establish, he said after Christmas. José Luis, she reminded him, was already looking for a home for them near the Gran Via.

"It's going well here, isn't it querida?" he asked, instantly wishing he hadn't.

"But it's not for ever!" she protested.

To encourage Rosario into forgetting about the passage of time, he introduced her to Gabi, a socialite in the town and sister-in law to her old flame Dionisio. From then on, for Rosario and Gabi, it was shopping, bridge and spending most afternoons at the Casa Port, the tea room for the famous. In the evenings they changed into their Rita Hayworth's style gowns in time for dinner and then nightclubs., with or without escorts.

The transient nature of the circumstances was what kept Pepa from admonishing Rosario. Her frivolous life, her neglect of the children's tuition and her lazing in bed until lunchtime to make up for her late nights pushed Pepa to the brink of desperation. Rosario hardly ever saw her toddler Miko, except when she flitted in and out of the villa and caught sight of him, sitting curled up like a kitten inside the gardeners' wheelbarrow where he took permanent refuge.

"Ay..Ay..Ay..Elias, Elias...How I feel for you..." Pepa bewailed, when Elias joined her for breakfast.

"You're not too well are you old friend?"

"Yaya...Yaya ..." he wheezed, with a pain that distorted his features.

"This place isn't for you Elias, is it?" Pepa said shaking her head.

"I'm in agony Yaya., and she hasn't even noticed."

"I know" she said, placing a cup of hot milk between his hands.

"She'll ask me again about Spain" Elias puffed. "And I can't bear it."

"It's been five months Elias! You promised..." Pepa said softly.

"Don't remind me" he begged.

"Wait until she asks again. My feeling is she won't, at least not for another month."

Something new was brewing in Rosario's life, Pepa sensed it when she returned flushed from one of her tea sessions with Gabi, mumbling something about Dionisio coming to Tangier. It was not too difficult to predict her daughter's determination to rekindle their romance, but this time, spent, with trying to supervise the children who roamed the hill all day long, teasing the goats and picking wild and sometimes poisonous fruits, Pepa had no energy left to intervene.

She demanded that a maid take over the household duties while she took charge of the children .

The girls had to clean their own bedrooms, whiten their sandals and wash their underwear daily, and for relaxation, Pepa gave each a metre of Egyptian cotton on which they learned under her supervision to embroider petit point. Alexi was made to whitewash the low walls surrounding the patio to prevent armies of ants from climbing up them, water the herb garden at sundown and write five lines of whichever word he loved best that day. Miko the toddler was allowed to just be. In the afternoons, when the sun was fierce, the children sat in a circle in the Gazebo to listen to their grandmother's vivid renderings of Berceo's "Milagros". She never explained or instructed them, and if they asked, she said that the storyteller's mission was to narrate, not to explain, and they each sank into a contemplative state of their own, long after she had finished reading.

Rasiz became an idol with the children. The stories and folktales he told them, as he drove on their outings, he said affirmed the value of faith, and to listen and learn. "Long ago" one story began, "when the world had just began, and all the people had tails." The children giggled. "No one would have dared make fun of a tail then" he chided, "because a tail was something to be proud of, like a beautiful mane of hair." Fearing this would be one of Raziz's darker stories, Pepa steered him to Abu Kassim's Boots, a tale from 'A Thousand and One Nights' and he began. "Once in the city of Baghdad..." until their ride took them to the Sultan's palace which enclosed an Andalucian garden. It surprised Pepa to see Phoenician graves, all dull and monochrome. Everywhere else there was greenness and Rasiz said that even in the middle of winter, Tangier still bloomed with bright red and orange bougainvillaea, scented arum lilies (or St Joseph lilies, as Pepa thought of them), humming bird flowers, frangipani, jacaranda, blue lotus, and the incredibly dangerous bugle-shaped datura which Rasiz told them, was a witch of a plant that drove people who took it crazy, or sent them into a long drugged sleep. Pepa's hair stood on end when Rasiz explained that the Judas tree, they had just passed, uncannily flowered every year between Good Friday and Easter Sunday, and Alexi shivered and said that its smell made his heart beat faster and his head spin. Raziz explained that gardens were miniature replicas of the world and had their evil spirits too, but in a garden, he added knowingly, the balance was always to the good. He stayed silent. "And even more so" he continued, telling them of the Arab saying about the desert where God removed all superfluous life from it so he might have a garden where he could walk in peace.

*

Most evenings Rosario visited the kitchen to gulp several glasses of icy water before heading for bed without visiting the boys to kiss them goodnight, or checking on Elias waiting for her, alone on the terrace. The icy water was to dampen the inferno that consumed her after she had been with Dionisio and Pepa did not know how to stop the accelerated momentum of theirp 229
entanglement. The worsening atmosphere at the Graziella disturbed the children's already precarious equilibrium and none more so than Paloma's who wanted life to be as it was in Ourika and to be loved as much by her mother as she was then. The cruel truth Pepa told her, was that her mother could never love her as she wanted, but that patience and trust would reward her, for she would, one day, be cherished and loved, more than she could ever dream.

After days of struggling against the pull of their mutual passion, Dionisio and Rosario gave in to it in the heat of an afternoon when Elias assumed Rosario to be with Gabi. That night, Rosario found herself revealing all to Pepa. Too weary to be outraged Pepa asked about Sarita, Dionisio's wife.

"He'll leave her for me" Rosario replied. "No question."

"And Elias? What of Elias?"

"Elias!" Rosario shook her head, unable to tell Pepa for a moment, that Elias hadn't been a husband to her for years and that the conception of their son Miko was a fluke.

But when they next met, Dionisio spoke of friendship and decency and how inconceivable it was for him to persist in deceiving his cousin and life-long friend Elias. He was not proud of having taken his wife, if only for one afternoon, but now, the only honourable option was for him to leave at once and never see her again.

Rosario had glimpsed at a life of passion and in the days that

229

followed Dionisio's departure, she revelled in the obsessive fantasy of herself as a widow. The only way out of her misery was to nudge Elias again to speed up their departure for Spain. Never in the thirteen years of their marriage had she witnessed Elias in such a state of desperation. A snivelling heap, he begged her not to ask this of him. The commotion brought Pepa to the scene with a glass of water for Elias. "It's alright Elias. We won't" she murmured. "We won't."

"Won't what?" bellowed Rosario. "Won't what?"

"Not now Rosario. Not now."

"I want to know!"

"Tomorrow... Let's leave it until tomorrow" Pepa pleaded.

"It's alright Yaya, let me tell her now" Elias said in a faint whisper of resignation. "Rosario, querida" he began, taking as deep a breath as he was able, "I cannot go to Spain. I know they'll arrest me at the frontier and have me shot."

"You've been cleared! Cleared! Cleared! God almighty Elias!"

"Keep quiet" Pepa warned her.

"I won't! Why should I? This is so childish!"

"Can't you see Elias needs peace" insisted Pepa.

"You've lost your balls Elias. You're a pathetic coward!"

"Out Rosario! Out!" shouted Pepa. "The door….." she said sternly.

"Cariño, don't make me go….. if only for Alexi's sake" cried Elias.

Rosario screamed, returning in a fury to his side. "Alexi? What on earth…..?

"I'm his father..."

"Blackmail now, is it? You've sunk that low have you?"

"Rosario..." he moaned, "you can be so cruel..."

"And I suppose you're not! You knew all along, didn't you, that you never intended crossing the straits. You got us all here under false pretences, didn't you? I see it all now—'I will follow you to the Pillars of Hercules,' you said—Romantic fool that I was! That was as far as you intended to go. Wasn't it?"

"I hoped I could do it. I swear I did. I tried so hard Rosario, but it's beyond me. I'm so bloody scared."

"You don't want to go... Is that final?"

"Rosario...I can't..!"

"Don't then!"

"Querida...My angel...I knew you'd..."

"We'll go!" she interrupted. "And I want a separation."

"Rosario..... I beg you... You're killing me!"

The children came running down from their bedroom to ask who was killing their father and Pepa sent them back saying their father was safe.

"Things will be clearer tomorrow Elias" she promised, escorting him to bed.

But in the kitchen, Pepa and Rosario talked the whole night. Pepa let Rosario unwind and talk of her frustrations as a woman at the peak of her sexual prime. As a woman who had loved, but without passion, how she thirsted for that unknown elixir. Tangier, she reckoned, had been her own Temptation of St Anthony, but unlike Anthony, she badly wanted to succumb. Spain too, had called her in her belly for a while. She could no longer ignore her needs and had to break from Elias and start afresh. She wanted another bite out of life. A juicier, spicier bite this time.

Pepa held Rosario's trembling hands, then she told her that Elias was dying. Not tomorrow or the next day but soon, and her duty was to be by his side. As if consumed by a lightening fever Rosario's body began to shudder and she screamed a long demented wail before she let herself cry quietly with a pain she knew was love. Sacrifice was what was asked of her. She had never given, not unconditionally. Others had for her and this reversal was starting now, for Elias needed to see her lying by his side when he awoke. She could not believe she had it in her to forgive so unreservedly and that she would allow another's needs to come before her own. In a way, it elated and surprised her that at this moment she felt lighter than she had done for months. There was no more longing to escape, and her return to Casablanca seemed fated and full of meaningful purpose.

PART THREE

All is included in transformation,
You too are subordinate to change,
even destruction.
So is the entire universe.

Marcus Aurelius

SIXTEEN

The Return of the Storks

The journey back to The Orchard was perceived as their destiny. Pepa remarked that they were like a family of storks returning home and that the stork was a sacred bird which symbolised birth and rebirth and was most certainly a bird of good omen. Elias' relief at his family's happy resignation allowed him to breathe again without gasping for his life.

The Orchard was as they had left it. Alcaya had placed fresh flowers from the garden in every room and gladioli and arum lilies in the Chinese vase on top of the piano as Rosario always liked it. Joaquín was there to greet them. Rosario detested him for his feigned surprise at their return and for his patronising chuckles that she could not keep away from the place, but he had entered Alexi's name at the local school and arranged for the girls to take their entrance examination at the Lycée de Jeunes Filles, and she was grateful for his foresight. The girls failed nevertheless and were sent to a school renowned for its tutoring of the academically deprived and for the disrupted education of children of travelling diplomats. 'École Aubusson' was a mixed day school in a very large 1920's villa, hidden away like a lunatic asylum amidst palm trees and gardens near the Cathedral. Paloma fretted that she would be the ugliest, puniest and hairiest girl in the school and at the mercy of cruel, teasing boys. But Carlota could not wait to be amongst the potent swirl of male hormones which she had not yet experienced. She was twelve, with slender still girlish legs, breasts that had developed faster than the rest of her, and auburn hair which fell shiny and dead straight over her rounded shoulders and down to her waist. There was not a boy who did not, from day one, compete for her exclusive attention. But Ruben Sidorenko, older than the other boys, the son of an émigré farmer from Mongolia, had eyes only for Paloma. For Ruben, Paloma was the most beautiful creature he had ever seen. She told her grandmother that his gaze aroused and disturbed her but Pepa said she was on the threshold of becoming a woman and to rejoice.

Rumours spread in the classroom that Monsieur Trompette (so called because of his chronic rhinitis and loud nose blowing) had it in for Carlota. Trompette was the deputy headmaster responsible for maintaining the school's reputation and delivering academic results in record time. Carlota's excessive interest in boys was of less concern to him than the boys fixation on her. A chronic lack of concentration paralysed the school like a sudden epidemic. At first, Carlota's seductiveness was dealt with by straight detention, then by lowering her grades. It was when none of these measures bore fruit, that Monsieur Trompette took to whipping her with his cane every morning after her Latin class. Anxious that her sister would be harmed, Paloma told Rosario, who dismissed Carlota as pathologically provocative. But when Carlota began to return violence with violence, Monsieur Trompette's excitement increased beyond his wildest expectations.

The academic drilling at Aubusson's was relentless. Paloma puzzled how could her sister succeed so brilliantly when much of her time was spent in flirtatious games with boys or submitting to Monsieur Trompette's sado-masochism, whilst she, herself worked so hard for meagre results. She thought her sister a genius, but she too passed her entrance exam to the Lycée, albeit in a class lower than other girls of her age.

Of more interest to Rosario were the comments on Alexi's progress by his form teacher. Though only seven, his logical mind she told her, could swiftly convert abstract thought into concreteness. Furthermore, he was seen to arbitrate disputes in classroom and playground with the ease of an experienced referee and she ventured to predict that Law was his natural métier since she had never met a child so young with so strong a sense of justice.

The moment Elias had dreaded since the onset of his illness had arrived. The shortage of oxygen to his brain his doctor explained, was limiting its function and this would result in serious blackouts and errors of judgement. His advice was that Elias should give up his business. Rosario could no longer look at Elias without loathing. His eyes, blood-shot, his face, purple and puffy, and his abdomen, distended and pendulous, were constant reminders of all she detested in life: ugliness, disease and failure. She had forgotten about the Elias of his heyday, his enigmatic aura and his exotic charisma. All that was left was Elias as he was now, and all that was left for her to do in order to survive the horror was to withdraw into the tower of her fantasy. She played Colette's music which took her into wild flights of fancy, where she saw herself with Colette in a Paris garret off the Rue Mansard where her friend had once lived. Or, in the semi-darkness of her locked bedroom, she drenched herself in the stories of Emma Bovary and Thérèse Desqueyroux, revelling in her acute identification of the heroines' disintegrating idealisations of the men they had chosen for husbands. Confined in a world from which she saw no escape, Rosario's thoughts wavered from wishing Elias dead, her own death (although it was never likely that she would pursue this option to its conclusion) or, and she couldn't fathom how this could come about, a breakthrough leading her to a journey of spiritual regeneration.

*

Rosario leaped into Samuel's arms. Pepa had sent him a note via Ahmed, expressing her concern over her daughter's outright withdrawal and rejection of Elias. It was this that brought Samuel to The Orchard, sooner than he had intended.

"What's up?" he asked, responding to her affectionate embrace. "Let's sit on the lawn and tell Sami" he said, "just as in the old days."

"I want to die..."

"Here?"

"Oh Samuel!" she pouted. "Seriously!"

"Tell me then." She breathed the freshly splashed Eau de Cologne from the nape of his neck . "He doesn't smell like this any more" she sighed.

"Elias is a very sick man Rosario. It could happen to any one of us."

"I miss it."

"What?"

"That smell."

"Well have another sniff!" he laughed offering his armpits.

"Samuel... I'm desperate!"

"Is it about Tangier and all that business?"

"That was the start. The betrayal. Him knowing all the time we wouldn't go to Spain. That is hard to forgive. I thought I could. I thought I did. And now, well, the anger, the resentment, it's all coming to me. And him. The way he looks, smells, it's so unlike him. You know how fastidious he was. I'm not cut out for caring for sick people Sami. I do care in my head, but I'm no saint. I came back to minister to him, I wanted to, I really did. And now I can't. I feel sick. I feel a prisoner. I can't breathe. I'm going to explode. I'm so afraid of his death Sami. And even more of his living! And me, my life, now, after!"

"I know how you feel chiquita."

"Of course... You, of all people. How did you cope, really?"

"There is only one way Rosario. After you've done with the self-pity, you've got to forget about yourself. That is the only way. Believe me Rosario."

"You sound like my mother!"

"Thank you for that! Yaya is the most generous and wisest person I know."

"I'll try" she said unconvincingly. "Cheer me up then......" she miaoued, resting her head on his shoulder. "Tell me about you whilst we were away in Tangier."

"It's been a good year for me Rosario. I wish you'd been here. I needed a woman's advice, you know..."

"Now, now...you flatter me Samuel" she whispered.

"Truly..." said Samuel holding her hands. "I've become

engaged Rosario!" She recoiled from him.

"You can't have! I won't let you!"

"Look at me!" He demanded. "I don't understand...!"

"You can't! That's all there is to it!"

"Can't what? Rosario... please..." he pleaded lifting her chin to look into her eyes. "Tell me!"

"Not after Colette!"

"It's been seven years, seven! I hate loneliness, you know that!"

"I'm here!"

"What does that mean, exactly?"

"I'm here! Me, here for you!"

"You're my brother's wife Rosario..."

Her voice grated. "Not for long."

"I didn't hear that Rosario. I-never-heard-that!"

Rosario came close to nest her head on his shoulder again. "So... who's the lucky one then?" she asked, feigning normality. "Do I know her?"

"You've not met her."

"A mystery woman eh?" she said, not sure she wanted to know, yet consumed with curiosity.

"Not exactly. It's Mme Dubail, Francine, my associate's ex-wife."

Rosario heaved, was sick in the flower beds and then ranted and kicked the bushes.

"Have you gone mad?" cried Samuel.

"You idiot!" she bawled. "How could you! I'll never be able to see you again. Is that what you wanted?"

"What are you on about?"

"She's a divorcée! Don't you see? Your marriage will be null and void in the eyes of God and I cannot have a couple living in sin visiting my house! See? See what you've done?"

"Stop that nonsense! You, talking like that. It doesn't become you Rosario. La Pia, Casablanca's number one religious bigot, yes, but you?"

"It's too late Sami. You've ruined something beautiful. It's over. And if you want to see Elias, check first that I'm not in.

And never, ever, bring that woman to my house!"

"Rosario..!"

How could she not have known of her love for Sami after all this time, and how could he not have sensed her wish to turn to him after Elias had gone? She shuddered at the thought that so vital a manifestation had passed them both by, and she was outraged that no sooner had she discovered a precious gem, it was not hers to hold.

It was that loss, unforeseen and unsolicited that had made her turn cold and vindictive towards Samuel.

She had to accept Samuel's needs for companionship Pepa cautioned her, and reminded her of her brief affair with Dionisio, a married man, and of her own double standards. Her feelings for Samuel she warned, had to be diffused, for his sake, hers, and especially for Elias.

Every day, since knowing of his engagement, Rosario drove past Samuel's small-holding in the hope of catching sight of Francine until she saw them emerge holding hands. Seeing her made Rosario resent Samuel all the more for choosing a woman so gauche and unremarkable after Colette's uniqueness. Samuel would surely tire of one so ordinary, and Rosario began to see herself as Colette's rightful successor, but the thought was shattered after Samuel married Francine just weeks after announcing his engagement to her.

She made up her mind to be so compelling that no man could resist her.

A hair appointment at Chez Stefan, the newest and most fashionable salon de coiffure in Casablanca was a good start. A Slav émigré and a lecturer in Slavonic studies before his escape from Czechoslovakia, Stefan's political views made him a persona non grata forcing him and his wife Susha to flee to Paris, learn hair-dressing to give them a livelihood, and then to set up their own business in Casablanca. His youth, virile handsomeness, and northern sobriety instantly captivated Rosario.

He wasn't like any other hairdresser she had known. He said little, but when he did, it was to talk about poverty, injustice, deprivation and world politics. Her appointments became weekly events, and even more frequent when she brought Carlota and Paloma to have their hair trimmed, one girl at a time. It was weeks before Stefan responded to her overt flirtation, and when he asked her straight out if she was after an affair, she was disappointed.

His approach, she told him, was uncouth and unworthy of a cultured man to which he replied that life was too short to be wasted in pretence and useless games. If it was yes, he would think about it, and if not, he would ignore her provocative teasing. "Once you throw the dice in the air, les jeux sont faits, Rosario" he said, combing a strand of her hair before cutting it. "You know this will be short-lived, don't you?"

"What do you mean?"

"I mean it's a divertissement. A turning away for a moment from our present emptiness, yours and mine. You must know this before you say yes. It's a diversion. Nothing more."

If that was true, how could she live with herself afterwards. She had never embarked on a liaison without wanting it to last. At least, she wanted an element of romance, but she shouted, "I've thrown the dice Stefan!"

"No going back?" he asked.

"Where to?" she said swivelling on her chair away from the mirror to face him.

"To the status quo" he replied. She shook her head. "OK then" he said. "When? Where? How?"

"You decide Stefan" she quivered.

"Next Friday, six a.m. at the Ain Diab beach."

"Come on..." she protested.

"I have to be at the salon at seven thirty, and Susha and I don't finish until nine in the evening. That's the only time."

"My husband will be suspicious..."

"That, my dear Rosario is....."

"Ok...OK...OK...I'll say I'm starting an early morning Novena and have to be in church for six o'clock" she stated, trying to emulate Stefan's matter-of-factness.

"And bring a towel. We'll swim afterwards."

The game was up when Pepa asked if she could join her for

241

the Novena, and had no for an answer. "Bravo Rosario. And with Elias so sick!"

"And that's perhaps why, haven't you thought?"

"And who is it this time?"

"My hairdresser. Satisfied?"

"What on earth are you thinking of?"

"He's not just a hairdresser!"

"That's evident! Using this poor man.... Mesmerising him, like a fallen prey!"

"Far from it. He's no prey. He's an exile, like you and me and we are using each other."

"How could you!"

"I had to. I was dying inside. Can you blame me for claiming some of my life back? Even if only for a brief moment?"

"It is wrong in the eyes of God."

"God? Religion? All lies that make you toe the line. Conspiracies, all of them! For better or worse I'm in the business of being my own person, shaping my own life, my own brand of morality. But you, mother, are too locked up in your own beliefs to understand what I'm on about!"

"It seems that you can forget about God and religion and normality when it suits you Rosario. But let me tell you, if I have erected walls in my life, I admit that they were of my own making. Anyway, I believe that whatever we do or not do, we'll all get there in the end, and that is only because of His All-Redeeming Compassion."

"You're uncommonly generous, why?"

"Because somehow, I feel that this is all you are able to do."

"You patronise me and forgive me all at once!"

"How could I not forgive you, when He already has?"

Stefan was not at the beach when Rosario turned up in a new bathing costume for their usual rendez-vous. She found out from the salon later that morning that he had left for a lecturing post in Canada without a word of warning to his clients or staff.

*

242

Rosario found refuge in Miko, her toddler with the bright eyes and enticing smile she had rejected in Tangier. Not unlike Paloma, Miko was undamaged. He had arrived whole and shiny in the world, lolled in the womb amidst the life-giving airiness of the Ourika valley. His beauty and amiability were constantly reiterated by all who saw him and he saw only his own perfection reflected in others. Naked in the garden all day to feel the sun warm his bare skin, Pepa said he was the innocent in the Garden of Eden, except, she added, this was no blooming paradise, and born to this earth in a state of grace, he too, would face his shadows before he returned from whence he came.

But Rosario was unable to visualise her small son beyond the vision of contentment she saw before her.

Short on solaces, after two romantic fiascos, eating became Rosario's consolation. She collected the girls from the Lycée for afternoon tea at the Salon de L'Esterel at the corner of the Rue du Jura. A choice of triple ice cream, a different one every day, and éclairs au chocolat were the girls' favourites. Rosario's choice was always a giant choux drenched in cognac, topped with a whirly pyramid of shiny chantilly cream, that looked as exuberant as the cupola of a byzantine church. She would grow fat and ugly, Carlota snarled, but it wasn't until Lorenzo, and her sister-in-law Lourdes (said to be lithe and chic), announced their impending arrival from Paris, that Rosario began a rigorous diet to compete with Elias' sister.

It was after her first husband, then Spanish Ambassador to Havana in Cuba was assassinated in an ambush, that Lourdes married Lorenzo, an exiled artist from the Spanish Civil War. They first met in a Monmartre's bohemian ghetto, and now penniless, they looked to Elias to rescue them. The basement of The Orchard, vacant since Alcaya had moved into her own accommodation would become their home until Lorenzo found work.

Lourdes, standing at the quay, looked as expected, as chic as a parisienne, and with a laugh cloned from Samuel's. No one had warned Rosario of Lorenzo's club feet, and she rushed into his arms to conceal her initial shock. Lourdes, he told her, was his sole model and sketches of her legs adorned advertisements all over Paris. He complained that legs were all that Paris wanted. Legs for stockings and shoes, legs for the bedroom, legs for the office, legs for the Trocadero. He said how he longed for the freedom of expression and from the need for money. Rosario liked him. She thought of him as Beaudelaire's albatross, ungainly on the ground and lofty and majestic when in flight.

Elias got worse. A couch was placed in the small ante-room on the first floor which had easy access to the terrace for air, and no stairs to climb. Carlota took over Pepa's upstairs bedroom for herself and Paloma and Pepa acquired Elias' old office he no longer used, also on the first floor to keep an eye on Elias at night when it was most needed. At eleven, Paloma was deemed old enough to raise the alarm should her father or grandmother need help. She did not find this a burden even though Pepa's only means of waking her in the middle of the night when she was out of breath was to hurl her clock, crucifix, slipper or glass of water at her.

Elias' agony deteriorated into a complex state of constant terror. He had not told Rosario that he would soon be bankrupt, nor that he had sold most of his assets to Joaquín. All that was left was Le Plateau—Papachito's plot of land by the lighthouse—and his share of the ancestral home. He watched Rosario spend as she had always done and he did not know how to stop her.

Catching up with years of absence and reliving the past to which Elias felt closer than the present, Lourdes could not have come at a more crucial time in Elias' life. She breathed new life into Elias' shrivelling heart, like no one else had the ability to do.

But after months of her and Lorenzo's constant squabbling and screaming, and their daily smashing clatter of broken china, Elias felt overwhelmed and no longer able to give his sister and her husband shelter.

They were like two mice in a small cage, down in the

basement, Lorenzo confided, and the claustrophobia was fast obliterating his inspiration and pretty much killing their relationship.

SEVENTEEN

Of Blood and Bliss

Paloma woke up early. She felt damp, and worried that she had wet her bed, which had not happened before. She turned around to show her grandmother the stains on the back of her nightgown.

"Virgen Santísima!" she cried. "Sweetheart," she said, hugging her, " you've just become a woman! It's your monthlies. That's all it is!"

"But this isn't blood!" contested Paloma.

"The first and last flushes of a woman are often messy. You'll see! tomorrow it will be bright red and beautiful" Pepa took her by the hand to the vast linen cupboard on the landing where Rosario and Carlota's terry sanitary towels were in two piles, next to each other, each, with initials C and R in red, embroidered in cross-stitch by Pepa. "There's yours Palomita. I've already embroidered them."

"It can't be that yayita! I've no breasts!" Paloma cried, her hands holding her flat chest.

"Your temper's changed" Pepa said, " and that's a sure sign."

She reminded Paloma of her responsibility for her own sanitary towels, that she must soak them in cold suds overnight to remove the worst of the stains before she washed them herself, rinsed and hung them out to dry and to feel proud of their whiteness, and to never let them get as grey as her sister's. She then sent Paloma to announce her new status to her mother.

"You haven't complained of any tummy ache" said Rosario, looking askew at her daughter.

"They didn't seem as bad as other aches" Paloma replied, in a tone Rosario read as full of innuendos.

"I see..." she said. "You'll have to tell your father. Fathers must know when their daughters become women." Paloma asked why, when he hadn't even noticed her being a child and Rosario said it was because fathers had to be watchful of their daughters, to make sure no harm came to them when they became women and that they were not taken advantage of. Paloma didn't remember Carlota going through this palaver. All she knew was that she lay moaning in her bed for days before and during her periods.

With the stained nightie as evidence, Paloma stood at Elias' bedroom door. "I am a woman." she declared, adding that her mother had sent her to say that she needed watching. Elias wriggled, incredulous that the diminutive creature before him and with no visible signs of womanhood could be proclaiming it with such disconcerting aplomb.

"A woman eh?" he said at last. "There" said Paloma, handing over her crumpled nightgown. He took it grudgingly. "A woman indeed" he conceded. "Congratulations" he said, returning the gown. And she was now officially a member of womankind.

Her temper had changed Pepa told her. It had come upon her slowly without her noticing it, like one of those stains that appear on a wall, and Paloma recalled Alexi christening her Bossy Boots and Carlota saying no boy would like her because she was such a pest. But Pepa had excused her behaviour saying that it was her juices gone berserk until they found their proper route.

With menstruation came the start of a trousseau: treble sets of sheets and pillow cases, table cloths and serviettes, towels and handkerchiefs, all embroidered from a girl's first bleed until her wedding day. Paloma began hers as soon as the crisp rolls of Egyptian linen arrived from Spain, on to which her aunt Carmela had already traced elaborate scrolls and initials in seamstress chalk for her to follow. She sat at her grandmother's feet when she embroidered them, and listened to her whispered stories of unfinished trousseaux that brought bad luck and of her worry that Carlota's refusal to start hers would lead to an unhappy life.

*

If Paloma was grown up enough to start her bridal trousseau, then she was ready to receive the sacrament of the Eucharist, and she was sent to Father Clement, the new parish priest. He had taught philosophy at Salesian seminaries in Brittany and been a 'Prêtre Ouvrier' in Lille before coming to Casablanca to take over from the very ancient Father Boniface.

When Paloma told him that she loathed the catechism after seeing what it had done to her sister, but that she wanted the Eucharist without the book of rules, Father Clement swept the books of Catechism he had prepared for her, off his desk. He smiled and explained that 'Katechizein' meant 'to din into the ears', and that the catechism was, in fact, a pure exercise in indoctrination only for those who could not think for themselves. He would instruct her differently, and said how excited he was at the challenge. She was to read Theillard de Chardin's Mass of the World and ponder on the meaning of the 'Mass', as she alone perceived it.

She did not understand all that she read and had no clue as to how to put her perception into words, but when Father Clement asked her what she felt on reading it, Paloma found herself saying that she understood everything because she knew she had once felt the mystery of the Mass when she was eight, in the valley of Ourika. She was certain it was what awaited her after death she told him, and because it was so sublime she had not been afraid, until recently, when she heard her father's agonizing cries at night.

Elias' life was wretched, trapped in a confined space where the past was irretrievable, the future fearful, and the present inescapable. Always cunning in business as well as in his private life he had never allowed himself to be cornered without an escape route or contingency plan, but the circle had closed in

248

on him regardless. Anoxic, he wandered the streets at night, often naked and friends, neighbours or the Police returned him home. Rosario played the distraught wife and the more anguished she appeared, the more Elias became mistrustful. He always gazed at Rosario's portrait as he paced the lounge at night, to try and soothe his wretchedness, but as time went by, all he came to see was a tentacled Medusa, and Pepa turned the portrait to face the wall every night to stop him panicking. She kept Elias' paranoid delusions from Rosario, but when he yelled that Rosario was poisoning him, Pepa told her about the portrait and Paloma became the one to dispense her father's medication.

Their daily and nightly encounters were like those of two strangers eager to please and impress one another. Elias thanked her for her ministrations, and Paloma replied it was a pleasure. Sometimes, and to prolong the ever so brief contact, Elias sent her for a glass of milk after he had swallowed his tablets, saying once that she would some day make a good wife. Her eyes bedewed, she asked him to repeat what he had just told her, as she wanted to hear it again. And when he did, she held his hand, swollen, taut and shiny in hers for the first time, and Elias wept without shame.

*

Paloma was apprehensive. She did not expect the announcement of the day of her First Communion to be so soon. Communing with her God, free of fuss and silly clothes was what she wanted, she told Father Clement. Rituals, he stressed, were important too, because they were spiritual signposts and codes that embodied the realities and truths we all sought, and that without them, he cautioned her, we could in times of stress lose our way.

Not certain of what to make of Paloma's accounts of the new priest, and in order to judge for herself, Pepa attended Father Clement's mass. It was his sermon, which had none of the usual blustery delivery of High Mass celebrants, that confirmed her approval of him, and though she could not understand every word he said, she came out of church with a gladness of heart she had not felt since the beginning of her exile. She might return to the fold she told Rosario if only she took the opportunity to hear him preach one Sunday, but Pepa chose not to tell Rosario that the sparkle in Father Clement's blue eyes were like light switches that set his parishioners souls alight.

Rosario remarked the next Sunday that the new priest had preached an eloquent but prosaic sermon, and said that she would introduce herself as Paloma's mother and as a dissident Catholic in need of spiritual re-alignment.

Rosario, Paloma requested, was not to play the piano and the boys were to amuse themselves quietly on the top floor. Her appeal for silence the day before her First Communion was so astonishing that everyone abided by it. She knelt before Pepa's small altar, invoking the bliss of one-ness that had once been hers in the Ourika valley and that was now inexplicably elusive. But in the aching vacuum of her isolation the yearning whisperings of her heart grew louder, so that when the solemn day arrived and Father Clement held the Holy Host to her lips uttering the Prayer of Theillard's mass, she felt, though she could not put it into words, that she dissolved into a love that was fire.

This was the most subdued celebration in the history of The Orchard. Paloma was the only First Communicant and Rosario, Pepa and Carlota the only attenders at the service. Elias' deteriorating health ruled out any chance of a family gathering afterwards and Father Clement declined his invitation to come back to the house, as he had a seminar to prepare for his 'vocations', as he called the young men of the parish who were contemplating the priesthood.

Joaquín appeared unexpectedly, twirling his tennis racquet above his head, in time to see Paloma still wearing her plain poplin white gown, and to slip a picture postcard inside the traditional pouch tied around her waist where her missal was kept. It was a Stupa—the explanation at the back of the card said that a Stupa represented the pure body, speech and mind of the Lord Buddha, and that it transmitted the limitless compassion of a pure heart. She knew the Buddha as a small, smooth and shiny ivory statue she liked to stroke in Joaquín's study sitting on top of a pile of yellowing books, but she had known nothing else until Father Clement told her the Buddha was another Christ, and she had puzzled how someone as sinister (as she thought her uncle to be) could be aware of such things and fail to become a good person.

Joaquín dragged Elias by the arm, away from everyone. Pepa had seen this steely look before in Joaquín's eyes and grasped that the purpose of the visit had little to do with Paloma's First Communion.

He chastised his brother for not complying with his recommended regime and prescribed a more drastic program. A no liquid diet, fruit—not citrus -, raw vegetables and cold boiled barley.

Compliant, Elias listened until Joaquín announced as casually as he would the retail price of a kilo of flour, that Elias' share of the ancestral home was now his, and then, their civilised meeting turned into a bitter confrontation.

He had to be joking Elias cried.

"Am I? And what about your debts, dear brother?"

Elias coughed, turned purple and shouted he had never had any debts in his life.

His mind was going and he had protected him all this time, Joaquín said in a sickeningly honeyed voice.

"I had millions in the bank, Joaquín" muttered Elias.

"Elias, you've lost all your money in failed business transactions. You owed money, big money, right, left and centre. To the Estebanis, the Rodez, even to your good friend Déchaumes. I've paid all your debts Elias!"

"I begged you before" moaned Elias, "never to take my share of the ancestral family home from me. It's my only legacy Joaquín, to my widow and children. And you've stolen it from them." He stopped breathing then gasped. "Tell me you haven't sold the land by the lighthouse?" he rasped in three laboured attempts.

"How could I. It isn't that I haven't tried, it's just not prime land, you know that. It'll take years before it's worth anything. You still owe me Elias!"

Elias shouted that it was he who owed him money from that time in Spain when he saved him from bankruptcy and that he wanted the money back now and with twenty years interest. Rosario came into the room to be marshalled out again. She cried to Pepa that it was like a fixed boxing match in there, without a referee to stop the kill. Pepa burst into the room, ordered Joaquín to leave, and said he was a disgrace and that she would personally see he would never harm Elias again.

EIGHTTEEN

The Silver Thread

Binot was coming home for Easter. Like his half-brother Josh before him, he had been sent to boarding school in the Pyrenees. Right from the start he enjoyed hero status with his cousins, but all at once he was turned into a demi-god to worship from afar. At thirteen, he had flown in airplanes, been in another country far beyond the straits of Gibraltar, seen mountains, rivers and cities they only knew existed from maps in their geography books.

A call from Joaquín warned that his son was on his way to The Orchard. "Calm down! Calm down!" shouted Pepa, not managing to settle the children and when Binot rang the bell, he heard Carlota and Paloma giggling and shuffling behind the frosted glass door, neither wanting to be the one to open it. Pepa pushed them aside and told Binot how silly they were and he was squeezed tight in her arms. He blushed. The girls tittered. They had never seen him blush before and he said nothing. Just stared. Alexi and Miko who came running down the stairs, stopped dead and looked up at him as if he was a giant. "Go on, kiss your cousins, Binotte!" Pepa urged. "I'll kiss him first" offered Paloma to make it easy for him, but Carlota was already pressing her body against his, and kissing him on the neck with her lips apart.

"Brioches in the kitchen everybody!" cried Pepa to break Carlota's incestuous embrace. They sat, dunking their brioches in the steamy chocolate. The silence, furtive looks and the intensity of sensations swirling in the ether informed Pepa that they were no longer children and that their predicament was all too new for them to grapple with.

Later, and in Carlota's bedroom the girls argued which of them Binot liked best. It had to be Carlota, Paloma conceded, because boys lost their heads over her, and anyway, she seemed hardly changed since Binot last saw her.

*

Lorenzo got into the habit of hobbling from his studio around the corner to The Orchard after his morning's sketching for his after-lunch pouce-café when he knew that Joaquín would be there. His flamboyance captivated everybody. Never without his gangster style hat, tilted slightly backwards to better see, he rolled, still moist marijuana leaves from his balcony crop, into a thin spindly cigarette only half the thickness of Rosario's Gitanes. The first puff he took was with his eyes closed; with the second, he blew a spiral of smoke through his thick pursed lips, which the children followed until it hit the ceiling and disappeared. His shirts, either indigo blue or bright orange, were left mostly unbuttoned, and over it he always donned the same diamond patterned waistcoat signed by Pablo Neruda on the back, as a thank you for his caricature of him, sketched during one of his poetry recital in Paris. He rang the maid's bell every few minutes for another café and a glass of iced water which he drank in two consecutive gulps before he started his hobbling, up and down the sitting room. It helped him think through his arguments and, with a vague gesture of his hand, he dismissed Joaquín's frequent requests for him to sit down. Out of the blue and as if exteriorising an internal argument he had carried with him all morning, he often introduced disparate elements into the discussion, and now, he shouted that expatriates were spineless, lost their passion and that their lives of spurious political stability and climatic bliss had turned them into gutless sheep. He rang for Alcaya to bring another café but Joaquín stopped her, saying that maids were strictly for colonials, and if he did not like them, why was he not in Spain?

"Why-am-I-not-in-Spain? he shouted, looking gawky. "And why are Picasso and Buñuel and many others not in

Spain? And why Antonio Machado lies in a grave in Collioure and not in Spanish soil? Shall I spell it out for you?" he asked,

"If you must!"

"Dictators" he said, "castrate the soul of artists. That's why. And we flee our beloved country to let our souls breathe and create once more. But there's a price to pay. The price we pay for our freedom to create is the gnawing longing for our soil, and at the same time hating it for rejecting us, and the pain of it is sometimes so imperceptible—like a corrosive poison—that we don't realise we are dying. And there's more. Do you know what it feels to be seen as a traitor Joaquín, or a deserter, or a coward by your countrymen and by those abroad, like yourself, who condescend to give us shelter? We, Joaquín, are birds in perpetual flight, only landing to rest when we are worn out." Joaquín clapped in slow motion to antagonise Lorenzo and said what a rousing speech that was and that no, he knew nothing of what Lorenzo felt. "I was born here and I'll die here" he stated. "This is my land. I love being here. I am grateful for this land's riches. But I tell you what" he exhorted, stroking his thin Hitlerian moustache, "I owe it all to my great-grandfather Eion when he landed in this continent from Ireland feeling just as dejected as you do, yet, he got positive about it. You, my friend, and all your melodramatic cronies create your own drought and you'll die in the desert of your own neurosis."

"Your ancestors did all the bloody work for you! All you do is sit and collect. You are colonialism incarnate!" Lorenzo shouted, losing control of his saliva.

"I understand what Lorenzo is saying" ventured Rosario following an uneasy silence. "I mean, about what it feels to be an exile."

"An ally!" sneered Joaquín.

"It's hard for either of you to know how the other one feels" she said, her voice strengthening. "You, it seems to me, are the lucky one Joaquín. Lorenzo and I struggle in your wonderful paradise. For us, it is not so wonderful, because it lacks vital ingredients, vital only to us, because we were fed them from the cradle. And after the honeymoon of newness is over, we suffer a withdrawal."

Lorenzo covered his eyes with the brim of his hat to conceal the stir he felt after Rosario's rescue. "And you're still here" he murmured.

"And I still get seduced by this country's luxuriance and charms" she admitted. "If you like, it's not so different from sleep-walking into a theatrical set and there you stay, enchanted, until the Grand Master snaps his fingers and you wake up, thirsty, hungry, and longing for what was never really there."

"Aren't you overdoing it a bit?" cried Joaquín. "You've been adopted by us all. Everyone loves you! You are one of us!"

"I'm an outsider Joaquín. Was from the start, and always will be. The adoration is a veneer. A cover-up to make me and everyone else feel accepted. The truth is, I have not been me since I left Spain."

"You chose to come Rosario. You chose to accept that veneer of your own free will. That was YOU, then, but now you're bored by it all, so out comes the martyred exile malady. It won't wash Rosario. Not with me." Joaquín rubbed his hands together in Moroccan fashion to signal his dismissal of her, and she squirmed, making sure he noticed.

"I wouldn't expect you to go beyond that veneer Joaquín" she said. "All I can say is that I was very young when I got here. I didn't question. I just was" Rosario said wearily. "You were not that young when you came here" Joaquín said, turning towards Pepa, silent in the corner. "Do you feel an outsider, an exile in a hostile land?"

"The point, Joaquín, is that it doesn't matter. Of course I feel an outsider, a different person to you and Elias. But what matters, is what you do with your feelings. If only to survive, you've got to turn things around and carve yourself a new life, like your own great grandfather did. You've got to be flexible. Inclusive." She paused, drawing a circle with her hand. "When that happens, well, you see with different eyes. You're no longer in isolation. You embrace others. You allow them to embrace you. You open your heart. And before long you are out of the I-am-an-exile groove. That's what it's all about. Not whether the culture and the people have to reflect your own image in order for you to be happy. That's narcissism. Not love. You've got to love whoever's around you. Love without conditions. Punto finito."

Elias had left the debate as soon as Rosario began speaking. It was sure to hurt him, whatever she said, and he did not want to hear. No one was aware of Elias' departure and alone on the empty terrace, he felt dead already.

He was joined by Pepa and Paloma when they noticed his absence. He looked at one, then the other, his eyes made tender with gratitude.

"Too many words in there..." said Pepa pointing at the lounge. "Like cloudlets obscuring the sun" she added with a half smile.

Only those close to the other side would understand that, Elias thought. He had drank Evian all morning, but his mouth was still parched and Paloma poured him a glass of water. It was water for his soul, she said. He asked, not expecting a reply, if she thought he had one. She did not hesitate to say that everyone had a soul and that it could not be ignored once we knew of its existence. He laughed, after taking his first sip. "You don't want to become a nun, do you?" he asked.

"Sometimes I think I do, or a nurse, but I want a family of my own, a real family, more than anything else in the world."

"Who do you take after, child?" he asked looking perplexed.

"La Yaya, I think" she smiled, putting her arms around her grandmother's neck. But Pepa said Paloma was her own person, even if she did take after her.

*

A slipper hurled across the room woke Paloma in the middle of the night. Pepa was sure a dreadful seizure was taking her, but after Paloma rubbed her head where the projectile had struck, propped up her grandmother on the pillows she had just fluffed, and sat at the foot of the bed, Pepa knew it was only a nightmare.

Paloma had never seen such agony etched in her grandmother's face. She stroked her feet under the sheets and asked what had happened. "Tell Mita" she pleaded.

"I don't know cariñito" she said after a time as if returning from far away. "But I know I've got to go."

"Where? Go where Yayita?" Paloma searched but she was absent from her grand-mother's eyes, when Pepa said at last, "Back home sweetheart. Back to Spain."

"You must never leave me! I want you with me until I die!" Paloma cried.

"Who do you think I am, Methuselah?" laughed Pepa to calm her down. "Listen, and don't interrupt. It's your grand-father Camilo. He came to me just now. You know, in my dreams. He was dying. He called me. He wanted me there. He begged me. A dying man's last wish. You know what that means?" and without waiting for an answer she said, "you've got to honour it. You understand, don't you sweetheart?"

"I'll come with you."

"I must do this alone Paloma. It's my pain" she said, framing Paloma's face with her hands.

"I can't bear it...I can't..." sobbed Paloma. "When will you be back?"

"I can't say Mita. I really can't."

"But you will be back won't you?" Paloma screamed.

"Mita, it is your test too."

"Another one?"

"There will be many more sweetheart. They are your learning posts."

"I need to see your face Yayita. I need to comb your hair in the morning before school and trim the hairs growing on your chin...I hurt so much.."

"You'll hurt for as long as you are attached to your suffering."

Pepa took her hand in hers. "Remember the river in Ourika? Letting it go...?" she said, in a soft whisper.

"It's so hard to let go of what you love most Yayita" she sobbed.

"That's the whole point. That's the lesson" Pepa said.

Leaving Paloma behind tore Pepa apart, and more than she was able or ready to admit. But her place was to be by Camilo, to hold him in her arms, to forgive and be forgiven. Only then, could she close the circle of their tumultuous earthly journey.

Rosario found it unbelievable that Pepa was to leave on the impulse of a mere dream and she suggested waiting for more positive confirmation.

The night Pepa left, Paloma dreamed of a silver thread that linked her with her grandmother, heart to heart. It stretched across oceans and mountains bonding them through time and space and she felt close and safe, yet exquisitely free. But when she awoke, the pangs of loss gripped her again, like death by strangulation.

Born into chaos, Pepa brought Paloma order. Born into indifference, Pepa imprinted her with love from that first contact at birth, until it became her staple diet. Paloma did not believe she could survive without that nourishment even though the separation was also to be a test, as her grandmother said. But every now and then, and when she felt herself die a little, the silver thread tightened to remind her of their love.

It was too late when Pepa arrived. Camilo was already dead. He had died at two minutes past two and at the precise moment on the night that Pepa had woken with her nightmare. Before he sank into a coma Camilo had instructed Maruja that he did not wish Pepa to travel all that way for him. Theirs, he told his daughter-in-law, was an ill-fated but miraculous love and that his Pepa would help him pass over, despite the distance that separated them.

Camilo was laid in bed in his Guardia Civil uniform, his Captains stripes on his sleeves and his arms folded across his chest with a crucifix Maruja had placed between his hands. Pepa sat on the small stool by his side in the room he had shared with no one for the last seven years. She was silent for a minute or an hour—she did not know—then she gave vent to her feelings. "I bless your brow" she whispered and paused before she was able to continue, "and all the thoughts that lived in it. I bless your eyes and the beauty you saw through them. And your lips for their sweetness. I bless the tenderness of your arms my Camilo, the strength of your thighs, and the pleasure that lay between them. I bless your feet for God knows I have worshipped every one of your steps!" She bent over slightly to reach his heart. "And I bless your heart most of all..."

She broke into unrestrainable sobs and called his name, saying she had never stopped loving him. "But you know that now" she cried. "I loved you Camilo, even with all the humiliations after we moved to Barcelona. Those painted women in the Ramblas, in the Barrio Chino. You couldn't help yourself, I know. You always liked beautiful things. You used to tell me I was beautiful, before we moved to the city—you compared me to the stars and the moon in the sky above the mountains and to the apples in the orchards—Remember? That was before... I should have tried harder to keep you mine and not thought myself better than you. I wasn't. I know that now. I should have dabbed on my temples that azahar perfume from Seville that excited you and wore black lace under my skirts. I should... I should have found more time for us. You, me, just us. To play together like we used to. I should have shown you my other side. I wanted to. I didn't know how. And that faded grey pinny I wore from morning til night. How you hated it! And church—for my escape, instead of you. My Camilo. I know..." She leaned forward to kiss his icy forehead and gaze at him as on that day in Arbucias when they first met. "How could they resist you anyway. I didn't!" she cried. "Rosario takes after you, you know. Love, men and adoration. Never enough. She needed someone like you. A strong figure. Elias is a darling, a good man, but he is weak and without convictions. No marrow in his bones. She despises him now. Men, women, what a charade! But we'll get together Up There one day. You and me, with our bare hearts." She paused, smiling at his face.

"Camilo, my love, I forgive you. Will you forgive me? Will you forgive me!" she shouted, forgetting for an instant that he was dead. And then she wailed.

"Mother, come and rest" whispered José Luis, entering the room. "We've put all the children in the one room. You can have Pepita's."

"Let her share with me" she pleaded, wiping her face with a handkerchief she found on Camilo's bedside table. "It'll be less lonely."

Instead, she stayed up all night talking to her son in the patients' waiting room. He was rolling his first cigarette, using as little tobacco as he could, when Pepa asked about life in Franco's Spain. He took his time and said glibly, that the olive oil was still rancid, the lentils and the bread maggoty. Maruja dyed her legs with brown shoe polish, as stockings were still only available on the black market, and she believed that buying 'black', was a capital sin, even though she knew that the Parish priest lived fatly on it.

"And life in the street. What's it like?" she asked.

"Twelve years on and you still see a lot of men my age wandering half-crazed, and screwed up. The poor buggers have never recovered." He sighed. "I'm one of the lucky ones."

"You suffered son, and never told your mother."

"And increased your agony?"

"You were innocent..."

"Who knows who was innocent or guilty in all this" he said, pulling a gossamer thin paper from a small red packet for another cigarette. "The fear hasn't gone" he continued, licking the edge of the paper. "It's there, as stubborn as a venereal disease. Even in cafes, they speak in whispers and they look over their shoulders expecting the barrel of a gun in their backs if they speak against the Movimiento Nacional. Even the harmless concièrge could be a 'watcher' and a whistle blower. They knew who went to Mass and who didn't, enough of a crime to be taken for a paseo, because Franco's cause is also God's and church and militancy is rampant to this day. And that's not just in Spain. In London, the Catholic Archbishop of

Westminster wrote to Franco saying he thought that HE was the Defender of True Spain. How sick is that! We will never know the full reality of what happened, and the truth, whatever it is, is beyond anything we will eventually read in books. The reality is where people were when it happened" José Luis sighed. "If only this had opened the way to a new egalitarian world, it might have been worth the suffering, the loss, even the atrocities." He looked at Pepa, then sat at the edge of his chair . "But what have we got out of all this? People's freedoms are still violated a decade later, even the freedom of speech is barred. Conversations are barren. No more gutsy topics like in the old days' tertulias. No soulful confessions every one could hear. Would you believe" José Luis said spittingly, "that the Vanguardia proclaimed that every citizen had to think like Franco, feel like Franco, talk like him—And those who dared not to, had their come-uppance. I tell you, repression everywhere. And prostitutes! Never have I seen so many on street corners and in broad daylight! Men using them, to prove whatever manhood they have left. Some girls are barely sixteen, some old enough to be grandmothers, all driven by hunger, destitution, and anomy!" He downed a copita de Ojen from the medicine cupboard in one go to stifle a cough. "Corruption, hardship and deceit everywhere you look." He croaked. "And youth! Zombies of greed. Bah!" he exclaimed despairingly. "We have such a long way to go!" And he gulped another Ojen.

"Whatever you do son, never, never lose hope" Pepa pleaded holding his hands.

"Hope" he whispered, anchoring his eyes on hers, "cannot exist in a vacuum, mother. It needs the seed of life for it to grow. We have lost ours here. We are still stunned, exhausted and some, yes, even now, are dying as the aftermath of this war." He paused to clear his throat. "And after years of physical and spiritual death we feel entitled to grieve for our losses and we are, at last, living a period of collective penance and bereavement. It is not all negative" he said, when Pepa shook her head dolefully. "We need this space, black as it might seem, because it is a kind of refuge where we are allowed to forget the smell of death, lick our wounds, regain trust, strength and energy. And when all this comes back to us, we can face both our collective and individual truth and then, we can think of rebuilding our lives and let in hope." His eyes clouded and he covered them with his hands. They were silent in their shared grief, grief for the past and grief for Camilo.

"And how is everyone?" he finally asked., after a long pause.

"Our Rosario's a disappointment" he conceded after Pepa had told him about Rosario's ignoring of god-given opportunities like the war and Elias' illness to give of herself to others and for self-growth, "And Paloma?" he asked, a smile loosening the muscles of his face. "How I long to know this child!"

"She's a struggler" Pepa stated. "She'll get there. And she owes it all to you."

After Camilo's funeral, Pepa spent a few bland days with Pilar, her middle and least favourite daughter from Madrid, before returning with her eldest daughter Carmela to Diputación. Now twenty, Mingo came to meet his grandmother in the street, swept her off her feet and laughing, carried her up to the flat, two steps at a time. Nothing had changed since Pepa was last there, more than ten years ago, except for Salvador's death. She stared at the table where they had shared their frugal meals during the first year of the war and she whispered Paloma's name. "She misses me" she said failing. Carmela sighed. "You're with us mother. She's safe now. You needn't go to her this time."

"I miss her too, Carmela" confessed Pepa her voice trembling, "but I'll stay awhile and see what happens."

Never before had Pepa been so aware of Carmela's inertia and she found it disquieting. Although she had always been inactive, Pepa realised she had abused everyone's sympathy to escape her obligations. Lalia, as in the old days, brought her mother hot milk in bed whilst Mingo swept the apartment and still fetched water from the old street pump. Carmela then rose and ate the lunch Pepa had shopped for and prepared, then slumped in front of her Singer, resigned and resentful, to tackle the day's sewing contracted from small hotels and guest houses, complaining all the while that her legs ached from pedalling and her eyes stung from their concentration on the delicate hand stitching. It wasn't just Carmela that disappointed Pepa. She was dismayed too, night after night, when she saw Lalia and Mingo return at dawn in their fancy clothes, back from their nightly excursions, and told Pepa if still awake, about the films they had seen, and the wages they would exchange for lengths of cloth on the black market to be replicated by the seamstress on the top floor, into the suits and gowns of their screen idols. Pepa recalled José Luis' despair about the 'war children's' apathy and materialism and she ached for Mingo and Lalia's father Salvador and for all the fathers, who had died for the freedom they were now squandering, and also for all the mothers, who had gone hungry to feed them.

Two short letters from Paloma arrived to say that she missed her grandmother and prayed for her safe return, and that she had made a new friend in school. Her mother, she wrote, was short-tempered and morose, and that Elias often called for la yaya, especially during the night.

Carmela's prying about the contents of the letter irritated Pepa and said she had to be alone. She found herself walking without a destination in mind and ending up at the Plaza Colomb, near the train station where she and Paloma had been met by Salvador in July 1936, after fleeing from Madrid on the first day of the insurrection.

Posters of   ESPAÑA
FUÉ, ES, Y SERÁ
INMORTAL

proclaiming Nationalist propaganda plastered the walls of the station bringing shivers of horror up Pepa's spine, but the station, unlike that day, was almost deserted. She sat on a bench and was soon lost in deep contemplation, with Paloma's letter strewn on her lap.

A voice from behind whispered her name and when Pepa did

not respond, the voice, louder this time, asked if she remembered her. "I do and I don't" Pepa replied, awaking from her rêverie. The woman, dressed in a nurse's uniform stood in front of her saying it had been a long time. It was a familiar voice, and Pepa could nearly feel who she was, but couldn't place her.

"I've never forgotten you. You are here for as long as I live" said the nurse, clutching Pepa's hand to place it on her own heart. Pepa's eyes widened and her face beamed.

"It's you sweetheart!" she cried, embracing her. "Esperanza-Luz! Bendito sea Dios!"

"Esperanza only," the nurse whispered, her eyes moistening with emotion.

"Why did you leave the veil?"

"I couldn't. Not after that."

"You were innocent, child."

"Damaged all the same. Soiled. Not good enough for Him. Anyway, here I am, here to meet you. And I'm off to Manresa just now, to the military hospital there, You know it?" Pepa raised her eyebrows. "I don't know what to say!"

"I know, it sounds crazy, seeing soldiers day after day after what happened to me that day, doesn't it?"

"Why are you punishing yourself Esperancita?"

"It's more like a cleansing, for them... Redeeming their violence...The collective thing, you know..."

"A hard task my friend. And are you married?" Esperanza shook her head.

"Not good enough for any man either?" Pepa asked.

"I haven't conquered the fear" she whispered, and asked Pepa if she was going anywhere. Pepa told her that she was sitting and thinking about teaching a dove to fly.

"The peace child"? she smiled, hastily kissing Pepa's hands when she saw her train arriving and she vanished as she had done years ago, on the same platform. "I'm still wearing your Sacred Heart, Esperanza-Luz!" Pepa shouted, touching the small medal that she had always worn since hat day.

"May He bless you and your dove and keep you safe!" she shouted back.

More than ever, and more so after Esperanza-Luz fortuitous meeting, Pepa was convinced that her place was not with Carmela, Mingo and Lalia and their limited life nor with her son whose happy and autonomous family could be upset by her prolonged presence, but elsewhere, back where Elias needed her love and skills to help him die, and with Rosario, to steer her and the children through the crises that would follow.

*

No one knew of Pepa's imminent arrival, nor that she had made her own way by taxi to The Orchard. Wearing the stylish navy polka dress Carmela had made for her during her stay there, Pepa let herself in and sat at the edge of her bed waiting for Paloma to come home from school. Everything was kept as Pepa liked it—the pillows inside their starched white cases, propped up on the bed in a treble balcony to support her chest, and a spare one to raise her legs at the foot of the bed; a set of three clean towels folded neatly on the bed side chair, and on her bedside table, the heads of fresh, yellow marigolds floating in a dark blue glass bowl, like stars in the night sky. But the window was wide open. Pepa covered her shoulder's with her shawl and smiled. She always kept the bedroom window closed for fear of draughts, but in her absence, her grand-daughter had indulged her craving for air, and Pepa left it as it was.

An urge, so irresistible, on the day of Pepa's return, made Paloma visit her room before her usual dash into the kitchen for her slice of bread, and four squares from a chocolate bar. She scrambled over Pepa's luggage near the door when she entered the room before they fell into each other's arms. Both started to say something at the same time, until laughter then tears stopped them. "There..." said Pepa, pulling a handkerchief from her handbag.

"Yayita..." yelped Paloma, wiping her tears, "I thought I was going to die without you..."

"But you didn't sweetheart!"

"Because I knew you'd be back..."

"I didn't..." said Pepa, sweeping her grand daughter's new thick fringe away from her face.

"If you hadn't, I would have become you, I know I would."

Pepa nodded. "Too soon for you, sweetheart, to take on that burden. You need to be YOU first."

"I think I found a friend Yayita" Paloma said in a secretive tone.

"You said in your letter... Tell me about her" Pepa whispered back.

"She's from school. Her name's Ondine and..."

"Ondina? Isn't that to do with the sea?" Pepa interrupted.

"It's a water-spirit, I think. And her birthday is a day after mine!"

"Twin souls! You see sweetheart, I had to go, so you could find Ondina."

"I was so lonely!"

"All's well that ends well, sweetheart."

"I told her you were my most favourite person in the world, and now she can meet you..."

"What does your mother think of her?"

"I haven't told her" she said, looking over her shoulder.

"Will she like her?"

"I don't know. She's not like us."

"Two heads?"

Paloma laughed and said Ondine was very fair, with blue eyes and that she was shy, very shy, and didn't talk to anyone, except her. "Her mother is from Paris" Paloma went on, "and her father from Poland. They live by Nôtre Dame in a tiny pavillon they call Le Bungalo and there's eight of them there. I don't think they're very rich."

"Is that why you think..."

"Maman likes people with nice clothes and things, doesn't she?"

"I thought I could hear voices!" exclaimed Rosario. "Why didn't you let me know you were coming?"

"I wanted no fuss" Pepa said, hugging her daughter.

"Catching up already, were you?" asked Rosario, scrutinising her mother and Paloma.

"Paloma was telling me about her new friend."

"Friend?"

"Ondine Hess, Maman. My friend from school. I want to bring her home to meet..."

"The family" said Pepa just in time.

"Hess? Interesting. Bring her over. By all means bring her over."

Rosario sat on the bed beside Pepa. She gloated that her mother had chosen to live with her and she took one of Pepa's crepey hands to hold against her own cheek. Paloma smiled. "You're happy to have Yaya back aren't you Maman?"

"Overjoyed" she whispered. "But we need to speak alone" she added, showing her the door.

"I've missed you!" confessed Rosario. "Desperately" she added.

"You needed me" replied Pepa kissing her daughter's hand.

"And that too..." said Rosario.

"What is it Rosario?"

"Your face is so full of Spain... My brother and the new nephews I've never seen. And Carmela, Pilar, Lalia and Mingo. I can breathe them all in your pores. I envy you!" she cried inhaling Pepa's clothes.

"Spain is not what you remember. It's a different place. The light hasn't shone there since you left it. It's in the shade. It's anaemic."

"After ten, more than ten years? Why so long?"

"How do you get over Guernica and the slaughter at the Ebro. If you'd been there, you would not ask that question. There was nothing left Rosario. They had to start from scratch with no energy and no money. Spain was not exactly popular with the world after Franco's victory. We were a dictatorship. We were pariahs, ignored, left for dead. Besides, other countries had their own wars to fight."

"I want to go back. After Elias. Take the family. Start again, in my land. In-my-land" she repeated. "I'm not afraid."

"You're not listening Rosario. You haven't got a clue. Your heart's intact. It hasn't been shattered to pieces. How would you know?"

"All I know is that I won't stay here after Elias. Joaquín's been snooping about every day, upsetting him, talking about money, helping himself to more of his assets to pay for debts Elias didn't know he had. People I've never heard of are claiming that he owes them. It's frightening. Joaquín said my jewellery will have to go. And the piano. He kept away before you left, but he came back. He's never respected me. And there's Carlota......"

"Carlota?"

"She's out of control. Seldom back home before nightfall. Paloma says boys pick her up outside school and off they go to the beach on their scooters. Love bites everywhere. Denying everything. Never looks me in the eye when I speak to her. She eats like a horse, raiding the fridge in the dead of night after her jaunts to God-knows-where, lying is her common language. And she's started having fits."

"Fits? What kind of fits?"

"I haven't seen them but Paloma has. Only the other day, she was lying in the middle of the road on the way to school, throwing her limbs about. The art teacher, on her way home, witnessed it too, and sent me a note. The doctor assured me it was nothing. Just a bit of adolescent hysteria. And Paloma. For the first six weeks after you left, I thought she was letting herself die. Wouldn't eat or sleep. And cried day and night. She accused me of not loving her properly, not like you. Look at me! These lines appeared since you left. My life's slipping away from me. I'm in a vortex. Something has to happen soon, or I'm leaving. South America—just me, free. You can take the kids back to Spain. I..."

"Self-pitying drivel! Stop it at once Rosario!"

"It's how it is. It's not self-pity."

"I'm only going to help you if you help yourself. I'm not here to take over from you, so that you can indulge yourself,

I'm here because I missed you all, to be here for Elias and to see that you have support and comfort for what is ahead. So get a grip on yourself Rosario or it's me who'll be off!"

"I've gone back to church" blurted Rosario to try and regain her mother's approval.

"The new priest?"

Rosario's nostrils flared, until they were thin and pale at the edges, a sure sign that she was concealing something.

"Have you introduced yourself?"

"I'm busy attracting his attention."

"What?"

"I want him to notice me first, he has too, then I'll say who I am."

Pepa shook her head. "Anyway, here" she said, "a mantilla from home."

"It's black" Rosario said, thinking of her looming widowhood.

*

When Rosario complimented her on her unusual name, Ondine puckered her nose into multiple creases. She flicked her tresses backwards and forwards but this attempt at camouflaging the not so prominent bone on the bridge of her nose, had the opposite effect. She would rather be called 'Ciel' she said, or 'Serpolet', and she erupted in a laugh that sounded like a thousand disordered hiccups. Despite her name, she believed she was not really a water person — more air.

Airplanes and horses she told Rosario were her passion (though she had access to neither) and adventure books fuelled her dreams.

Her father, a Civil Engineer, had met her mother in Paris where she had been a psycho-analyst of the Jungian school, but had given up her work to care for their six children, and to help pay the bills, she taught the piano from home, as did Ondine's grandmother, Madame Michaud, who lived with them. Money was scarce. Ondine's patched up school overalls and the self-mended soles of her sandals bore witness to that. But the household in which she lived was a hive of enterprise and creativity which more than compensated for any privation.

NINETEEN

"He Who Lives Well, Dies Well"

Joaquín came bearing tragic tidings. Geraldo, their younger brother had died. Elias could not take in the news. It was a mistake he kept saying; he knew no one stronger than Geraldo. Elias' breath grew laboured and left him with one unstoppable gasp. The oxygen cylinder was rushed in from his room and it was an hour later before Joaquín could tell him what had happened. Geraldo had collapsed whilst chasing a run-away stallion from his stables. A subarachnoid haemorrhage killed him, with his poor brain floating in a pool of his own blood. They looked at each other in disbelief. It was obscene. He was only thirty nine and the youngest of the crew. And they had abandoned him at eighteen. Family honour required that they support their brother's wife Marina, but the walls erected all those years ago to keep her out, were now insurmountable. They could not even have their brother's body buried in the family vault, and even more distressingly they feared not being asked to the funeral. It was Rosario's offer of mediation that brought the two families together.

No Butler had ever visited Geraldo's house when he was alive and when they sat by his coffin waiting to be carried away, Elias wept tears of regret. Serene and dignified in a plain black dress, Marina was nothing like they had imagined, and her poise bewildered them. Fate had this day brought them together in her kitchen where a noisy coffee pot percolated on an old stove. Voices, in Italian, French and Spanish harmonised as if they were one—they were of Marina's circus people and Geraldo's adopted family. They had loved Geraldo and he had cherished them back. Rosario watched their bond. It was the

Butlers, she thought, who had been the losers all along.

Geraldo would rest in Marina's parents vault at the El Hank cemetery, not far from the shade of Elias' beloved lighthouse. On foot and in a cortège, Trini and Carlo, Lourdes and Lorenzo, and Joaquín followed the open coffin laid on a horse drawn carriage to the burial ground. Elias and Rosario had gone ahead by car. At the short ceremony, the Pavorotis played the circus opening fanfare. Trini wailed, fainted, and fell into the open grave in a fit of hysteria.

A cruel sense of finality shrouded Elias on the journey home. He mumbled that waving at Geraldo when he passed The Orchard would not have hurt anyone. Recriminations were pointless at such times rebuked Joaquín since there was nothing anyone could do. Elias half listened and once home, fell asleep with Pepa sitting by his bedside, soothing his brow each time he began a nightmare.

The children felt deceived by the death of an uncle they had never met but only knew through Trini's poignant account of his absconding from the family. The reasons for his rift made little sense to them, and for weeks, they talked about nothing else but of their uncle Geraldo—El Supremo, Lion Tamer Extraordinaire—until he grew into a mythical hero, so colossal, not even Trini could have recognised her brother.

Samuel returned from Switzerland too late for the funeral. Ignoring Rosario's visiting ban for marrying a divorcée he called to see Elias without her permission. He would miss Geraldo the most. Their mutual passion for horses had brought them together and unknown to anyone, they had over the years, secretly met at the races, but Samuel was even closer to Elias and he foresaw that his brother would plunge into despair when he announced that his recent move to Arcachon for the summer months was to become permanent and he was not taken aback when Elias implored him to return and stay one more year.

Death, was the most frequently discussed topic at The Orchard since Geraldo's passing and for Elias' sake, the conversations took place after he had retired to bed, when only

273

Lorenzo and Joaquín were left on the terrace to pursue their disparate exchanges. They always ended up jaded, irritable with each other and frustrated, but they derived a sado-masochistic enjoyment from their vociferous contests. Lorenzo who had perfected the crafty toreador's art of catching his bull unawares caught Joaquín by surprise one day in the middle of a banal argument on motoring without a licence when he asked him what he thought about slavery. Joaquín laughed at this unexpected probe and sleepily replied that this was the twentieth century and slavery didn't exist. It was the likes of him, Lorenzo contested, that still perpetuated it. The proof surely was that his servants were landless and had no choice but to accept his bonded labour as a means of survival, and was that not slavery he asked.

"I've rescued these people, not enslaved them." stated Joaquín "And, what's more, they know it. They're grateful. We understand one another."

"How colonialist!"

"Go and talk to my servants then, and hear what they have to say!" offered Joaquín. "But first, why don't you read the history books. It's all there. You'll see that the country was a theatre of cruelty and torture until 1912 when the French took over. For the first time in centuries, the Arab nation experienced a sense of order, justice and even an opening up amongst their own people, from one tribe to another!"

Lorenzo listened. Grudgingly, and after dipping into the history books Joaquín recommended, he conceded that Joaquín might have had a point. The servants themselves, he learned through his questioning, believed that they were indeed salvaged from the cruel bondage of masters of their own kind, but nevertheless he also discovered that they remained unaware of their rescuers wallowing in their well-meant deliverance and paternalism. It was, Lorenzo felt, a kind of marriage of convenience which should never have taken place. But since it had, this inadequate union he reasoned, might well be the only available mechanism at this point in time, and therefore the first inescapable step towards securing their final freedom.

Elias was glad Joaquín found a worthy debating opponent in Lorenzo. He had never been one to argue, always preferring to listen, and he was now too weary even for that. His son Alexi was his one solace and when Alexi was not by his bedside, he withdrew inwards, to some stark and remote part of himself he had, up until now, kept carefully tucked out of sight. He was fearful of lingering there, for he could hear his voice echoing the words, "he who lives well dies well" This, he knew to surely be a warning from On High to clear his conscience before he met his reaper. Flight was his initial response, but his extreme fatigue prevented him from attempting it. He had come to the end of his journey and was now at the ante-room of death, and there he had to stay. He held his breath and waited, but he did not escape the sudden litany of recriminations that came pouring inside his head, from ear to ear and more inexorably still, to that triangular space between his eyes. He had been weak. Very weak, the voice said as through a wall of water. Never should he have allowed Joaquín to get away with Geraldo's banishment, nor should he have ignored Rosario's selfish and often cruel handling of the girls. He had not partaken in the fatherly upbringing of his children and he saw that they had been orphaned long before his death. That was not all. As a citizen, he had neglected his responsibilities by his laissez faire attitude during the wars he had lived through and escaped from. His helping of Carmela, José Luis and the beggars, were mere gestures to appease Pepa. He had squandered his assets mostly on Rosario and high living, instead of seeing to his family's future security, and when he tried, it was too late. In conclusion, he had not been a good patriarch, even though Pepa thought him to be a "thoroughly good man." But the most desperate and gnawing of all recriminations were for her, the one person he truly trusted. Madrid 1936, when he fled to safety and a life of luxury, leaving her and Paloma amidst chaos, and later, once more, deserting her on her sick bed whilst he and Rosario went night-clubbing. Tears, the last he had, came, which he could not with-hold. He felt cleansed by their saltiness, feeling the same lightness as confession did long ago .

At night, when Pepa sat by his side, she saw that his incoherent ramblings no longer tormented him and two nights after the voice had gone, he could not hear her whispered prayers nor see the thin lines of light caught in the bedroom blind, nor did he smell the pungent scent of the eucalyptus leaves burning in a clay pot in the corner of the room. One by one, his senses left him and Pepa knew the doctor and the priest would soon be needed. Samuel called to reminisce in a rambling whisper about their childhood as Pepa had asked him to, and more importantly to recall their days as altar boys when they were close to the redeeming spirit of the Eucharist. He held Elias' cold hand and stroked the blue, smooth curve of his fingernails and told him that he loved him. Doctor Baldous came every two hours for the next day and then told Rosario to be brave as the end was near.

Pepa filled the room with scented arum lilies, lit candles and prayed. Rosario could not pray and lay curled up by his side like a sleeping snail, nor could she look Elias in the face.

In his white plimsolls and smelling of freshly splashed orange water, Joaquín breezed into the room at dawn to relieve Samuel from his vigil. Samuel stumbled as he got up and held on to the headboard to kiss Elias' forehead. Joaquín opened the window wide and snapped his fingers several times signalling Rosario to help him raise Elias into a sitting position, which, he said would make him look more dignified. But propped up by pillows on all sides, Elias had acquired the vague appearance of a ventriloquist's dummy, looking anything but dignified. Adept at the art of helping the dying as she had been at birthing, Pepa cautioned Joaquín to think carefully about his every movement and to be more respectful of the most delicate of transitions that was death.

Elias stirred, it was only a thought, but so powerful in its essence that he gasped for more breath from inside his oxygen mask—HE HAD NEVER LOVED ROSARIO. Not as he had loved his son, Alexi. Rosario had been the sheath and the container for that gift of the son that he had always wanted from her, even before Alexi's conception. He panicked,

276

wrenched at his mask and called Rosario by name. He would have done anything to prevent that cruel truth from striking while it still mattered. The air he breathed was thick treacle and his chest hot enough to burst into flames. He winced and shook his head from side to side until the movement itself allowed his mind to shift elsewhere and onto a swirling carousel, a happier place, with faces he had long forgotten. He struggled to halt and freeze the images and to relive them once more. No one in the room captured Elias' distant smile when the carousel of his mind stopped and his father Zac appeared, teaching him, aged two, to ride bare-back on his russet horse Zalamea, and his mother shouting from the Portuguese-style balcony overlooking the courtyard, to put him, for God's sake, onto a saddle. His parents drifted away in a frozen mist, which became a sea of shimmering dunes, where his grandfather Joseph, wrapped in tuareg garb and mounted on his white horse, bobbed up and down, beckoning him. He opened his eyes, afraid to see a gaping void, but he could fathom Pepa's contours by his side and he allowed himself to move out of consciousness.

"It's time" Pepa whispered inside his ear, threading a rosary through his coldly fingers. "I am with you. My breath is for your peace" she said breathing in and then out. And then, in a voice that was at once firm yet sweet, she told him to let go of all that still held him back, to surrender his heart to the serene unknown that was opening for him, to trust it utterly and to let himself float into it. Without a change in modulation, she repeated the same words until Elias drew the last one of his breaths. Asleep, Rosario and Joaquín missed Elias' passing. They woke up half way through Pepa's chanting of the Psalm of Praise and Thanksgiving that her own mother chanted when she was called to someone's deathbed. Pepa eased their minds saying that in the end, Elias had died a good death. They knelt together for the act of contrition before leaving Rosario on her own with Elias. Numb and willing herself to feel intensely, she stood at the foot of the bed, her limp arms dangling by her side. Her remoteness from Elias at that moment was as vast as it had been in the desert of their last five years of shared life. She left his side without shedding a tear, and Pepa comforted her, saying it was too early for tears—that crying came before, or long after. Corpses, Joaquín decreed, needed disposing of quickly so that negative entities that impeded liberation did not enter the body and it was his and Rosario's task to lay Elias' body which would remain in the open coffin for mourners to see until it was time for the burial. The close family would keep vigil, but there would be no wailing, no church service and no memorial. Pepa was emphatic that there should be a priest's last blessing, in keeping with the Catholic tradition into which Elias had been born. And it was not a wife's place she contended, to lay her husband's body, but Joaquín told her it would be the most valuable and long-lasting memory Rosario would keep of Elias. As Rosario and Joaquín washed Elias' cold and blotchy body down with a flannel, shaved him, trimmed the protruding hairs of his nostrils and ears, blocked each of his orifices with cotton wool and dressed him in his silk cream shirt and favourite pin-striped suit, a kind of tacit, uncanny intimacy grew between them that was as effortless as it was unexpected.

Pepa told the children of their father's passing on their return from school. She gathered them together and showed them into his room. Paloma tip-toed to her father's bedside and felt his brow. His skin felt different, the colour and consistency of wax, shiny and taught so that the wrinkles on his face had vanished. Death was more of a stranger than she had anticipated. Her father had lain dead for over five hours without a movement of his body and though she tried, she could not conceptualise the absoluteness and permanence of the immobility brought about by the cessation of life. She was disappointed that this was where her mind stumbled but she felt certain that sorrow would strike her, even if she had not really known her father. She forced herself to look at him longer than she wanted, brushed his frozen cheek against hers, and told him to have peace. She heard her mother hum and wondered if she was in a trance, like a magician she once saw at the souk in Marrakech. She looked at Pepa who reassured her that it was grief and it was fine, as long as uncle Samuel was in the room with her to keep her earthbound. The boys had to be lifted up to the coffin to kiss their father for the last time. Miko said he had never seen his father asleep before, but Alexi who knew he would never kiss him again, cried. Carlota saw no point in kissing a dead man and later complained that instead of her joining the boys, during the days of mourning who were at Marina's (whom Rosario had befriended since Geraldo's death) she and Paloma had to stay at The Orchard and usher the visitors to Elias' coffin to pay their last respects.

The mourners arrived in subdued trickles of ones and twos. Some wore black from head to toe, even though it was not the day of the funeral and others held their handkerchiefs to their noses to simulate grief.

A piercing wail broke the stillness and reverberated throughout the house. It was Trini. She had clambered inside the coffin and taken Elias into her arms calling him a saint. Her husband Carlo tried to prise her away but she only let go when Joaquín tickled her under the arms and Elias' body fell back in the coffin with a hollow thud.

*

Father Clement arrived to give his benediction. Rosario ran to open the door herself just as Paloma, already at the door, was letting him in.

He had a haunted look Paloma had not seen during her preparatory communion sessions or at any other time, and never had she seen her mother so flustered. Pepa could feel the throb and rippling heat radiating from their respective bodies as they faced each other without saying a word. She backed away from them as if to avoid burning and told Father Clement to follow her, but Rosario side-stepped her mother and escorted him instead. "My husband was not a practising Catholic for many years" she said hoarsely. "I hope you can still administer..."

"A final Absolution is everyone's right" Father Clement

replied not looking at her, adding that everyone without exception, needed forgiveness.

This was the first death at The Orchard since the family had lived there. The black velvet drapes on the front door, and the presence of a verger in full regalia standing at the gate looked out of place. Rosario appeared behind Elias' coffin in a full-length black dress (ordered from Paris long before the funeral). She wore it with a black silk veil over her face, which floated down, skimming her waist in a scalloped edge. She had more of a mannequin look in a fashion parade than a stricken widow, and the mourners without exception, gasped. It was, she said, when Pepa disapproved, the last time she dressed up for Elias, and that he would have loved her looking stunning for his last journey.

Samuel came to visit the next day. He gave Rosario a long embrace, pinched her chin and wearily sat down on the sofa before announcing he would be moving to France next week with his wife Francine. Rosario pleaded with him to wait. "I promised Elias I would stay another year Rosario. I've kept my word" he said uncompromisingly.

"You belong here Sami."

"My wife's French. She feels edgy here—you know how that feels. And besides, my leg still needs frequent treatment these days."

"And your godson?" she asked. "He needs you Samuel, now that Elias is gone."

"I'll keep my eye on Alexi for as long as I live, Rosario. You have my word."

"And me? What about ME?"

"You, Rosario, are a survivor. You'll find someone to care for you and dote on you."

"Elias would have wanted you to stay."

"I think Elias knew you wouldn't be alone for long. I think you know that already."

"It could have been you..!"

"But it isn't."

"Did you ever love me Sami?" she asked, bringing her lips

a breath away from his.

"I could have" he replied unperturbed.

"What happened?"

"You were my brother's wife."

"So you did love me."

"I don't let my feelings run away with me Rosario. You were unobtainable. And that was it" he said, moving away from her.

"Do you love her?"

"Francine's a kind and generous woman, a good companion, and I deeply care for her."

"And what of Colette?"

"The love of my life. The one love."

"I loved you Sami."

"I know." He paused to look at her more closely. "Even before you knew it" he added. "But not now" he said, staring at her. "Now your eyes are on fire for someone else. Ssh..." he hushed, "I don't want to know. I never want to know."

*

There was nothing but praise from the boys when they returned from their week's stay at their aunt Marina's after their father's funeral. Marina's garden was a playground of magical happenings where Alexi and Miko had, for the first time, connected with each other as brothers and playmates. But this was to be Alexi's last day of childhood. "Sit down Alexi, and you too Miko" said Rosario. His mother's ominous tone made Alexi's small features stiffen, arch his eyebrows and widen his eyes to help him concentrate. "You are the head of this family now Alexi." She paused, so that he could ponder on the significance of her statement. "You are responsible for us all" Rosario said, "and especially for me, your mother, and your little brother Miko. He and I need you the most." She bore his eyes with her own. "Do you understand what I'm saying, son?"

"For God's sake Rosario!" shouted Pepa. "He isn't even nine!"

But Alexi stood up, declaring he understood and pledged to care for his mother and family.

"Good" replied Rosario. "And now come and embrace me."

In the weeks that followed, Rosario did little else but reply to hundreds of black-edged letters of condolences. "If I see this sentence once again I shall scream!" she squealed.

"Which one?" asked Pepa sorting the letters into various piles.

"Despite everything, dear Rosario, life continues..." Rosario read exasperated.

"Well" said Pepa, "it's the form. People mean well... "

Rosario had gone quiet. She had come across a very different letter and she began to read it.

New York 15:2:1950

My dearest Rosario,
It was with great sorrow that I heard the news of Elias' passing. He was one of the rare individuals I greatly admired, a consummate gentleman and the epitome of kindness and good manners. I loved him dearly. My heart sank when I found out I could not attend his funeral. I so much wanted to pay my last respects. But now I think of your situation—a woman alone with an elderly mother and a young family to support and I cannot but worry about your future. I know it may not be the time to say that I am entirely devoted to you and at your disposal, but I can easily ask General Motors to transfer me to Casablanca, Rabat or Tangier if you would consider my proposal. Sarita died last year and I am asking you to marry me Rosario, as soon as the official mourning is over. Think about it.

Your loyal servant. Eternally yours, Dionisio

"Why so quiet?"

"Let me think, mother!" cried Rosario turning around to hide her face.

She called Dionisio's name inwardly and struggled to conjure a picture of him, to capture a smell, an intonation, something. Not even his voice came through as she read his letter without a flicker of excitement. She thought of the fury of their passion in Tangier and of the intensity of their last few days together, but her thoughts were like charred images after the ravages of a summer sun and the more she tried to revive the contours of his features, the more another face appeared, unsolicited, but deliriously welcome. "Well?" asked Pepa. "Who is it?"

"It's Dionisio..." she murmured.

"Dionisio?"

"Mm..." uttered Rosario. "Isn't it extraordinary! He wants to look after us all. He wants to marry me, mother!"

"And?" Pepa said, not sure of the implication.

"Only that the things you want in life always come too late!" Rosario said.

"How late?"

"You already know..."

"Well there's nothing much you can do about this one, is there?" said Pepa.

"Maybe not. But I can't marry Dionisio or anyone. Not now. Not ever."

"That's a bit final! You're not yet forty and you want to be without a man for the rest of your life!"

"Who said I would?"

"I hope you know what you're saying Rosario!" Pepa cried with an uncontrollable tremor.

"I can't help feeling as I do" Rosario mumbled looking pleadingly at her mother. "I loved Elias, mother. In my own way. And shall always love him."

"I know" whispered Pepa, "but..."

"What?" interjected Rosario.

"It's those fantasies of yours. You've done it all your life— missed real opportunities to learn, just to follow your desires,

283

forever veiling your true direction. You must wake up Rosario" commanded Pepa. "This time, the stakes are too high, the danger is not yours alone!"

"This one is not a fantasy mother, what is happening is as real as me standing here. I know it is.."

"Not a fantasy..." whispered Pepa. "Dios!" she despaired, realising the might of her daughter's resolve.

TWENTY

Marina's People

The drama that shrouded The Orchard after Elias' death was the platform for Rosario's most challenging performance, and, as in any successful play, she made sure it would run for at least a year. She only wore black, but when at home, slipped into a red and emerald green silk satin kimono, embroidered with dragons and stylised lotus flowers that Elias had lavished on her during their week in the Canaries. It was an exhilarating switch which the children thought disconcerting until the discovery that their mother's mood depended upon whether she wore her kimono or black.

A kimono, Joaquín admonished whilst on one of his visits, was a frivolous garment and quite inappropriate for one so recently widowed. She was to stop lounging around the house like a geisha and find herself a job since Elias had left insufficient reserves to support the family. Elias would never have allowed her to work when he was alive and she was not about to disturb his wishes from the grave. But a month later, she looked nothing like a geisha in her grey overalls, typing at Joaquín's Real Estate Agency being bullied, humiliated and reminded every single day of her good fortune in finding work after decades of unemployment.

"That stinks" said Pepa, when she heard Rosario's account of Joaquín's sadistic behaviour at work. "I'll give him a piece of my mind" she added.

"I must fight my own battles" Rosario asserted. "He thinks I can't fend for myself. He thinks Elias protected me from everything."

"Didn't he?"

285

Rosario said that she wasn't afraid of his sick and pathetic games and that she would show him that she was as good as any man. Pepa's advice was to ignore him. It had to be tit for tat with him Rosario replied.

Looking defiant, Rosario returned early from work the next day. She had put an end to her abuse. Though relieved, Pepa wondered how the family would manage without an income. The servants had been dismissed, except for Alcaya who begged to be retained for nothing, and Samuel's gardener whom he had paid for another year's service in advance, before he left for France. She would rather sell her jewellery Rosario said than seek further employment, and within the week her near perfect, cherished, black pearl necklace, the proceeds of which would guarantee to keep them for a couple of months, went to Mme Daubigny who had coveted it for years.

Anticipating that it would be Joaquín, no one answered the door bell though it rang three times, until Pepa quickly opened it when she recognised Father Clement's cassocked figure through the glazed panel. His smile was diffident and before he could utter a word Pepa showed him into the lounge. He had never been there before and his inquisitive gaze circled the room until his eyes met Rosario's in the Cruz-Herrera portrait.

"Do you like it?" she asked, appearing at the door in bare feet and her loosely belted kimono.

"It's routine. My visit...I hope I haven't called at an inconvenient time" Father Clement mumbled, vaguely gesturing at her appearance.

"How are your children and yourself, after your.....?"

"Husband's death?" she said, helping him out. "Good and not good. But," she pronounced, looking pious "I seek solace in prayer. You have seen me in church, have you not, Father?"

"Indeed. So glad you find it a consolation Madame Butler"

"Rosario. Please" she said, revelling in his shyness. "Yes. Well..." he mumbled, making his way towards the door.

"Would you care to join us in an apéritif?" she asked, as Pepa entered with a tray of pastis, three glasses and thick, uneven slices of saussison piled roughly on an hareera bowl.

She had won. The ice was broken. He would be back, Rosario had no doubt. And next time the ice would melt.

*

Marina was coming to The Orchard. Rosario needed a friend who, unlike Pepa, would not judge or fret at every move she made. She arrived on time on an ancient, adapted circus bicycle. A large wicker basket at the front carried her oversized mock crocodile bag and various other bulky items covered with a red mousseline shawl. Her black dress and plaited bun held together by giant tortoise-shell hair pins made her look haughty but she smiled a full smile and when they saw her dismount as gracefully as she would have done from her horse in the circus ring, they all smiled back. She pulled off her gloves with her teeth, then handed a paper bag with still warm goose eggs to Pepa. From the rear of her bicycle a bunch of marguerites from her garden, the size of which took their breath away, materialised for Rosario, and for the boys, a day old chick birthed out of the cup of her hand. For the girls to dress up in, a mountain of garish garments from the old circus days, sprang out of the mock crocodile bag. Pepa remarked that she could easily have been a conjurer had she not been a horsewoman.

Rosario and Marina were different. Opposites even. But their widowhood and the alienation that separated them from their respective roots had clinched their friendship. Rosario felt the same connectedness with Colette, Ludwig, Stefan, and now Lorenzo. That feeling of fellowship was like nothing else she had encountered in the whole panoply of emotions she knew. Every single time it happened, it exhilarated her, and she came to realise that this unequalled feeling of kinship was only possible with another from the continent of Europe. Pepa approved. Unlike Colette, Marina was unadorned, reliable, generous, had a love for the land and a puritanical taste for the simple life—the perfect foil for Rosario's moody, selfish, excessive and fanciful temperament.

It was every other Thursday afternoon that Marina visited

The Orchard, when the children were home from school, and every time, she brought with her a loaded wicker basket of weird and wondrous gifts. Her garden, she told them, with her eyes wide open, was now a vast magical meadow, filled with huge and brilliantly coloured butterflies, and wild flowers, some so rare that they were listed in books on the shelves of the Librairie des Sciences Naturelles. There were, she said, daisies as sunny-faced and tall as Paloma, untamed brown rabbits dashing in and out of deep burrows under the spiky hedges of barbary figs and she insisted Rosario bring the children the following Thursday before the summer heat overwhelmed the poppies in bloom.

They could hear music long before arriving at Marina's which they thought emerged from a nearby fairground, but when they got closer, it was clear that the sounds they heard came from her back garden. Waving their tambourines for the children to join in, Señor Fraiz, his Bostonian wife Lulu, Piero, Chouchou and Marina danced the Saltarello. Someone played the accordion, another the drum and a dwarf was sitting on an empty wine barrel, playing the trombone. The accordionist was Bertrand who had left the travelling circus for Paris to become a lawyer, and made a dash for Rosario as soon as he spotted her. He let her know that she was the most enigmatic woman he had encountered and that he wanted her. Rosario was in mourning and already lusting for another man, but she saw no reason to resist the temptation to flirt. That was before Carlota, miaouing and licking Bertrand's face like a kitten came to sit and rock on his lap, until he rose in a hurry to seek relief behind the stables and Carlota staggered like a drunk, falling to the ground in a faint after Rosario shook her senseless.

Rosario could not sleep that night. Caught in a maze of convoluted fantasies arising from Carlota's seduction of Bertrand and the bizarre erotic tale Señor Fraiz, aficionado psychologist and interpreter of dreams had told her that afternoon. Whatever Señor Fraiz motives were for recounting this tale, it had so inflamed her imagination that as she waited for dawn to break, she felt the volcano of her senses swell, ready to erupt.

Rosario would not make the first move to see Father Clement, not ever. Not after the Stefan fiasco, but she rose before Pepa one morning to attend what she called the old crows mass. When Father Clement beheld her from the altar, partly concealed behind the statue of Don Bosco, Rosario's bowels twisted and churned like frenzied eels in turbulent waters. She held his gaze and he could not let go of hers.

Looking romantic and pristine in his desert monk white summer cassock, he called the next day. Rosario's excitement grew at the thought of his impetuosity, but it was Paloma he wanted to see. Something about a deal they had struck—Latin lessons in exchange for monitoring small girls during the long procession of the Pentecost through the streets of the parish. He asked Rosario how she was, but before she could answer, he was off on the terrace with Paloma carrying a bundle of books under her arm.

He was very kind Paloma said, when Rosario enquired about the priest. He had listened to her reading, she told her, which was more than she had ever done for her. Rosario retorted that she had sent her to the best school in the country or had she forgotten, and Paloma walked away muttering how could she ever.

"Give him my thanks for the Latin lessons!" Rosario shouted back. "And I'll help you read too, if you like" she added. "I'm reading Henri Bergson, one of Father Clement's heroes" she said, walking back towards her mother.

"A Catholic priest teaching Bergsonian philosophy! Wasn't he Jewish?"

"He said 'God is love and love is God'" Paloma said as a way of explanation.

"I know what the man said!" Rosario snarled, thrown by the discovery of Paloma's maturity. "You're far too young for all that. You should be reading Loti! Pagnol! Acreman! Les nouveaux Russes! Forever Amber—which she had not read herself but seen at the Rialto, starring Linda Darnell with whom she identified—Detective stories even! You should read for fun! But whatever you read..." she added, "come and tell me first... Come and share your thoughts with me... Will you?" For the first time her mother had noticed her, as boldly as she would a bunch of red gladioli in a room. She did not pause to question how or why it had come about. She was far too elated that it had happened at all, and until late every night, she devoured Rosario's recommended list of authors so as to hasten her next tête-à-tête with her. Nevertheless, she acknowledged to herself that the tap of goodness her mother had opened for no apparent reason, would one day run dry, and she consciously stored all of her mother's solicitude, knowing that she would sink again into the depths of emotional anaemia. But Rosario did not fool Pepa. Who better than Paloma to shepherd her to the desired and elusive priest. It was a move that Pepa had not foreseen and she blamed herself for not protecting Paloma from Rosario's treachery.

Mother and daughter became inseparable—even to the point of eating together, just the two of them, and separately from the rest of the family, and it troubled Pepa that when their precarious and bogus closeness was exposed for the lie it was, it would imperil for good, the chance of them becoming truly closer one day. Pepa watched the fierceness of Paloma's undivided devotion to Rosario turn her grand-daughter into an exclusive, secretive and distant child, and hurtful as this was, Pepa drew back. Whatever pain her own distancing from Paloma caused her, Paloma's friendship with Ondine, she was determined, would not be jeopardised and she vowed that it would continue to flourish. She was even grateful to Joaquín who collected the children from The Orchard to spend Sundays at his beach house with Josh and Binot and his friends. It gave Paloma a break away from her mother, but one Sunday, as she packed Paloma's bathing costume, Pepa noticed her reticence which Paloma later confessed was because Binot and his friends jeered at her pubescent body. Something else happened at the beach house which disturbed her, and she was undecided whether to relate the incident. Her grandmother had always been her confidante, but her mother demanded that she be told everything first. In the end Paloma kept it a secret, until it happened again and this time she told Pepa.

Joaquín and the boys, routinely pitched a large bedouin tent between the beach house and the sea shore to store the small gas stove and cool box away from the sun. No one went there except at lunchtime, and only after Joaquín's call on his conch. Concerned at Paloma's reddening skin in the mid-day sun, Joaquín ordered her to shelter in the tent. It was before lunch and Carlota and her cousin Josh,who should have been on the beach, crept into the tent. They did not notice her presence as she sat, curled up at the opposite end, unable to avoid witnessing their blatant intimacy. When Pepa later questioned Carlota, she feared that at sixteen, Carlota had made up her mind to carry on just as she fancied. If it kept Carlota away from The Orchard, and out of Father Clement's sight, Rosario did not care. Joaquín had long known of Carlota and his son's shenanigans in the tent. He had even discussed it with Rosario that should their relationship take a more serious turn, a dispensation from the church might be de rigueur. Two Butlers coming together, had to be the ultimate union and he was unreservedly in favour. For Pepa, the idea was preposterous. Only royalty were licensed to commit incest and that was for reasons of greed and self-perpetuation, and for which they often paid the price with imbecile offspring. But all was resolved when Joaquín's suggestion of marriage drove Josh into hiding and he did not return until the start of the next school term, by which time Carlota was dating Max, an aspiring Olympic long distance runner.

TWENTY-ONE

"In Such Oblivion Immersed"

Ondine came to The Orchard every other Saturday afternoon when it was not Paloma's turn to visit Le Bungalo. They left their respective homes from the opposite sides of the town at precisely the same time and met at a half-way point previously calculated by Ondine. A formal handshake was their usual form of greeting, and then there was silence, until Paloma, without exception, broke it. "I read somewhere..." she often began, which aroused Ondine's interest more than any other overture. This time Paloma talked about Carlota, which never failed to fascinate Ondine. She was always with boys, one or two at a time, whilst she herself, only a year younger, had never managed a romantic rendez-vous, except once with petit Jean whom she had met at La Jeunesse Catholique in the parish hall and who followed her home after Saturday confession until one day Carlota told him that Paloma had hairy legs which she secretly shaved.

Her sister Chantal, Ondine said, saw an American Officer in the piano room every Friday afternoon but she never played it and when she and her other sisters pressed their ears to the door to listen to their courting, there were only sighs. After a pause Ondine added that she could not flirt like Chantal because she would only love once. He would be a flyer, like her lost hero Saint Exupery and it would be the most romantic idyll in the history of the universe. In the meantime she said, switching to a matter of fact tone, there was Chopin and Robin Hood to think about.

"Who?" queried Paloma, her head still floating with the image Ondine's statement had conjured.

"Surely you've noticed them! And Chopin is most definitely keen on you."

"You don't mean the one at the Marquise's private school opposite the park we pass when we come out of the Lycée!" Paloma blushed. "I don't mind his limp, I even like it!" she conceded wistfully. "But he must be at least nineteen!"

"Twenty." corrected Ondine. "He had polio as a child which gave him the limp, and delayed his schooling. And that's why he is at the Marquise's, to catch up and prepare for his Bac."

"Do you know him then?"

"'Course not. I just know about people. Observation, that kind of thing."

"And he looks at me?"

"He slows down or hangs about until you come out."

"Could be for you!" cried Paloma agitated.

"Robin Hood is mine."

"D'you know about him too!" exclaimed Paloma

"He's seventeen, arrived from France last year, his father's a naval officer. He lives in Anfa and he rides in the woods."

"He must be yours. You love horses!" exclaimed Paloma.

"But I don't own one" she said. "He does." They walked fast to keep pace with their soaring emotions. "We should spy on them."

"Ondine!"

"We must find out more about them. Be like detectives. Like Miss Marple."

"Who?"

"Agatha Christie."

"Oh her! I didn't know you read detective stories!"

"They teach you about people."

Paloma preferred it when they talked about make-believe romances such as Le Grand Meaulnes which they had read together and had kept them in dreamy speculation for months. Or when Ondine recited whole chunks of Saint Exupery's La Citadelle, Vol de Nuit, or Terre des Hommes, and exalted that his heroes had everything. They took risks, were dutiful and disciplined, and often sacrificed love ties to discover hidden inner treasures. Or when she proclaimed that she wanted to be lost with no name, so no one could find her, and would remain a mystery, just like her hero St Ex.

"How can we spy on them?" asked Paloma.

"We'll assign each other tasks."

"Tasks? What tasks?"

"You make a detailed list of what they are wearing."

"What's clothes got to do with anything?" Paloma asked, looking a tinge guilty for not being as sharp as her friend.

"Personality. It tells you what they're like. For instance, Chopin always wears a long red floaty scarf around his neck. That means he's delicate, romantic and passionate. A Chopin figure. And Robin Hood.. Well he's got a horse!"

"And your task?"

"I'll enquire at their school to see if they'll have me as an evening cleaner, when I can rummage around in the files ."

"You're mad! Maboul! Completely maboul!"

"Who's mad?" asked Rosario bumping into them at the gate of The Orchard.

"Nothing" mumbled Paloma. "It's..."

"It's a secret" whispered Ondine quickly covering one side of her face with a wisp of hair.

"There's no secrets between Paloma and me, Ondine..." uttered Rosario.

There was something burlesque about the way Rosario said this that made Ondine burst into hysterical laughter. "Later..." she said when she had stopped. "We'll tell you later Madame Butler, and can Paloma come with me to see La Belle et la Bête next Thursday?"

"And I'll come too!" cried Rosario. "I adore Michelle Morgan."

What Ondine saw in Paloma baffled Rosario—like the rest of her family, Ondine was very bright. Rosario had lost interest in Paloma's academic evolution—she said it was more like a steady involution and she wondered about the girl's conversations since she knew of no male admirers, nor were they keen on fashion or rock and roll, or had any other diversions. What Rosario did not know was that they read Camus and Cocteau in Ondine's father's converted garage and listened to the freedom singers Brassens, Brel, Ferré, and Greco—star and muse of Sartre, who embodied rebellion, freedom and individualism and was also their own star. Rosario did not know either that they were crazy on Strauss' waltzes which they practiced on Ondine's lawn and read War and Peace aloud to each other. She would not want to know that they had played truant at least one morning a week, since the beginning of the Easter term, stopping without exception at the 'open all hours' small épicerie near the racecourse for their breakfast of two individual tartes au citron and a shared bottle of coca cola. They then walked six kilometres to the beach at dawn to watch riders on horseback or horses without mounts galloping at the edge of the ocean, and the early birds scrutinising the wet sand for insects and worms. There was so much to see, hear and feel, during their time on the beach, that it was seldom they spoke, but if one of them did, it had to be potentially worthwhile. "I've been trying to build a bridge" Paloma once proffered, with her last mouthful of tarte. "Are you an engineer then?" laughed Ondine until the laughter became uncontrollable. "Sorry... must be the ocean air" she added quickly, aware of her inconsiderate remark. "But I know what you mean. I think."

"In my head." said Paloma. "The bridge is in my head" she repeated, peeved.

"That's what I thought, but you'd better explain just the same."

"You know St John's verses written on 'ecstasy'?" Paloma saw her friend acquiesce. "I felt it, Ondine! Me! Just like he did, when I wasn't even trying" she said intensely. "And then it vanished and I can't get it back."

"I know" said Ondine brushing pastry crumbs off her bathing costume. "Poetry, music, nature, that's where you'll find God but go to Church and you'll stay glued to the ground. And they tell us otherwise. Crooks, the lot of them! And animals. Look what they did to the Jews! Rome!"......

"Back off Ondine, Father Clement isn't like that!" interrupted Paloma.

"Maybe not, but just the same, if you can think for yourself, you shouldn't be a practising Catholic" Ondine said. "It's the religion of the weak. It controls you and takes away your free will."

"What of St John of the Cross and Ávila. How do they fit in then?"

"Oh them, they are above religion."

*

When Father Clement called at The Orchard, he stood smiling behind the blue and white beaded curtain hanging from the open kitchen door to keep out the flies. He begged them to continue their game of cards when they stopped, but Rosario sprang from her chair, showed him into the living room after asking Paloma to bring them tea, with two slices of lemon.

Carlota jeered at her sister and called her a creep, whilst Paloma told her she was jealous. Rosario wound down the persiennes of the sitting room complaining the sun was blinding though they both knew the room was always in shade at that time of day. She and Father Clement sat facing each other on the squashy brown leather armchairs. He talked about the needs of his Parish and bemoaned the narrowness of the French bureaucratic system. Not even the Ministry of Education he said, listened to his plea for the education of the indigenous population of his own Parish. But his hands were tied, adding that the Bishop himself had reminded him that his ministrations were to do with religion and for the faithful only. He continued to talk compulsively and without a pause as if to protect himself against dangerous silences or Rosario's abortive intimate comments. Paloma knocked and entered the dim room with the tray of tea which she placed on the bridge table next to Rosario and waited. She was asked to pour, serve, and leave.

From then on, Father Clement visited most Thursday afternoons. Instructed to stand guard at precisely two o'clock, Paloma was to meet him in the street as soon as she heard his

Vespa draw up at the gate, and to accompany him back to the gate, in silence, as he left. If questioned by neighbours about his visits, she was to say that the Father came to counsel the family after their recent bereavement. Something indefinable was unfolding between her mother and the priest, she knew that, but she did not want to believe her sister's damning innuendos. Theirs had to be a special relationship. She caught them reading poetry every time she came into the room with the tray of tea, and to her that was proof, but the more Paloma revelled in this tacit and strange complicity 'à trois,' the more she alienated herself from the rest of the family and Ondine, and although she was aware of it happening, she felt fuelled and driven by the very nature of its complexity.

*

The summers in Casablanca were grim after Elias' death. Gone were the long spells in the temperate Atlas mountains. The children had nowhere to go and stayed at The Orchard most afternoons, lying flat on the kitchen floor to feel the cold mosaic tiles against their backs, keeping close to the open refrigerator, underneath the whirling coolness of the ceiling fan, or best of all, they ran naked into the garden to soak in and venerate a rare summer rainstorm.

A supervisor was required for the summer camp at Azemour Father Clement disclosed, and there was also a vacancy for one more boy. Paloma, whom he knew was familiar with children from her involvement with the Guides, and Alexi, puny and in need of a change of air, were chosen. But days later diphtheria struck Paloma and only Alexi left The Orchard that summer.

José Luis had nearly died of it when a child. Distraught, Pepa reminisced the horror of it. Paloma's own immunity, if good, the doctor said, was her best chance of survival. A horse serum injection to neutralise the toxins in her blood was a possibility if her condition worsened, but he warned that it could also lead to kidney failure. Paloma communicated in a feeble sign language and was considered so infectious that only Pepa and Father Clement visited her. For over a week she was delirious, lost the physical awareness of herself, felt insubstantial and as if having traversed, with unimaginable ease, a density of matter unknown to conscious man. She did not know how long she would be there before she made it back to where she had come from. The thought arose, woolly as it was, that she would rather dwell in that other place where the burden of weight did not exist. Her skin felt tight and as if not her own and, or, as if her body had expanded and could not fit into her old shell. "Open your eyes" a voice, she recognised from where she had been, told her, "and it will be as it was." But so acute was the pain when she opened them that she closed them again and fell asleep, a sleep without dreams. Matching each of her own breaths with Paloma's, Pepa sat by her bed and prayed, not for her grand-daughter and not for herself, but for the Will of God to be done, even though she could not bear the thought of losing her. Good Thoughts she believed were messages of healing and she was convinced that Paloma would pick them up. Finger movements, light at first, filled Pepa's heart with hope, then sobs of relief when her granddaughter spoke in stifled whispers for the first time in a week. Paloma smoothed her grandmother's hair and apologised for neglecting to comb it. She began to drink through a straw the bouillon that Pepa made for her. When she smiled in gratitudd her lips bled, but her eyes glowed and Pepa gave thanks.

She had seen visions Paloma told her. Some were blissful, others tormented her. Most clearly, she remembered coming from another place. Pepa listened. What she needed now to be earth-bound was good food, fresh air, her family, and Ondine by her side. Paloma sat up in bed and scribbled:

Ondine, my dear friend,

I do not know what day or month it is, and though weak, I am well again. I owe it to my grandmother who stayed by my side. I am now ready for something

different from what I have known up until this day,
though I cannot think what. I'm missing you—I think
it is now safe for you to visit me. Please come by after
school one day—even if I haven't much to say.

With my loving friendship,
Greetings, from far, far away......
Paloma

Ondine was there at Paloma's side almost as soon as she had finished reading the letter. She too, had had other worldly dreams during Paloma's illness Ondine confided. They were kindred spirits Pepa said.

The procession of well-wishing visitors exhausted Paloma and visits only from Father Clement were permitted from then on. Endeavouring not to be subjected to Rosario predatory charms, he came at daybreak before Mass and was greeted on the terrace by Pepa every morning. There they stayed awhile whispering the latest on Paloma's recovery before he went up to her room. Miko often sneaked in after Father Clement's visit, but before that he had peered through the open door whenever Pepa entered the room. He now sat cross-legged at the bottom of Paloma's bed like an endearing elf saying that when he was not allowed in he had breathed out something that came from inside his chest through the keyhole of her bedroom door to reach her heart and make her well again.

TWENTY-TWO

Things Are Not What They Seem

"It's most definitely a new chapter in our lives!" proclaimed Pepa whisking egg yolks in a bowl for the egg custard. Rosario and the children sat around the kitchen table busy shelling broad beans.

"St Joseph's today and Easter next week!" Pepa shouted to overcome the din of her whisk.

"I want a turn!" cried Miko climbing onto the table to spin the handle. "Perfect" she said, snatching the silky mixture away seconds later and pouring it into the almost boiling milk.

Father Clement appeared unannounced through the back door and it gave him a thrill every time he caught the family unawares. "What a sacred sight!" he marvelled, embracing them all in turn.

"Will you come and break bread with us this Easter, Padre?" Pepa asked.

*

He arrived on his vespa at noon, the distant bells of Easter cheer still ringing in his parish church after the High Mass in which he had officiated. The boys were sent to greet him and he gave them each a ride around the block before coming in. Carlota was still in bed. She had been out until late, though no one knew where or with whom. After a while she appeared naked in the kitchen where everyone had joined in an apéritif. Pepa threw her a tea towel to cover her most intimate parts, and told her to get dressed.

"She is a free soul" Father Clement said benignly, finding

it hard to conceal his blushing. "She is plain provocative!" snapped Rosario. "There is nothing free about what she just did!" She wished Carlota had gone off for the day with Joaquín or Josh, Tom, Dick or Harry. She didn't care who. When Carlota next came down to join the family, dressed, as she had been told to do, but wearing one of Rosario's most glamorous dresses, unworn since Elias' death, Rosario screamed at her to take it off, which Carlota did, on the spot. Father Clement cast his eyes down and squirmed. He could not make out whether his embarrassment was to do with Carlota's brazen nakedness or with the patently uneasy relationship between mother and daughter, but struggling out of his quandary he ordered Carlota to behave, and to come down with her own clothes on next time. The boys laughed at Carlota for being scolded by a priest. They had seen their sister roam naked through the house so often that they failed to grasp what the fuss was about. Pepa and Paloma busied themselves with the finishing touches of the blue, red, green, and yellow painted duck eggs that they had been decorating over the week, and which now filled a straw nest for the table centre-piece. Nothing about Carlota surprised them, except that this time, they thought she had gone too far.

As they always did, Rosario and Father withdrew to the lounge for their pouce café after lunch, Rosario pulled the persiennes down as she did every time, and burst into the tears she had been saving, telling Father clement that Carlota had wrecked her life and had been her bête noire from birth. Everyone knew that Carlota was the culprit, and that her own endless efforts and prayers for the betterment of her daughter had not borne fruit. She begged him to say something when he remained silent. But all she heard him whisper was "Poor, poor Carlota..."

"Poor Carlota? Poor Carlota! You don't see, do you?"

"I see Rosario, if only partially."

"She's a witch, a horrid witch! She's always done that, ever since she was a tot."

"Done what Rosario?"

"Get people to feel sorry for her, or seduce them. You just have no idea!"

"Let me talk to her" he pleaded.

"She'll twist you around her little finger in no time, and you'll be at her mercy before you know it."

"Thanks!" cried Father Clement.

"That's the truth. I know it!"

"You can't leave things the way they are Rosario" he said, "for her sake and others. I can see," he acknowledged, "that she's hell bent on destruction, but why? What started it all Rosario? You are her mother. You were there from the start. You, of all people should have an inkling about such matters. You must search your soul. It's important."

"That's how she was born. Nothing to do with me. Ask my mother, Paloma, even the boys!"

"Look Rosario, I fear that Carlota is fast becoming a scapegoat, yours and maybe even the family's. We must try to dispel that before it is too late. Come on, let's open our hearts to her, and let's make it a priority."

"She has ruined our day" Rosario moaned.

"She has not. Things happen. We mustn't become a folie-à-deux, you and I, Rosario. Each and everyone in this family counts, equally. Today Carlota took centre stage. That's all."

She coaxed him to read her some poetry to cheer her up, but not before she had sulked at his laying equal priority on each member of the family.

"As it happens" he said (and a pensive look overtook him) "I've brought the 'Pensées' with me."

"Pascal's?"

"Of course."

"That sanctimonious dry old stick, telling you how to think. I want something soft and undemanding and ridiculously romantic."

"Like Verhaeren?" his voice smiled... and she curled up on the sofa. "I know it by heart" he whispered, before reciting it in the hollow of her ear.

'Oh ce bonheur, si rare
et si frêle parfois
qu'il nous fait peur............'

but now, ma jolie" he said standing up, and sounding like a
stranger, "I must leave you". He slipped on his robes over the
mufti he now wore when visiting The Orchard. She watched
him avidly, as he always did this in absolute silence and she
never knew if this was part of the reverential ritual of putting
on his priestly robes, or to do with the sorrow of their parting.
She rose from the sofa to kiss him as if this might be the last of
their encounters. They probed each others burning gazes until
alarmed, Father Clement looked down to break the spell she
was wilfully casting on him and left.

An unusual weariness settled over him when Paloma
escorted him back to the gate and he told her, as if to himself,
that things were not as they seemed, and to love Carlota, to love
her with all her might. Paloma nodded and held her hand out to
shake his, but he bent down to kiss her forehead instead, not as
a priest might, but as a father. No word or suggestion from
Father Clement was ever lost on Paloma. She was meant to
ponder upon what he had just uttered. 'Love Carlota. Love her
with all your might' and 'things are not what they seem'. That
was what he said. Was Carlota then, her mother, or herself, or
himself and Rosario, not what they seemed? Or, was that which
appeared evil, good. And vice versa? Or was there something
else he intimated, beyond her understanding?

*

"Two more families gunned down, Madame Rosario!"
shouted Alcaya, waving La Vigie Marocaine.

"When?" asked Rosario snatching the newspaper.

"Yesterday. Look. Its headlines. In their sleep. They
stunned the dog with a brick and bang! bang! The Désusclades,
gone!. Did you know them Madame? And a couple in the Sadi
souss. They were picnicking by the river. Trouble stewing

everywhere, like Tadjine in the pot..." she said.

"God help us all!" exclaimed Rosario.

"And another rape in Le Parc Lyautey Madame! Only thirteen ... Halouf!" she added, spitting on the ground.

"Same man?"

"The same, Madame. The naked one with oil smeared all over his body so no one can catch him!"

"Halouf!" Rosario said, without spitting. "Pig!"

*

It was 1952 and the second week of December when alarming riots broke out in Casablanca, following the assassination in Tunis of the Arab nationalist Ferhat Ashid, killing some five hundred people. Rosario did not quite understand how it had all come about. She knew little of politics and cared even less. She had, after all, not shown much interest or unease for her own country and countrymen during the civil war, and was only concerned now that her personal welfare was at stake. All she knew of the Moroccan problem was from her vague recollections of snippets of news she had heard on the radio when at Marina's and from the discussions that followed amongst the circus people. From this she had gathered that trouble was brewing, and that it was the growing demand for Independence sweeping colonies in Africa, Indo-china, India and neighbouring Algeria that fuelled terrorism in Morocco. Unbeknown to her until this moment, unrest had been smouldering for the last three years since the French government had turned down the request for self government put forward by the Moroccan nationalist group—the Istaqlal Party. Supported by the sultan Muhammed V, most colonials chose to ignore the implications of this, until the protestors began to target Europeans and their properties.

Joaquín would know what the next step would be. All anyone had to go by he said, were the conflicting and often contradictory accounts from La Vigie Marocaine and Le Petit Marocain. One claiming thirty five Moslem deaths in one riot, the other, a dozen Europeans. And to confuse matters, their stories of arrests and internments clashed. "That's Morocco for you Rosario!" he told her wryly. "You'll never know the truth. Least of all in black and white!"

"The Déchaumes are leaving, did you know?" she asked.

"What do you expect! They're not true colonials! They panic at the slightest brouhaha, and rush home to their motherland. But we won't budge. This is our place... It's home... Has been for well over a hundred years. 'Here I am and here I stay!'... as somebody or other once said" he exclaimed.

She rang around to make sense of what the faux colonials like herself felt. Many were planning to flee within days or weeks, and if she was intending to stay, an old friend of Elias advised her to employ a resident armed watchman. Marina had to move out of her isolated villa by the sea after terrorists smashed her windows one night and she now lived with her sister and Piero above their Café Saltimbanco in town at the edge of the harbour. More civil unrest was likely but Pepa felt certain the insurrection would die down, at least temporarily, while the resurgents regrouped, which would give the family enough time to plan their move.

✳

Carlota was in love. Again. She told the family it was special this time. Norbert, her new love had said so, and he was coming to see Rosario for permission to become engaged. Handsome, in the Robert Taylor mode, Rosario nevertheless thought him as exciting as a turnip, so much so, that she couldn't be bothered to indulge in a spot of flirtation. Devolving her parental responsibilities, even to a total stranger was like seeing the collapse of an insurmountable wall. Her approval and blessing, without consideration of the suitability of her daughter's fiancé, was given without question.

At seventeen, Carlota was far too immature to contemplate marriage Father Clement said. She needed to find, and then affirm her own identity first. On the other hand, he also knew of Carlota's licentious tendencies and hoped a steady relationship might provide her with the love and stability she had not found at home.

After the engagement was made official, Norbert began to visit The Orchard daily after school. A teacher, his serious intent was to coach Carlota for her baccalauréat in the coming June. But she diverted him from her desk to the shade of the covered terrace near Lobo's kennel, knowing the dog would bark obligingly when anyone approached. Later, after Carlota had taken her exams, they met outside the confines of the The Orchard and every day after school Carlota sprang onto Norbert's motorbike to drive to the beach. Seldom home before midnight, Pepa worried for her welfare but Rosario turned a blind eye hoping pregnancy would precipitate an early wedding.

Only a year separated the two girls, but a huge gulf appeared between them after Carlota's engagement, Carlota was on the verge of marriage, whilst Paloma secretly nurtured the romantic dream of her Celtic Knight predicted by Alegria long ago in magical Ourika. There was Binot's friend Julien, with whom, for a while, she had attended weekly confession, but even when Paloma had longed, on a few occasions to keep Julien's hand in hers for longer than a normal handshake allowed, her dream stopped her every time.

"You'll end up an old maid like Mademoiselle Avril at this rate" Carlota warned her, fondling her own voluptuous curves, and then she confided that there was someone else in her life. He was Marco, who came each day to watch her come out of the Lycée. He was blonde with piercing blue eyes and very athletic. All she wanted was to experience Marco once. Norbert need not find out. She had thought it out, made her mind up and swore Paloma to secrecy. After Marco came Eugène, then Malou, Dédé the boxer, and others. Norbert never knew, nor Rosario nor Father Clement. Not even Pepa.

Pepa was Paloma's confidente, but life was changing. She had to keep secrets for Carlota and talking to her grandmother about her own evolving sexuality did not come easily. Only Ondine could listen, she was good at it, but even so, all she thought about of late was obtaining her pilot's licence to enlist as a recruit for when the war of Independence broke out, which she said would be soon.

Paloma hesitated, Ondine's body did not appear to scream for the calls of the flesh as hers was beginning to. But she was bursting to talk. She just had to. They arrived at the deserted Lido beach just after dawn, undressed on the sand and ate their breakfast, this time of figs, plums and grapes before a swim. Paloma wore the apple-green bikini Ondine's sister had sewn for her in the spring from an old skirt of Rosario's. "I don't remember this thing being so scanty when you last tried it on" remarked Ondine pointing at Paloma's belly button.

"I just turned it down, a bit" Paloma said sheepishly.

"But there's no one here to see!" laughed Ondine looking all around.

"I know that..." Paloma replied rolling her bikini up to her waist. "I just feel a bit...I don't know..."

"You ARE changing!" said Ondine scrutinising her.

"It's Carlota's fault" Paloma said vexed. "I don't want to be left behind."

"Behind?"

"An old maid, I mean."

"At sixteen? Come on!"

"She's engaged!"

"That's insane!" cried Ondine. "Carlota's not the marrying kind. She's far too crazy about boys for that!"

"She told me I would never have anyone."

"Do you believe that?"

"I don't know anything" Paloma replied despondent. "Tell me your most secret secret Ondine!" she cried. "I need a treat!"

Ondine stood up all at once, gave a loud yawn, stretched and shouted "I have no secrets Paloma. Be free! Be yourself!"

Paloma watched her friend run to the sea and drew her knees up to her chin to gaze at the horizon. Why could she not feel at peace as she had been as a child? She would have called God or an angel or something Out There for help, only a couple of years ago. Now, she had lost her links and felt empty.

307

She shivered and waited for the mid-morning sun to warm the water before diving in. The fine sand filtered between her toes as she walked to warm herself up, and she watched the soles of her feet leaving an imprint that the high tide would wash away forever. "life....!" she murmured to herself.

*

They stood in the street after one of Father Clement's visits to The Orchard, when Paloma asked if he believed in spirits and guides. She had considered seeing someone other than a priest, as Ondine had advised her to do, to guide her out of her turmoil and she wanted to know about the clairvoyant in white robes by the Post Office everyone talked about. "Be wary of charlatans" he warned her. She would know them because their egos gave them away. He looked at her closely. She should learn to watch out for wolves clothed as holy men, he said, "but" he told her softly, "there's a place you can always go to, which is yours and which is safe—your soul." They said nothing and smiled, just smiled, until Father Clement started his vespa with one thrust of his foot. "Stick to the old soul" he said, revving up his scooter, "that is your link with God. All the rest is window dressing. No more than that!"

TWENTY-THREE

Cria Cuervos and the Rose

An air of neglect, almost dereliction, pervaded The Orchard. Lobo, Carlota's Alsatian, was the only remaining animal. Alexi's pet donkey, too costly to keep, was sent back to Ahmed-Zeen on Samuel's old small-holding he had bequeathed him. As the chickens were eaten they were not replaced, and fresh eggs were supplied from Joaquín's farm.

Rosario heeded the advice about protection and hired a guard who did little except rest and sleep with his gun between his legs. Even when the boys tickled the soles of his bare feet he did not respond.

Alexi and Miko grew closer after Elias' death, spending their days roaming the souks alone with the few coins in their pockets that they had pilfered from the Sunday Mass collection, to buy small trinkets, like colourful paper windmills, marbles or tin soldiers, and honeyed pastries they were never allowed to eat at home. They had too much freedom, Pepa said, all the more so now, as terrorism in the streets, mainly aimed at Europeans, increased. But Rosario, looking more pale and gaunt with each passing day, was oblivious to Pepa's concerns. She sat all day in her room reading the books that Father Clement left her after each visit. The latest, George Bernanos' Diary of a Country Priest was the one she had to read, as his unalterable Catholicism and profound concern for spirituality gave her a flavour of how Father Clement might feel about his own priesthood.

She should go out more and renew contact with Marina, Pepa repeatedly said, but Rosario made no effort to see her or anyone else. As a concession to Pepa, and for the fresh air, she took to reading under the fig tree. Paloma joined her after school with a cup of chocolat au lait, always in silence, but not this time.

"I'm reading!" Rosario said grumpily, turning away from Paloma."

"We must talk. I've got to know before five o'clock!"

"What? Know what?" growled Rosario putting down her book. "What could be so important? Has Chopin or whatever his stupid name is, proposed to you?" she mocked.

"I don't want him anyway" replied Paloma offended, sorry that she had ever confided in her.. "I've come to say that I've been invited to an Arts and Craft Fair in Rabat".

"Really" mumbled Rosario half listening and starting to read her book again. "There's only one every two or three years" Paloma insisted, her voice growing louder with excitement, "with Berber tribal art from the High Atlas, and rugs, pottery, jewellery and calligraphy from Fez. It's like a live theatre and an Aladdin's cave, all in one!"

"I didn't know you went in for that sort of thing" Rosario said, scrutinising her daughter's face "Who's invited you?"

"Ondine's mother. Ondine's sisters are going too."

"That's all right then. You can go" she said still trying to read.

"I'll need money for the train fare" Paloma said.

"Ask your grandmother, she's the housekeeper." Paloma wanted to hug her mother but scarcely patted her shoulder instead. "Thank you Maman" she said, moved with gratitude. "And when is it?" asked Rosario.

"Thursday. All day Thursday. I shall have to get up at the crack of dawn. We'll take our own picnics to save money and Ondine's father will bring me back in the evening if it's dark. Or they'll keep me overnight. Everything's been planned to the last detail!"

"Not Thursday. You know you must be here on Thursdays." Paloma screamed why!

"Why? Why? Think, child! You're my chaperone, that's why!"

"Could you not miss one Thursday!" begged Paloma.

"They are my life blood."

"I'm sure Father Clement wouldn't mind missing ONE Thursday" she persisted.

"He mustn't know!" she snapped, at last looking at her.

"I know he'd want me to go….." Paloma pressed on.

"Only if he finds out. So not a word! That's final!" Rosario decreed.

"It's not!" Paloma yelled. "It-is-not!"

"I beg your pardon?" Rosario said, peering over her book.

"You're not getting away with this" Paloma uttered quietly, despite feeling her face turn pink, then bright red and she shouted, "You are nothing but a mean, selfish and self-centred monster! Have you ever cared for anyone, anyone at all? Who were you visiting when we were hungry and frightened in boarding school? Not us! And who's been a real mother to Carlota and me? Not you! And where were you after I was born? You think I don't know? Well, I know all about that! I know more than you think.!"

"What is this? An Auto da Fé from my own daughter?" Rosario sneered. "And from the sweet one at that! Maybe you're a bad little egg too! Are you a bad little egg?" she goaded.

"Your tricks don't work on me" Paloma continued to shout. "Not any more! I won't be your fetch and carry slave. You'll have to find yourself another mug to do your dirty work!" Paloma saw Rosario stand up as if in slow motion and before she took the full force of a slap on the one cheek and then on the other. She swayed. Her eyes glistened with tears that clung at the edges of her lids and she pressed them hard with her fingers to keep them at bay. Her voice trembled. "You'll never, NEVER, forget what you've just done. I'll make damn sure of that!"

"You are nothing but a worm" Rosario hissed. "And you'll worm your way back to me, yet!"

"Start counting the minutes!" challenged Paloma, "and watch yourself grow into a sad old hag!"

Pepa stood beside them unnoticed by either. "I wish you hadn't threatened your mother like that" she admonished. "It was very cruel, very cruel, what you just said. It doesn't matter how much she hurts you, you owe her your respect. Remember that, she will always be your mother, no one else but her."

"You are my mother" sobbed Paloma wiping her nose against her grandmother's apron. "YOU ARE MY MOTHER!" she screamed.

"Paloma" whispered Pepa, holding her quivering granddaughter in her arms . "Listen."

"I can't!....." snapped Paloma "I just can't! I wish she fell ill, a long and painful illness. Sudden death is too good for her!"

"Sweetheart...You don't mean it"

"Yes I do! I really do!"

Pepa bowed her head. "We all have negative parts. It's human nature..."

"It's all a matter of degree, is it not?" Paloma retorted.

"Of course it is. Just like trees."

"Trees? What about trees" intercepted Paloma, not in the mood for one of her grandmother's morality tales.

"Even the diseased parts, I was going to say" said Pepa, taken aback by her grand-daughter's impatience "are of that tree. Love is the same." She paused to search for Paloma's eyes. "Do you see sweetheart?" Paloma grunted uncompromisingly. "You can't" said Pepa, I can see that, because you're all tied up in knots. But you will, cariño. You must. It is the only way."

Locked in her bedroom until Rosario was ready for a truce, Pepa each night, tucked the sheets around her grand-daughter's body as if to protect her from further assaults and watched her sink into the sleep of the tormented until at dawn,she tapped her gently on the shoulder . "Daylight sweetheart" she'd say tunefully. "Time to comb my hair."

"It's greasy, Yaya. Where's your eau de Cologne?" she asked, pulling and tugging it.

"It's not like you to be so rough sweetheart....." moaned Pepa holding her head. "That anger of yours, it will eat you up!"

"I can see it all." Paloma muttered to herself. "I wake up with it, sleep with it—it's there all the time. Me, being a pawn. She never cared about ME, my life, my welfare, who I AM, what makes me tick, what I become." And she turned to face Pepa. "She's just unnatural! Mothers are not supposed to be like that! Are they?"

"You have to try to understand Paloma. Your mother is like the Queen Bee in La Tia Tula."

"And who's she when she's at home?" Paloma asked losing her patience.

"She's a character in one of Unamuno's stories."

"And the Queen Bee?"

"That's your mother." Paloma laughed. "My mother, a Queen Bee?"

"D'you want to hear the story or not? And stop pulling or I'll be bald."

Paloma acquiesced and sat opposite Pepa. She bit her nails and fidgeted and Pepa knew she had to be brief.

"The story is about the caring ministrations of the Worker Bee which gives more of herself than the Queen Bee ever could. Their two roles" she paused to increase her attention, "are different and pre-determined, and in a way, Paloma, I am, for you, one of the Worker Bees, a carer, and your own personal Tia Tula."

"A bit unconvincing, your metaphor Yaya" Paloma sniggered.

"Why?"

"It's too simple. Bees are bees, and humans are humans!"

"So?"

"So, there's a bee culture and there's a human culture. And as a human mother, mine rates zero!"

"All I'm saying to you Paloma is that your mother's purpose in life may not have been that of a carer at all, but she was made to assume that role when she became a mother, probably by mistake".

"Whose mistake?" goaded Paloma.

"Society! Religion! Conditioning! Hers! Mine! Who

313

knows! Any of these and all of them!"

"You're letting her off the hook, aren't you!" Paloma objected.

"Of course not! We all have to face up to our own mistakes. We can't escape that and I'm not condoning your mother, if that's what you think. But at the same time, if her attitude seems unimaginable this minute, it could be fully explicable at another level." Pepa paused for thought. "Who are we to judge, eh? Mita?" she asked.

"Judge..." muttered Paloma to herself as if the word weighed a ton.

"So have you a final verdict on your mother?" asked Pepa, sensing a softening in Paloma's heart.

"I have pain, Yayita. Pain from as far back as I can remember. And it never really goes away. But judge..?" Paloma said wearily, "What do I know about it!"

"See it as a lesson and not a conflict to resolve sweetheart." Then Pepa took Paloma's hands in hers. "You must forgive yourself and your mother" she murmured. Paloma buried her head amidst the umpteen layers of her grandmother's skirts and asked for help. "Before I do, return to the beginning and bring your rituals back into your life" Pepa advised. "It'll work, I promise you."

"I've neglected them" confessed Paloma. "Things always go wrong when I do."

"Take your time, and remember, you can't build a palace wearing a cowboy suit." She had not heard her grandmother use this aphorism before and she did not understand it, but she knew it had to mean something important, like bringing rituals back into her life, but with proper awareness. What she needed was something concrete, like an altar on which to focus her determination to daily clock herself back into inner balance and joy.

"Now we can begin" said Pepa taken aback by Paloma's progress and the simplicity of her altar piece.

"Now? You mean now—now?" cried Paloma incredulous.

"You are ready" Pepa said. She knelt, and when she heard

Paloma's breathing steady and light, she said, "Repeat after me:

The past I now release.
I am strong and bold.
And my true self will I hold

Breathe the words in sweetheart, and make them yours. And again repeat:"

The past is done.
Time to forgive
For me, and my mother, most.
So the petals of my rose,
One by one, can open and glow,
Deep in the cave of my heart.

Do you see your rose Paloma?" Pepa whispered. "It is the rose I promised you long ago when I told you the butterfly story. You have won it all by yourself because it is your pain that brought it there" and she let Paloma weep. "Now the last bit" said Pepa, "you can chant it, sing it, or shout it! Ready?"

'I am happy to be ME! Now that I'm FREE!
I AM THAT AND THAT I AM!'

"I hope it is penance you are practising child!" cried Rosario bursting into the room as Paloma chanted.

"Penance is a gloomy word Maman!" she said.

"You can come out of your room and greet Father Clement. He's waiting in the lounge for you" she said in a sugary, whispered voice "And not a word..!"she mouthed.

"No time for that. I'm off to Ondine's" said Paloma unflinching.

"But it's Thursday!" rasped Rosario.

"I'm going anyway!"

"You will not!" ordered Rosario.

"I am strong and bold" Paloma sang looking tantalisingly into her mother's eyes, "and I will not be told," and she began to dance, fairy fashion, "or be as good as gold," and facing her mother after the last twirl she shouted "but my true self I will hold!"

"Did you see that mother!" cried Rosario. "Cria cuervos!" she screamed like a virago or a fury in a greek tragedy. "Enough!" cried Pepa, "Paloma is merely learning to assert herself, and about time too, and I will not let you call any of your children 'crows' Rosario. They feed on no one. If anything, YOU are the crow that feeds on them."

"Shut up!" bellowed Rosario. "I'm getting sick and tired of your know-all, see-all, bloody sanctimonious goody-goodyness! You can't open your mouth without some pearl of wisdom gushing out of it. Can you?" She was spitting and paused for a moment to swallow her saliva. "And I've had it up to here with your wretched candles and your holy images, your stupid Ave Marias and your bloody novenas! It's all a bag of shit and I've had enough of it all!"

"Father Clement's behind you, Rosario..." said Pepa very collected.

That Thursday, he did not spend long with Rosario and it was Pepa who escorted him out. "What's wrong" he asked, his voice unusually hollow. "Can you tell me Yaya?" She told him and he cried Paloma's name inside his hands. "She'll be alright Padre" Pepa said. "Paloma has hidden resources."

"And Rosario?" What of my Rosario!"

TWENTY-FOUR

Mal D'Amour and Other Realms

The urgent petition to his superior for a week's retreat deep in the bled was granted without question. Father Clement chose a remote refuge in the Ouarzazate region and rang Rosario on the eve of his departure to cancel their next meeting. She hung up on him without a word, and he knew that a distance between them was essential.

St Augustine, it was said, ordained the refuge around 390AD when he returned from Rome to North Africa to establish a monastic community. Now six priests from mixed denominations were allowed there at any one time. Each brought his own supplies for the duration of his stay and a gift to leave behind. They lived in total silence except after their evening meal when they could converse for no longer than one hour and ten minutes, before the bell by the fountain in the courtyard rang for the resumption of silence and bed.

It was already dark when Father Clement arrived. He had travelled since dawn by coach, mule, and the last lap, on foot. No one came to greet him, but his name was scribbled on the back of an empty packet of Camel cigarettes and nailed loosely to one of the cell doors.

The mattress was the only object in the two square metre cell and it lay thin and compacted on the brown crumbly earth. A now faded cross was painted in cobalt blue on the white-washed wall and an empty, coarse earthenware bowl sat outside on the uneven stone floor, for water to be collected from the well at dawn. He sat cross-legged on the mattress to eat the bread, and a chunk of gruyère cheese he had brought with him, and washed it down with a swig of red wine from his tin gourd.

He gave thanks, read his breviary, did not bother to get undressed and settled for the night.

The bell rang at dawn. There was no one about when he pushed open the worm-eaten wooden door which opened onto another smaller courtyard. The magnificence of the scenery he witnessed on his way to the well slowed down his steps. The palm groves, verdant along the riverside below, contrasted with the clear desert sky beyond, as if they were landscapes from separate places. He found this disparity astonishing and beautiful to the point of aching. Man—Woman he thought. It was all there. He gazed into the distance, Rosario too, became part of that vast, ancient world. He called her, and found that the sound of his own voice echoing her name amidst the wilderness was the most erotic, yet most spiritual act he had ever performed. He begged her image to stay away, but amongst the bruised saffron scent beneath his feet, he could smell her longing. Her body was always provocative to him yet he had never penetrated it. They learned to dance with their desires, each to their own tune. Slow and graceful or made ungainly by the irrepressible rush of lust. He saw their lightly clad bodies strewn on the Moroccan rug of The Orchard's lounge floor and their thoughts reflecting upon the mysteries of its symbols. From them, they made up their own love stories as they became lost in the ecstasy of an unbroken caress and the burst of their mutual climaxes, separated only by the unshakable wall of his Church. She thought it unnatural. He told her their limitations induced a beauty to their love-making few other lovers could ever know. That's how it was. That's how it had to be. He was a priest. He loved being a priest—not the churchliness of it, but the pastoral work. Being a father to one and all. But what of denial?—Detachment—that was a better word. It allowed participation with non-attachment. A foot in both camps. To be of the world and not of it. Divine indifference. Desire—that was the root of all suffering—he had read it in the Buddha's scriptures and he liked it, because Christ could have said it too.

He gazed at the blasting of pinks and reds of the oleanders

below by the river bed, and remembered that its first flower grew from Fatima's tears and that its leaves were poisonous and unbearably bitter. He closed his eyes and his contemplation took him back to when he and Rosario first met, reliving the same exhilarating panic and stirring feelings that had swamped him then, and that he previously knew possible only from the whispered confessions of his parishioners. His cousin Marie, a shiny-cheeked milkmaid in his Brittany village was the first woman to disturb his pubescent youth but the seminary had already claimed him for life and from then on, he was compelled to bring his longings to heel. No one explained to him how to transmute the volcanic desires and fiery emotions of his manhood that threatened the integrity of priesthood, other than through prayer. He knew it did not work, because he had tried it but he had read books, hidden in the deeper recesses of the Vatican library during his probation period in Rome, about how Eastern monks were edified in the art of transmuting sexual energy. For them, arousal was not forbidden, but when it struck, it became an act of great concentration and spiritual will to send that raw energy upwards, through the spine and up to the head, where it was transmuted into spiritual fire which was then released as a kind of cosmic music. It was a lifetime of dedication for the monks who practised this form of purificatory exercise, and it resolved the sinister consequences of enforced chastity. But for the Catholic priest, chastity was a monogamous marriage between his soul and God, and the intrusion of a woman into this sacred union was the most profane of adulteries. He smiled at the glorious thought of so sublime a ménage-à-trois, failing to see how God would not enjoy partaking in the joys of his own creation.

Pascal was right in saying that man is neither angel nor beast, and that it was unfortunate that he who imitates the angel becomes the beast and he had never realised it as much until his love for Rosario. It was in the mystery of Man and Woman that lay the whole schooling of mankind, and in the word Love: a love freed from personal ego—there lay the key to all

319

understanding . He wanted a love that was pure and simple, like the lilies in the parable, which grew and toiled not, but simply were. He wanted Rosario to be a lily. She must have been one at the start, he was certain of that. But then, she became a lily tampered with, made to seduce, and her fragrance had evaporated with the subterfuge. His heart shrank. But still, he could not live without her. That was love. And if it wasn't, he did not want to know. But in an unsolicited flash the answer burst upon him. That-was-not-love-that-was-possession, and he knew he must free himself from this bondage which was not soul-to-soul-love. He whispered Paloma's name. Paloma was Rosario's sacrifice. He could see it now, captured in Rosario's seductive net and thrown into a cage. Used and abused, and he was an accomplice — her adolescence robbed to serve the secrecy of their relationship. Carlota too, another morsel, eaten up by Rosario before she had a chance to be. And Alexi, a mere boy, made old before his time. He felt sick, and tried to swallow his ache.

On his return from the bled Clement wrote,

Dear R,

I am back. Come and meet me in the Oasis district, off the Rue de Sompy. Bring Paloma and your bathing costumes. We are off to the sea. C.

He could not meet her in the shadows. Not any more. Not after the limitless space out there in the Atlas. The light seemed blurred indoors, and he had made up his mind always to meet her out in the open. Except for feast days at The Orchard, when the whole family was present and celebrating. The note mystified Rosario. Something had to be brewing, otherwise why could he not come to see her? Whatever, she was certainly not wearing a bathing costume. She had always pulled the persiennes to conceal her blemishes and flawed proportions, even though he thought her sublime.

He jumped into Rosario's car, turned around to squeeze

Paloma's hand and thanked her for coming. She returned his smile, happy that he was back. They drove along the Avenue Mermoz in silence until Rosario pulled up in a wooded lay-by where he took off his cassock. "To the Tamaris Plage!" he shouted, once he had changed into his muftis. Paloma knew the beach from her camping weekends with Joaquín, Binot and friends, and enthused that it was the best. Rosario wondered how Clement knew this place, only frequented by old settlers. "We bring the scouts here" he said, "it's a safe sea."

He had never learnt to swim. Paloma teased him and pulled him by the hand further into the sea and when she couldn't see his chest she lifted his chin up with one finger and told him to let go. He wanted to, but he coughed and spluttered and said he was still learning to swim in the waters of life. Paloma swam alone. It was not often that she had the chance. She, her brothers, cousins and friends always swam together in great shoals. She drifted on her back, beneath the sun, insulated from reality and dreaming floating dreams without any beginning or end. Rosario remained dressed, excusing herself and saying she had a cold. Clement took the towel she offered him and knelt in the sand to face her. "Rosario..." he whispered "I have missed you so.." Her eyes explored his to divine all that she had missed in his absence, and also the future. "I've been thinking that things must change Rosario"

"My love..." she said softly caressing his untanned shoulders, "I know what you are about to say..."

"Only some of it" he said, with a finger on her lips. "You were not in the bled. Things can happen under those luminous skies. Things that can alter your perception, for good..."

"Is it goodbye Rosario then?" she said spikily and drawing back.

"That can never be. My pledge is that I am forever committed to you and your family—my family, Rosario" he said, bringing his wet body closer to hers. "And I will care for you" he whispered, "until I die" .

"Are you..?" she hesitated. "Are you leaving the Church for me?"

He lowered his gaze to the sand, searching and waiting for the right words to manifest. Words Rosario would accept and understand. But she was so far from his own present state of consciousness that he doubted he would reach her without a struggle. "I will not leave you, nor the Church Rosario" he said at last.

"Nothing's changed, then!" she jeered. "Not-a-thing!"

"Oh yes," he whispered "much has changed Rosario. Much."

"I see now " she glowered, "meeting outside is to avoid temptation. You're just like the rest of them. Wanting your cake and..."

"Yes! Yes! Yes! I admit it! I want my cake!" He paused and took her by the shoulders, "but I won't eat it. I know that now."

"You never took large portions of it anyway!" she said with contempt.

"But I took.. and took.. and always wanted more.. you know that Rosario.."

"So what's next?"

"I want to love you differently. I want to learn to see you from another angle. I want to get closer to you, but further from your body. I want a love that bears all things... believes all things... hopes all things, endures all things. A love that never ends. I want.."

"It's not real. It's repression. Sick!"

"It's not Rosario. What I am saying is voluntary suppression. I, consciously have chosen something out of another, and that, Rosario is not repression or morbid masochism as you imply. That is spiritual maturity."

"It's inhuman."

"No! Rosario, no. I am talking about human love, initiated by the flesh and transfigured. Rosario, be my Sophia!"

"I want to be your Eve, Clement!"

"You are my Eve! Now let Sophia have a go! Eros first and now Agape!"

"Spoken like a medieval monk!" she exploded. "What

322

happened to you under those 'luminous skies' and the sonorous universe of your precious bled, Clem? What is so wrong with desire?"

"If it's not transmuted, it is lust."

"Yes, lust! And so what? Lust, for God's sake! He invented it too!"

"No he didn't. Why do you suppose the Bible says 'Thou shall not lust? I'll tell you why, because if you do, you put another into the role of a thing—a thing of pleasure. An object. And when that happens you leave love behind—cut yourself off from God and you create a separation between you and Him." He stopped. "And who can afford to do that?"

"But that's how it is. That's how it's always been!"

"It is the starting point, yes. That, which attracts two beings, but then... then we must transcend it! At least, I must."

"Transcend! Ha!" she laughed. "And you think you can? Not if you see me Clem! Not if I'm there..." She murmured this while caressing his groin. He let her stay until the fullness of his desire swelling in her hand sent him running to the sea.

"I can, Rosario!" he said, back by her side. "And I want you to help me."

"Why should I? I want you! All of you! For myself!"

"And so you shall. When we have learned to marry our souls together."

"You won't leave the Church then?" she asked down-hearted.

"I must serve it. It has been ordained."

"What if we became lovers then. Real lovers?"

"No, Rosario, no! Because it would turn into a tragedy."

"Like Abélard and Héloïse?" she asked aroused.

"Theirs was a doomed love and I won't let that happen to us. We shall rise above it. We will transform it before it destroys us." He held her hands and kissed them. "Beloved," he said profoundly, "for that is what you are, let me take you to the heights of passion until our two souls have united with God."

Rosario dare not object when Father Clement agreed to

Paloma's chaperoning—only if she consented to it, always meeting outdoors, and never more than every first Thursday of every month. But the dampness of November put an end to their meetings on the beach and if Rosario longed to see Father Clement, she had to be content with the distance that separated them from the pulpit, as it was in the beginning, looking from afar and measuring the significance of each reciprocal gaze.

Rosario grew frustrated and Pepa and the children tired of her melancholia. The boys had worked out long ago that Father Clement was the lynch pin in their mother's life and they begged Pepa to call him back for peace's sake. He relented and came for Sunday lunch most weeks, declining to stay for the pouce-café which implied lounging alone in the shadows with Rosario afterwards.

"Enjoy things as they are!" Pepa told her when her daughter bemoaned his early departures. Rosario said it just wasn't enough. Pepa reminded her of Ludwig, Samuel, Stefan, other numerous flirtations, and her fury for Dionisio, paling into non-existence as soon as Father Clement appeared in her life. Clement, she replied (she now called him Clement brazenly to Pepa's face and sometimes just Clem), was the love she had waited for all her life and she would have him yet. He would die of guilt and sorrow Pepa warned her, if he was made to break his vows. "See that he never does" she cautioned. "That is your true gift to him."

Life made little sense to Rosario or so she convinced herself. Colette had once taught her not to accept the world's scale of values. One, she often said, should be free to live as if actions were inconsequential, and what Clement asked of her was antithetical to Colette's attractive libertarianism. Rosario knew about discipline, control and sacrifice. It was inculcated in her as part of her Catholic conditioning, but accepting it at that point in time made her feel cheated, for when the miracle of true love dawned on her, it was snatched by a mischievous thief called Irony.

*

Several letters from José Luis arrived before the end of the year, all urging his mother and sister to leave Morocco. Trouble was fermenting there and should the situation deteriorate, the fourth floor of his house at Calle del Oro was available until Rosario found a suitable position to earn her living. Pepa was persuaded that the timing was right to return to their homeland, but with her attachment, Rosario wasn't, and she made sure that Father Clement did not find out about José Luis' offer.

In seventeen years at The Orchard, it was the first Christmas without any of the Butlers. Instead, Clement was invited to dinner after the midnight mass. He disrobed as soon as he walked through the door, and like a child, he piled his gifts, one by one under the tree and sang loud Noëls (not always reverently) with the children by the candle-lit crib. The milk and chard soup arrived at the table in a heavy silver soupière, and after the briefest of blessings, the champagne glasses chimed around the table.

Clement returned the next day with a crate of Heidsick a parishioner had left him at the sacristy door. The first cork popped to hit the ceiling as he came into the lounge and the children went on all fours to lick the golden juice fizzing onto the mosaic floor. Pepa slapped their heads and told them not to behave like animals.

Clement laughed saying he wished he could join in and had his head slapped too. She shooed the children into the kitchen. He and Rosario had not been alone, indoors, since his retreat in the Bled and Rosario trembled when she reached up to his lips. "We are so close already" he whispered, resisting her advance.

"I want fun Clem!" she demanded and he popped open another bottle making her drink straight from the neck. Their laughter brought the children back into the lounge. "You're not at all like a priest!" challenged Carlota.

"I am and I'm not!" he giggled, drying Rosario's wet face with a napkin.

"You'll stay for tea, won't you?" Rosario asked breathless.

"Isn't she just like a little girl" he mused, cradling her.

"She's only pretending" snapped Carlota. "She's good at that."

"You'll behave, at least until after tea" Rosario lashed out (a response that seemed disproportionate) knowing that Clement would stay only if the entire family was present.

"I'm meeting Norbert" defied Carlota, pulling a sick face behind her mother's back, and mouthing Lady Macbeth, to make Paloma laugh, but Paloma frowned to warn her to stop.

Clement stayed for tea and watched the children unwrap the gifts he had placed under the tree the night before. Miko and Alexi practised jumping in their new basket-ball boots that replaced their smelly and disintegrating old ones. There was a diary with small red hearts raining on both covers for Carlota to help her keep tabs with her paramours and Paloma rushed out into the street to show off her hoola-hooping skills to passers-by. A rosary blessed by Pope Pius X11 made Pepa weep, but Rosario kept her gift on her lap to open later, until the children shouted "O-pen! O-pen! O-pen!" and she opened it very fast in the end to stop their frenzy. A necklace of polished shiny pink stones lay curled up in a spiral inside a leather box and when Rosario lifted it out she played with it over and around her hand and wrist, then tested the quality of its smoothness on her lips.

"Is it the only one in the world?" she asked.

"There are no two the same" Clement replied confidently, because they are from my homeland where semi-precious stones have magical powers. These" he said solemnly, putting the necklace around Rosario's throat "are rose quartz and release their note of universal love to those ready to receive it."

He knew he did not sound much like a priest but he came from Brittany, the most magical part of France, and decided he was entitled to sound at least a little whimsical. "Not personal then?" she asked.

"The universal is also personal Rosario" he replied.

"Sop-py! Sop-py!" shouted Alexi. "Sop-py!" repeated Miko, unaware of what it meant.

"It's Christmas! Let's play charades!" suggested Carlota,

sickened by Rosario's and Clement's display of mutual adoration. "Me first!" implored Miko stamping in his new boots. "I'll be a painter!"

"Silly" chided Carlota, "you're not supposed to tell! They," she said pointing at everyone else, "are supposed to guess what you are."

Miko didn't understand and hid himself under the table.

"I'll start," Carlota said, bending down to cajole him. "It's not your fault, you're only small." She left the room with a look that Rosario recognised as trouble and breezed in again within minutes to pace up and down the lounge floor, swaying her amphora-like hips.

"You're a prisoner!" shouted Alexi.

"Not with that walk!" said Paloma. "She's a model!"

But Carlota continued walking up and down, swaying her hips, then she stopped, facing Clement and licking her lips. He smiled without flinching and the boys laughed without knowing why. Rosario shouted to stop it at once.

"It's a game" said Clement. "Just a game" he added, feigning a calmness he was losing. The swaying went on but now Carlota lifted her skirt right up to her waist, and still facing Clement, she began a slow to-and-froing movement of her pelvis and with each, Clement's breathing deepened to a groan.

"Witch!" shouted Rosario "Stop her Clem!"

But Clement stood up, open-mouthed, dazed and as if in a fog. Carlota clasped his hands and they wrestled. The boys shouted "Come on Clement, she's only a girl!" and when he overpowered her, she fell to the ground taking him with her, the full weight of his body now over the whole length of hers. He lay there still clasping her hands and looking at her face as if he did not see her. His eyes flashed, he opened his mouth and roared like a lion in a cage. "How come you didn't guess Clement?" she teased, rolling him aside, "I was a fille de joie. Have you never seen one Clement?"

"Out!" cried Pepa. "Go to your room and stay there!"

Still crouched on the floor, Clement clung to Pepa like a

life-buoy. "Oh my god..." he sobbed. "Dear, dear God!" he cried.

It was an aberration she assured him, kneeling beside him, nothing more. She looked towards Rosario and saw her slumped in the armchair. "You know Carlota ..." Pepa hazarded to say, "how she enjoys to shock and provoke...She didn't mean......"

"It's us two I'm worried about" said Rosario in a daze, "not that bitch!"

"Pot of strong coffee coming up" said Pepa, making her way to the kitchen. "You two need to be alone. And," she turned back to tell Clement, "I don't want you to leave before you've talked to my Rosario. She needs to understand what's happened".

"How can she, Yaya, if I don't" he lamented.

"Just be silent" she said gently "and pray, then talk, talk and talk! And if you can, keep away from guilt and reproach".

In a silence that was more paralytic than reflective, Clement flopped in Elias' armchair. He felt a stranger to himself. Someone ex tempore he vaguely knew and had never met. An invisible hand had pushed him close to that stranger, and when he looked closer, he saw that the stranger was him, asleep and dreaming in the pit of his being, abandoned in the cold land of shadows. Sadness overwhelmed him, and he felt as if he had lost and found a friend all at once. He wept softly and murmured "I love you" to the stranger. A lightness of being floated within him and he shouted "Deo Gracias!" His voice was triumphant. "That's it! That's what it's all about Rosario! Do-you-see?" he pleaded, when he saw that she looked vacant. "Carlota is a shadow raiser, Rosario! THAT IS WHAT SHE DOES!"

"Must we talk about her?" asked Rosario hoarsely, refusing to wake up into a nightmare that had already started.

"Yes, Rosario! Please listen! She has helped me uncover that part of me I have separated out from myself and denied access to for my entire life! It is not the best part of me, but it is a part of me and I know that I must love it, and then let go of it. She,

Rosario, has a kind of darkness that sheds light. She, without her knowing it, is an agent for good!"

"Is that what she is?" sneered Rosario. "Carlota, a saviour? Whatever next Clem?"

"And she must be guided to find her own light."

"Let's forget about her for a moment!" Rosario shouted, suddenly revived. "You've discovered your own shadow whatever that is, and now you love it. Good for you. So what?"

"If you had understood what had happened this afternoon you would not be angry. You would rejoice with me, and for me!"

"You're right Clement. I haven't a clue about what you've experienced, but tell me one thing, is there room for both, she and me after all this?" He reached for her hands. "This.. Revelation," she continued, "has it changed anything between us?"

"It has strengthened me and my resolve Rosario..." he said softly.

"To continue as you had planned?"

"It must be the right way. The right way for me"

"That's it then. Les jeux sont faits, rien ne va plus!" she cried. Her hand spinning an invisible roulette wheel. "You've dealt with this thing whatever that was, after one moment of foolishness and everything is alright." "Think of Absolution Rosario. How speedy is that! It takes seconds to dish it out and seconds to receive it, but does it bring the recipient any revelation or wisdom?"

"Your revelation was better than Absolution? Is that what you're saying?"

"Yes! I'm saying precisely that! Absolution is only a pale imitation of it. Absolution is there merely to remind us all of the need to cleanse oneself and to be forgiven. It is a powerful metaphor for forgiveness. But it is still a metaphor. What has happened is the real thing! Instantaneous! No intermediaries! No escape! The clear arrow of revelation, straight to the heart!"

"You'll be ex-communicated next, Clement!"

"Thankfully, the Vatican chooses to ignore the likes of me" he laughed.

"And at the end of all this, what?" asked Rosario.

He thought for a moment. "Neither light nor shade shall be" he said, "but that which is the Lord God, will be in all."

"Grace, you mean?"

"More than that" he said. But he did not elaborate.

"And what about me? You have forgotten me in all this, haven't you?"

"Rosario, forgive me for having hurt you, but what I want you to believe is that what happened had nothing to do with Carlota. Someone else could have taken me to the same place. It happened to be your daughter. So let us not personalise this event Rosario. There was nothing evil about it, on the contrary, it was an opportunity for good."

Something about his choice of words—not evil, but an opportunity for good—brought an echo of hindsight from Ludwig's own words all those years back sitting on the bench, by the fountain of Night and Destiny in the garden in Meknès, and in a flicker of lucidity she saw that the role of Mephistopheles, as Ludwig had explained it to her then, was bringing meaning in the very situation in which she now found herself. "It will take time..." she murmured.

"I understand that..." he said, placing his hand on her shoulder.

"You wish we could forget the whole thing, don't you Clem?"

"That's the very last thing I want us to do, Rosario. But we must remember this event for what it truly was. And then, we must move on, and climb up that spiral staircase, singly and together."

TWENTY-FIVE

Myrrh, the Little Prince and the Amethyst

It had been ages since Paloma was last at Le Bungalo and when she visited she was fêted as if she was a long-lost relative. Small tartes au citron, especially baked by Mme Michaud, Ondine's grandmother, sat gleaming on a red and green flowery enamel plate which they had rescued from their native Poland, and by its side to welcome her back, a wine bucket with crushed ice, in which stood a bottle of chilled Mousseux.

When Ondine's father came home from work looking tired and still wearing his overalls, Paloma sensed it was time for her to go, but she was captivated by the curious look on his face and she stayed. With the latest issue of Paris-Match held at arms length he read the slogan sprawled in red across the centre page. 'The Sultan must change, or we must change the Sultan'. He put the magazine down on the sideboard to look at the reaction this had on his family, but all were silent and expectant. There was more trouble to come he predicted, waving his flimsy half-moon spectacles, and it was religion, as always, he said, that was behind it. Monsieur Hess could not agree with the slogan he had read. He had no quarrel with the Sultan; in fact he admired him. He thought Muhammed V a good ruler, an innovative and progressive politician who had taken a stance against the anti-semitic Vichy Government and refused entry to any ex-Nazi into his 'land of the Setting Sun' after the war was over. Whatever happened, Monsieur Hess told his family, they would not budge when Independence came. Not after twenty peaceful years of living in that house.

And as he spoke, a silent agitation spread over every face in the room, the sort captured on the rugged features of pioneers seen in films of the American mid-west, over their fear of losing what they had worked so hard to call their own.

News of more unrest blackened the newspapers over the days that followed. In France, Le Figaro boasted pro-Sultan, anti-colonialist intellectuals, namely Mauriac, amongst critics of the French position in Morocco. Because the Sultan's popularity had so risen in his homeland and abroad, the French believed that they had no alternative but to exile him to Madagascar. The consequence of this deportation was far from what the Government had intended. Morocco re-erupted into increased indigenous violence and in a panic, Rosario phoned Joaquín. He told her to keep calm, that the whole thing was nothing more than a pantomime since the majority of Arabs in the street knew little of what was going on, and that made it impossible for a true insurrection, and because they had no strategy and no plan. He added that in any case, the intractable disagreements that prevailed between the Berber and the Arab populations, mostly over landownership, made it necessary for a prolonged French presence, simply to keep the peace.

*

Epiphany day. Of late, Clement called at The Orchard without warning, but seldom at mid-morning and never in the middle of a major feast day. Sensing a crisis, Pepa left him alone with Rosario while she had it in mind to retire to her room to pray her litany of All Saints. But Clement, looking drained and sombre, asked her to stay. He sat down, a letter resting on his lap. "Bad news?" she asked, scrutinising his face.

"I've been transferred, yaya. They're sending me away!" He buried his face in his hands and whimpered, like a very small child. Rosario stood up, saying nothing, and paced up and down the kitchen, her high heels hammering the mosaic floor with an even rhythm. "Epiphany eh! Well thank you, you happy trio up there!" she mocked.

"The Myrrh they brought for the child Jesus was for his suffering and our sorrow" said Pepa.

"And thank you too, mother! Trust you to brighten things up with le mot juste!"

"Your mother is right" Clement said, buoyed up by Pepa's relevant intervention. "Gifts come in all shapes and meanings. This is ours, and we must see the hidden treasure beneath its prickly wrapping."

"And where is your new parish to be, my son?"

"It's not a parish. I've been given charge of a Salesians boys' school, in northern France!"

"Virgen Santisima..!" she whispered.

"They know..."

"How did they..?" cried Pepa, sliding her chair closer to his.

"We've been seen outside a lot this summer, and I've been recognised by several parishioners, wearing my muftis, frolicking on the beach, sometimes with two women at once, it was reported!" And he laughed feebly.

"Serves you right. Safer indoors!" growled Rosario.

Ignoring the remark and removing his cassock he asked where was the bubbly and said it was time to celebrate a new start. Rosario stopped pacing.

"Bubbly? A new start? Who for?" she yelled.

"All of us!"

"All of us?" she repeated meeting his eyes.

"I've promised to look after you Rosario, and your family. And I will."

"Priests can't afford to make such promises!" she snapped.

"I know" he murmured, "I know."

"So then?"

He made Rosario sit down and poured the very last of the Heidsick left over from the Christmas crate.

"Listen to me." His conspiratorial whisper was encouraging and she came closer still. "The political situation is worsening here. Hundreds of Europeans are leaving this place every day. Many think a Coup d'État for Independence is imminent. It's time to leave Morocco. Now!"

"Not for France!" dismayed Pepa.

"Spain Yaya. Spain first. Rosario and the children can join me later, when I've found a job for Rosario, a school for the boys, and the girls can train as teachers or something, we'll see. And you Yaya, are welcome too," he said, looking into her dewy eyes, but I know your heart belongs to Catalunya."

He touched her shoulder, "Yaya," he called softly, "are you alright?"

"The circle is about to close, my son" she said trembling, "and that is something to celebrate." Her voice was flat, but she raised her empty glass as she spoke and smiled a sad smile. "When do you begin your new assignment?"

"My parishioners need time to adjust. The new priest arrives in a fortnight. Easter I guess."

They sipped from their glasses in silence, each lost in the jumbled images of their respective past spent in this foreign land, and in the formulation of their hopes for the future. Change always excited Rosario, even if this time, separation with Clement had to come first. "We'll keep it quiet from the children" she said, cutting into their separate rêveries. "They'd get too excited. And you know Carlota, she'd tell..."

"And Joaquín?" asked Pepa.

"What if he tries to stop us, him and his patriarchal rights!" agitated Rosario.

"He can't!" cried Clement. "He's your brother-in-law. Not your husband or Svengali for God's sake! Wait a bit" he advised. "Get your visas, papers and whatever else is required. Present him with a fait accompli."

"Svengali..." pronounced Rosario in a mesmeric tone. "Will you be my Svengali, Very Reverend Father Clement?"

"Tease! Is that all you can think of Rosario!" reprimanded Pepa. "Did you hear what the Padre said, get our visas organised first."

The Spanish Consul thought it a wise decision to leave as he predicted a mass exodus before the end of the year and promised to have everything sorted and ready for a mid-June exit. It was as Rosario told Pepa, that the reality of their leaving hit her. She, Rosario, thirty eight years old, widow and mother of four was about to drive them and her elderly mother through a troubled land, and then, the length of Spain at the height of summer without a male escort or counsel. Taking on a man's role made her adrenalin flow. Her spirit, she often thought, had been trapped in a woman's body, and if she had believed in re-incarnation she would have said that she had come into the wrong body, but she recalled Olympia once saying that no incarnation was wasted, each having a pre-determined soul plan, and when a tough life came along, the purpose was to overcome the challenge and not blame it on some indeterminate error outside of oneself.

"What will we do with the furniture?" asked Pepa.

"Furniture?" asked Rosario still caught in her ruminations.

"The furniture! This house's furniture!" Pepa cried tempering her impatience.

"Try to sell it, I guess. We need every franc we can get!"

"The lot?"

"Books, china, glass, silver, linen and rugs. The Kosighin sculpture Samuel gave me before he left, the Bruneau still-life, the piano, and the Cruz-Herrara portrait of course, we'll take."

"It will still mean a lot of packing, Rosario. How on earth can we conceal this sudden flurry of activity from the children?"

"We'll pack while they're in school and keep the boxes in the basement."

"And what about a farewell for the family?"

"We'll only tell Marina" Rosario said categorically.

"And Joaquín?"

"I hope I never see the old goat again! But I must, I suppose, about The Orchard, Le Plateau, our share of the house in Mazagan and see if he'll sell the furniture for me. I hate asking him for any favours" she grumbled. "He'll make me grovel, as always."

Pepa told her she must swallow her pride. Rosario pulled a face. "I hope it will be the last time."

"The children won't forgive you if they don't say goodbye

to Binot" said Pepa. "We mustn't lump him in with his father!"

"I never liked the wretch myself!" Rosario admitted.

"You intimidate him with your grand airs Rosario. It's a miracle that the lad is as normal as he is. He's a good egg and the children adore him. Take my word for it he's the only one of the tribe that you can trust!"

"Your word against mine" Rosario replied "but we'll have him around anyway, nearer the time."

A note from Marina arrived announcing her intention to leave Morocco soon, and Rosario hastened to see her. Clement called, not to see Rosario, but Paloma about her progress in school. He knew she lagged behind and had been stuck in the same class without significant progress for two consecutive years. Paloma told him her mother did not care, and had made up her mind that she would at best, end up as a nanny. Paloma confessed, that despite her efforts to feel otherwise, she still hated her mother. It was not hate she felt, Clement said, but resentment, and rebellion, both legitimate emotions for her to feel, in view of her age, the past and her more recent experiences.

She had always hated her she insisted, even though she wanted to forget that she had been abandoned at birth and sent to boarding school at three. He knew nothing about it, and she told him everything as if it was someone else's story. She had gone over it so often in her own mind that it had assumed a kind of distance. She said she must have picked the wrong mother when her soul wasn't looking. He hugged her and reassured her that there was no such thing as the wrong person. And that if anything, it is gratitude one should feel for such challenging people in our lives who in truth were our teachers, like Carlota had been for him. He smiled. And as for love for your mother, it will come one day, out of compassion. She rested her head on his arm for a long while. He was the most tender-hearted person she knew and she loved him. What she felt certain about was that with Pepa, he had given her love, a love without conditions, a sense of purpose and had taught her to look at life with sacred eyes. "Paloma!" he called, making cloud shapes above her head. "Come down from up there!"

336

She smiled and blew him a kiss.

"Sing me that song you sang on the beach last Summer... You know, the Constantine one!"

"That one? You like that one?" she laughed. Flicking her pony tail in the air and releasing it deftly from the constraints of the elastic band that held it up, she sat cross-legged on the cool floor, her elbow on her knee and holding her hand under her chin to show how relaxed she was, and after clearing her throat, she sang:

> *Je ne me fais pas de bi-le*
> *Et n'occupe aucun empl-oie,*
> *Je mène une vie tranqui-lle*
> *Et ne fais rien de mes dix d- oights...oi.*

"Bis! Bis! he clapped." She sang it again, louder.

> *I don't worry about a thing*
> *I have no job.*
> *I lead a peaceful life*
> *And just twirl my thumbs all day.*

"Ça, c'est le Haut Ideal eh, Paloma?" he said heartily. "You make me feel so uncomplicated and young Paloma" he added fervently. "Something I have never allowed myself to be. Thank you." He kissed her forehead and left unescorted.

*

It was the last time Rosario would see Marina, as she would be boarding the Koutoubia within a week to live in Paris with her nephew. It all happened very suddenly after her house had been looted and vandalised for a second time, whilst she stayed at her sister's for safety. It was only a matter of time, the gendarmes warned her, before the same thugs returned and set the house on fire. For Marina, the thought of her Geraldo's stables in flames was like him dying all over again. The house would be sold, or more

337

likely, appropriated, without her receiving a single sou for it.

Clement was leaving and the family broke their Lent fast two days before Easter to celebrate the meal which would be their last supper together at The Orchard. He said lesser rules were made to be broken, and that few knew that flexibility was a spiritual virtue, but nevertheless, he gave himself a flippant absolution, to be on the safe side.

Pepa saw a basket, more like a treasure trove, on the floor outside the kitchen which she guessed Clement had left for her to find. He had noticed the frugality of their meals since Elias' death whenever he had called unannounced.

In the basket was a plump capon, a bag of Spanish rice and a few strands of saffron in a small glass jar from La Casa Española in the Marché Central, a water melon, and a gâteau au chocolat reeking of cointreau from the Patisserie Blanchard.

Rosario made everyone dress up and Pepa was cajoled into wearing her polka-dot dress under her several layers of pinafores. Clement discarded his cassock in a deliberate slow motion to reveal an orange and green stripy shirt he was wearing with velvet pantaloons—the baggy sort, gathered in at the ankles. They clapped and giggled (none more than himself) and took photographs of each other. Each of the children presented him with a wrapped gift. The boys had carved him a cross for above his bed from a piece of driftwood for which they had spent weeks combing the shore. He pondered at the significance of Carlota's painting depicting his parish church, with a winged black cow on the belfry, larger than the church itself, but he thanked her all the same though he soon understood that Rosario was the cow. Paloma had written a poem that made him laugh, of a priest who could not swim but could not drown either.

He kissed them all and gave them each their present before bedtime. He whispered something in Carlota's ear which made her sullen face beam, and when he lifted Miko up, he was called 'Papa Clement' for the first time. Alexi shook his hand and Paloma said nothing, burying herself in his arms as if she wanted to nest there.

"I want you to stay Yaya!" he called to Pepa who was also off to bed.

She sat down again. It was a while after the children had gone before he regained his composure and with a voice that was barely audible he said that they were his children, borne of his heart, and that he loved them.

"And they love you back, Padre" Pepa uttered. He touched her dry, wrinkled hand.

"I want to know as soon as you get to Barcelona, Yaya" he said, "and I'm coming to see you, no matter what." He looked at her intensely. "It will happen. I know it will" he said trembling. He caught Pepa's far-away gaze. She was the victim in all this. Always a giver, fate decreed that her time to administer was up.

"Are you alright Yaya?" he whispered, knowing that she was not.

"Circles are very neat but they can also be painful" she struggled to say.

"Because they close..." he added, feeling her agony reaching him.

"It's all for the best!" exclaimed Rosario.

"Yes it is" Pepa replied standing up. "Con Dios my son!" she cried, hugging Clement as tight as her breathing would allow. "See you in Barcelona!"

"Families!" cried Clement when Pepa had gone, intentionally leaving the door wide open, as she knew Clement would have wished it.

"What about them?" asked Rosario.

"They are the most precious organisms in the world!"

"And the couple?" she asked pressing her provocative body against his. "Is it a precious organism too?"

"It's where it all begins."

"Show me!......"

"You know it already.."

"Let's make the most of this moment" she pleaded, feeling the quivering flesh of his chest beneath his ridiculous striped shirt.

"It's au revoir time" he said almost hastily and rolling his pantaloons up to his knees to hold them there with elastic bands. Then there was that silence as he slipped his cassock over his head. He wanted to be unflinching but his arms encircled Rosario crushing her enticing body against his. "You see? You see how excruciating this is for me?" he cried between his clenched teeth. She stayed trapped in the fury of his embrace wishing for a lifetime of it, until he released her.

"Ma grande passion..." she breathed. "Mon Grand Amour, toi, Clement."

Alexi could not be found the next morning. Miko told Pepa he left before breakfast with the book Papa Clement gave him, tucked under his arm. He saw him reading it all night with a torch under the sheets because he said he had to finish it.

But Miko said his book was best. He sat on his grandmother's lap and opened it to reveal a radiant image of the Archangel Michael, armoured and bearing a lance and shield ready to slay the dragon beneath his feet. Pepa said that Angels were beings created by God to bring light, and to remember that Mickael was his very own Angel Protector for the whole of his life.

When he surfaced, still clutching his book 'On Duties Three,' Alexi told everyone in the kitchen that although he only understood some of what he had read, he wanted to be a man of law, like Cicero.

Carlota was in love with Clement she confided to Pepa, and she knew that he loved her back, as he had given her a book called Love in Art Throughout The Ages, which was evidence of that. The Padre, Pepa told her, was a loving man who could not help but love and be loved. But Carlota said that he had chosen to love her and not Paloma, whom he knew better, nor Rosario who tried so shamefully to get him. "Yes" Paloma replied, when Rosario asked if the book she was reading was Father Clement's gift. "He knew I wanted it. Everyone talks about it in school, and Ondine can't stop reciting whole chunks of it aloud."

"I didn't know St.Exupery wrote for children" she said almost critically, gazing at the picture on the cover of the book. "He doesn't, Maman. The Little Prince is for grown-ups who will always stay innocent or grown-ups who have forgotten how to be children" Paloma replied. "And it's about love, the sorrow of loss and flight."

*

It was lunch time and all the family were together. Rosario had an announcement.

"I bet you it has something to do with Father Clement!" whispered Carlota in Paloma's ear.

"What I am about to say is a secret. A family secret. At least for a few weeks."

"You're pregnant!" joked Carlota.

"We," declared Rosario ignoring Carlota's outburst and bowing a little, like an advocate at the bar, "are leaving Morocco." She paused, expecting a reaction like 'Hooray!' or 'Oh no!' or 'when?' But when nothing happened, she asked loudly if they had heard what she said.

"Why does it have to be a secret?" Carlota complained. "I need to tell Norbert."

"You can tell him, and you Paloma, can tell Ondine, but you must make them promise to keep it quiet."

"Are you telling anyone?" Alexi asked his mother. "Father Clement knows and I have to tell Joaquín for obvious reasons. And you boys, don't mention it to anyone, least of all the guard or any of the old servants you might meet. Except of course, Alcaya." And she explained that when the terrorists found out which Europeans were about to leave, they became targets for theft, arson, rape and even murder.

"When will it be?" asked Paloma.

"As soon as the visas arrive. Your grandmother and I have started the packing and I will ask each of you to take charge of your own belongings and to select one—and I mean ONE— special toy or whatever, to take with you. And Paloma, you will be responsible for Miko's things and for checking on Alexi's."

Paloma knew that she would take her Red Cross first aid kit, her collection of shells and pebbles from the Lido beach

341

and dried leaves from Ourika and a secret matchbox filled with uplifting thoughts and proverbs she had copied on wafer-thin rolled up sheets of cigarette paper during her convalescence.

*

The first of Clement's letters arrived (too brief for Rosario) to say that he was safe. He was teaching philosophy to eighteen-year-olds (who knew all about anomy and existentialism, or thought they did) and he would soon transfer to the Alsace region to take up the directorship of a Salesian school.

Rosario announced their impending departure to her brother and accepted his offer of the top floor of his home.

*

"May all the storks in the Maghreb crap on your head as they fly past and horses shit before your path, and may you be whisked away by aliens and never come back" said Alexi in a tedious recital.

"What's this?" asked Pepa. "A futuristic Arab curse?"

"Carlota told it to me. I think she's horrid."

"And what did you do to warrant such a foul malediction?"

"She stole my egg!" he cried. "My fried egg, from—my—plate! And she swallowed it whole in one go. Down her gullet, just like a pelican!"

"Where was I then?"

"You'd gone out in the garden to feed Lobo."

"I see..." she said picturing the scene and trying not to smile. "And then?"

"I was so furious! It was so unfair! I was saving my egg for last. After the bit of chorizo. And..."

"You hit her, right?"

"I threw my knife at her!"

"Alexi, you must learn control! Did you hurt her?"

"I hope so. She held her arm and cried that it was bleeding and would need amputating."

"How on earth did she come out with a curse like that?" asked Pepa, still thinking about it.

"Maman says she's evil. That's why."

"Your sister is not evil" Pepa said. "SHE IS NOT EVIL. She repeated. Remember that, always."

"But she's a pig!"

There were several other incidents between the children since the announcement of their going, signalling a tension which Pepa fought hard to diffuse before the long exodus to Barcelona.

"Beware of Greeks bearing gifts" hissed Rosario between her teeth.

Joaquín was on his way up—three steps at a time—carrying crates of oranges and bananas.

"Take it easy Rosario" whispered Pepa. "No need to make things worse."

"If it isn't my beautiful sister-in-law!" he exclaimed, followed by a series of chuckles.

"Flattery!....You know what they say about that Joaquín..." she groaned, embracing him minimally.

"That's what I like about you Rosario!"

"What, do you like about me?" she asked icily.

"Your fire! That's what Elias saw too!" The way he said that made her feel exposed, naked almost.

"I've asked you to come because of business" she said curtly.

"When did you call me for anything else Rosario?"

"Come inside" she ordered. "I want my mother to be there."

"That serious, is it?" he tittered. "You're not getting married again are you?"

"Joaquín!" she cried. "How could you!"

"I'm listening ..." he said, lifting his arms in surrender.

"We are leaving the country. Our time has come to return to Spain" she stated outright. He did not object or tell her she was out of her mind. He sat there eating a banana from the crate he had just brought. "Have one..." he offered. "From the Canaries you know. Elias used to trade there. The sole importer he was. At the time anyway."

"Well?"

"Your place is here Rosario" he said, still chewing. "No question."

"I'm not from here, I'm a Spaniard Joaquín!"

"Your children belong here. Remember they are Butlers. And who are the Butlers?" he asked, throwing the banana skin back into the crate. "I'll tell you who they are" he said, now peeling an orange, "they are an old family, here for over a hundred and fifty years,. They have made their mark here and they are respected. Everyone knows who the Butlers are. You owe it to Elias. You owe it to his progeny!"

"Elias promised to return to Spain years ago! He was ready to leave himself!"

"But you're still here aren't you? And where did Elias die? Eh?"

"Elias was paranoid. That's why I'm still bloody here! And anyway, all this is irrelevant. You're not my jailer!"

"Elias asked me, on his death bed, to take care of you" he said with a sugary drawl.

"Not in this way. Not in this way AT ALL! He wanted you to make sure my children and I would not want of anything for as long as we lived. And he knew you owed him Joaquín. From that time in Spain. You never paid him back and you know it!"

"You never give up, do you sister-in-law" he said shaking his head. "Let me explain. By law I owed nothing to Elias. Nothing was written down. There is no document to prove what you say. It's a figment. Nothing more. I've helped Elias already. I paid some of his debts..."

"With HIS property Joaquín! With HIS share of the house in Mazagan! You paid his debts with the only security he had. Where is this sense of honour you always talk about. He asked you to safeguard that for me and the children's future! And if one day...if one day Joaquín, I die in poverty, you will go to hell! I'll see to that!"

"See what I mean Yaya? Passion!" he laughed through his

tonsils and against the well of his throat like a nutmeg rubbed against a grater.

"Joaquín" said Pepa sternly, "Rosario asked you here today out of respect for Elias. She knows how important eldership is to this family. We could have left without telling you, but you are the first of the Butlers to know of our leaving. In return, we don't seek your approval nor your help if you don't wish to give it, but we would cherish your good wishes."

"You have them...All of you...You have my blessings. There..." he said with a magnanimous gesture.

"Thank you" replied Pepa politely. "That is all."

"I can help too..." he said with a singing Mexican accent he used on certain occasions, like a talisman.

"Rosario!" called Pepa, "Joaquín is offering his help."

"Our furniture needs selling" said Rosario, without looking at him, "and I need the proceeds sent to me as soon as possible. The trunks will need shipping to Barcelona, and I thought of selling Le Plateau."

"Dead land Rosario! You'll be lucky to ever sell it. Your children, maybe! Or grandchildren..." he said with a long sickly smirk.

"What of The Orchard?" she asked, ignoring his last remark.

"I can close it down" he said, "no problem."

"And then, can you advance me what mortgage Elias has paid?"

"What mortgage?"

"We've lived here for seventeen years it must have amounted to something!"

"I'm sorry to disappoint you, dear sister-in-law, but the house was never mortgaged. It was rented from the start."

"Rented? Elias rented our house? How? We..."

"Whoa there..! Brakes on Rosario! Elias never bought property, except Le Plateau. Never. You must know that!" He laughed his grating laugh again. "Elias was a spender, not an investor! If he had been, you wouldn't be in this wretched

345

mess. This," he said staring around the room "is-a-rented-house! And when you leave, it-will-be-put-up-for-rent-again! C'est la vie...Rosario. Not always en rose..."

He was a sadist and she could smell his rotting pleasure climbing up her nostrils. She had no money, and without it she could not leave. The piano. She would have to sell it for a pittance to finance their exit. And if he thought he had her trapped, he could think again.

"I will do my very best of course..." he said, his words like syrup in a vinagre glass, adding as an afterthought "you could always come back to work for me, if you badly need the money!"

"I'd rather walk the streets" she replied laconically.

"Same old Rosario!" he laughed. "I'll miss you, old girl!" and he said it as if he really meant it.

"The fruit is wonderful Joaquín. Thank you." said Pepa. "And send that boy of yours when he returns from Foix. The children must see him before they go."

"Will do..." he replied, waving goodbye with his back turned.

The piano was going. Throughout the night Rosario played her old favourites and Colette's entire repertoire, leaving Chopin's 'Farewell Waltz'—which she performed flawlessly for the first time—to the end. As in a trance

she played it again, and now the sounds burst into colours of pink and gold and into the luscious fragrance of Jasmine, the Jasmine that lived its scented life on Colette's balcony.

Drawn and taut as the man from the Playel showroom came to collect the piano in the morning, Rosario remembered,with a twinge in her gut the day it was bought. The money would cover the exit expenses to the last sou. She took the money and ran upstairs, slipped the elasticated bundle of notes under her pillow and sobbed herself to sleep.

Everyday, a painting or rug came off the wall ready to be packed and stored. Every room in the house sounded hollow and haunted. Alcaya's time at The Orchard was over. She said there would never be another Madame Rosario. The necklace of polished lapiz-lazuli with an amber stone in the centre, which Dionisio had given Rosario in Tangier was now Alcaya's. Rosario embraced her and said not to come back to The Orchard as she could not bear more than one emotional farewell.

*

Norbert's promise that he would write to her about marriage plans as soon as she reached Barcelona uplifted Carlota's spirits to an hysterical pitch. Clement had begged her to postpone the marriage on the day before he left but she had interpreted his plea as his need to have her for himself and this made her more determined to plan her wedding day, if only to tease him.

Should her wedding dress be three-quarters or full-length, frothy mousseline or broderie anglaise, she asked Paloma but before she could reply that a full decolleté and red satin was more her style, Pepa came to say Julien, her friend from the beach house weekends and confessional Saturdays, had come to see her. There was a coyness between them that stemmed from not knowing for certain the true essence of their relationship. Even though there had been a chemistry there, they had not interpreted its significance until this moment. They shook hands. His was moist and she released it from hers slowly, taking pleasure in its dampness penetrating her own skin.

She waited for him to speak.

"I...I mean we..." he stuttered. "My family and I, are leaving Morocco for good." He came closer as he spoke to create a focus of intimacy. "And I won't see you again" he added, without waiting for her response. "And I will miss you Paloma..." She had not noticed before how different her name sounded when uttered by a French voice, with the inflection on the last syllable and she found this incredibly arousing. Her head swam. He was going away, he was saying goodbye and he would miss her. This was the closest she had ever come to receiving a declaration of love . "We are going too, Julien" she murmured, and they drew closer to each other in small,

347

faltering steps, until their trembling finger-tips met and they breathed each others' breathing.

"Where?" he asked dry-mouthed.

"Spain first, then France" she gasped, amid the warmness of his longing. "And you?"

"Monté Carlo. Monaco, because of the sailing. Will you... Can I visit you when you've settled in France?" he asked, his lips now made damp and red with the rush of desire. She came closer still to better inhale the Savon de Marseilles scent of his neck, then she stiffened. The thought of Alegria's Celtic Knight prediction came caressing her brow like the wing of a returning swallow from the northern clime, and she said "maybe."

*

Ondine did not voice any emotion at Paloma's imminent departure when she visited her at Le Bungalo, for the last time. But her body language, the way she sat hunched, her head bowed, and furiously twirling a strand of her hair betrayed the fact that she was angry, bereft, and afraid to lose her.

Paloma had a secret wish. It was to share her poem 'The Lamp in the Desert' with Ondine.

But when Ondine returned it and said nothing after she had read it, she wished she had never bothered.

"Is it that awful?" Paloma asked with trepidation.

"It depends."

"On what?" Paloma asked defensively.

"On whether you call your piece 'poetry' or 'therapy'" she said bluntly.

"Meaning what, exactly?" Paloma challenged.

"I read the other day that Genet said to your compatriot Goytisolo, that in a poem or a story, if you know the point of arrival as well as the point of departure, then it's not an adventure you are writing, but a bus ride. Your 'Lamp in the Desert' is a bit like that, a predictable and personal journey. But poetry," she said slowly "must take you by surprise and it has to appeal to every soul in the world."

"My heart was in it, and my whole being, but I'm not Hugo, Valéry or Breton, if that's what you mean!" Paloma said, trying not to sound peeved.

"That's fine then. Except" she added as a considered afterthought, "that verse." Lost on the back cover of the booklet she reclaimed from Paloma, Ondine read a stanza, just one, in such a way, that Paloma did not recognise it as her own. "THAT is poetry" Ondine said. THAT is sublime. Will you give it to me?"

"And I have something else for you" Paloma said, still flushed by the compliment she felt had fallen straight from heaven. "It's a farewell present."

Ondine took a small but weighty package of crunchy brown paper from Paloma's hands. "This one's yours" Ondine said, after she had put Paloma's on her lap. And as they unwrapped them, they cried with one voice, "An amethyst!" and they laughed a lot and cried a little.

"When did you get yours? I mean, which day?"

"Last Friday afternoon, around three o clock at the Marché Central" said Paloma, drying her eyes.

"I knew it! I was buying yours at exactly the same time, at the Safi Fair! It means it works Paloma! It really works!" She then poured a glass of panaché for each and explained that ancient civilisations used gem stones not only for healing but for communication over long distances and even to enable the possessor to fly wingless anywhere they wished. It meant they wouldn't need telephones or letters as their thoughts, impregnated in the sensitive crystals could be transmitted over mountains and seas, and they would never lose touch. And Ondine's ache of parting was lessened by their telepathic link.

Paloma revealed that she was afraid that once she left the land of her childhood she could no longer dream and that she would miss her, as she too was a dreamer. As they started to walk away from each other in opposite directions for the last time, Ondine turned to shout "Remember St Ex and you will dream forever!"

TWENTY-SIX

The Exodus

Saying goodbye to Binot was the most heart-rendering of all the farewells. This was made all the harder, for neither Binot nor the girls knew how to express their feelings of desolation and separation, nor did they have any idea of how to come to terms with the brutal suddenness of the event. To resolve this impasse and to bear their loss more easily, Paloma said, see you soon.

Pepa packed her crucifix, a framed photograph of Camilo, her copy of Ávila's Camino de Perfección, her poems of St John of the Cross and those of Campoamor, that Camilo loved. They all fitted tightly inside a large tin where Marie biscuits were once kept, but she held on to the rosary that father Clement had given her, for Thanksgiving prayers before leaving Casablanca for good. Rosario preferred to travel map-less and when Joaquín turned up offering her a bundle of guides to facilitate her travels, she told him to keep them for when he had to leave, which triggered one of his cynical chuckles. Josh accompanied him. He believed that the splintering of a branch of the Butler tree was weakening its roots, and though critical, he said nothing. Pepa hugged him and whispered in his ear that love was the vital ingredient he must seek in life. His chartreuse green eyes filled instantly with a jelly-like substance which made them look larger and sadder, and he left, mouthing something about her being a good person. Joaquín promised to return the next morning to supervise their departure and Rosario made sure no one revealed their intention of sneaking out in the dead of night, and that she was seeing him for the last time.

Norbert arrived after dark as arranged, to check the car and help with the loading, making sure Alexi noted where each item was placed on the roof rack so that he could relocate them in exactly the same order every time they had to unload. He and Carlota had a lingering and cinematic last embrace and when Rosario drove straight out of the garage and away into the night without even a hoot for her forlorn Norbert, Carlota moped and called her mother an unfeeling monster. The sound of the engine on the deserted street increased their pervading sense of unreality. Half an hour on, Miko asked if they were nearly there and the others, disorientated by the strangeness of the event, felt like bit actors assigned to the wrong set and hadn't the skills to improvise.

For Rosario, the exalted feeling she experienced as she left The Orchard for the last time was as intense as it was private. She sighed, then took a breath that was long and deep and which released pent up emotions she did not know she harboured. For all the vastness and emptiness of 'The Land of the Setting Sun' and its long history, she recalled Mrs Fogg saying it was a place of tribal divisions and of a society that was cloistered and suspicious. Those remarks had made little impact when she first heard them in Tangier but she now clearly saw that this was Morocco, and as she was distancing herself from it, she realised how her own limited and claustrophobic life in The Orchard, a mere house, was nonetheless a mirror image of the greater landscape that had surrounded her.

Rabat and Safi were passed without a break, but the breakfast in Kenitra revived them. Larache was their first real stop and where Elias' relatives welcomed them for the night. They complimented Rosario for taking on such a formidable task single-handed, and she was surprised to receive, from people she had never me, financial help to cover the basic costs of their journey, and their advice to be extra patient and diplomatic at the customs where long queues of travellers from the French Protectorate often waited for days to pass through.

All her documents, checked and double-checked by Pepa and Rosario were in order and Rosario was reassured by those already in the queue that she would cross the border without delay with an old woman and children as passengers, and because she was beautiful. An official approached her. He scrutinised the documents and mumbled that one amongst them lacked the exit date. He shouted that it had to be stamped, back in Casablanca. Feeling sick, Rosario swallowed the brash rising from her gullet and gave him a smile before asking to see the Chef de Douane. The official pointed to his door. "His name is Gutierez" he said, wagging his tongue.

"Rosario Iriondo de Butler" she announced at his office door, looking as haughty and awesome as her Guardia father. At his beckoning, she walked into the middle of the room. It stank of cigar smoke, garlic belches and stale cognac. Gutierez wiped the sweat off his brow with the grease-smudged cuff of his uniform and ordered her to stay just where she stood, and at a distance where he could gawp at the whole of her. He walked slowly towards her, until his body, oozing lust, touched hers. Her jaw and shoulders stiffened .

"You want to cross the border….." he panted, undoing his flies.

When Pepa saw her daughter run towards the car, her sullied hand held away from the rest of her, as if scalded, she understood the degradation she had endured to guarantee their exit. "Animales!" she seethed, looking towards the Douanes buildings and crossed herself.

They boarded for Algeciras on the first available boat. It was the only adventure of this odyssey that the children had eagerly anticipated since leaving Casablanca—a sea crossing they knew would be turbulent, separating one continent from another. The Moulay Idris was a small cargo boat, the kind used for transporting merchandise, and all but a man in a panama hat like Elias's, were sea-sick. Only when looking back across the straits from the harbour, did the measure of their undertaking dawn on them. But what most overwhelmed Pepa and Rosario was knowing that they had touched Spanish soil— home—and the mood was instantly made lofty inside the Traction Avant. The boys blared out the marching songs they had learned at the Colonies de Vacances, and Rosario sang "Palomita blanca, Reblanca. Dime la verdad soledad" in a coy little girl's voice, saying it was for Paloma's ears only. Her mother had never sang this, or any other song to her before, and Paloma found it irritating and far too late to matter.

The Sierra Morena, with its crushing July heat and dust was nonetheless enticing. Whenever they stopped, they were fêted. This was Andalucia, the land of merriment and Pepa could not remember such effervescence and friendliness not even in her own Catalunya. The heat and the burden of weight, hampered their progress and sight-seeing was cut to a minimum, but Toledo with the Cristo de la Luz church, once a mosque with water gardens, and the old Jewish quarter, had to be seen, before heading off towards Pilar's home in Madrid.

Seeing her middle daughter sent no flutters of excitement up Pepa's spine, and she was not ashamed to admit it, since Pilar had distanced herself from her family years ago after her marriage to Gustavo Mercadero.

Gustavo was a rag and bone merchant with a horse and cart until the purchase of Limoges porcelain seconds during a chance visit to France changed his life. In his poky kitchen cum workshop he then replicated the few pastoral figurines he had brought back with him and soon his facsimiles became so extraordinarily fashionable that his business expanded into a factory, then another, and made him a fortune. Franco, or Paco, as he familiarly called him, for he claimed it was he who made him wealthy, was Gustavo's hero. A full-sized cardboard cut-out of the smirking Generalísimo in military regalia stood in the entrance hall which Rosario thought not only vulgar but offensive and told him so, but her remark was dismissed as churlish.

Excessively cherished, their three sons were older than Rosario's children and were assigned the task of escorting Paloma and Carlota around the capital's national monuments and museums during their stay.

Paloma asked Rosario afterwards if what they had done all week with their cousins was called culture and she replied that it was, and that it was only the beginning.

It was six o clock in the morning, a few days after their arrival in the Capital when Paloma woke up with a jolt. The first celebratory gunfire of the day had just detonated, commemorating the eighteenth of July and Paloma knew that she was now eighteen. Her grandmother was already in the kitchen reminiscing over the drama that had separated the family all those years ago, only a few kilometres away from Pilar's apartment. Paloma looked pale and agitated. "Drink the milk you didn't have then" Pepa said, pouring the hot liquid into a bowl.

"I feel wretched Yaya, I can hardly breathe" Paloma gasped. Pepa rubbed her cheeks.

"I know" she said softly. "Get dressed. We're returning to the scene."

"The scene? What scene Yayita?"

"The Galdós Clinic."

The clinic was no longer there; it had since become a small hotel. They sat on a bench near the Puerta by the bear statue nuzzling a madroño, whilst Pepa reconstructed every stage of her grand-daughter's birth. Her hand rested on Paloma's head so lightly, she hardly knew it was there. She told Paloma to breathe in and when she expired to feel new, reborn to the world, a world of freedom and happiness. Paloma breathed until she felt a swirling of water fill her being, washing away the agony of her birth in waves of crimson, and then escape into misty bubbles of blue from where Pepa held her hand.

*

They reached their goal, Barcelona. This bustling city made Casablanca look like a frontier town. People seemed grim and in a kind of compulsive hurry. Soot covered the buildings and the clatter of trams was deafening. Bewildered and lost, Rosario drove twice, and at considerable speed, the wrong way around a Plaza. Traffic guardias appeared, converging on Rosario in swarms, gesticulating, blowing on their whistles after every word they spoke, like clowns in a circus. For the children and even Pepa it was hilarious, but Rosario, mortified, whined that things had changed beyond recognition. Once she sited the Bull Ring, she would know that they had arrived. Pepa searched her bag for her Eau de Cologne which she sprinkled like holy water over everyone. "Watch for the balcony with the most geraniums. It'll be Carmela's!" she cried, when they circled the Plaza de Espana. Miko spotted it first, and amongst the pink blooms were the sparkling smiles of Lalia and Mingo. They were waiting for them in the street by the time the car stopped. In disbelief the children looked at the two adults who had always been their first cousins. It was Mingo who beckoned them out of the car. He was dark, with sleek, shiny hair parted to one side, with a small, Errol Flynn moustache highlighting his sensuous mouth.

"Smooth..." whispered Carlota, elbowing Paloma.

"He's like an actor..." Paloma responded, mildly trying to conceal her approval.

"You fancy him then!" teased Carlota. But Mingo had eyes only for Pepa as he climbed the stairs to the third floor with his grandmother cradled in his arms. "My bride has come home at last!" he laughed breathless, dropping her without ceremony onto the sofa. And Pepa giggled like a fifteen-year-old. An old record scratched out 'Ojos Negros' on Salvador's ancient gramophone and a cork popped, hitting the ceiling as Rosario entered.

"Carmela!" They hugged, cried and hugged again. "The same old party-loving Carmela!" Rosario cried.

Lalia poured the drink into small glass coffee cups, apologising that they were not proper glasses and that it was only espumante. "Salud!" coughed Carmela getting too excited for her own good.

Alexi, now twelve, could not avert his gaze from Lalia's pool-like blue eyes, and her golden hair, plaited into two convoluted buns covering her ears, as two ear muffs. "Shall we tango?" she asked, bending down to hold him by the waist.

Miko sat on Paloma's lap. He could not figure out how the

room they were in could be so dark in the middle of the day. In the corner the scruffy two-seater sofa was piled up with laundry. The mahogany table and four chairs lived in the same room. A bird cage—too small for the two canaries, gone mute since Salvador's death, hanged precariously from the battered shutters on the balcony. The master bedroom had no windows, but a large, oval mirror on one wall reflected the dim light from the corridor, only when the door was left open. Whoever slept in the other room was favoured with a small porthole of a window looking down into the inner courtyard, only if they stood on a stool. But there was no visible bed. Four thin mattresses, stacked in one corner, waited to be used, as and when required. Staying there would be like camping, except for Carmela and Pepa who were to share the double bed in the master bedroom. With standing room for one, the kitchen had a single vent for the cooking fumes to escape, whilst a frayed curtain, converted it into the bathroom. Once a week, Lalia washed her waist length hair there, but she recommended using the Public Baths around the corner in the Plaza de España near the Bull Ring for a proper bath on Fridays. Paloma could not believe that she had began her life there, sharing that very same gloomy space with Pepa, Carmela, Salvador and her then small cousins.

"We'll make it here" Paloma whispered to Miko curled up on her lap. "Somehow" she added, to convince herself.

*

"It has to be champagne! espumante won't do. And not one or two. I want three bottles. And Langues de Chat" Rosario ordered Mingo. "Serrano, that goes without saying. Olives, black and green, the big fat ones that fill your cheeks. Vol-au-vents filled with truffles, and caviar, of course." Mingo struggled with the spelling and the speed of Rosario's inventory of goods. "Got that?" she asked, snatching his shopping list. "I can see I shall have to teach you some French!" she said in a tone full of innuendos that only Pepa understood.

Carmela had listened aghast. Their last champagne was a bottle Camilo had kept from Rosario's wedding to celebrate José Luis release from prison almost eighteen years ago, and caviar was something they knew only existed in romantic Russian novels.

When Mingo returned from his shopping spree with shrivelled dried olives, finger wide strips of fatty serrano and espumante, Rosario shouted that he could have tried the black market.

"I wouldn't know where to go for stuff like that!" he mumbled, downcast.

"Elias would have known..." she said, sweeping the goods off the table. "All I can say is....."

"Don't." interrupted Pepa.

"......that I hope José Luis won't......"

Pepa stopped her again. "He won't."

"Why this glowering all of a sudden?" rasped Rosario, looking at the faces around her.

"You haven't got it, have you?" said Pepa. "This is Spain 1954 and still recovering."

"I just want a fine welcome for my brother. That's all"

"The welcome doesn't depend on quantity nor quality, Rosario. And you know that, at least I would like to think you do."

"But it helps." she argued.

"Espumante is fine. The bubbles are a symbol of how we feel. That's what matters."

*

José Luis had telephoned a message to the Café Montjuic on the corner near Carmela's flat the night before, to announce his visit the next day and the house was a bedlam of anticipation. Only Paloma was serene. The prospect of meeting her uncle did not agitate her. Quite the reverse. All expectations built over years of listening to Pepa's stories about his war-time heroism, and her own remote memory, made her reflective and convinced that she was about to meet one of the seminal figures in her life.

Rosario's peevish outburst over the shopping had soured the jolly atmosphere. Carmela, who had been immersed in the flurry of her mother and sister's homecoming, was reminded of how petulant, selfish and spoilt Rosario could be. Rosario had pleaded poverty on her arrival, but in the same breath she also warned them of a fleet of trunks filled with books, silver, rugs, linen, artifacts, and clothes arriving at the port. Now, she was squandering her money on luxury goods on the black market. Pepa told Carmela that Rosario was living in a fantasy world and had better watch her purse, or she'd be knocking on doors for work sooner than she planned. Carmela didn't believe her sister could ever hold down a position and Rosario confirmed that she would not.

*

"It's your godfather at the door!" called Pepa, who wanted Paloma to be the first to welcome José Luis, but she was already there, facing him. "Palomita..." he whispered, his arms outstretched to embrace her. Rosario elbowed her aside, threw herself into his arms and would not let go, until she dragged him into the lounge in a kind of hysteria. "What do you think of them? Are they Iriondos or Butlers?" she asked about the children.

He had no idea, but thought them beautiful, and he wanted to hug them. And if she let him examine them later, he would tell her exactly what he thought of their hearts.

"I loved it when you examined me..." breathed Rosario. "You were my hero you know... There was no one like you..... No one in the whole world."

As if for the first time, José Luis recognised Rosario's flattery as manipulation, and felt uneasy.

"So then," he said casually, "what are your plans Rosario?"

"Plans?" she asked, wary that his question might spoil the party.

"You can't all stay here" he said looking around. "It's far too crowded, unhygienic even. Either you all come with me, as we already agreed in our letters, or you'll have to split up."

"La yaya and me will come with you!" Paloma rushed to say before anyone else had a chance to think. "We are best at keeping house. We can help aunt Maruja. And Miko must come too. I know how to take care of him." Persuasive as Paloma was, her uncle said "No, Palomita" and said her name very softly so as not to upset her. "You see," he added, "it's the wrong combination. I suggest Rosario and the boys come back with me. I'll take care of their education and you, Rosario, can look for work. Mother can stay here and keep an eye on the two girls."

"Champagne?" asked Rosario.

"Later, after we've sorted this out" he said, taking the bottle away from her hand. "What's the problem?" he asked, listening to the silence. "Am I missing something?? Well? "

"I've only just got here!" moaned Rosario. "I'd like a little time with my sister. You can take the boys back with you if you like!"

"No!" shouted Pepa. "It's better to stay together here for another fortnight son, until we've all talked things over."

TWENTY-SEVEN

Seeds of Chance

Barcelona. Rosario's favourite city. She had lost it in a haste once before, and she wanted it back. A hunger for revisiting old haunts, the cinemas of her childhood, bodegas, chocolaterias, the museums, the Barrio Gótico, and the Ramblas at night devoured her. She needed not a fortnight, but weeks of indulgence to satiate it. Besides, she knew this could be the last of the good times. Mingo, whom she had made her accomplice, was the only one at Diputacion to know of her intentions to spend indiscriminately and relish life as she saw it, even though money was scarce.

The car had served its purpose, public transport was efficient. Pepa said it had to be sold, but as she was talking, Rosario removed the triple row of pearls—Elias' last gift—from around her throat and pouring it into her hollowed palm said she'd rather sell it at the Bisuteria Escobán in the Gran Via, than be without the car.

*

At the end of the deadline set by Pepa, the family split up. Rosario took the boys to her brother and dumped them there, explaining how much more likely it was for her to find employment in the metropolis. There was wailing and tears of disbelief from Miko at his mother's desertion without warning, whilst Alexi vowed that no harm would come to his younger brother as long as he was there. She drove back through Montserrat and the barren countryside, with the boys far from her thoughts, until Mount Tibidabo beckoned her from a distance in such a persistent manner that she took the road to the funicular railway before returning to Diputación. She had gone there alone many times in her youth. It was in that very site that she had climbed to think over Elias' proposal of marriage. And she was drawn to it again. She was standing at its highest point, her long scarf billowing in the cross-wind, and her eyes trying to encompass all at the same time, the city beneath, and further across to the Sierras.

'Haec omnia TIBI DABO si cadens adoraberis me.'- All things will I give thee, if thou wilt fall down to worship me.' She remembered they were Satan's words to Christ in the wilderness when he led Him to a high spot offering Him all that He could see beneath His feet—the Temptation of Christ. She shrugged her shoulders to shake off any personal implication, and looked at the palm of her hand to divine her future. She called for a concrete sign to spell out her fate, and when no sign came she picked four tear-shaped seeds from amongst the pine needles coating the ground and named each one after her children, and closing her fist on them she shook it like a gambler would before throwing dice. Seeds are to be scattered, her voice said in her head, before she blew them off her opened palm, watching each stray seed spiral into the air, then float to the ground. "Seeds of chance that's all they are" she muttered rubbing her palms together.

*

"Right," she stated, back at Diputación, in that singular way which made her listeners feel threatened. With her legs up on a small stool, she sat on Pepa's low peasant chair by the balcony "Café!" she ordered Pepa. "And then I want the girls here!"

"In my presence or not at all" Pepa said. "And get your own coffee."

"With or without you, it won't make a bit of difference" hissed Rosario.

Carlota and Paloma heard their mother's request and came without prompting; they waited, standing a few steps back, for the café to be consumed, looking at each other and pulling faces. Paloma always did it when she smelled trouble, and could not stop herself once she started.

"You, my girls" said Rosario ominously, unaware of the clowning behind her back "have come of age and..!"

"What? All of a sudden?" When did it happen?" interrupted Pepa with unusual sarcasm, looking around as if it had occurred that second when she wasn't looking. "And you are on your own" continued Rosario ignoring her mother's comment. There was silence until Paloma burst into an hysterical laugh.

"See if you still laugh" yelled Rosario, getting up from her chair. "Here's the last money you'll get from me" she shouted, throwing two duros each towards the girls. "It's for newspapers, and don't think of coming back until you've found yourselves positions!"

"Rosario..." whispered Pepa, "How could you..!"

"I've waited long enough. They are off my hands, and that's legal."

"They're unprepared!"

"They've been to the best schools."

"And what about life? What does Paloma know about life outside her own family? She needs easing out gently. You've kept her indoors to suit your selfish needs and now you want to turf her out."

"She'll learn!"

"Or die!"

"Her choice!"

"And what do you suppose they can do with that best education you gave them?"

"They can be gouvernantes and teach French. There are plenty of wealthy families here in Barcelona who want well brought-up girls like them for their children. It's a status symbol around here."

*

The Mozarans, a family of industrialists, liked Paloma instantly and retained her. She lived in, wore a white uniform with pale blue stripes around the collar and cuffs and taught French to Ursula, a thirteen-year-old sickly girl, and had complete charge of Tito, a busy bespectacled toddler with lenses half a centimetre thick. The pay was abysmal but all her living expenses were met. The promise of holidays in their Swiss and Italian villas more than compensated for it. Monday afternoons were free, which Pepa reserved for her. Paloma combed her grandmother's hair like in the old days and they played El Tute, but realised their time was too limited and precious to waste on trivial card games and when Carmela left the bedroom to sew, they whispered their week's events. Tito's overactive temperament, Paloma reported, kept her awake until all hours of the night and the housekeeper's bell outside her door rang every morning at six o'clock for breakfast. The señores did not help as they often took the liberty of leaving her to care for the children, whilst they visited friends.

Pepa said she was being exploited, but Paloma assured her that she was used to looking after Miko and did not mind. She liked her charges and the Señores, when they were there, especially Don Isidro who often brought her ensaimadas to eat and a hot drink in the middle of the night, when Tito came into her bed and kept her awake.

*

A letter for Carlota arrived from Casablanca. Her Norbert was coming in three weeks time.

When he saw her in her scant bikini pacing the edge of the swimming pool where she worked as an attendant, lusted over by voyeuristic swimmers, he begged her to marry him there and then and to return to Morocco with him, where she truly belonged. She did not tell him or anyone else that she had been spotted by the owner of Tricot Fashions, who, impressed by her ample bosom and sinuous beauty, had offered her a contract to model his winter collection in Madrid. All Carlota told Norbert was that she would join him as soon as she had saved enough money to travel.

It was José Luis who first found out about her modelling when he learned from the wife of the 'tricot man', also his patient, that she was grooming a young lady from Morocco for a modelling début in Madrid.

Within a fortnight, Carlota had seduced and ran away with her new boss, no one knew where. Rosario was informed of Carlota's escapade, but she laughed it off and told her brother that it was nothing new, and when he asked her to visit the distressed wife to offer sympathy she said there was little point in it, since she knew already that the estranged husband would be back repentant within a month. Carlota, Rosario told him, was a huntress who overpowered her prey then left it to bleed, and the wife should be grateful her usurper was not a nurturer.

A night's crawl at the Barrio Chino's tapas bars flirting with Mingo, revived Rosario's humour. Nothing Carlota did could upset her, and she exulted that she was free of her forever. Her harshness surprised Mingo who commented that a mother never ceased to be one, no matter how old were her children, or how awful their behaviour. If that was what he thought of motherhood she replied, he was dim and a stick-in-the-mud.

*

Paloma did not turn up at Diputación one Monday afternoon. Pepa knew something had prevented her from coming. She was being over-protective, spurned Rosario—Paloma had surely been asked to work on for a special function at the house that afternoon she said. But Pepa sent Mingo to the Mozaráns that evening, to investigate.

La Señora Mozarán looked flustered and told him that Paloma had left on Sunday night. She did not say where, but she had left her belongings behind. She was not there herself when Paloma left so could not answer any of Mingo's questions. She shrugged her shoulders and suggested Paloma was most likely in town having fun and spending her wages.

Mingo thought the story unconvincing as Paloma brought her wages untouched to Diputación for Pepa to keep. He was alarmed to find the neighbours had never seen a young gouvernante at the Mozaráns nor anyone of Paloma's description on the street or in the park with a bespectacled child.

Hours later he found Paloma at the police station. She had spent the night huddled in a confessional in a nearby church said the Guardia and had not spoken a word, not even her name. She had a sprained ankle and sat listless on a hard bench in her torn nightdress. Mingo lifted her up and carried her in his arms to the tram and then up the stairs to Diputación.

Pepa laid her down on her own bed and then laid beside her. A vacant glassy look was all Paloma could manage before she closed her puffy eyelids and fell asleep, whimpering words which Pepa could not fathom. She stroked Paloma's brow with her forefinger to erase the anguish, but it startled Paloma and she sat upright, her ankle hurting.

"You are safe sweetheart" whispered Pepa. "Mingo will bring you some hot milk. Would you like that?"

Paloma nodded. "I'm fine" she said, "really," and she began to tell the story of what had happened that Sunday night. Pepa showed Mingo out after he had brought her a glass of hot milk and carefully cut thinly sliced bread. She held Paloma's hand. "Go on..." she encouraged, squeezing it. "In your own time.."

"It was out of the blue and it took me completely unawares" started Paloma. She pulled the collar of her nightdress up to her ears and the hem right down to reach her ankles. Pepa shook her head. She did not know whether she could take what she foresaw. "Are you ready to speak about this?" she asked.

"I must" she replied, drawing in a deep breath. "La Señora Mozarán's mother," she began, "was taken ill on the Sunday. She received the phone call late that night and la señora had to go in a hurry. The commotion woke Tito up and la Señora brought him in tears to my bed and after he had calmed down, we both fell asleep." She paused.

"Take your time Mita" said Pepa stroking her own face with Paloma's hand.

"I woke up all of a sudden in the middle of the night and saw Don Isidro looking wild—I mean I never saw him like that—with an ensaimada in his hand and without any clothes except his shoes. He leaned over me, it was awful. He was as big as Pericles in the Spring."

"Your mother's horse?" interjected Pepa dismayed. Paloma nodded. "And he forced the ensaimada into my mouth, really hard until I choked and then he lifted my nightdress over my head, saying no one could hear me now. I pushed him away with my feet, and he fell on his back. I could move faster than him and I ran down the stairs through the house and into the park. He was still following me with nothing on, but I could hear that he was getting out of breath and he lost me, and after I fell and couldn't run anymore, I hid in the church around the corner until morning, when the charwoman found me asleep curled up inside the confessional and called the Guardia to pick me up."

"And here you are, safe, amongst those who love you" said Pepa hugging her. She held her a long while. It was not easy to assess how much Paloma had been marked by her experience, but the unthinkable had not happened, though she feared that the episode could affect her perception of men and scar her grand-daughter for life. She let go of her embrace. "What a thing!" she exclaimed lightly. "Thank God there aren't many men like this animal around. He should be locked up!" Pepa said in jest.

"SHE locked me up!" cried Paloma sitting up. "She did!"

"Who?"

"His wife, la señora . She said it was a strange neighbourhood and I was safer indoors. So she locked all the doors and I never went out or saw anyone."

"What about Tito?"

"He never went out either in case he got snatched."

"Snatched? By whom?"

"He's not perfect. It's his eyes. He's almost blind, the poor mite."

"So?" asked Pepa.

"When I asked la Señora, she said it was Franco."

"Franco? What does he want with blind children?"

"I'm not sure. They, that awful lot, you know, his people, the Movimiento Nacional, the Falange, the Secret Service, whoever, they find out about imperfect children and babies and take them to special laboratories for experimentation."

"What is this story?" cried Pepa outraged. "You've not dreamed that, have you?

"I read about such things in my school books."

"About Franco?"

"No, ancient Greece."

"That..." said Pepa with a frisson. "Is that why no one ever saw you, then?"

"Only on Mondays when I left the house to come here. And even then, I was made to use the back door which opens onto a busy street, and no one noticed me."

"We should report these people" said Pepa concerned.

"No one would believe us. They look normal. No one could guess he... I mean he's respected. You should see the visitors who come to the house. Like our guests at The Orchard when we had big parties, but there's no laughter and they always talk in whispers."

"You're not going back there Mita! And that's that!"

"Hope Maman wont make me!"

"I'll see that she doesn't!"

*

Pepa thought it best to omit the details when she told Rosario about the incident, but enough was said to convince her that Paloma was in danger at the Mozaráns. She had not been raped stated Rosario, and Paloma had better return or she would be out on the streets, begging.

And Pepa said "over my dead body."

*

When Rosario ordered Mingo to collect the crates from Morocco that had arrived at the port, he replied that he was nobody's errand boy. Pepa winked at him, proud he could

367

stand up to the aunt he had once thought a paragon, and without Rosario's consent Pepa wrote a note to José Luis asking for Paloma to stay and recover from the Mozaran affair.

*

Alexi and Miko sprung from their chairs and tumbled over each other when they saw Paloma appearing through the living room door of their uncles house. Maruja sat at the dining table as she did every evening, to help her two nephews and sons with their homework; Paloma melted at the sight. A family. Together.

José Luis called her to his private study on the fourth floor, after he had read Pepa's note. He wanted to hear the Mozarán story in her own words, and she told it in a voice that was monotone and matter-of-fact. He lifted her chin and smiled. "You've told me what happened" he said taking a pause, "but I still don't know what you feel."

"I feel... I feel... I don't know... overwhelmed." she said flatly.

"What does 'overwhelmed' mean to you?" he asked, aware that the meaning of the word did not match her tone.

"It means I feel lonely. Alone. Rootless. A nobody. Yes, a nobody. Unwanted. Broken. Scrambled. Empty. Heavy—and light. Light, like a fallen leaf on a path in a sudden gust of wind, spiralling up into the air one minute, then down on the ground the next. I hurt and I don't hurt. I feel numb. Dead. I think I feel dead, like nothing matters any more."

José Luis placed his hand on her shoulder. "Thank you Paloma, now tell me about Don Isidro. That's why you are here."

"I don't feel much about that" she said shaking her head.

"Don't you want to cry Paloma..?"

"What for?"

"You look sad. What is it that is making you sad Mita?"

"The boys and Yayita."

"What about them?" he asked pushing her long fringe off

368

her forehead to see her eyes. "Tell me."

"I'll never see them growing up, not properly, not like a family together, like here. We're broken into bits like a sugar cone for sale in the Souk, whole one minute and shattered the next."

"And it hurts?"

"I can't stand it!" she exploded. "And she's the culprit."

"You mean your mother, don't you?"

"She loves only herself. She's breaking all our hearts" she snivelled.

He rocked her in his arms. "You'll stay here with us for as long as you need to Paloma."

"I've left all I have in the Mozaráns. I have no clothes other than these" she said pointing at her skirt and blouse.

"Maruja will kit you out. That will be fun, won't it?"

Paloma beamed. "You mean shopping?"

"You bet!"

"And will I see the boys every day?"

"Every day. And you can help with their homework."

"And Yayita, when will I see her again?"

"Yayita wants what's best for you. She wants you to be here, even if she pines for you." He looked at her melancholy face. "You love her very much don't you?"

"She's my life" said Paloma filling up with tears again.

"I know, Palomita. She once was mine, and I had to let go."

*

José Luis had kept it quiet from Rosario and Pepa that there were daily squabbles—often violent—between Alexi and his own children. After one of his worst fits of rage, Alexi confessed to his uncle that he missed his father since his death. But when asked what it was that he missed, he did not know and repeated that he just missed him. José Luis comforted him saying he needed time to adjust to his new circumstances and added that no one could replace a father, but that he was there to love him. What troubled Alexi most, José Luis had gathered, was having to co-exist on equal terms with his cousins when he had previously been spoilt by his father, and he was concerned that since his arrival the natural rhythm of the household had been disrupted. He recognised also that Maruja's innate laissez-faire nature did not do much to redress the situation, especially now that she withdrew from the crisis to find solace in Paloma's company.

Her aunt was everything Rosario was not—effacing and giving, asking nothing of José Luis but his presence as a companion and father to her children. Maruja knew that his work was his life, but his family was his lifeline, vital to his functioning, and she was proud and grateful to be so indispensable. Paloma came to appreciate this unassuming woman who once disclosed that she knew that her husband had lost his religion, but to let him realise that she knew, would kill something in their relationship and in him, for good.

*

Every evening after surgery at a quarter past eight and just before supper, José Luis walked arm in arm with Paloma to the bustling town square to sit in his usual bar. Friends and patients stopped to pat him on the back or enthuse about their recovery or, lowering their voices, express concern about new symptoms. He said he was never off duty but he never failed to add that doctoring was not doctoring unless it was given with one hundred per cent dedication, and he was happy to give that.

Unless he had something useful or good to say, he kept, what he termed 'noble silence'. He said it with a half smile, adding that it was not only Trapist monks who could achieve it.

Post-war Spain under Franco was a topic never far from his mind, and for which he was prolific with his words, but when Paloma questioned him about his imprisonment, the reply was always the same -he had recovered. There was still a brittleness in him born of a sad recognition that his country was not evolving in the direction that he had hoped. He wanted liberation, but not at any cost, and although it was coming, he said it was in the guise of a flitting butterfly in a rose garden, when the awful reality was that a monster with the sinister face of totalitarianism lurked amidst its scented petals. The police in Spain, he was convinced (and was not afraid to say it out loud) was a military force trained by the Gestapo. Their idols—Hitler and Mussolini—whom they called 'The Defenders of European Civilisation', were still there and alive. Except for Catalunya, he always added, which believed Francoism to be a festering wound in the side of Spain, and he was proud to affirm that Catalans had consistently protested against the fascist regime. Paloma asked him about the yellowing newspaper clippings she had seen on the wall of his private study. They were of La Pasionaria, he said. He was silent for a while as if he needed a moment's reverence after speaking her name, then he added that if there had to be saints, she was his kind of saint. She was not always called 'La Pasionaria' he said. Her name was Dolores Ibarruri, she was Basque and it was selling fish from door to door in her youth that had taught her how to use her voice. Education was not essential, he remarked, if there was passion, and she had an abundance of that, no more so than when her speeches reverberated through loudspeakers in streets everywhere at the onset of the war. "People of Spain!" she called, "Keep tuned in. Do not turn your radios off. Rumours are being circulated by traitors. Keep tuned in!" Everyone listened, especially those who feared her.

José Luis kept copies of all La Pasionaria's speeches in the drawer of his filing cabinet and knew them by heart. "Listen to this Paloma. This is what she had to say of those who fought for their ideals and came to fight our war". And he stood up as a mark of respect. "She called to mothers and women everywhere and told them with a passion impossible to ignore that when time had healed the wounds of war, when sorrow and rancour had died away and pride and freedom was in the heart of all Spaniards, then it would be time for them to speak to their children and say that THE INTERNATIONAL BRIGADE was there for them, that many had lost their lives for them, and were now in Spanish soil for their shroud. She told them that they were the True Crusaders for freedom and that now and always we, Spaniards, will remember them."

Still moved by the recollection of her words, José Luis continued with another recollection of her speeches which she had addressed directly to the men of the Brigades who had sustained heavy casualties.

"What happened to her?" asked Paloma, stirred both by the passion of the speeches and by her uncle's emotion.

"There was chaos throughout Spain, especially in Barcelona where she was at the end of the war. Franco's forces were everywhere. Nowhere was safe for Republicans after their defeat by the Nationalists under Franco. Her life was threatened. She waited for as long as she could, before recognising that their cause was lost and she and others finally escaped to exile in France. But her legacy Paloma, was that she sowed a seed which has yet to bear fruit: the seed of democracy."

Now that the war was over, and Catalans were made to speak Castilian, Paloma wanted to know, did José Luis feel that he had lost his identity and was alienated from his own country. He replied that alienation was a metaphysical question he was not qualified to answer. The philosophy of mind, he told her, required a specific training which he had not acquired. But he said Miguel de Unamuno theorised that a man's identity depended, not upon his existence as a personal being, but more as the being he believed himself to be, that others thought him to be, or that he wished himself to be, which came close to that authentic being that God would perceive in him. He explained that there also existed a national identity and that the lack of it brought about a kind of alienation. He confessed his soul no longer belonged to Spain where he had been physically rooted, and if not Spain, he knew not where. It belonged to no country, Paloma said, but to that part of the self where God dwelled, and after she had said it, there followed a long silence. José Luis shook his head and finally let it rest to one side. "I don't believe in God" he said quietly. "I am an atheist, but no one knows. Least of all my mother and Maruja who could not live with the